INCITATUS

Incitatus

Jakub Wisz

Double Proficiency

ISBN 978-952-69894-5-7 (softcover)
ISBN 978-952-69894-6-4 (PDF)
ISBN 978-952-69894-7-1 (EPUB)
ISBN 978-952-69894-8-8 (AZW)

Cover art by: Holly Humphries
Editing by: Teresa Grabs

First Printing, 2022

Prologue

The distant Solar System's lights reflected in the coffin's glassy, tear-shaped surface as the body continued the slow journey towards the stars. The gaunt, dried face gazed peacefully into the infinity with unseeing eyes, almost as if the deceased was merely resting after a long day.

Tap. A pulse of light touched the coffin—once, then again, and soon the pulses increased in frequency as the distant instrument realized it had found something. A long-forgotten longing awoke within the tomb at the gentle prodding of a ladar. A spark flared inside the golden crown of implants protruding from the mummified corpse's skull, then turned into a song, reaching out in pulsating waves of an electromagnetic greeting.

The Wanderer stirred.

1

Shao had been off-world before—Jupiter, Neptune, even Earth once —but nothing had prepared her for this view. Hollowed out and turned into a floating megacity housing nearly a billion people, Pluto-Charon Spaceport bristled with the frantic activity of the last port before the Frontier—the vast Lethe Bridge spanning between the tidally locked planetoids. The sight took her breath away as the distant Hydra Waystation powered its multimegawatt laser, sending ships towards the Great Beyond in a flash of brilliance. She exclaimed quietly with every burst of light, consumed by the spaceport's seemingly chaotic business.

The quiet hiss of opening doors and a familiar smell announced Mai's approach: industrial soap that almost succeeded in masking machine grease residue.

'Nice view, ain't it?' Mai asked, sitting next to Shao and embracing her.

'Yeah, it's mind-boggling. I mean, I've read all about it and saw it on vids but being here... It's almost too much.'

'You said it. I always thought the Titan's Crown is big, but this is something else.'

'Just looking at it makes my head spin, you know.' Mai giggled and ruffled Shao's hair. 'You can't even look up without falling over.'

'Not everyone was born in a spacesuit, swinging from antennas.'

'Swinging from antennas? You're thinking monkeys, love.'

'Monkeys, floaters, same diff.'

Mai put up her hand in a theatrically offended gesture, but her cybernetic eye flickered with joy. 'Oh yeah? In that case, I'm not telling you what I did to the Sōngshǔ.'

'Now that's just not fair! You didn't break anything?'

'Not unless you think overclocking the main drive is breaking.'

'You did it!'

'Sure did. Told you the specs are a load of drivel. Now we can race with the best of them.'

'Won't the capacitors overheat?'

'Maybe with sustained thrust, but on a race track, she's golden.'

'A race track?'

Mai winked, her eyes flickering from blue to pink. 'What, you wanna just look at the Styx track from a distance?'

Shao jumped to her feet excitedly, stumbling in low gravity before her magboots caught the floor with a click. 'Hell no, I'm booking us a spot. I'm sure Dad won't mind.'

Mai hesitated. 'Wait, just like that? Won't that figure on the travel expense listing?'

'Sure, sure, it's gonna be fine,' replied Shao absentmindedly, already opening the augmented reality window in the air before her and sharing the image with Mai's HUD. She compiled a message with the pole position lease request to the Styx arena through the Pluto CommNet node in a heartbeat.

Mai glanced at the display, and her face sunk, eyes dimming into pale orbs. 'Looks like the home office couldn't wait until we arrive.'

Shao sighed at the incoming stream notification's sight but didn't pick up the call. 'We won't be staying long enough, I bet. Bummer. I always wanted to run the Styx.'

'They're gonna run us through the hoop before we even set foot on the mothership. Prolly should cancel the lease.'

'Maybe we'll get shore leave. We just need to make sure to tie everything up to the last button, so they let us off the hook.'

Mai leaned over to Shao with a mischievous smile. 'Oh really? What about this button right here...'

Shao paid no heed to the Sōngshǔ for a while as it continued its landing pattern on autopilot, directed by the NaviNet's guidance system. When she and Mai looked back at the vidscreen, the jumper already maneuvered between the traffic. Sōngshǔ weaved its way between freighters waiting for permission to dock or depart and swarms of smaller service ships hawking their wares on broadband comms.

'Feel like snacking?' asked Mai nonchalantly.

Shao shook her head. 'Nah, I already did.'

Mai giggled, blushing. She opened her mouth to reply but froze up awestruck as their craft skittered past a freighter, revealing the Lethe Bridge's enormous spire spanning twenty thousand kilometers across looming above the jumper.

Shao's eyes raced between the megaconstruction, its docks and dome habitats, and hundreds of ships swarming around it—seemingly tiny in comparison.

'It's pretty big, eh?' uttered Mai finally.

Shao chuckled at the absurdity of her statement. 'Yeah, quite.'

'Where's our dock?'

'I don't know, give me a moment.' Shao brought up the course information onto the screen, putting it in a side window in a practiced motion. 'Here it is.'

The vidscreen rushed across the Bridge's length towards a scaffolding erected a distance from its structure. Inside it, the Yusan mothership anchored, its hull far too expansive to fit inside any of the docking bays, yet still dwarfed by the spire behind it. The escort frigate, Jīnlóng, loomed near it—a sleek and dangerous white and gold wrath.

'Ever been aboard?'

'Once, when it was built. Dad took Mom and me with him to see the decks when it arrived in the Crown.'

'Must've been quite the sight then.'

'Yeah, I was scared it'd fly off and take me away. What, I was seven, don't laugh at me!'

Mai covered her mouth to hide the smile. 'You were right, though.'

'About?'

'It is gonna fly and take you away. Just a bit later than you thought.'

Shao laughed, but the feed from Sōngshǔ headed towards the Jīn-lóng's shuttle bay caused her stomach rise to her throat. The jumper looked like a speck of dust compared to the hundred and fifty meters long warship. Sōngshǔ slid inside and vibrated gently as it landed in a designated space between angular boarding shuttles and drone racks, holding a small army of fighter drones and armored insertion bots intended for boarding actions.

Shao took her time putting on the white and gold jumpsuit adorned with Zhengdao insignia.

'You're not changing?' she asked, seeing Mai slipping back into her work fatigues and a worn leather jacket.

'Nope. If I have to stand and listen to the committee's drivel, might as well be comfy.'

Shao sighed. 'Wish I could do the same.'

'Nobody's stopping you, love.'

'If only.'

They exited the craft through a vertical airlock. It cycled slowly, giving Shao an extra minute to make sure the uniform is impeccable—Dad hated sloppiness more than anything. The airlock hatch slid open with a hiss, letting in a breeze of fresher air—an improvement over the jumper's pump but still carrying the arid quality of sterilized atmosphere. Shao stepped onto the white docking bay deck and fought not to roll her eyes ostentatiously at the sight of three security guards in white and gold Zhengdao uniforms led by a black-haired man with golden eyes, wearing a two-piece black suit with golden finishing.

She brought up a comm window with Mai on her personal HUD, adjusting its augmented reality display to hide the conversation from others. 'At least they didn't bring the red carpet.'

Mai giggled nervously and affixed her jacket as she caught a disapproving look from the man in the suit. Her cybernetic eyes changed color from blue to deep purple, reacting to her mood change, but she withstood the glare.

The rush of anger reddened Shao's face. Arrogant bastard. She coughed quietly in her hand, which the suited man mistook as a sign to speak.

'Good day, esteemed Shao Zhenya. My name's Jin Sun, your father's aide.'

'Hi there,' replied Shao through gritted teeth.

She zoned out to a private chat with Mai as Sun continued the welcoming speech as if Shao's occasional nods and half-words were an epitome of protocol. Sneaking away to the arena will be much more difficult from the Jīnlóng than it would be from the busy mothership, that's for sure. She could always count on Dad being too busy to watch her, but his aide seemed determined to hold the fort until the old man's arrival.

'She wasn't alone, you know.' Mai's sharp tone caused Shao to focus back on reality.

Jin Sun smiled briefly at Mai. 'I wasn't made aware of that. Although I'm glad esteemed Miss Zhenya had the foresight to bring along an underling to pilot the jumper back to Titan.'

Mai's now crimson eyes flashed as she glared at Sun. 'I'm nobody's underling, you slimy...'

Shao stepped forward, raising her palms defensively. 'Mai Wren is a first-class software specialist assigned to the Yusan. She's not going anywhere, and by the way, neither is the Sōngshǔ!'

'My apologies,' he stated unapologetically. 'It is my mistake to assume one's role in the corporation based on their demeanor.'

Shao raised her hand toward Mai, who had stepped forward, clenching her fists. The guards averted their eyes when she glanced at them.

'You'll know better in the future. I believe you were about to make introductions, yes?'

'Indeed I was, esteemed Miss Zhenya. Please, meet your father's chief of security, Sarah Lowe, and her best men...' Sun paused.

One of the soldiers, a short-haired blonde woman with a strong jawline, stepped forward and bowed slightly. 'Tommy Leng and Henry

Thompson,' she said, saving Sun the trouble of learning their names from the ship's database. 'Pleasure to meet you both.'

The soldiers saluted with a stone expression, though Shao noticed both blushed awkwardly. She felt for them; second-hand embarrassment caused by the stiff, "casual" protocol used by Zhengdao Corporation's higher echelons was known to her all too well.

'Likewise, Miss Lowe. The pleasure is only slightly marred by its unexpected nature.'

Shao smiled when Mai's eyes' red glare softened to a mild green as she composed herself. She was sure Mai would learn to ignore the buffoonery displayed by corp executives soon; Zhengdao rank and file living and working in Titan's Crown kept to the same informal language as the outsiders they interacted with more than with the corporate elites. She faced the adjutant again. 'So, where's Dad? Too busy to come say hello?'

'I'm afraid the most esteemed captain is, as they say, swamped. Allow me to assist you in assigning quarters and giving you a tour of the port in his stead.'

As if I had a choice, Shao thought. 'Are you sure your busy schedule allows the time for babysitting?'

'I made it a point to make room, just for you,' replied Sun with an ingratiating smile. 'It'll be my treat to guide you...'

'And Mai.'

'And Mai, around. What would you like to see first?'

Shao glanced at Mai who shrugged slightly and rolled her eyes. 'How about an arena?'

Sun smiled charmingly. 'Sounds like fun, esteemed Miss Zhenya. Please allow Miss Lowe to take you to your quarters so you can freshen up while I arrange for the tickets and transportation.' He motioned as though he wanted to add something else but nodded and walked away instead.

Lowe dismissed the troopers and led both women through Jīnlóng's sterile, white and gold corridors.

'Sorry about Jin Sun, Miss Zhenya,' she said. 'He means well, but meet-and-greet isn't in his job description.'

Shao shrugged gently. 'I liked Miss Kovalev more; too bad she retired.'

'Captain's Zhenya's old aide? I never met her. So, where would you like to start the tour?'

'Wherever,' replied Mai sheepishly. She cooled off after the confrontation, and her eyes raced between high-tech gadgets splayed on the decks.

'As long as you adopt a strict no-esteemed-whatever policy,' added Shao.

Lowe grinned. 'Yeah, I can do that. So, how about we start with the bridge? Captain Powells will be glad to meet you.'

Shao clapped her hands. 'Uncle Ed is here? Finally, some good news.'

'I'll take you right there, then, and tell you all about the ship on the way. You won't be staying here long, but you know,' replied Lowe and saluted theatrically.

'Aye, aye!'

Shao idly listened to their guide's methodical explanation, supported by maps, images, and video projected to their HUDs by the ship's computer. Mai, on the other hand, was consumed by the data. Good, Shao thought. Tech and relaxation, that's better.

Lowe guided them through the decks, bringing up the frigate's technical details to their HUDs to support her explanations.

Mai interjected eventually, 'That's nice, but where are the toilets?'

Lowe smirked. 'Your quarters have all the amenities, Miss Wren. Sorry, I always forget that not everyone is in love with military tech.'

Mai shrugged with a devilish smile. 'Who said I'm not in love with it?'

Lowe let out a short laugh. 'Fair enough. Anyway, your temporary quarters are just around the corner. You can freshen up and get something to eat before meeting Captain Powells if you want. You'll be assigned a station on the Yusan once we're en route, but for now, our humble abode will have to suffice.'

'I'll take what I can get,' said Shao simply. 'Please let my dad know we've arrived.'

'Oh, he knows. I imagine whatever delayed his arrival on the Jīnlóng couldn't wait.'

2

Yuan Zhenya closed the file and shut down the mental link to Yusan's computers. The corner of his HUD still blinked with a growing number of notifications to address; all marked as "urgent"—they're going to have to wait. He got up from his desk and stood in front of a wall, commanding the ship's computer to switch the AR display into a mirror Sun reported that Shao arrived, and Zhenya wanted to look good when he greeted her. Zhenya examined his reflection—preparing for Yusan's journey kept Zhenya up the last forty sol hours, but stims and biosculpting made sure he was sharp as a razor. There were days, like today, when he did feel his age—he was nearing fifty, after all. At least he made sure to reroute Shao's ship to the Jīnlóng; the last thing he wanted was for his daughter to wait in a docking queue with service crews and common employees. Now, with all actually urgent matters taken care of, Zhenya thought, I can relieve Sun and meet Shao.

He brought up an itinerary onto his HUD, and double-checked a prepared plan of activities before Yusan's departure—restaurants, sports events, a tour, and racing, can't leave without having a go with a rented speedboat on Nix.

He got up to head for the shuttle to the Jīnlóng, and as if on command, a comstream request appeared on his HUD.

Zhenya sighed heavily and brought the message upon his AR display, moving the queries aside for a moment to make room for the stream. To his surprise, the footage he received was a full HD video feed from a drone cam deep underwater. Rays of light streamed through the liquid, illuminating icy walls, and a small flock of bioluminescent fish swimming by the drone. Half a second later, an Outer woman drifted in front of the lens, scaring the fish into a panicked retreat.

She didn't wear a scuba mask, and Zhenya could see her bright blue eyes and fluorescent hair standing out on the background of her light-gray skin. She wore a blue diving suit with stabilizers allowing her to remain in the camera's view once she got there. 'Greetings, Mister Zhenya,' she said, bubbles escaping from gills in the sides of her neck. Water distortion made her voice sound hard to comprehend, but the drone's audio synthesizer made up for the audio loss. Zhenya could barely notice the lip sync being off by a fraction of a second. 'It's a pleasure seeing you this lovely day.'

'Greetings. I will reserve my opinion of the feelings' mutuality until I know the purpose of the call, Miss...?' Zhenya sent his reply and minimized the comm, filing away the overdue messages while awaiting a response. It's a good thing Sun volunteered to keep Shao busy when she arrives, he thought. It doesn't seem I'm getting out of the office yet. He resigned himself into the chair. Whoever the woman was, she opted for enduring the wait between comm pulses instead of sending a single concise message, so she obviously wanted something. I, too, can play the long game, Zhenya thought and opened a broadcast in a different corner of his HUD. A sweaty, emaciated floater talked at the cam drone about the mysterious lights she saw while spacewalking on the Bridge, while an amused reporter nodded vigorously.

Eight minutes later, the response arrived.

'Delacroix, Mister Zhenya. And the purpose is business, naturally.'

Zhenya smirked and shook his head. 'Why else would you hail me from Nix without an appointment?'

Delacroix's eyes widened in theatrically overdone surprise before disappearing in a cloud of bubbles. 'How did you know where I am?'

Zhenya frowned with feigned impatience. 'Really, Miss Delacroix, where else would there be open water within one AU from Pluto?'

'I could have been in a ship.'

'With ice walls? Please, don't waste my time,' responded Zhenya sharply. 'It would cost you so much cred; you might as well have bought off my shares and approve whatever it is you want instead of talking to me.'

'Well deduced, Mister Zhenya.' She hesitated before continuing. 'I am, in fact, on Nix. I only aimed to impress you with the display, nothing more. I'm comming you with a very profitable proposal if you find time for me in your busy schedule.'

Amateurs, thought Zhenya, hiding his curiosity under an expression of feigned disinterest. The Outer woman fell for it; she deduced he was hiding interest in her unusual methods and quickly began her pitch. 'The Helikaon refinery currently contracts me to fit and dispatch one of your firm's mass transit haulers, the Incitatus, headed for the System. As I'm sure you're well aware, the hauler is over a quarter empty. I wish to buy space on the ship, which I would fill with my cargo, twenty thousand TEUs, to be unloaded during the slingshot maneuver around Jupiter. Are we talking about price?'

Zhenya grinned like a hungry wolf. The hauler could carry a hundred thousand TEUs of cargo, twenty-five tonnes each. The reports he received just a few hours ago did indeed indicate that only sixty percent of that in raw materials were harvested this decade, as increased pirate attacks and bad luck kept the mining ships from filling their quota. If he could fill that ship up with the woman's cargo, it could be the pinnacle of his career. He'd tie up the project he spearheaded and oversaw from inception on a high note, bringing billions of unexpected revenue to the company. Not to mention also skimming the added cred to his secret bank accounts and retiring, supporting Shao's ascent to the board from behind the scenes. 'The offer does sound tempting,' he said with polite, nonchalant interest. 'The question stands on the nature of the cargo, and of course, the price.'

Bringing his fingers together into a bridge in front of his face after sending the message, Zhenya smirked with delight. The woman didn't seem very bright, thinking she could fool him with the comm delay, the exotic locale, and using water to distort her voice so that he couldn't gauge her reactions during the bargaining. She was using all the advantages she could muster against him, thinking her masquerade was so sly, but she did, unknowingly, betray her ineptitude.

Taking such extreme measures meant she was aware of being outclassed. Showing that to a trade partner was a rookie mistake. All he had to do was pretend to have fallen for the ruse, fumble on purpose, read her reactions wrong. Delacroix will unquestionably believe her ploy worked and become confident. Overconfident, if he had any say in it.

A live comstream request appeared on Zhenya's HUD. 'What seems to be the problem, esteemed adjutant?'

'Your daughter has arrived on board the Jīnlóng, esteemed captain.' Jin Sun's tone was an example of etiquette, as always.

Zhenya nodded, gauging his aide's smooth face and golden eyes. The adjutant was vying to advance in the corporate society, high enough to see the top but not yet ready to reach for it. Always ready to serve and always willing to use any information given to him as a tool... Or a weapon. Zhenya always needed to be wary of every word when his aide was around. 'Very well, esteemed adjutant, thank you.'

'If I may, esteemed captain, I see from your schedule that you are extremely busy today, and your daughter would like to see the local attractions—'

'Yes, I'll join her as soon as I can.'

'By all means, esteemed captain, perhaps I could personally escort the young miss on her tour. That would allow you the time to finish with your duties for the day before seeing her.'

'That would be most kind of you, esteemed adjutant, but I cannot expect you to go beyond your duties—'

'Oh, it would be my pleasure, esteemed captain. You have so many more important things to deal with today; it would be a shame if they distracted you during quality time with the family, would it not?'

Zhenya started thinking of a reason to say no, but a reply notification started blinking on the Delacroix window. What harm could it be to work just a few hours longer and be sure his daughter wasn't bored? 'You would know, esteemed adjutant, you arrange my schedule.' Zhenya paused. 'Very well, please make sure Shao has fun.'

A weaselly smile spread across Sun's face. 'Naturally, esteemed captain, I will do my best.'

As the call disconnected, Zhenya couldn't shake the feeling his aide had outmaneuvered him somehow, but the matter would have to wait. He turned back towards the conversation with Delacroix, bringing her stream window back into his HUD.

Shao will understand.

3

The battered raider struggled to slow down before approaching the station. The recent skirmish had left its ugly hull pockmarked with burns and impact craters; its shielding peeled in places, revealing the metamaterial beneath.

The station was an old, angular model; its central ring made up of a haphazard collection of various modules attached to a central, rotating spine like grapes to a vine. The outer ring was nothing more than a hexagonal rim of scaffolding with several blue-lit docking bays and service modules attached.

Milosh doubted more than fifty people were living there.

Inside the raider, the comms sounded, insistent, demanding that the ship identify itself.

'Shut that bloody thing down,' demanded Milosh. 'It's breaking my concentration.'

Muldoon, the red-haired mercenary piloting the ship, showed him a finger without turning around. 'You do it, I'm busy trying not to crash us.'

'And I'm doing a sudoku.'

'Can't you finish later?'

'No, I wanna get it done before we land. Or crash, either way.'

A third mercenary, an Outer known only as Chatty, reached out and swiped the tablet from Milosh's hand. It immediately flew backward and slammed into the rear segment wall, the screen cracking into a thousand pieces.

'Oopsie daisy,' he said cheerfully. 'Am I clumsy today or what?'

Milosh glared at him. 'The hell did you do that for? I almost had it.'

'Stop crying, you found it on the shelf. Easy come, easy go.'

'That reminds me of someone,' added Muldoon.

'What's that supposed to mean?'

The comm station rang again demanding the craft to identify itself.

'What are we gonna tell them?' asked Muldoon. 'We won't get clearance to land if we don't respond.'

'Nothing, what are they gonna do?' asked Milosh. 'Cry themselves to sleep?'

'Well, for one, they locked the defense turrets onto us.'

'Did you lock ours right back?'

'Yup.'

'Good.'

The raider shook with turbulence as one of the maneuver drives choked and died. It had been hit with a plasma discharge a few sols before when the mercs broke out from the Pan American Coalition's frigate, hijacking the craft on their way out. They swerved in a tight turn towards the docking bay's open door. The raider was severely out-gunned, even against a backwater junker like this one. Milosh hoped whoever was in charge of the defense didn't know it.

Space stations, sporadically spread throughout the explored sectors of the Oort Cloud, were unilaterally armed to the teeth to ward off pirates and other vagabonds, but their gear was often in disrepair, and their supplies were short. They also needed the cred and barter that visitors brought with them, and, as such, were careful not to open fire on random travelers. Milosh was sure they wouldn't consider a small raider vessel to be much of a threat—and he wagered he was correct; otherwise, they would have opened fire by now.

The raider drifted into the dock, carried by inertia. Muldoon put her down gently in a free net, and the three mercs prepared to egress.

They geared up in a PAC Navy suits and railguns from the ship's armory. Milosh would prefer not to get into a scuffle with whatever security they have, but it never hurts to bring a gun.

They exited through the airlock and kicked off through the bay, floating ahead in zero-g, moving through the blue-lit kelp-like forest of docking nets towards the passenger airlock.

They didn't have to discuss their entry plan; Milosh and Chatty took cover on both sides of the airlock hatch while Muldoon initiated the entry protocol. Milosh was willing to bet a welcoming committee was bound to attempt an interception, but they couldn't know how many intruders were inbound. Not unless the security cameras were functional, but that was a calculated risk. Maintenance in the Frontier was an art of balancing needs and available means. Internal security cameras were a low priority.

The airlock opened. Milosh watched Muldoon raise his hands and back out of the corridor. A zero, a human bioaugmented to survive accelerations far beyond a regular person's limits, in a brown duster long coat on top of an armored space suit followed, aiming an ancient slug thrower pistol at Muldoon. 'That's far enough, cowboy.'

Using his magboots to stand still on the station's wall, the zero stopped dead in his tracks. 'Oh, no, you ambushed me,' he said phlegmatically. 'Who would 'ave thunk it.'

Milosh and Chatty stepped out of their cover, railguns trained at the man.

'Them's the brakes,' said Milosh. 'I take it your associates have their guns ready to blow us up?'

The man nodded. 'You betcha. The name's Jim, by the way.'

'Hi there, Jim. You can call me Stepan, and the two goons over there are Muldoon and Chatty.'

'Pleasure. You mind telling me what's your business here, and what's the fuss with the guns and the junk you flew in on?'

'It's a long story,' started Muldoon.

Jim shrugged. 'Make it short, then.'

'Aight. We stopped by for a drink.'

'Long as you keep them cannons holstered, fine by me.'

'Deal.'

Jim lowered his gun, prompting Milosh to signal the mercs to do the same. Milosh knew the locals were outgunned, but it was no reason to escalate. Fragile as it was, the situation boiled down to them needing to fix the raider and get out. Antagonizing the locals was pointless; they already knew who held the cards.

They headed towards the airlock and into the station.

Jim, the station guard, was an impressive sight up close—scarred, angular facial features, massive, muscular limbs, and a barrel chest. Zeros' bones were grown to form a type of internal armor to support overgrown organs and genetically engineered muscles. Yet, the guard was clearly on edge.

From his perspective, they were a threat—a large merc with a handlebar mustache and mean eyes, a tattooed, red-haired Earther, and a grey-skinned Outer bruiser with a cybernetic eye, all armed to the teeth and armored to match.

We should be fine, Milosh thought. As long as nobody pushes a wrong button, everyone's walking out of here in one piece. 'We're not pirates, Jim,' said Milosh as they waited for the airlock to cycle. 'We just need some repairs and a drink, that's it.'

Jim shrugged, his massive shoulders making the gesture seem threatening. 'I take you don't need questions asked, am I right?'

'Right.'

'In that case, let's make a deal. I won't ask you what gives or tell you to put them armatas in a locker. You stay in the bar and don't give us any shit, capisce?'

Milosh nodded, grinning. 'Works for me. We do need that engine fixed, though.'

'I'll send somebody over. Stay in the bar.'

'Yeah, yeah, heard you the first time.'

The station was a typical Frontier outpost built from cheap components and jury-rigged to last. The corridors and streets were made from printer concrete slabs laid out on a cheap, steel mesh. There was no augmented reality overlay preset, no comm network. As far as Milosh could tell from cardboard and neon billboards, the modules housed a mechanic, a clinic, a casino, and a cantina.

The bar was a true staple of the Oort Cloud—printed plastic and metal furniture, faux-wood counter, a beaten-up jukebox playing country hits from a hundred years ago, and a row of AR gaming machines at the far end.

Muldoon's face lit up with boyish joy. 'Sweet! They have Astral Commando here.'

Milosh shook his head and smirked as the ginger merc immediately booted up the game. He and Chatty approached the bar, where an ancient drone "howdy pardner"-ed them and poured their drinks.

'Think we're gonna get outta here in time?' asked Chatty, sipping his white Russian.

'Not a chance. We'd be lucky if they're half an hour behind us.'

Chatty sighed heavily. 'I figured. Was just kinda hopin' you'd cheer me up.'

'Tough diddles. Best we can do is send the word out to the crew, and wait for the jarheads to come can us. Might as well relax until they do.'

'Still, I'll keep an eye on things.'

Chatty's cybernetic eye wiggled out of the socket, sprouted eight segmented, spidery legs, and crawled down the Outer's arm, making its way out to the station.

Milosh connected to the station's comm service using an ancient keyboard and monitor terminal and wrote a message to Gál Tibor, captain of the Hussaria mercs' mothership, the Querub, explaining their situation. He knew that the PAC Navy will search the hard drives and find the message once they're captured, but the fiasco on Sedna was too great; Tibor needed to know about it.

He sent the message through the CommNet system to one of the many relay beacons the company stowed in the sector, hoping they'll pick it up.

Before long, Chatty's drone pinged, displaying a meeting between a group of four PAC marines and Jim. The marines wore powered armor suits, turning them into hulking giants barely fitting in the station's corridor as they stormed towards the cantina.

'Let's get captured then,' said Milosh calmly, commanding his suit to slide the helmet on via internal HUD.

Muldoon turned off the game and took a position. 'Can't we just kill those bozos?'

'We sure can,' replied Chatty, collecting his eye, which slid back into his empty eye socket. 'What are you planning on doing next? Stealing whatever ship they came in on and running?'

'Why not?' asked Muldoon.

Milosh crossed his arms on his chest. 'Cause they didn't come here alone. Whatever they landed on, it came from a frigate, at least.'

Chatty chuckled behind a makeshift table barricade. 'Wanna punch a frigate, mate?'

'Watch me.'

The cantina's door blew inside in a fountain of shrapnel, followed by a grenade. Chatty slammed the canister with a table before it landed, causing it to explode in a cloud of caustic smoke. Milosh and Muldoon dove into the mist, dodging the stray bullet from a surprised soldier.

Milosh rolled over, aimed, and fired. The slug from his railgun pierced the marine's armor. Sparks, blood, and pieces of bone splattered across the concrete floor. The marines fired, their bullets ricocheting off their fallen comrade.

Muldoon wasted no time and charged the nearest marine, somersaulting over the raised gun, placing his own rifle on the soldier's chest, and pulling the trigger. The soldier's powerful metamaterial carapace did little to stop a point-blank supersonic rail. A bloody flower erupted from the exit wound.

The mercs scattered, disappearing from sight.

Milosh ran into the nearest side alley, knowing at least one marine was on his tail. He kicked the door in and dove, barely registering the thudding of bullets searing scars onto the metal frame above his head.

A terrified Outer woman in a pink toga ran screaming when he slammed into a slot machine, overturning it in a rain of sparks. Golden coins showered from the slot accompanied by the virtual pirate's mad cackle. Milosh's boots slipped on the tokens, slowing him down a few seconds. He heard a blast behind him, and a powerful force slammed into his lower back. The armor withstood the impact, but the force carried his body over the coin-laden floor. He rolled over, aiming his rifle, expecting to see an armored marine but found Jim staring down at him; rifle barrel trained directly at Milosh's face.

'I told you not to start shit,' he growled, gritting his teeth.

Milosh smiled apologetically. 'We didn't start any, technically.'

'Trouble just so happened to follow you, eh?'

'Kinda like that, yeah.'

'Not gonna lie, I like your style. But you dragged pigs into this, and I gotta turn you in. I'll be sorry to hear about your execution. Might even shed a tear.'

Milosh looked around, wondering where his rifle fell. 'They won't kill us,' he said, hoping to stall for a moment longer. 'If they wanted us dead, they'd have nuked us outta the sky hours ago.'

'Shame they didn't, I woulda had a pleasant morning instead of this.'

'Sorry to disappoint.' Milosh shifted his weight.

'Aight, enough of chit-chat. I gotta hand you over.' Jim motioned with his revolver for Milosh to rise.

Instead, Milosh pushed himself off the ground, knocked Jim down with a roundhouse kick to the knees, and slammed the falling guard with a knee to the face. Broken nose cracked, blood spurted on the golden chips. Milosh grabbed the revolver from Jim's hand and ran out of the casino.

He raced through the corridor towards the docking bay, knowing the other mercs would do the same.

Suddenly, he felt his body lift off the ground, pulled forward by a powerful gust of wind in the back. The module's ruptured, he thought. They decided to flush us out. Turning around the corner, Milosh saw the airlock was no more; only a gaping hole staring into the docking bay remained and the black void beyond it.

Muldoon stood next to it, attaching his armor's magboots to the station wall. 'It was locked, and I had no time to look under the mat.'

'Understandable. And Chatty?'

'Already in.'

Milosh nodded and jumped into the docking bay. They headed through the web of docking nets, using them as cover during the approach. The crew inside had surely scanned the bay carefully, counting on a second of carelessness to get a clear shot and vaporize both of them, and yet, the shuttle didn't open fire; its twin laser turret remained cold and silent.

Chatty awaited them by the hatch, working on an open panel with his multitool. 'The bitch is locked tighter than a sailor's ass after a year-long cruise.'

'You can open it, though?' asked Milosh pensively. 'We can't stick around here.'

'Don't worry; I got this.'

The hatch eventually gave up, and they entered the shuttle, guns trained and ready to fire.

Empty.

Its jingoistic interior contained only the absolute necessities—four empty gel pods, weapon and armor lockers, cockpit, gunnery station. Not a soul aboard.

Chatty quickly got to work on the electronics, turning the system online and breaking any locked systems open, while Muldoon prepped the pilot station for departure. Before long, the shuttle burst out of the docking bay, heading towards the sleek corvette looming nearby as if it belonged there.

Milosh reckoned the marines probably had time to report resistance and casualties, but a few seconds of confusion would be enough to swerve to the other side of the station and hit the road. Milosh knew the PAC Navy wanted them alive, wanted them bad, and there was only so far the mercs could run. The marines were hunters, and Milosh the prey. That didn't mean he should make it easy for them.

The corvette launched a swarm of canisters to intercept the shuttle. Muldoon did his best to avoid them but to no avail. The shuttle drifted into range carried by its velocity and inertia, no matter what the merc did to maneuver away. As soon as it did, canisters released powerful EMP pulses, devouring the craft, and the station in an electromagnetic storm. Milosh shuddered involuntarily as the shuttle lights went off, and they were left in a dark coffin drifting through space. His mind went to the station's crew and civilians left without power without any warning.

'Looks like the jarheads want to play hardball,' he said.

'They sure do,' replied Chatty. 'Now it's nothing but waiting for them to pick us up.'

Milosh sighed heavily. 'And I left my sudoku in the raider...'

The mercs burst into laughter and laughed still when the shuttle hatch exploded, and the marines stormed in.

4

Jin Sun made good on his promise, much to Shao's surprise. She and Mai barely had an hour to rest before he came back, with a big smile and two white-clad security guards.

'I have arranged for the shuttle and purchased tickets for the nearest game, Miss Zhenya.'

Shao raised her eyebrow in surprise. 'Really? I expected Dad to assign me some tedious task or at least come say hello.'

'I'm afraid the esteemed captain has a lot on his mind before Yusan's departure.' He smiled apologetically. 'I asked for permission to show you around while the duties occupy his attention, and he agreed. It's the least I can do after our less than fortunate first meeting.'

'Oh, does that mean you're going with us?'

'It is my pleasure; think nothing of it, miss.'

'Oh, great,' said Mai without enthusiasm.

Sun ignored the jab and smiled politely before gesturing for the women to follow him. He led them down the deck towards the shuttle bay, keeping up the appearance of casual friendliness.

Shao nodded and smiled whenever Sun paused telling his story and replied to direct questions, but didn't really listen, focused on the private comm.

'That's not great,' messaged Mai. 'Want me to cancel the reserv?'

'Over my dead body. Maybe we can talk him into letting us race.'

'What if he doesn't?'

'I'll call the Sōngshǔ to follow us.'

'Thinking what I'm thinking?'

'Always.'

The guards followed a few steps behind, silently. Shao guessed they were probably having their own conversation on a private link, muted from the group.

Sun led the group to a luxurious, white and gold shuttle—a long, smooth state-of-the-art limousine. Shao heard Mai whistle quietly when they entered.

'Holy shit, love. Your fam has rides like that at work?'

'Oh, this old thing.' Shao winked at Mai when Sun wasn't looking, getting a shy smile in return.

Sun turned to the escort. 'Troopers, man the steers, would you? I don't think we'll need armed retinue during the flight.'

Shao followed them into the spacious airlock, complete with leather-bound benches to sit on while the air cycled.

The commlink node on Sun's temple blinked, and a biodrone—a white and gold semi-organic squid-like machine with segmented arms —served tall glasses of sparkly champagne.

'That's what I call luxury,' said Mai out loud, earning a favorable glance from Sun.

'The company provides the best commodities to its valued personnel,' he replied.

Shao scanned the aide's face searching for irony but found none. I guess he does try to make up for the first impression, she thought. The inner door slid open, letting them into a spacious passenger cabin, where more opulence awaited. The takeoff lights turned green just as Shao sat down. The craft rose from its bedding with a gentle vibration of the magdrive and headed towards the spaceport. 'So, which arena would you like to visit first, Miss Shao?' asked Sun. 'The news bulletin announced the Styx Arena opened a new game recently. We reserved a pass for everything they have.'

'That sounds fine,' replied Shao, trying to keep a straight face. 'Not that we'd know if it's new; we've never been here.'

'Won't we stand out like a sore thumb... With the bodyguards, limos, and all that glitter?' asked Mai, glancing up from the display streaming the outside camera footage.

'We sure will, miss. Nobody will bother us unduly, though, I assure you.'

Mai shrugged slightly, avoiding looking into Sun's face. 'I guess. Making a show out of us will make it kinda hard to blend in.'

'Why would anyone want to do that, dear Miss Wren? The space-port is full of criminals, swindlers, and lowly truckers.'

'Lowly truckers like me?'

Sun hesitated, spreading his hands apologetically. 'Forgive me, miss. I didn't mean to slight you.'

'No, of course not.'

Shao quickly stepped in. 'I'm sure you only have our best interest in mind. Does the pass include racing?'

Sun shook his head. 'I'm afraid your father would order my head on a plate if he found out I allowed you to put yourself in harm's way.'

'If he found out? Doesn't Dad know we're going?'

'I was told to make sure you have fun, miss,' replied Sun smoothly.

I'm not the only one skimming the rules, Shao thought. Well, that makes it easier. She decided to be particularly polite during the flight to lull Sun's alertness and found herself actually enjoying the conversation, perhaps thanks to the private comm with Mai. They listened to Sun explaining Styx's history while coordinating their jumper's auto-pilot, secretly shadowing the shuttle and planning how to slip from the aide's keep.

The luxury shuttle took another half an hour to reach Styx and dock in one of the restaurant stations orbiting the moon.

'If you'll allow me, I'll make sure our table is ready.'

'Please do,' agreed Shao. 'We'll be right behind you.'

Mai nodded enthusiastically and gave the thumbs up.

Sun raised an eyebrow, puzzled, but left through the airlock sleeve. The receptionist greeted him from afar, bowing with respect. Shao and

Mai lagged a bit behind. Once Sun was out of the shuttle, Shao turned to the guards.

'Oh, I forgot... A thing... Inside the shuttle. I'll just pop back in for a minute. Can you wait here?'

'Of course, miss.' Not that the guards had any authority to say no.

'I'll help you.' Mai followed Shao back inside the shuttle.

The guards turned and stared at the airlock hatch closed behind her.

Mai quickly booted the prepared software, locking the hatch.

'Got everything?' asked Shao.

'Yup, they'll have to input a captain's override command to open that door now.'

'How's the...?'

'Already here. It is way faster than this painted mule, you know. Especially without passengers.'

'Awesome, let's get going then. Where's the...'

'Right behind you, let me get it for you.'

Mai gave the shuttle a couple of commands through a hand-held terminal, and the craft's augmented reality filter shifted, removing the illusion of an aquarium.

Shao opened the closet and took two emergency spacewalk jumpsuits from it. She handed one to an already undressing Mai and started changing herself.

A couple of minutes later, both women were dressed in the Zhengdao white and gold space suits with tight hoods and flat, opaque metallic facemasks. The suit's faceplate linked up with Shao's HUD contact lenses, and the stream from the helmet camera allowed her to see the Styx Station in real-time, together with all the ship ID signals and data traffic.

Giggling into their comms, they opened the emergency hatch, venting the shuttle and escaping with the quickly crystallizing oxygen. Shao unbuckled a hand-held torch from her suit's utility belt, grabbed Mai's hand, and the two flew towards the Styx race track.

A commlink window opened in Shao's suit's faceplate, on the back-drop of the helmet camera's stream. 'What do you think you're doing, miss?' Sun's face was red with fury and humiliation.

'Just going for a walk. We'll be back before you know it.'

'I already know it! Return immediately, or I'll have to relay this whole debacle to your father!'

'You do you, esteemed Mister Sun.' Shao shrugged and disconnected the stream.

'We're almost there.'

The Sōngshǔ's airlock opened, letting them in. Shao took her mask off and quickly sat down on the pilot's chair, blushing with excitement. 'All right, let's win a race.'

'What's the time?'

'T minus thirty minutes, babe.'

Shao uploaded the coordinates to the jumper's autopilot and en-gaged the magdrive before moving the inertia pod at the back. The tank's transparent hatch closed behind her as soon as Shao put on the facemask. The pod filled with green, elastic inertia gel just as the mask pumped the PFC liquid into her lungs. Shao fought the impulse to rip it off her face and run—even years of pilot training aren't enough to remove the self-preservation instinct fully.

The moon's automatic guidance system led the Sōngshǔ towards the launch pad, where three other ships were already positioned, waiting for the run to begin.

Shao zoomed her HUD view from one to the next using the jumper's external cameras. 'Wanna give me a head's up on the compe-tition, Mai?'

'Sure thing, boss,' replied Mai, jokingly. 'Let me run the scan real quick.'

The first ship was a modified jumper, just like their own. The owner had installed heavy armor on theirs, though, and Shao suspected some hidden weapons onboard. Better be careful with that one, she thought. The second ship was a straight-up racer—a tiny cabin with powerful fission drives dwarfing the rest of the hull. It would easily beat the others in a speed run, but by the looks of it, speed wasn't the most critical factor here. The last ship seemed really out of place—just your run-of-the-mill shuttle, bulbous and awkward-looking when contrasted with the other competitors.

Styx control tower uploaded the race map and the countdown to the Sōngshǔ computer as soon as the ship hit the launch pad bracers. To Shao, it looked as if the designated track was laid out over a Moebius strip plan. Easy-peasy. She ran a check of the primary ion engine and the maneuver magdrives, just in case. According to the ship's sensors, all systems were green, and it seemed the track was laid out with a maglev padding. If nothing else, that should help even out the speed difference between Sōngshǔ and the rocket over there.

The countdown reached thirty seconds. Shao saw the others start to burn their engines and set her ion engine ready but didn't start the thrust yet. Instead, she pulled the magdrive power to the maximum, causing the Sōngshǔ's hull to tremble under pressure induced by the magnetic fields trying to push Styx's walls apart.

'This is gonna hurt,' said Mai over the comms. 'But the hull should hold.'

'It doesn't have to hold on long.'

The countdown reached zero, and the docking clamps let go. The pressure caused by the jumper's releasing magnetic drives on the mag-lev field flung the Sōngshǔ forward like a bolt from a railgun, leaving behind even the fission-powered rocket.

Shao's pod staus turned from green to yellow as the acceleration compressed the inertia gel faster than the ship could compensate. The overdrive pressed on Shao's body, threatening to crush her, and the pod administered steroids and reaction enhancers into the bloodstream, preventing her from slipping away in pain. She kicked in the ion drive and shook in turbulence when the jumper sped up even more. Short-range sensors indicated the turn was nearing fast, and the rocket ship was catching up, despite the armored craft firing laser pulses after it.

'Looks like the others aren't wasting any time,' said Mai. 'They're already slugging it out.'

'I figured as much. I wanted to get at least a bit of space between us; Sōngshǔ can't take a pounding.'

'Not much, no.'

Shao initiated the maneuver drives to lean gently into a curve ahead of them. The computer suddenly signaled the track had shifted—the walls moved, and the turn now arched in the opposite direction.

'Son of a...' grunted Shao, realizing she won't be fast enough to switch the engines. She braced for sudden deceleration, but instead of brutally bouncing off the maglev padding, the Sōngshǔ flipped around its axis, taking the turn backward, then barrel rolled and sped on as if nothing happened.

Shao watched with a tingling of fear as the gel in her pod slowly turned orange, and she felt the crushing weight against her body.

'Neural interface, baby,' laughed Mai over the comms. 'Told you, you should get some.'

Shao didn't reply; her stomach was going up to the throat. The pod's software diagnosed her condition immediately and injected stimulants through the induction needles in the mask. 'You saved our butts,' she agreed as soon as she could speak without fear of vomiting into her mask through the tubing. 'I should have known the track looked too simple.'

'Looks like our company didn't expect it either. The speeder is down to one engine, and the other jumper is looping to bounce off the maglev and catch up.'

'Where's the shuttle?'

'Dunno, can't see it.'

'The pilot probably resigned,' stated Shao, preparing to hit another curve.

'Either that or they crashed.'

Again, the track shifted at the last second, and the course now headed straight down at a sharp angle. Shao expected the sudden turn this time and coordinated the approach angle with Mai. Her pod still blinked in the orange as the Sōngshǔ flipped and pounced down the hole, but with the aid of Mai's computer-assisted reflexes, they managed the plunge with relative ease.

'Found the shuttle,' reported Mai all of a sudden, pointing to the icon on Shao's HUD.

The icon split in front of her eyes, the smaller radar signature falling behind the parent vessel.

'It fell apart?'

'No, wait, it's...' started Mai, but her words drowned in electromagnetic interference. Shao realized the smaller object was a laser buoy, firing its payload into the shuttle's solar sail. The narrow tunnel bounced the accompanying EM discharge off the maglev padding, overpowering their sensors. The clunky-looking craft rushed past them like a thunderbolt of heat, rapidly taking on the next unexpected turn and blinding Shao in the process.

'What the fuck,' cried Shao in surprise and pain as the sharp turn overloaded her pod's capacity to compensate for thrust. 'Son of a bitch sailed past us...'

'So that's why we didn't see him.'

'Madman, who sails in an enclosed space?' Shao felt blood dripping down her throat and the pressure mounting on her eyes, despite the protection of the inertia gel.

'Well, at least we kept the other jackals at bay.'

Mai was right. Shao took turn after turn without seeing the other competitors on the radar display. They must have been slowed down by the abandoned probes just as much as the Sōngshǔ, if not more. The track swiveled and snaked erratically until she had no clue where she was anymore. The best she could do was to try and stay conscious during the crazy spins and stunts they had to pull off to keep the jumper from getting stuck on a maglev bumper along the way.

The race ended suddenly, forcing Shao to hit the burners to slow down. The pod overloaded at the end of it, and she could feel the deceleration crush her lungs like an empty paper bag despite the PFC filling it.

Mai gave up as well but managed to command the autopilot into a mooring sequence before passing out.

The computer drove the Sōngshǔ into the landing bay, administering painkillers and stims to both women. When the atmosphere equalized, and the bay's airlock opened fifteen minutes later, both Mai and Shao were already conscious and cleaned up from the gel crust.

A small crowd cheered as Shao and Mai stepped onto the platform. They were quickly swept by the celebration heading up the hallway to join with a larger party.

Shao wasn't exactly sure how she ended up at the table with a tall, dark-skinned man, whose dreadlocks waved like snakes in the low-g and the commotion in the hallways. One moment she was handed a plastic suction cup with alcohol tasting like grease and acid, which made her swollen eyes water, and the next, she was sitting down. Somebody played fast-paced, electronic music, constantly changing tempo and style in a loud, psychedelic mix.

'Hi,' said Shao a little awkwardly, clasping her moonshine cup with both hands. 'It's some party.'

'Aye, tha's normal after a race... Even a friendly bout like this one,' replied the lean stranger in a melodic drawl.

'It is?'

'Yes. I ain't a fan of drunken crowds, but what can I do. Always a slave to the currents of space, wherever they may lead." The man shrugged. 'Wa's your name?'

'Um, Shao,'

The man grinned, his thin mustache twitched mockingly. 'A pleasure to make an acquaintance, Um Shao. The name's Silver, John Silver.'

Silver's drawl constantly changed, seamlessly shifting between dialects in a confusing but jovial manner.

'Yeah, it's just Shao, Mister Silver,' she said with a shy smile. 'Who are all these people, anyway?'

'Jus' some fans we made. The locals are always hungry for spectacle, no matter how much the vidfeeds saturate the market.'

'We? Do you mean us? You a racer too?

'Da's rite.' Silver nodded.

Their conversation was interrupted momentarily when a group of Outers stopped by, loudly asking for Silver's autograph on various items ranging from helmets to underwear. Silver dutifully signed them all and chuckled with content when the tourists bought him and Shao a round of drinks. He raised the toast, and Shao had no choice but to drink it up, grimacing at the awful taste.

'So you're the asshole who beat me?' she managed after catching her breath.

'Hush, girl. I'm just a poor sailor with spare time and bills to pay.'

'Oh, come on. It was awesome... Except the part where I almost crashed because of you.'

'My bad—didn't mean to bounce your boat. We can drink to your survival, at least!'

He raised another toast, and Shao downed her drink in one go. The booze started to grow on her. She struggled to keep up with Silver's strange speech pattern but found herself enjoying the company.

'I did come second, though.'

Silver grinned in response. 'Tha's the best place to be, they say.'

Shao joined him in laughter. 'We should exchange jackets like the pros do.'

'I think yours is a tad small.'

'Come on; we'll switch back.'

Silver hesitated for a second before agreeing. Another shot glass later, Shao was buckling under the weight of Silver's brown synth-leather jacket with faux-fur coating while laughing hysterically at the man's attempts to squeeze his chest into her white and gold jumpsuit's top. The jacket smelled like smoke and machine grease.

A realization struck her. 'Oh, shit, where's Mai?'

Silver resigned from his attempt and hanged Shao's jacket on a chair. 'Your mechanic friend? I think she was swaggerin' some punks at the bar.'

'I better find her...'

'Why, she can't handle her drink?'

'No, it's just... She's...'

'Say no more,' agreed Silver knowingly, reaching out to help Shao stand up. 'I'll help you look, come.'

They left the table and headed to the improvised bar, where she expected to find Mai in the crowd. They pushed their way through the tightly packed mob of dancers, and Shao almost fell face-forward when the crowd suddenly parted—Silver caught her in the last second.

Shao straightened up, giggling, and was about to say something funny to Silver when the reason for the clearing in the tightly packed deck became apparent.

'Oh, shit,' she muttered, sobering up immediately.

The crowd passed to let a group of eight white-and-gold clad soldiers armed with needler rifles. Silver disappeared without a trace, but between the armed guards stood terrified Mai Wren, accompanied by Jin Sun and Shao's father.

Without a word, Yuan Zhenya motioned for his daughter to follow and turned to leave.

Crushed by the disappointment on her father's face, Shao obliged, avoiding Mai and Sun's questioning looks.

5

Delacroix stepped out of the projector panel and leaned over the technician finishing the edit of her final message to Zhenya. The man just finished adding the fish playfully circling Delacroix's head. 'That should keep him busy,' she stated, more to herself than the techie.

The technician was focused on his job, erasing any signs of the footage tampering with speed brought only by routine and experience. His hands moved with certainty between the icons, cooperating with the neural interface connecting his cybernetic eyes with the computer using a high-speed laser link. The control light blinked green and yellow, casting odd-colored shadows on the man's gray skin. The work slowed long enough to maintain a conversation with an offhand comment. 'Sure, if you say so, boss.'

Delacroix knew the technician only cared about what she had to say out of idle curiosity, but she didn't mind.

'Why bother with the subterfuge at all, though?' asked the techie. 'Not that I mind or need to know. Cred is cred, right?'

'Right.' She considered not telling him, but the tendency for theatrics took the better of her. 'I wanted him to think I'm hiding something. That way he'll never catch on to me not being entirely honest.' The technician listened to her conversation anyway, so there wasn't a point in keeping secrets from him. She liked to retread and reiterate ideas anyway. It made spotting the flaws easier, even if the plan was already ongoing.

'I don't get it,' he said after a while.

'Don't get what, Miguel?'

'Like, so he thinks you're on Nix, enjoying a spa,' he said, watching the export bar progress quickly on the finished work. 'But you're on Charon, boohoo, big whoop. And why the underwater ef-ex?'

'Well, I want him to think I went with an overly elaborate negotiation scheme to hide something,' Delacroix explained patiently. 'He'll want to find out what it is, and that'll consume time and effort that otherwise might be spent elsewhere. Like finding out what I'm actually trying to hide.'

'Ah, I get it. Something's fishy with your cargo. Nice. Clever, clever.' He pushed a few buttons and sent the message on its way.

'Something like that.'

She paid and left his cabin. The man was wrong, of course, but explaining everything to a random hacker hired for one service only was too much, even for her. If I did that, she thought, I might as well grow a mustache to twirl.

She headed towards the docks, passing restaurants, casinos, and omnipresent virtual brothels.

The Charon station's main road running along the asteroid's hub was divided into four lanes—two for the arriving traffic and two for departures. The inner ones were excluded from pedestrians and serviced by magpeds. Delacroix headed straight there, calling a rental vehicle on the way. Masses of people passing these halls gave it the characteristic spaceport smell, sweat mixed with antimicrobe spray, and cheap air conditioning. Charon station's system was well-maintained and lag-free, and so the levitating chair waited for her the moment she stepped onto the boarding platform. Delacroix rested her weight on the seating with a sigh of relief. She let the magped ride the maglev rail towards the station's docks. Passing other commuters. Pilots. Vagabonds. Free-traders. The station maintained a steady one-g of rotational gravity, pushing Delacroix down. Aromas of hundred different fast foods printed by passing gastrodrones mixed with cleaning products, irritating Delaxroix's throat. She shifted uncomfortably, her body unused to the exercise.

Delacroix watched the crowds passing her in both ways. Brightly clad Outers in loose tunics and ponchos, wearing wide-brimmed hats and HUD-goggles. There were a lot of spacers in the crowd - zeroes and floaters. River of people in hundreds of different jumpsuits, spending their hard-earned cred on booze and hookers on short shore leave before departing again. High-pitched laughter pierced above the general noise—drunk freighter crews or chipped prospectors, Delacroix couldn't tell. Sprinkled here and there were serious businessmen in suits fitted to form, hurrying to their meetings and transits. Delacroix let the murmur drown out her thoughts and tried to relax, but she couldn't stop nervously scanning the halls. Her eyes hanged upon a small group of people moving through the human river like icebergs—their body language always betrayed them, whether dressed in suits or djellabas; mercs could never hide who they were. This group seemed unaware of her, busy making shady deals with an Outer wearing nothing but a speedo and a transparent coat, demonstrating his chromatic skin pulsating in a kaleidoscope of colors.

Finally sure no one was paying any attention to her, Delacroix focused on her HUD's communicator. 'About damn time, Silver,' she said when the pirate finally picked up.

'Deepest apologies, admiral. My hands were tied elsewhere, but I'm free to obey your commands now. I'm just a poor sailor, bound to obey the whim of chance.'

Delacroix rolled her eyes so hard her HUD goggles almost slid off. 'Cut the shit, Silver.'

'Fine, suit yourself,' he replied, dropping the act and chuckling. 'You never did fall for my lucky charms.'

'And I never will. How's the prep? Did you get what I asked for?'

'Sure, sure. Wasn't easy though. She's waiting for you on my ship, no stress.'

'I'll stress however much I want, and it's none of your business.'

'It's just a saying, no stress.'

Delacroix imagined his stupid grin. 'I take it she's onboard of her own volition, yes? I won't have the Rangers on my ass because of kidnapping?'

'Absolutely, no force was applied in obtaining the actress, just cred.'

'Good, good. I'm on my way to the docks, to rehearse the role with her before you depart. But be ready to lift off today, got it?'

'Never been readier. We can head to the Cloud in twenty hours if that's cool with you.'

'Perfect. I'll wire your waystation fees right away then.' Delacroix disconnected the comms and got off the chair.

The station's navigation software uploaded the directions to the shuttle via her HUD as she headed for the docks. She followed the augmented reality arrows leading to the right bay, ignoring the station's AR system warning her it's closed for maintenance. The road was blocked by a sealed hatch, red light, and AR floaters warning her of the dangers of an open space bay. Delacroix just sighed and uploaded the code. The hatch slid open with a quiet whir of servomotors, letting her in. The inside was well lit, and not at all exposed to vacuum. Could actually use a bit of fresh air, she thought as the mixed odors of fuel, grease, and stale booze hit her nostrils.

The green shuttle sat on the burned-up floor, bulky and ugly. It reminded Delacroix of the tailed frogs from Callisto—clumsy-looking oafs whose robust body hid their speed and voracious hunter instincts. The comparison fits on more than a superficial level, she thought. The pirates were ambush predators, just like the frogs. They might be on her payroll at this moment, but she'd be a fool to trust them further than she can throw them.

The shuttle hatch opened slowly as she approached, and the pirate swaggered down the gangplank, accompanied by a chubby Outer woman with a mess of short, black hair.

Silver bowed with a mocking grin, tipping an imaginary hat. 'Welcome aboard our finest craft, boss woman.'

'That's *not* your finest craft, Silver. At least you dropped that badly faked dialect.'

'Perhaps it's a goodly faked dialect, made to look fake to confuse the—'

'Right, and I'm the queen of Canada.'

'Fine, be that way.' Silver shrugged. 'This is the actress you asked us to peruse, Miss Porshe.'

'Samantha Porshe,' added the Outer woman with a coy smile.

Delacroix eyed the woman up and down unkindly. 'She looks nothing like me.'

'I'm not wearing any stage makeup yet, but I assure you I'm a professional, Miss Delacroix.'

'Please, call me Emma. And speaking of which, here's the data.' Delacroix uploaded a set of files to the actress' icon, raising an eyebrow in surprise as Porshe reached into her pocket for a hand tablet. 'It's a list of directives, comms you have to send, deals to make, places to be. Also, a few hours of footage and intel about me, so you can pull it off convincingly.'

Porshe scrolled through the list using her finger, frowning a little. 'It seems like I'll be organizing a prisoner transport? And overseeing the launch of a hauler ship?'

'That is correct. Make the meetings already scheduled, get as many prisoner contracts as you can, make sure the hauler is modified to hold them, and see to it that it launches as planned. That's it.'

Porshe pocketed the tablet with a shrug. 'Sounds easy enough, especially since none of the people there know me... You, personally.'

'Great. I'm looking forward to hearing about your success. Make sure to speak with as many prisoners as you can.'

'I'm sorry, but why?'

'Because I pay you to. And get rid of that tablet, I use a HUD, like everyone in the System who didn't just crawl out from under a rock.'

'Tablets are top shit in the Cloud, boss,' interjected Silver. 'You need network connectivity for the HUD goggles to work, and the Cloud is not called a Frontier because of well-entrenched infrastructure. A tablet's got all the functionality with none of the limitations. Plus, it can store the data locally.'

Delacroix eyed him up and down. 'Look at you, an IT salesman in disguise. Missed your calling, huh?'

'Very funny. Keep it up, and people will almost mistake you for a person from time to time.'

'Are you two always bickering like that, or are you just married?'

'See, boss woman? You have nothing to worry about; you two are practically twins already. By the sound of it, at least.'

'I trust she will do a great job. Yours, however, ends when you drop Miss Porshe off at the Helikaon station. Your fee awaits you there, and you will receive it when my associates confirm she has arrived safe and unharmed. Just keep it quiet, got it?'

'No worries, I'll lay low. Unless my admiral needs our services, we'll be spending our paycheck sitting pretty.'

'Pirates have admirals now? What next, a pope?'

'Careful, boss woman. Someone less amicable than I could "pope" that grin right off your face. Along with the rest of your head.'

Silver's eyes were suddenly dull as two pieces of glass, losing all expression and illusion of humor. Delacroix felt a sudden heat wave, her lips shuddered. Keep it together, she thought, trying to stave off an oncoming panic attack. The pirate was a dangerous man, and she could only provoke him so far before she crossed the line from seeming daring and unafraid to being dead in a ditch. 'Now, now, Mister Silver,' she managed, almost without her voice trembling. 'Don't let your emotions get in the way of business. It wouldn't be healthy.'

'Not for you, that's for sure, boss woman.' Silver menacingly leaned slightly forward.

'Right, I'd love to stay and compare dicks, but I have timetables to keep.' Delacroix backed off towards the bay hatch, gave Porshe a last glance, and turned away. A cold drop of sweat slid between her shoulder blades. She was pretty sure that Silver wouldn't shoot her just for the fun of it. Almost sure.

6

Shao stormed through the decks of the Yusan, uncaring about other crew members, who had to step out of the way to avoid a collision. She had spent the last month learning the ropes of prospecting in the Cloud, studying the nav charts, piloting the mining craft used in harvesting raw materials, operating machinery, protocols of conduct when dealing with frontiersmen and freelancers—all with Mai. They had worked almost an entire month. One-third of the long journey through the Great Beyond, a vast stretch of interstellar space between the Heliopause, marking the end of the Solar System, and the Oort Cloud. Now, after not mentioning it at all, hell, after barely making the time for a few stiff dinners together, her father had the audacity to assign them to different ships?

Shao couldn't believe her eyes when she checked the full crews' roster; she wasn't supposed to, but what is the point of knowing the captain's passcode if one doesn't use it? At first, she thought there must have been some mistake; after all, her father's adjutant assured her that there would be no problem with her and Mai being on the same crew. The expert system chooses people best suited to work together, he said on multiple occasions. Since Shao and Mai are already good friends, as he put it, the computer would take it into account.

Sun even went out of his way to get to know Mai and give her priority access to the mothership's training facilities together with Shao.

Now that Shao stopped to think about it, Sun must have done so on her father's bidding, to spy on the two. Perhaps he even found out about the few times when the simulators had "power outages" arranged by Mai so they could spend some time alone without surveillance?

Fueled by those thoughts, Shao became gradually more enraged, and by the time she reached her father's cabin, she was angry enough to storm past the secretary without so much as acknowledging her existence.

Yuan Zhenya looked up from his desk. 'Can I help you in anything?'

Shao glared at her father's regular, biosculpted features—the smooth bastard looks not much older than I am, she thought. She barely recognized the father who thought her how to fly a jumper, took the family for vacation to Venus... The corp chewed Yuan and spat him out changed, since he became the chairman.

'Help me? You...' Shao cut herself off, grasping for words. 'How long are you going to punish me for running off? It was my last day of freedom, for fuck's sake!'

'If you're referring to the incident on Styx, I was under the impression the matter was behind us?' her father replied, slowly but deliberately. 'You're not a teen to be grounded for misbehaving.'

'Then why are you doing this? Out of spite?'

I'm not doing anything. I already told you, I'm sorry for not being able to come and greet you, I was held up by work. As for your escapade and endangering your own and your friend's life, you're an adult. That's all I have to say.'

Shao leaned over the desk, poking the air in front of her father's face with a finger angrily. 'Don't pretend you had nothing to do with it! You're the captain of this piece of junk!'

'Honestly, my dear,' replied Yuan, letting irritation sound in his voice. 'Either sit down and tell me what you're going on about or let me work in peace.'

Shao paused and sat down, more or less, on an involuntary impulse. She took a deep breath before continuing. The air in Yuan's spartan office smelled of sandalwood, just like their home on Titan. 'I'm talking about you reassigning Mai to a different ship, what else?'

'I did no such thing. Your assignment has been taken care of by the computer, based on your profile and career prospects.'

'And of course, you didn't interfere in any way to make sure we're not on the same tour,' Shao said, her words dripping with sarcasm.

'I did not. Here, let's see.'

Yuan brought up an augmented reality display into her view listing all twenty mining ships and their prospective crews, organized into neat columns. Yuan selected Mai Wren's name together with Shao's and magnified them, highlighting their dossiers for her to see.

'There's no mystery here,' he said. 'You're my daughter and a skilled pilot on the fast track to a promising officer career, so the system assigned you to ZMV Seventeen. Its tour of duty is short since it's going to venture into a rich rare metal deposit. You'll fulfill the mission parameters quickly and reach the quota of work in the field, then return to the Yusan and undergo command and management training. That way, you'll not only head into a great first year of your career in the corporation, you'll also make fine captain material, and we'll get to spend more time together. When we return to the Solar System, you'll have a bright future ahead of you.'

Shao bit her lip, looking at the data carefully. 'What about Mai? We both graduated the same year, and you can't tell me she doesn't have a future in the corp.'

Yuan nodded thoughtfully, weighing his words. 'Listen, Shao. I know you two are... Close. But you must think of her best interests as well. Mai finished the IT degree, specializing in communication and navigation software. She will need the work experience, not just a glory tour in the field, to satisfy the pencil-pushers back home. She was assigned to ZMV Five. Sure, she'll be out the entire journey, but the expert system decided correctly. Mai will score hundreds of hours of fieldwork more than she would on Seventeen, and will quickly get a job as a navigator on a mothership like the Yusan. After a few years, maybe even as a fleet coordinator. This is a good prospect for her.'

'And just by sheer coincidence, that good prospect will lead to a career in the Cloud, as far away from me as possible?'

'I can't help how you feel,' replied Yuan softly. 'This is best for both of you, I won't overrule the system.'

'I hate you so much sometimes.' Shao stood and left, feeling the tears gathering in her eyes.

The white corridors of the mothership passed before her eyes in a blur as she ran, unconsciously following the directions displayed by the ship's augmented reality filter on her HUD lens.

Shao sat down on her bed, her face hidden in her hands, trying to think of something to do or say. Hot tears ran down her face, her throat gripped by sorrow and anger. Her eyes fell on the leather jacket hanging from a rack in an open closet—a memento from her last day of freedom with Mai.

'It's too big for me...' she muttered irrationally but got up to put it on anyway. She curled back onto the bed, covering herself with the jacket—it still smelled vaguely of engine grease. Her hands felt something hard in the pocket, and she pulled it out. Surprised, she sat on the bed, examining the unmarked info chip. Curiosity killed the cat, she thought. Then again, she could use a distraction right now... Shao shook her head. 'This is stupid, what am I, five?'

She tossed the jacked haphazardly into the closet and was about to throw the chip into the recycler, but hesitated. What could the mysterious racer carry in his pocket? Maybe it's important, and he's looking for it? It's probably porn, decided Shao. Still, checking it out can't hurt, and it will stave off the moment when she'll have to comm Mai and tell her they won't be on tour together. She has to call, do the responsible thing, as Dad would say—like he ever had to sacrifice anything.

With those thoughts, Shao ran an antivirus scan on the chip, and when the results came in negative on malware, she uploaded the contents to her HUD.

7

Shao watched as the footage unfolded in a panel of her augmented reality feed. The compressed video must have been corrupted sometime between being beamed and loaded onto a chip, large pixels, and discolorations making it hard to read the details.

It must be a ship security feed, she figured. The date stamp marked it as January 17th, 2280—over a year ago.

A slim, jaunty Outer man in a sagging technician jumpsuit stared directly into the lens with a haunted expression in sunken eyes. His rubbery, gray skin seemed gaunt and malnourished, even his dark eyes and a mess of rainbow-colored hair—not unlike Shao's own—looked odd in the decompressed, glitchy footage.

'Right, where should I start?' he muttered. 'My name is Adam Redding. I've been fighting with the nav systems since the last time, but the shit's deep-fried.'

Shao tensed immediately, something in the feed made her skin crawl. Not the man, it was something else. Something in the footage was deeply disturbing—not the cabin either, as far as she could tell it was some sort of control room, full of screens, panels, and keyboards. And yet... It's like fingernails scratching on the ship hull, she thought. Same feeling, but without the sound.

'I wore the same jumpsuit for days now, and it itches,' continued the man incoherently. His eyes kept darting to the corners. Like a panicked rat in a trap. 'I wish I could muster the courage to use the showers, but I wouldn't dare after what happened to Chucky.'

Redding ran his long fingers through his hair. Shao noticed the fingernails were black and crusted in old blood. Chewed. Or scratched.

'Right, where was I? Everything works. Kinda. Except for the software. It ninja-plots a course to the far side of the Cloud instead of back home every time I try to reset it, so basically we're lost. The ship's computers don't reflect that change, so it looks like we're headed towards the buoys. We'd been following the navs for days before we even noticed something was wrong. We may be pretty much anywhere now.' His head dropped, and he covered his face with his hands, fighting a panic attack.

'I guess you should see for yourself. From the start. Computer, play security footage from this cabin, start January, the fifth.'

The screen went dark for a moment.

When the footage returned, a cleaner, healthier, and relaxed Redding sat on a chair in a cabin filled with instruments, screens, and control panels. He leaned back on a magchair, legs on the control panel, watching a jumper race stream, only sporadically looking at the numbers flying by on the screen in front of him. The pilots in the feed were navigating their craft through a labyrinthine track full of sudden turns and power-ups, competing aggressively. The gut-wrenching, almost subliminal dread from the first part of the footage was gone, though Shao couldn't quite shake the memory of Redding's haunted expression. No, not haunted, she thought. Hunted.

The radar console beeped suddenly, and the graphs spiked.

Redding barely looked at it, but the footage displayed a side window with information—a single return signal, from what seemed to be an advanced ladar array.

'All right, lemme scan you real quick, baby,' said Redding in a bored tone. 'Another damn rock.' He paused the transmission, brought up a radar control panel into his field of vision, and commanded the network to triangulate. Shao watched the commands Redding gave recorded on the feed in the form of text input—whatever the ship was, they were monitoring the crew pretty tightly.

It wasn't long before the radar's laser beam located the object again, along with the size and vector estimate—a tiny object, barely two meters long, drifting idly through the Cloud, on its way out. Redding seemed uninterested until the EM scan data arrived, showing impressive spikes in the signature.

A second later, he sat up in a chair and hailed the commanding officer. 'Cap, you better come take a look.'

A second stream joined the recording, dubbed Cpt. Juarez.

'Found space whales again?' said a female voice over the commlink.

Redding rolled his eyes. 'I told you it wouldn't happen again, ma'am.'

'What is it then? I haven't got all day, you know.'

'EM readings, off the charts for predictions. We're supposed to find ice cubes out here mostly, nothing magnetic.'

'Hit me up,' commanded the captain. Redding must have sent the data to her commlink, because a moment later she added: 'Be right down,' and disconnected.

'Yay, just what I needed,' muttered Redding.

He unzipped the restraints on the chair, pushed himself off, grabbed the edge of the console, and pulled himself closer. He quickly shoved empty food ration packages into the trash compactor, rounded up floating equipment and personal items, and just managed to lock them up in a drawer when the cabin door opened with a hiss and Captain Juarez entered.

Shao couldn't help but smile watching the young Outer scramble. I'm not the only one having to deal, she thought. It wasn't much of a consolation, but it beats suffering alone.

Redding looked innocently at a tall, muscular woman who must have been spending all her free time at the ship's high-g gym. Juarez floated awkwardly in the navigation room. Her red hair floated around her head, an aureole of ginger braids, as she looked around. The beige walls were clean, and all the junk stuck into tool drawers.

'I see you picked up on the workspace cleanliness regulations,' she said, suspicion coloring her tone. 'I'll drop by for a thorough inspection later, rookie, now show me the data.'

Redding sent over the data excerpt to the captain's HUD. 'Here they are, mom, err, ma'am. The readings are bizarre; I don't know what to make of it.'

Juarez gave her subordinate a stern look, but not bereft of sympathy. 'Afraid you're gonna make another whale mistake? Good. Never jump to conclusions, rookie.'

Redding just shrugged it off and pulled himself to the side, letting the captain get to the consoles. Unlike his commanding officer, he moved with grace indicating that he was used to zero-g. He reminded Shao of Mai, who always floated with effortless grace as if she was born in the void. The captain on the other hand moved heavily like a rhino without the gravity supporting her motions. Shao saw she had to use magpads on her feet and hands to make the short trek from the door to the console.

'What are you smirking at?' she grumbled at her subordinate as she passed by slowly. 'Having a giggle at the commanding officer's expense, are we?'

'No, ma'am. Never.'

'You Outer kids have no respect.'

'But we have good balance,' replied Redding—faster than he could stop to think about it, judging by his expression.

Juarez chuckled and wagged her finger at him. 'And a sharp sense of humor, too,' she said. 'Just don't make a habit of talking back to officers.'

'No promises, ma'am.'

Captain Juarez looked over at the consoles, studying them intently, her focus giving her face a stern look. No, not only focus, thought Shao. Something else too. Fear.

She opened a ship-wide commlink, a small status window immediately popping up in the corner of the recording. 'Wake up, boys and girls. We have a priority one find.'

Three more icons popped into the feed.

'Space whales again, cap?' asked a man described as engineer Paulson, whose voice over the comms was drowsy with sleep.

Redding groaned loudly, 'Oh, come on. I made one mistake, and on the first day!'

'It was hilarious, though. Ooh, captain, I think I found life, ooo. Singing like whales, I peed my pants, oh my.'

'Piss off,' started Redding, but didn't get to finish the sentence before Juarez interjected.

'Knock it off, both of you. The sensors picked up a mutating frequency EM field, and we gotta check it out.'

'Yes ma'am,' both men agreed in unison.

'Jake, get the engines up.'

'Of course, right away,' agreed Paulson.

'Track our prize,' continued Juarez, to Redding this time. 'Keep a long-range sensor on it and don't let it slip.'

She turned to leave the navigator's cabin, accidentally catching a drawer with her elbow. The shelf opened with a silent click, releasing a tangle of tools, posters, uneaten food, and energy drink bags. The clutter expanded rapidly into a cloud of junk when the tightly packed items were suddenly freed, releasing the pressure.

Juarez gave Redding a long stern look promising trouble later but left without saying a word.

'Computer, send a long-range stream to the nearest buoy. Relay the fastest possible route to HQ on Luna,' Shao heard the captain say, she must have forgotten to switch to personal comms. 'This is OSEE Deep Cloud Five exploration vessel, Captain Martina Juarez speaking.'

'You're still on the open comms, cap,' reminded someone named Chuck, apparently the ship's pilot.

The captain switched off without a word.

A few minutes had passed before the hull trembled. Redding had barely had the time to finish pushing the last piece of clutter back into the drawer when the acceleration formed a gravitational pull. He quickly sat down on the chair and strapped in, not wanting to have to struggle to reach the console. He quickly unlocked the keyboard and typed a command, transferring control to his HUD, then unbuckled and waited.

As soon as the ship's movement paused for a second, he leaped towards a long compartment in the cabin wall. 'Wait, don't go yet,' he cried to the commlink.

Chuck's icon muted for a moment, and Shao imagined the pilot cursing under his breath. 'The procedure is already on the countdown, Whaleman. Please tell me you're in the tube...'

'Well, yes,' said Redding, scrambling to get into the compartment. 'But actually, no.'

'Bloody hell, kid, you wanna get smooshed?'

'Let me guess,' added Juarez. 'You were tidying up a mess?'

'Jesus, seriously,' spat Chuck angrily into the comms. 'You tryna sit through acceleration in a chair or something?'

'I'd rather not,' admitted Redding. 'Almost in.' He pushed himself into the tube and ordered the computer to lock him in, while simultaneously calibrating the sensors to take the ship's turning and acceleration into account, to make sure they won't lose the find.

Without a word, Chuck sent him the plotted course and calibration data, along with a countdown informing how long before the acceleration blows Redding's brains out.

The tube's hatch closed with a rubbery smack, transparent alloy separating Redding from the rest of the cabin. The footage became grainy as the ship shuddered and accelerated noticeably, preparing for the final thrust. Shao saw Redding put on a mask as his tube filled with green gel, gagging a little when the long tube made its way down his throat. She also saw a small tool floating up towards the center of the cabin. A screwdriver.

Redding must have noticed it as well, 'Oh shit,' he muttered.

'What happened,' asked the captain. 'Are you in the tube?'

'Yeah, yeah, it's just. Nothing. All good.'

'You sure?'

'Yup, everything's tip-top.'

Gel filled the pod just as the counter reached zero. Shao watched in rising panic as the screwdriver spins around, slowly drifting to the height of Redding's face, aiming the sharp point right at him. She saw the Outer trying to wiggle to the side, but the gel held hard—the pod intended to protect the passengers from being crushed by acceleration trapped him in front of a blade. The cabin shook as the ship accelerated rapidly, and the screwdriver fell with a tremendous force, skewering the cabin door.

Shao exclaimed unwillingly, but she calmed down hearing Redding sighing with relief.

'That coulda gone badly,' he muttered.

'What could have gone badly?' asked Juarez on the comms.

'Oh, nothing, everything's fine.

***

The footage became too corrupted to watch afterward, so Shao set a notification on her HUD to tell her when it's clear again, and printed herself a cube of coffee. By the time she finished preparing the drink, the recording blinked back into her view.

Redding shuddered as he exited the gel tube, and removed the mask. He looks like he's about to vomit, Shao thought. She knew being confined during the acceleration caused some people, even Outers and some floaters, massive claustrophobia attacks. She always found it kind of funny—one would think claustrophobia is the last thing to expect in space. She personally loved the rush, the weight of hundreds of g's crashing down on her, while she's safe in the pod, piloting.

She watched Redding as he scrubbed the remnants of the hardened gel off his uniform and ordered the cleaner drone to get rid of them, wondering if that's there is to the recording, just a technician doing his job on a ship somewhere.

Redding stepped to the nearest terminal screen, low-g created by the deceleration barely enough to prevent him from floating away, and looked into the black screen, staring at his reflection for a moment.

He gave a command through his HUD, and the screen booted with a click, displaying a logo with the ship's name, Deep Cloud Nine. The ladar reading indicated they jumped precisely into shuttle distance from the object, which didn't change its relative position since they detected it. The mystery thickens, Shao thought while sipping coffee.

Redding brought up the chat window and pasted the coordinates into it for the crew to see. 'Doesn't look like our catch moved,' he commented. 'It's sitting pretty.'

Chuck's icon flickered as he scanned the data. 'Doesn't look like a ship. Too small, and no heat readings.'

'It's barely warmer than the background,' agreed Juarez.

The ship's engineer's icon joined the conversation. Paulson greeted his colleagues drowsily. 'Morning crew. How long have we been?' asked Paulson.

Chuck brought up the flight plan in response, with the ship's course marked in red line over the stylized background of the Oort Cloud. 'Almost fifteen hours, at half a percent,' he said. 'We're a little off course, but it's no biggie. We'll pick up the find and hop right back on schedule.'

'Great, another delay in the mission,' grumbled Paulson.

'It's only a few sols; you'll live,' reprimanded Juarez.

Chuck sneered. 'Just grit your teeth and think of the bonus pay-check. I, for one, am planning to buy a nice little house on Venus when we get back—'

And farm sweet potatoes, we know,' interrupted Redding. 'You keep telling us.'

'What about you, Outer boy?' asked Paulson. 'Gonna spend your paycheck on a boat and go hunting space whales?'

'I would, but your mom's already taken.'

Juarez cut in before the situation escalated. 'How long 'till we're in pickup range? Let's not make this detour longer than it needs to be.'

Redding rechecked the radar readings. The object, whatever it was, neared fifty thousand klicks. 'We should be good to go now, ma'am.'

'Good. Chuck, park the boat here and take the shuttle. Paulson, keep the engines warm and ready the bay—in fact, prep the autolab while you're at it. Redding, keep the comms running, and monitor the object's position.'

The crew acknowledged the captain, and Redding got busy setting up a macro updating the shuttle on its relative position between the Deep Cloud and the target. The program came online once the shuttle departed, allowing both Redding and the shuttle pilot to monitor their progress. The Cloud kept its course carried by inertia, firing the maneuvering thrusters every now and again to keep it steady.

'You're doing great, Chuck, keep the course, and you'll get there in an hour.'

'Thanks, mate. I guess I'll watch a movie or something. Got anything good?'

'I have Space Jockey 3, I can stream it to you.'

'I thought the captain locked the smutfeeds?'

'You want it or not?'

'Aight, hit me up.'

Shao observed the shuttle's trajectory on the recorded displays. The distance between the mysterious find and the shuttle was shrinking, but still considerable. Curious, she sped up the footage sixty minutes.

'All right, keep it steady and keep your hands on the blanket,' Redding said, then unbuckled himself from a chair and rummaged through the drawers. It took some effort, but he managed to liberate a bag of self-heating soup. He opened the cap and started sucking the liquid. He sat back down and stared at the sensor readings. Hesitating, Redding brought up his commlink again. 'Captain, the field is gone.'

'What do you mean *gone?*'

'Just like that, it was there one second, gone the next.'

'Maybe you misaligned the sensors?'

'No, ma'am. I'm positive.'

'What's going on?' Chuck enquired. 'Is the object still there?'

'Yup, still there.' Redding sighed heavily. 'Should I abort?'

'Negative, continue the mission.'

Redding shrugged. 'Whatever,' he muttered, muted the commlink, and looked at the readings again, narrating them under his breath for the mission archive.

'Computer, compile data. The object's EM field isn't strong enough to interfere with sensors. Its influence distorted the readings slightly, but all the indications were otherwise in order. There's just one thing—the comms between the shuttle and the mothership were out of sync just a tiny bit. It shouldn't look like this... The shuttle comms seem to take double the bandwidth, almost as if they were mirrored, or something was hijacking the comm laser to add data.' Intrigued, he opened a maintenance connection, which immediately popped into the recorded feed.

'Right, coming in on five hundred meters now,' Shao heard Chuck report.

'Do you have visual confirmation?' inquired Juarez.

'Roger. It looks like some kind of silvery tear. It's definitely not an asteroid, way too regular.'

Redding listened to the pilot inattentively while examining the bandwidth. He eventually shrugged and closed the maintenance window.

'Opening the hatch, captain,' reported Chuck. 'I'm going to intercept the object in ETA two minutes.'

'Good look, Chucky,' replied Juarez. 'Everything five by five there, Redding?'

'Yes, ma'am. All readings normal.'

***

The footage went dark. When it returned, Redding was floating in the cabin, bent and spitting bloody bubbles.

'That door could have cut me in half,' he whispered through thirsty, cracked lips. 'Gotta be more careful.'

The lights flickered, and the hull shuddered as a heavy moan of machinery ominously pierced the silence. His shoulders slumped as he cast a terrified glance somewhere outside of the frame. 'It's happening again,' he said. 'I don't have much time. I rerouted all the security recordings and personal feeds onto a small recording unit.'

'Our ship was... *Is* on an exploratory mission beyond the furthest reaches of the D sector. I'm hoping someone will find the footage eventually. We're, um, further than any human has ever gone.'

Shao realized she's holding a half-empty coffee mug only when the self-heating liquid spilled and burned her fingers. She put it away.

'I've started this log to, um, document the events,' started Redding again after a frame jump. 'I'm afraid I won't be there to relay the account of what happened in person.' He waved his hand, and a map of the Oort Cloud displayed itself as an overlay in the corner of the footage. The Deep Cloud's position was marked with references to the nearest human-made stations in Sector D. 'We were sent to map the space and place the laser buoys, making way for prospecting in the future. Part of the recent deal between Colonies and OSEE, you know. Earth is allowed to send a ship partially crewed by their people; Colonies fill the rest of the ranks and get access to all the data. I guess it works out cause I got the job on this can.'

Redding was interrupted by a hum of opening doors as Captain Juarez entered the cabin, her red-hair disheveled and her military uniform smeared with black oil and in disarray. 'What's the sitrep?' she asked without a greeting, apparently unaware of the recording camera.

Redding gave a quick annoyed glance towards it before turning to the captain. 'Same as before, cap. We can't contact the NaviNet. What do you want me to do?'

'I don't know,' said the captain, exasperated. 'There's gotta be something.'

'I plotted the course back the way we came; maybe our sensors will pick up one of the buoys, best I can do.'

'Mierda. Think of something better, rookie!'

'Aye, aye, captain.' Redding saluted mockingly. 'I'll pull a set of new microchips straight from my hat. Anything else I can do for you on this beautiful day?'

'Don't fucking test me.'

'Aye, aye, cap, I'll do my best.'

Juarez grunted, unsatisfied with the answer. 'Fix it.'

Redding hunched, as if expecting a blow, but the captain just left without a word.

'I'm making this recording as a letter in a bottle or something,' he continued after regaining composure. 'We're fucked, and we aren't gonna make it. The mission went to a crapper when we found that... I don't even know what it is. A freaking flying saucer. That's what I've been telling them, but they don't believe me. Earthers, the fuck do they know, right?'

Redding paused to take a breath. He brought up a feed from a different security camera.

A group of five scientists in vacuum suits oversaw a drone forklift emerging from the craft. The camera's overlay labeled the box carried by the drone as a container holding the anomaly. The excited scientists speculated wildly about the contents of the crate—their theories ranging from strongly magnetic minerals to some sort of a beacon. Their discussion displayed on separate windows tagged by name and wave-form added to audio logs played in the background as they moved the crate through the bowels of the ship, followed by camera footage.

'The object was unusual enough, and the docs were happy like rabbits during spring,' Redding said. 'It's a shame I've no idea what's in-side the crate; I don't have access to the comms there. The mission had to go on, weird rocks or no, and so we kept the course—going where no man's been before. Or so we thought.' He returned to the screen once more.

The lights in his cabin flickered and dimmed, causing him to drop on the floor in panic. He got up after a moment with an embarrassed look on his face and hair in disarray. 'Sorry about that,' he said. 'The ship's been acting up lately. Where was I? Oh, yes. We continued our mission for a few sols before I noticed something was wrong. At first, everything seemed to be in order—except for the added weight on the comms, but it wasn't enough of an issue to investigate. Then the lights started to flicker for no reason, the doors and hatches locked and opened randomly... I almost got cut in half when the servo exploded in my cabin doors. So we had our engineer grab a few docs and run a full-ship diagnostic, and it turns out our navigation is no longer informing the ship's computers about our course.'

'I've done my best to manually steer the Deep Cloud towards the buoys we left behind, but I don't believe we'll make it back. I think all the electronics onboard are fritzed—can't prove it, but the ship just feels wrong somehow. Anyway, that's my message in a bottle. Redding, out.'

***

The recording didn't stop. The dark screen remained, and the feed kept playing, filled with distant echoes and noises. Shao listened intently, trying to make something out of it. The interference sounded vaguely rhythmical, almost like whispered chanting.

Eventually, it skipped to the next part of the message.

The camera feed displayed a charging battery symbol on a black background. Over a minute passed before it came online with a click. It was still in the Deep Cloud's cabin, except the computers were all dark and silent, and the only light source came from the LED lamp on a helmet's solid faceplate. The man in an armored suit attempted to hack into the device. A console window obscured part of the camera's feed, awash with hundreds of commands, and override attempts. Another click announced the man's success, followed by a message informing that the audio channels have been linked to a mobile commlink network. The man reached out with a hand gloved in rust-colored protective plating and picked the camera up from the ground. The display window marked a data file download directly to the user's HUD and playback as he floated through the vacuum of the Deep Cloud's desolate decks.

'Oi, boss man! Got somethin' juicy for ya,' the man said in a coarse voice. 'Take a gander.'

'Wha' you got there, Stevens?' came a reply in a dialect with a heavy accent. Shao knew that voice—it was Silver's.

'Looks like one of them birds, left us a letter, and it flew away with the treasure. Take a look at this.'

A pop-up window marked the transfer of information to another HUD.

'Shit. This might be worth a penny or two,' came Silver's reply after a while.

'My thoughts exactly,' agreed Stevens. 'An anomaly like that's gotta be worth a good mil. Hell, maybe the poor sods found aliens, no? That'd be something. We gonna stray off course to pick it up?'

'Nuh. We have the coordinates. Let's get this boat to Pluto for a refit an' swing by the treasure trove on our way to the rendez-vous.'

'Whatever you say, boss man,' replied Stevens. 'I thought we're gonna salvage the boat, though?'

'Change of plans. It's in good condition. We can arm it and run with it.'

'What the hell do we need this junker for?'

'Damn it, Stevens, you never plan ahead. Never take the long view. I, for one, do. It's a Monday, and I'm already thinking about Wednesday... It is Monday, right?'

'I think so,' agreed Stevens. 'Taking the long view is why you're the boss man, not me.'

'And don't you forget it.' Silver's jovial tone carried the slightest hint of threat.

'Aight, if you downloaded the data, I'll just scrap the recording.'

'Do that.'

The footage went dark for the last time, only a set of coordinates with a Deep Space Nine shuttle IFF tag blinked in the corner.

8

The doorbell chimed, bringing Shao back to the real world, and to her sadness. She glanced up, displayed a "do not disturb" sign on her quarters' augmented reality window, then hid her face in her palms once more. The momentary distraction found in the jacket calmed her nerves but did little to remedy the anger and sorrow. Her HUD comm window chattered with a notification of an incoming message.

'It's me, Jin. Please let me in, miss,' she read. Sighing, Shao stood and headed towards the cabin's washroom. Jin Sun probably won't go away without talking to her, but he doesn't need to see a dumpster fire of a person. After cleaning herself up and letting the personal assistant drone put some makeup on her to conceal the swollen eyes, she said: 'Come in!'

The door slid open. Sun wore an immaculate corp-fashion suit as always, but a worried expression replaced the usual polite smile. A HUD sensor light blinked green on his left temple. Shao wondered momentarily why didn't he simply get an implant like everyone else. Some people didn't like body mods for whatever reason, but Shao couldn't imagine how a pinhead-sized chip could bother anyone. She couldn't even feel hers, sunk deep into the temple bone. She only knew it was there when it interpreted her brainwaves to work with augmented reality interfaces, like her HUD contact lenses. A sensor glued to the skin did the work just as well, but was visible and less convenient. Focusing on trivial observations allowed Shao to compose herself enough to speak calmly.

'Hello, Mister Sun. My father sent you, I presume?'

Sun bowed slightly in a greeting. 'Hello, dear Miss Zhenya. You are, of course, correct.'

'Spare me the lecture, please.'

'I did not intend on lecturing you, Miss Zhenya. Your father is merely concerned with your well-being. He sent me to talk with you, since he understands that you may not wish to speak with him right now.'

Shao sighed heavily. 'If he's so concerned, he shouldn't be such a tyrant.'

Sun walked over to the chair and sat opposite Shao. 'You know of course that our corporation was founded on Earth, yes?'

'By my grandpa and Misters Dao and Nguyen, yeah. What's that got to do with anything?'

'Bear with me, this is a bit of a long story. But it will help you make sense of your father's decision.'

'So a lecture after all, eh, Mister Sun?'

'I suppose so.'

Shao threw her arms up. 'Fine, let's hear the ancient wisdom of my dad and his dad and all the dads before them!'

Sun chuckled, in a rare moment of authentic emotion, usually hidden behind corporate etiquette. 'I'll try to be quick, then,' he said. 'Do you know why we adhere to a strict protocol of courtesy in the corporation?'

His question made Shao pause for a moment. 'No, actually. I never thought about that.'

'It's a story so minute that history teachers in the academy usually omit it. Which is also part of the lecture.'

'I hope it is going somewhere then.'

'Oh, it does. Long story made short, your grandfather and esteemed Misters Nguyen and Dao started Zhengdao corporation from a small firm producing mining equipment and software. That story is, of course, taught in the academy program, so I won't bore you with it.'

'Thank the heavens.' Shao laughed, her worries at least somewhat scattered by Sun's efforts.

'Anyway, the software produced was mostly sold to Pan American Coalition and Europe, and as such used western naming conventions and honorifics. When Zhengdao grew enough to buy our own ships and field crews, we adopted stricter protocol, to remind us that we, citizens of Zhengdao, are a community separate from Earth. That we need to put the greater good ahead of our own selfish ambitions. Do you know why the Board never issued an order to correct that and loosen the etiquette, now that we're a megacorporation and don't need such reminders?'

Shao shrugged, perplexed. 'Cause they don't give a damn?'

'They do give a damn, Miss Zhenya.' Sun laughed. 'But enforcing a sweeping update to Zhengdao software in the entire fleet would be impractical, and the expense and work time spent for no other reason than to adapt to Earth's informal etiquette. The Board and senior staff members would feel much better if they could loosen the protocol among themselves. But it does not warrant taking actions inconsiderate towards the corporation as a whole.'

'So what you're saying is how I feel is meaningless because emotions are suboptimal for the corporation's bottom line?' asked Shao. 'If that's supposed to make me feel better...'

Sun raised his hand in a plea for her to wait. 'Why no, this is but a tale your esteemed father asked me to tell you,' he said when Shao paused. 'As his father told it to him, many times, I bet. He also asked me to do what I can to lessen your suffering. So, Miss Zhenya, what can I do for you?'

Shao hesitated a moment before shrugging. 'I can't see how you could help me, short of transferring Mai to Seventeen.'

The light on Sun's temple flickered orange and red before turning green again. 'Done and done, Miss Zhenya.'

'What? You can't just override my father's orders. Don't get me wrong, I appreciate it, but he'll bite your head off!'

'He'll do no such thing,' reassured Sun. 'Your father didn't give an explicit order assigning Mai Wren to ZMV Five. The system placed her there based on her merit and career prospects. Your father only ordered me to do what I can to make you feel better. Overriding an automatic decision made by the expert software is well within my authority.'

Shao shot up from her bed energetically, causing Sun to raise as well. She hugged him on impulse. 'Thank you, Jin, really.'

Sun took a step back, embarrassed by the outburst of emotion. He swiped an invisible speck of dust from his suit. 'I'm happy to help, Miss Zhenya,' he said. 'I'll leave you to your duties now if you don't mind. I'm sure you'd like to tell your friend the good news.' Sun bowed lightly and left Shao's quarters.

Shao waited a few minutes, nervously pacing around the room, before calling Mai's commlink. Mai responded immediately, her face brightening a window in Shao's HUD. She moved the window to the center view to look Mai in the eyes and see her reaction to the good news. 'Hi there, got the news about the assignment?'

Mai gave her a quick grin, cybereyes glowing bright green. 'I got the Five! Gonna make enough navigation hours to end the tour with double the minimum needed to apply for bigger ship duty, livin' the dream. How about you?'

'I got Seventeen,' replied Shao, faking sadness.

Mai's smile faded a bit. 'Ah, shit. But at least we'll see each other on the downtime, no?'

'I'll get you one better, babe. I got you a transfer to Seventeen! We'll spend the whole tour together!'

Mai's eyes dimmed as she looked away to the side. 'Oh, cool. I mean, that's great. I was kinda hoping to—'

'I know, right? We'll have all the time in the world—just us and two other guys.'

'Sure, sure. Seventeen is only out for half a year. Isn't it a fast-track ride for officers?'

'Yeah, I'm sure they're boring as hell. But it's only six months, not like we need to send each other postcards and shit.'

'Yeah, but what am I gonna do the rest of the tour?'

'Don't worry about it; we'll figure something out.'

Mai shook her head in disbelief. 'Figure what out? Where should I apply for janitor training?'

Shao felt the heat of a growing blush, surprised by the outburst. She looked in vain for something to say, thoughts racing. Why was Mai like this? 'I... I just thought you'd want to stay together...'

Mai's soft features hardened as she clenched her jaw. Her eyes flashed crimson, and Shao thought Mai's going to yell at her. Instead, she spoke quietly: 'Of course I do. But you can't make decisions like that without even asking me. Didn't you think I'd want to make the best of this tour too?'

Shao looked down in embarrassment. She fought to compose herself, eyes burning with the promise of tears. Everything went wrong, she thought, from the moment the Yusan left Pluto. 'You know I want you to be happy... I just thought you'd be happy on Seventeen, with me.'

Mai hesitated before answering. 'It's not about that,' she started, then paused. 'You know what, let's go with the Seventeen. What's done is done. I'll get my hours on supply ships, or maintenance, or something.'

'Are you sure? I can talk with my father and—'

'Nah, babe, it's all good. Got any plans for the rest of the day?'

Shao smiled, relieved. 'Wanna meet up in the hangar, check out our new home away from home?'

'Yeah, sure, let's go.'

They met half an hour later in the expansive control deck of the Yusan. White and gold walls gave way to more subdued tones of gray. The deck was filled with hushed chatter and the smell of industrial soap. Simple, yet comfortable workstations hid hundreds of computer terminals and monitors used daily by the crews. Soon enough, most of the stations will be empty, but for now, Shao had to share the space with almost a hundred people in Zhengdao uniforms milling about.

They found each other in the crowd using the commlink's minimap function. Finding an empty terminal to take a look outside proved to be more of a challenge.

'Looks like all the terminals are in use,' Mai said, finally giving up. 'Seriously, people need to get a life.'

'Well, they did just reveal assignments; everyone wants to see their ships.'

Shao stomped on the metal floor. 'The system should let everyone use external cameras from their HUDs, I mean, come on... This is a madhouse.'

Mai gently grabbed her by the elbow. 'Let's get outta here. We'll see the ships in a few hours when everyone gets bored.'

Shao shook her head decisively. 'Forget it. I'll get us a terminal even if I have to do it the old way.'

'The old way?'

'Watch me.' She stormed off, going from station to station, leaning into and asking people which ship they're watching. By the fifth terminal, a young, chubby man approached her as she was heading towards the next one.

'Hi, um, sorry,' he said. 'I heard you're looking for someone watching the Seventeen...'

Shao looked the man up and down. The guy was wearing a casual outfit, his shirt wrapped around the obese body was stained with food. His bald-shaven head and sweaty cheeks didn't do him any favors.

'Yeah, so what?' she replied. 'Doesn't have to be Seventeen, if you're leaving your terminal, that's also good.'

'Um, sorry, but no. I'm also looking for Seventeen. Lasse Toft.'

'Lasse who?'

'Lasse Toft... That's my name.'

'Oh, okay. Guess we're crewmates, then. Shao.'

'Might as well look for a free spot together?'

'Sure, I guess.'

Before they headed further, however, a comm message appeared in Shao's HUD with a message from Mai. 'Station 51.'

Shao motioned Toft and followed the directions. The augmented reality overlay on her HUD lenses displayed arrows hand-made by Mai, decorated with unicorns, and for some reason, pink alligators eating flowers. Shao couldn't help but smirk. She feared Mai's going to be upset longer, but it seems she got caught up in the excitement. Or maybe she's just doing it to cheer me up, Shao thought suddenly. She must have frowned, cause Toft gave her a surprised look.

The terminal in question was occupied by a lean, brown-haired man, seemingly in his early twenties, and Mai. They both laughed, busy comparing notes about the images on the screen. Mai looked up as soon as they neared. 'Looks like the old way did the right thing, went the way of the dinosaurs.'

Shao bowed theatrically. 'Well done; you proved the superiority of digital approach. Who's this then?'

The lanky man gave Shao an off-hand wave without looking. 'Hi. I'm Jared Green, your captain. Isn't she a beauty?'

'Well, yeah, but I called dibs,' replied Shao.

That got Green's attention. He straightened up, looked at Shao, then decided his feet are the most interesting sight in the world. 'I meant the ship,' he said. 'Take a look.'

Shao stepped closer and looked at the display. It took a second for the sensor to register her HUD lenses, then the opaque gray screen turned into a three-dimensional view from the Yusan's external cameras. ZMV Seventeen was one of many bulbous ships docked to the mothership's "stalk." Its white hull was fresh and unmarked by space trash burns pockmarking most of the other mining craft near it.

'Looks brand new,' said Shao absentmindedly.

Green nodded with enthusiasm. 'Yeah, we'll be its first crew!'

'From school, straight into the field, whoosh,' giggled Mai.

Shao couldn't help but attribute Mai's uncharacteristic openness to their argument. Or maybe she was just nervous, as the only floater in a group of oners; her lean, long-limbed body with fragile bone structure identified her immediately as a somebody who grew up in zero-g. Shao knew Mai was often stressed around colony-hailing corporate higher echelons, even though nobody ever gave her grief because of her place in the firm or strictly tech education. Shao swallowed the growing uneasiness and turned back to the Seventeen on the screens.

The ship's frame was similar to that of the mothership itself. A wide rim of a living module, built to provide rotational gravity for the crew —with a glimmer of the folded solar sail on the underside. The "cap" was set on a long, thick core providing structural integrity and housing all the modules that didn't require gravity.

'It looks like a mushroom,' noticed Toft.

'It's a pretty ship,' replied Shao. 'I bet it's a joy to pilot.'

Green shrugged in response. 'As much as any truck can be, I suppose.'

'It has enough room on the stalk to dock the Sōngshǔ,' said Mai, pointing at a spot under the Seventeen's living module.

'What's that?'

Mai smiled broadly, and her eyes turned sky-blue. 'Our jumper — Shao's and mine.'

'Whoa, we can't take a second ship on board,' protested Green. 'That's against regulations!'

Mai's smile vanished again, but Shao met his gaze with determination. 'Why not?'

'It's against regulations. Besides, we have tonnage to think of; we can't haul a fleet with us.'

'We could ditch the lifepod,' proposed Toft, earning a grateful glance from Mai. 'I mean if we get a permit.'

Green struggled for words, exasperated. 'Are you mad? What if we get hit by pirates? Or suffer a meltdown?'

'The jumper is better than a lifepod,' argued Shao. 'It can carry eight people in the tanks; it can do interplanetary, even has a solar sail. What, you want to exchange that for a lifepod and starve to death if we get hit by pirates?'

'Not to mention that the pirates would just cut the pod open and catch us anyway,' said Toft.

'And eat us,' added Mai with a shy grin. 'Or worse.'

'Captain Zhenya will never agree to modify the ship.'

'I'm sure Dad won't mind if I ask real nice.'

Green gave Shao a puzzled look, then a realization dawned on him. He threw his hands in the air. 'Fine, sure, put your ship in place of the lifepod. You'll be the death of me.'

'I'll get the clamps adjusted, thanks, cap,' said Toft, happy as if it were his own idea.

'I'll help,' volunteered Mai. 'We have plenty of time to modify the Seventeen before we reach the Cloud.'

Green shook his head. 'Amazing. Just when I thought my day couldn't get any worse when Patrick got reassigned to Five.'

'Who's Patrick?' asked Mai, raising an eyebrow.

'My brother. We were going to hit the officer training together after this run, and now he'll be on a tour half a year longer than I. Fucks with our plans something fierce. One of us is gonna have to skip a year if we want to work on the same ship. Needless to say, it's not gonna look great on our resumes.'

Mai gave Shao a stern look. Shao shrugged, feigning ignorance. 'Sucks, man,' she said. 'Those computers, huh? They make stupid choices sometimes.'

9

Lederman ducked into cover a split second before the shrapnel ripped the door frame into shreds, sending spikes of bent polymer spiraling outwards. He was wearing an armored jumpsuit reinforced with ablative plating, but the blast of this force would turn his guts into mush regardless—if it had hit him directly.

The asteroid's near-zero-g surface was pretty much hard space and the decompression combined with the shockwave tossed him aside like a ragdoll. Spiraling away in a geyser of quickly solidifying ice and molten metal, Lederman scrambled. Gotta get a grip, he thought, fighting to focus his vision and silence the ringing in his ears. The explosive masked into the frame seamlessly and almost cost him his life. Still might. The declining trajectory shoved Lederman into the dark-brown icy crust. His HUD blinked with red warning lights. Visor fogged. Oxygen leak. No, it's just eyes losing focus. Hit my head, he thought. Didn't even feel. Lederman's body bounced a few times before he managed to stabilize on all fours. Breathing heavily, he got up and headed for the dome again.

The airlock's hatch lay bare before him now, blasted open. The white metaceramic coating was torn asunder. There was no way of knowing if the enemy trapped it further.

'Hold on five, squad. There's maybe more explosives in the 'lock, gotta find another way in.'

The reply from Dassler came in almost immediately. 'Roger, captain, standing by. Fabian, push Europa into a flyby and drop another eye in the sky. Lara, how's the frontal assault going?'

'The drones are keeping the bogies busy, so far,' replied Lara Tomasson. 'We made it the other side of the module, covering cap's approach.'

A light blinked urgently in Lederman's HUD. The Europa finished the orbital scan. He brought up the footage streamed to the squad from orbit.

A housing dome placed in the center of a crater, with several agridomes and mining facilities nearby, connected with surface life support pipes and a tiny fission power plant supplying energy to the complex. The scene would almost fit onto any corporate poster glorifying the life in the Frontier, Lederman thought. If someone would shut those turrets down.

A dozen round drones, marked with green tokens on the stream, maneuvered around the edge of the crater, playing hit and run with the dome's defenses. That's where the complex's automatic defense system core must be, Lederman thought.

Usually, the right to defend themselves was supported by Frontier Rangers like Lederman and his crew who often made sure the outposts in the Cloud were well supplied, and their PDS turrets were in good shape. Sometimes, on days like this, Lederman cursed them to hell.

'Aight, listen up. I have an idea,' he said. 'Get down here and join me.'

'Got bored of walking into booby-traps?' asked Tomasson calmly.

'It's not like I knew they were there, okay? Move in, but keep it safe. Send a drone first, and keep it at least five meters ahead of you.'

'Roger, roger.'

Lederman saw the other two blue tokens representing Dassler and Tomasson move down the crater, covered by a barrage of laser fire from the drones at the edge of the crater. The turrets returned fire, railguns sending long streaks of shards towards the crater edge. The towers weren't precise enough to hit a fast-moving target like the

Thomasson's scout drones but that didn't mean much. They had tons of rocks and trash to fire at them and keep them at bay.

The Rangers ran from cover to cover, stopping behind ceramic structures when one of the dome's turrets tried to lock onto them. Within a hot minute, they joined Lederman by the main airlock.

Dassler saluted lazily. 'I take it the negotiations didn't go that well.'

'Not really, no,' replied Lederman stoically. 'It was going well; the perp even invited me in.'

'Tricked you into activating the mine,' stated Tomasson, ending the sentence with a puff. Lederman imagined her blowing a loose blonde lock from her face as she did so.

'Yup,' he replied. There wasn't much else to say.

'What's the diagnosis then?' asked Dassler. 'Drunk or crazy?'

'Nutcase, definitely,' decided Lederman after a moment of hesitation. 'He didn't seem so, at first.'

Tomasson chuckled humorlessly. 'Trying to kill you was a dead giveaway?'

'I mean, it is our captain,' Dassler joined in. 'Everyone reacts to him like that.'

'Hilarious, really. I'm dying of laughter.'

'Ready when you are, cap.' Tomasson got serious instantly. She did that sometimes, joking around at the most inappropriate times, then back to business. She didn't waste time on nonsense. It was one of the many things Lederman liked about her.

'Hold on; I need to think,' he said, raising his hand. 'We have to assume the perp is holding his family hostage. Plus, it's not the poor schmuck's fault.'

People sometimes snapped, out here in the cold darkness of the Frontier. The harsh conditions of prolonged space habitation, often without proper medication and safeguards, got to people, especially with loneliness and isolation typical for deep Frontier outposts. Outbursts of paranoia, schizophrenic behaviors, and suicide were common. Sometimes people just disappeared without a trace; sometimes, they took their families hostage. Such is life.

'Hell, seeing the same three faces month after month, I'd snap too,' said Lederman seriously.

Tomasson and Dassler exchanged glances on the chat window theatrically—people spending most of their time in space suits took to treating their HUD commlink windows as real human connection.

'Aight, here's the skinny,' said Lederman after consideration. 'Perp busted the outside hatch, but the inside is still kosher. We can only assume there is another explosive there. We're gonna send in a drone to eat the bait, and head in after it bubs. Questions?'

Dassler raised his hand in objection. 'I have a better idea. Let's mark it as though we do just that, while we set up a tent and get through the wall, why don't we?'

'It's gonna take some time,' said Tomasson. 'What if the perp drops the hostages?'

'What if the blast from the inner airlock vents the module and the shockwave splats them?' replied Dassler.

'Good point,' Tomasson conceded hesitantly.

'It's decided then,' said Lederman. 'Europa, this is Lederman. Fabian, do you copy?'

'Copy, loud and clear,' replied Fabian Van Alst, the Europa's pilot. 'Wachu need?'

'I need a field airlock down here, pronto.'

'What else, an elephant playing trombone? Can't drop you anything until you shut down their PDS. It's old junk, but I can't blind it without damaging the dome.'

'I'll take care of it. Have a drop ready on my mark.' Lederman activated the mag pads on his boots, knees, and gloves.

Dassler patted the dome wall for good luck. 'Careful up there, captain.'

'Gotcha.' Lederman started scaling the dome.

The near-weightless climb onto the pockmarked dome was a breeze. As long as he didn't float off into space, Lederman should be fine. His energetic but careful crawl was practiced to perfection. Still, he couldn't stop thinking about the madman inside the dome noticing his shadow on the ceiling and firing a gun at it. He bit his lip, a coppery taste of blood in his mouth.

The defense towers caused plenty of vibrations to mask his approach. The inside of the dome must be drumming like a laundry machine, Lederman thought. He reached the top of the dome without breaking a sweat and headed towards the twin tubes of the PDS laser. He got to them in two quick leaps and slapped on a jammer box to the machinery, effectively blinding the laser canon. 'Aight, Europa, drop the load.'

'You won't even take me out for dinner first?'

A new dot appeared on their HUDs—a drop marker. The pilot aimed the package to fall meters away from the dome, dangerously close.

'Careful, Fabian, you have competition,' said Tomasson. 'The perp already tried blowing the cap.'

Lederman shook his head and headed down towards the ground in long, calculated leaps. 'Will you people ever grow up?'

The laser-propelled package rushed past Lederman and slammed onto the ground, raising a cloud of gray dust. Tomasson and Dassler picked it up and placed it by the dome wall, and before Lederman got down, the field airlock tent had been erected.

Lederman headed towards the dome entrance. The airlock was probably mined on the inner hatch, but he only needed to cause enough of a ruckus to distract the frontiersman long enough for Lara to cut through the outer wall.

The scout drones maneuvered themselves into the crater proper and were now engaged in hit and run tactics against the stationary defenses. Lederman called one over and ordered it to run a scan on the inner hatch. The moment it entered the blasted airlock, a man's wild face appeared in view of the transparent part of the door.

The frontiersman's jaw was unshaven, dirty hair sticking out wildly on his balding head, eyes bloodshot and bulging. He yelled something at the drone, waving a rifle around, but the machine's sensors didn't catch it through the thick alloy. Lederman could only observe as the frontiersman disappeared, then came back, dragging by the neck a terrified dark-haired woman with a rifle aimed at her head. He ordered the drone to stop the scan and hold the position. The fear in the frontiersman's eyes said all Lederman needed to know; the airlock wasn't trapped.

The perp's full attention was at the standoff by the airlock, and he couldn't see the wall behind him, slowly turning white-hot and melting away. The burned-out circle flew inside the dome propelled by a hefty kick. Dassler rolled into the dome, bulky pistol in hand. The man turned around, face twisted in rage and surprise. The barrel raised towards the struggling woman's head. Dassler was faster—a dart from his taser struck the woman square in the chest.

The hostage collapsed in a heap when an electric charge shocked her, but so did the man holding a gun to her head. Both spacers twitched in agonizing fits, their limbs flailing in the hab dome's messy interior. The man rolled into a cabinet, overturning it. Its contents, mostly printed nutripaste and tools, drifted away. Tomasson and Dassler disregarded the trash and scanned to room for more targets.

By the time Lederman made the rounds to enter the dome through the field airlock, the woman was slowly regaining consciousness under Dassler's care. Tomasson pushed the spacer into the ceramic wall, his hands cuffed behind his back.

Lederman looked around the dome—unmaintained beddings, dirty clothing, and empty food containers lying around. The floor strewn with brown residue and discarded utensils. Broken gastroprinter, smashed in with a fist by the look of it. A picture of a smiling prospector couple in front of a brand new mining hab hanging above the disheveled kitchen table. Happy, productive life in the frontier. Lederman looked at their faces, so different than on the photograph, and felt an unpleasant pull in his stomach.

'Bag 'em and tag 'em,' he said dryly.

10

Shao toyed with her fatigrade steak, poking it with a fork.

'No appetite?' asked Yuan. He sat on the other end of the oval dining table, white with gold trimmings, of course. Shao shifted uncomfortably on the chair, and the maglev motor adjusted to the center of mass moving. Captain's lounge offered no help in the conversation —standard white and gold furniture and opaque augmented reality screens, a few potted plants, a sandalwood incense slowly burning, tracing a thin wisp of smoke circling to the unseen air conditioning currents. Shao's graduation picture on her father's desk was the only sliver of personality in the office.

Shao shook her head. 'I'm just not hungry.'

Yuan nodded, his golden eyes and biosculpted face unreadable. 'Hmm. I saw you convinced Mister Sun to reassign your friend, Mai.'

'I didn't convince him. He offered.'

'How nice of him.'

'He said you sent him with an authorization, to make me feel better.'

Without a word, Yuan cut a thin slice of his synthato, as if it was all that mattered to him. Shao hesitated. It was just like when she was a little girl. Her father suddenly became still and silent, and she was left there, thinking she did something wrong.

'Jin Sun said it wasn't a problem.'

'Did he now?' replied Yuan slowly. 'How kind of him.'

Leave a message after the beep, thought Shao. Was he even listening to her? 'Why would you send him to make me feel better if you didn't want him to actually do something about it? About Mai?'

Yuan's cybernetic irises contracted and expanded again. 'No matter. How's the ship? Seventeen, was it?'

Typical. Just change the subject when it gets uncomfortable.

'It's fine. Looks new.'

'It is. Getting along with the crew, I hope?'

'Yeah, they're all right.'

Yuan hesitated as if he were about to ask personal questions. Shao discovered the cooling fatigrade steak suddenly looked more appetizing. They ate in silence. Quiet guzheng chimes played a slow melody.

'Actually, Dad,' Shao said eventually. 'We did have a favor to ask, as a crew.'

That wasn't entirely true, but close enough. And Mai would be so happy, maybe she'd forget about Shao's blunder.

'As a crew? I see you're becoming a unit quickly.'

'Yeah. We were considering requesting a permit for replacement of our lifepod.'

'Is there something wrong with it?'

'No, no. It's just that we wanted to clear it and dock the Sōngshǔ in its place.'

Yuan raised an eyebrow. 'Really? Captain Green's file never suggested a propensity for playing loose with regulations.'

'We kind of overruled him. Majority vote.'

Yuan shook his head disapprovingly. 'Command is not a democracy, Shao. You can't just vote on...'

'We all agree, okay?' she interrupted. 'Sōngshǔ is only a little larger than the lifepod, and it has better drives. If anything bad happens, we can get out of dodge quickly.'

'What could go so wrong for you to need a racing jumper?'

Shao shrugged, 'Nothing, I guess. Think of it as a team-building exercise.'

She watched Yuan's face intently—her father was hard to read at the best of days. Now he was an enigma. He's probably thinking how to say no without me storming off, Shao thought.

'Fine, you have the permission,' he said to her surprise. 'But fill all the paperwork yourself, and request Yusan's engineering team to double-check your work. And please tell Captain Green he needs to sign in for aptitude tests again.'

'What, why?'

'I can send him a direct order if you will.

'No, I'll tell him.'

'Good. Would you like some dessert?'

***

Filling the forms took forever, but Shao would rather do that than be in Green's shoes right now. She felt a pang of guilt—after all, it was a little bit of her fault their temporary captain was in trouble. She considered going to Dad and asking him to undo the entire mess, but remembered the constant preaching about responsibility and following through with her actions. She's going to follow through, even if she has to go against the protocol.

After dealing with all the bureaucracy, Shao found Mai and Toft measuring the lifepod bay with remotely controlled drones from the Yusan's cantina, mostly empty at this time. The two sat on a white bench, snacking on mycofries regularly supplied by the drone waiter hovering above them like a mother hen. Their laughter carried far in the echoey deck designed to hold over a hundred people at a time.

Shao's eyes narrowed. She increased her pace. It's not that she was jealous, she just wanted... Wanted *something*, especially after their fight a few days ago.

'Getting busy, I see?' she started, forcing a smile.

Mai took off the remote control rig, unplugged it from the neural interface ports in her cybereyes, and moved to embrace her. Toft also removed his rig, waved a casual greeting.

'Sorry we started without you,' he said. 'Catch a can and join us.'

Shao missed the cue and a drink tossed by Toft flew past her, soft can landing with a splat a few meters behind her.

Mai giggled. 'Sorry, I know you wanted us to wait for you, but we knew you had tons of paperwork to fill. The mining ships are still sealed for the crew, but since we got a permit, we can work on them remotely.'

'It's fine,' replied Shao. I guess I just got used to Mai only being comfortable around me, she thought. 'How's the progress?'

'It's going great. Lasse has a knack for spatial reconstruction.'

Toft blushed. 'Yeah, it was my major. Optimizing cargo hold layouts and such. Boring stuff, really.'

'Oh, come on, it's not that boring.'

Shao was inclined to agree with Toft's assessment. 'Yeah, don't sell yourself short,' she said instead.

'Anyway, we won't actually need to do that much,' he changed the subject and displayed the AR feed from the drones onto the table. 'Your jumper is larger than the pod but slimmer. So if we move the docking moors here... And here...' Toft moved the plates to explain his plan.

'Then we should be able to fit the Sōngshǔ diagonally without having to recombine the docking bay,' finished Mai in his stead.

'Nice. And I filled all the paperwork, so we should be good to go.'

They talked over the details over lunch, after which Green joined them in the cantina, following a small crowd of Yusan's crew heading for their break. He sat down heavily on the bench.

'You look miffed,' noticed Toft.

'That's one way of putting it,' replied Green. 'How's the jumper?'

'It's a perfect fit,' smiled Mai.

'Good, because this change earned us an unscheduled co-op training.'

'What, why?'

'Apparently, there are doubts about our ability to maintain the chain of command during the mission.'

Shao cringed internally. Father just has to punish me even when he agrees to something, she thought. No carrot without a stick.

'No, you're a perfect captain,' said Mai.

'I was just about to say,' agreed Toft, as always playing second fiddle.

'Well, you aren't a captain,' reminded him Shao. 'You're the captain of this mission, but not a ranking officer.'

'Is that supposed to make me feel better?'

'Give him a break, babe,' added Mai. 'What bit you?'

Great, I'm already loving this crew, thought Shao.

***

Shao woke up and went through her morning routine, barely noticing the service drones assisting her. Days trudged by, and responsibilities piled up, leaving her exhausted each evening. Countless hours on the mining drone simulator, learning the remote controls, procedures, and they didn't even get to work on flying the ship yet. She was reading the new training roster and cursing under her breath. The new schedule included five hours of group training daily.

She made her way through the Yusan's white and gold corridors to the cantina, where Green and Toft were already eating breakfast.

'Have you guys seen this bullshit?'

'Oh, hi Shao,' said Green.

Toft waved a greeting. 'Grab a snack,' he said, tossing a fatigrade burger her way.

Shao walked past the flying bun. 'I'm not hungry.'

'Yeah, you're angry,' noticed Toft with a grin.

'Damn right I am, aren't you?'

Green raised his head slowly. 'You're right, this is bullshit. First, they reassign Pat, then they call my command in question, and now Pat—a neural network specialist—tells me that the ship he got assigned to doesn't even have a neural network.'

Shao felt the heat of a blush climbing up her neck. 'That's... Suboptimal.'

Green nodded with fervor. 'Apparently some bigwig, Jin Sun, personally requested his transfer. I don't even know who that bastard is, but I swear I'll...'

'Oh, come on,' interrupted Toft. 'That Sun fellow was probably just filling some quota. You know how it is.'

'Yeah, don't blame the man,' interjected Shao quickly. 'Blame the system.'

Toft waved a fork in agreement. 'I was about to say, yeah. Anyway, Mai's not coming?'

'No, she called in sick,' replied Shao. 'We have gravball practice today, as a team-building effort. She hates sports.'

***

Morning routine was torture after only four hours of sleep. At least Mai got to stay over tonight, for the first time in over a week. She finished programming most of the drones' software for the bay reconstruction, and they finally had the time and opportunity to make up. Of course, thought Shao, now she sleeps like a bear, whatever that is, and I have to wake her up.

Shao poked Mai with a finger, but the only response to the assault was her wrapping herself tighter into the blanket and pulling it over her head.

'Time to get up, sleepyhead.'

'No,' replied Mai from her puffy fortress. 'Go away.'

'Fine, I'll head out without you. And ride shotgun with Green. He loves piloting drones.'

That finally got Mai's attention. 'No, not the esteemed captain,' she said, getting up. 'I'll move, but only 'cause he'd crash us into an asteroid again.'

Shao understood the sentiment—failing another practice meant yet more hours and more supervision. 'He's the worst co-pilot I've ever had.'

'It's like he's failing the tests on purpose.'

'Yeah. Let's go play happy miner. Have you seen my sock?'
'Right here, under the pillow.'

***

Shao drowsily headed to the simulator deck, passing other crews practicing in large sensory deprivation tanks. Their additional training started less than two weeks ago, but Shao was already ran rugged by it. She climbed into the nearest free tank and waited for the virtual reality landscape to load. The pixelated feed clarified itself, turning into a virtual ship deck. Green sat in the brightly lit control chair, looking at Shao disapprovingly. Mai smiled a greeting and blew her a kiss. Toft waved casually and tossed a set of gauntlets over his bald head.

Shao ignored them, and the object despawned, returning to its original position on the pilot console.

'You gotta stop doing that, Lasse,' she said. 'Sorry I'm late.'

Green scoffed, 'Yeah, what do you care if we fail and not get greenlit to live practice, right?'

'Come on, I just forgot to reset the alarm. The schedule is killing me.'

'Did you forget how to fly the ship, too?

The stress was putting everyone on edge, Shao thought, but come on. 'Why are you such a bitch, Green?'

Green scowled at her. 'Why are you such a bitch, captain, sir,' he corrected. Shao tried to keep a straight face but burst into a giggle.

'No, really, what bit you?'

'The evaluation from command bit me,' he replied. 'We're getting substandard scores. It'll affect my results.'

'Shit, sorry, man,' said Shao. If Green gets canned, he'll lose the whole tour and won't catch up with his brother. Not to mention they'll get a replacement captain, probably some veteran jarhead instead of a trainee like Green. That'd be a blast. 'I'll get on the chair and we can start the practice. We'll get you the straight As, don't worry.'

'Sorry, I know you're doing the best you can.'

'Don't worry, I get it.' The simulations started, and Shao focused on running the virtual ship as best she could.

**

The alarm clock rang just as Shao was about to leave the cabin.

'Too late, sucker,' she told the machine and closed the door. She headed straight for the cantina, where Green argued vehemently against Toft and Mai. He was gesticulating vividly, waving a fork around and garnering occasional looks from the Yusan's crew and other mining teams eating breakfast.

'What's that all about?' asked Shao. The three of them started talking one over another, Shao blinked confused. 'What the hell is wrong with you today?'

Green commanded silence, gesturing with a fork-armed hand. 'They want to break protocol, again!'

'Not break,' opposed Mai. 'Just bend it a little.'

'A little?!'

'Okay, a lot. So what?'

'It's against regulations, we could get in trouble.'

Shao sat down, looking at their breakfast. Fatigrade burgers, printed salad, and a can of protein soda. Yummy. 'You mean, more trouble?'

'Yeah. You can't just hack into the testing system,' continued Green, lowering his voice to a whisper. 'This is ridiculous.'

'It's piece of cake, actually,' replied Mai matter-of-factly. 'And it's not like we'd be cheating. Just a free afternoon in VR playing a game. Then we get to work.'

'Exactly,' agreed Toft. 'I got From Outer Space Three on a drive, got it from the guys at Eight. They did it, and they're fine.'

Shao considered it for a moment. 'That does sound fun. It's the one with icefield deathmatch?' Anything's better than another repeat of the same exercise—they'll be watching real drones do the same thing over and over every day soon enough. For months. She fleetingly considered telling them about the Redding's chip and the coordinates. No, not yet, she decided.

'Yup, and dogfights. So we technically would be training. Just not... Mining.'

'We'll call it a group exercise!' exclaimed Mai.

'Yeah, I was about to say.'

Green sighed. 'Fine, you win. I dream about piloting mining drones by now. Every night.'

'You mean crashing the drones,' teased Mai.

'That does it, it's guys against gals, we'll demolish you.'

***

Shao woke up at the same time as Mai. 'The alarm,' they said in unison and dashed to turn it off, almost falling off the bed. Twenty minutes later they marched into the cantina, exchanging pleasantries with mining teams from Seven and Twelve heading out for training.

Toft waved a casual greeting and lobbed a can of soda towards Shao who caught it without even looking.

'Thanks, Lasse,' she said. 'What's on the agenda today?'

Toft shrugged. 'More of the same. But hey, our score is up.'

'No wonder,' replied Shao. 'They're running us to the ground with this training.'

'At least I'll boost my work hours,' said Mai. 'VR doesn't mean as much as hard space, but it's something.'

'Yeah, there is that,' agreed Shao. She wondered if her dad had a hand in overburdening them with tasks and training. She knew he was petty, but that seemed a bit extreme. 'Where's Green anyway?'

'He skipped breakfast,' explained Toft. 'Went to catch up with Pat, you know.'

'Yeah.'

'It really sucks. The corp just bearing down on us like that. Like, where is our agency, aren't we valued employees?' continued Toft.

'Sure, we are, Lasse,' said Mai. 'As long as we're doing what they tell us and nothing else.'

'Don't forget about the esteemed Mister This-and-That and his bottom line,' added Shao.

Toft smiled in response. 'Aren't you going to be an esteemed this-and-that after this tour, though?'

Shao tossed a synthato at him. It splattered on his bald head in a very satisfying way, garnering laughs from the few people in the cantina. Toft collected the vegetable, blushing fiercely.

'Anyway, Mai, wanna take the drones for a spin and finish the bay?' he asked. 'We could move the Sōngshǔ there tomorrow then.'

Shao gave Mai a look. 'Weren't we supposed to take an afternoon off?'

Mai looked into her plate, eyes darkening into a deep blue. 'Yeah, but... We do have to finish the work.'

Shao held a grimace but tossed a deadly glance at Toft. 'Yeah, sure, no problem. We can hang out later.'

11

Milosh felt a heatwave drop on his face, causing his skin to tingle and itch. A reddish glare penetrated the darkness, and for a moment, Milosh thought he was on fire, then realized his eyes were closed. He opened them, immediately getting blinded by a bright light.

'Ah, you're finally awake.'

Milosh shook his head to clear his vision, scowling at the throbbing pain in the back of the head. It didn't work, but the ache brought clarity to his thoughts. Enough to call up the HUD display in his cyber-implanted eyes and lower the gamma to block out the glare. He looked around, slowly gathering the pieces of his consciousness.

The room's walls were white, padded with some sort of sculpted cushions. Soundproof, Milosh thought. He tried to move and discovered straps tying him to a hard and cold bedding, magnetic bracers on wrists and ankles denying any hope of getting out. Its bolster has been raised so that the occupant can see more than just the ceiling and the powerful lamp flaring right into Milosh's face. The smell of ozone permeated the air, and something else mixed in. A sweet aroma, reminding Milosh of tropical flowers.

An older man with gray hair, a thin mustache, and narrow glasses sat in a simple, metal chair in front of his bed. A blue military uniform covered the lean silhouette. The dense smoke from the man's cigarette spread the tropical scent across the room.

'Yeah, I guess I must be,' Milosh said finally, his voice coarse, throat dry and sore. 'I'm not dead after all. Unless you're the devil, and this is hell.'

The man chuckled gently. 'I'm not, but soon enough, you'll wish I was.'

'Now, you sound like my ex-wife.'

The man didn't seem at all moved by Milosh's remark. He looked at the tablet on his lap, no doubt browsing the data displayed on his own HUD, unseen by Milosh.

'You may refer to me as Mister Crowley if you will. Tell me, why did you do it? And where is it?'

Milosh let out a short, raspy laugh. 'Yeah, the resemblance is just uncanny.'

The man looked up from the tablet, affixed the glasses on his nose with a patient expression, and continued. 'Let's start from the beginning, shall we? My employer hired your company—'

'The PAC Navy, you mean.'

'My employer,' repeated Crowley with emphasis, slowly chewing every syllable.

'Fine, your employer,' agreed Milosh, rolling his eyes. He felt relaxed and calm, despite his bonds. Weirdly inert. There was a way out of the mess he was in, and he'd find it, but he couldn't force himself to try.

'You've been hired to investigate an asteroid in sector D of the Oort Cloud, Sedna, I believe...' Crowley paused, awaiting confirmation. He was met by Milosh's blank stare instead. 'Instead of acting according to the obligation,' Crowley continued eventually. 'You and your crew double-crossed my employer. I'm interested in learning the details of it. Why did you do it? Where did you hide it? Is it still with your crew on the Querub?'

'Your employer hired us to investigate a death trap,' replied Milosh, deciding that he won't learn anything about his situation by refusing to cooperate. Stoic silence and resistance during interrogation are all well and good, but they don't help in planning an escape.

'What do you mean by that?'

'Simple. Your commander wanted us to explore a shipwreck filled with illegal bioweapons. Don't pretend you don't know that. He wanted my men and I to be his guinea birds.'

'Guinea pigs.'

'Guinea go fuck yourself. The only reason we breached the contract was because he breached it first by sending us on a suicide run.'

'Why didn't you call for a cancelation, then?'

'We had to be sure. So, I went on and got some randos to go there first.'

'And yet you and your men landed on Sedna before the, as you say, randos, and explored the wreckage. Several of your men were exposed to the contagion, you included. You were fortunate, Mister Milosh. If our soldiers had left you there, wounded and infected, you would have died.'

'Gee, whiz, thanks, mister.'

'Why don't you tell us where you hid the canisters? You owe us that much.'

Milosh frowned and shifted uncomfortably. He was well aware of Crowley's inquisitive stare reading into his body language and probably biometrics. He could do nothing about that. It was best to play up to perceived weakness. 'There were... Complications.'

'I see,' replied Crowley patiently. 'Care to elaborate?'

'I wanted to get proof first.'

'Proof? Of what?'

'Proof that PAC military tried to recover the bioweapon and used my men as expendable pawns to get it. Unwilling to send the soldier boys to their deaths.'

'That sounds plausible,' admitted Crowley. 'Except that Pan American Coalition troops are well compensated for risking their lives. Why pay double and hire mercenaries? Assuming, of course, for now, at least, that the story about the so-called bioweapon is true.'

'No idea. Ask your employer. Maybe because a hundred dead PAC soldiers leave a paper trail; gotta explain to the ones up the chain what happened to them. There are PR issues. And an expense on hiring mercs can be hidden with side-spending. Get a nice tax write-off on top of that, and voila. None the wiser.'

Crowley nodded to himself a few times. 'Interesting, very well thought through. Wouldn't you say that sending a drone would have provided you with that data, however? Why did you send half of your ship's crew to the wreckage? To recover the alleged bioweapon?'

'Why don't you search Querub's black box and find out?'

Crowley didn't miss a beat. 'We can't, the entire ship has been destroyed in an explosion.'

Milosh forced himself to not smile triumphantly. The interrogator played up to expectations, but his initial questions proved he had no idea where the Querub was. And that it was intact. Tibor fixed it in time and dodged the bullet. That gave him a chance. He just needed to stall until Tibor and the rest of the crew figured out where Milosh, Chatty, and Muldoon were. Crowley, however, needed to know where the bioweapon was. That gave Milosh a tool to use... And every tool is a weapon.

'We expected resistance,' Milosh said dryly. 'Automatic defense systems, drones, maybe PAC troops. And we had to displace the canisters, so your soldier boys don't take us out when the job's done. Maybe next time think about it before hiring pros to be your expendable assets.'

'Perhaps, perhaps,' said Crowley, patting his lip with a finger. 'Or maybe you simply meant to sell the weapon on the black market.'

'If we did, we wouldn't be having this conversation.'

Crowley shifted in his seat and sent an ice-cold stare over his glasses at Milosh. 'I don't enjoy your dodging the answers, Mister Milosh. Where are the canisters?'

Milosh did his best to shrug nonchalantly. 'You're not enjoying your cigarette either, Mister Crowley.'

The interrogator glanced at his cigarette quickly, covering the action by affixing his glasses. That look confirmed what Milosh already suspected. The interrogator must be using the cigarette smoke as an inconspicuous way to deliver a truth serum or other drugs to his system. They could have just plugged him into an IV, Milosh thought, but that would immediately raise his suspicions. As is, they hoped Milosh will slip without realizing the chems loosened his tongue.

'You know... My employer could have your court-martialed for the breach of contract, not to mention endangering civilians in a military operation—'

'And risk implicating himself in an illegal operation?' Milosh interrupted without hesitation. 'I doubt that, somehow.'

'We could just toss you out the airlock,' said Crowley coldly, staring Milosh in the eyes.

Milosh withstood the stare with calm certainty. 'Do it.'

Crowley let out a short chuckle. 'That's enough for now. I have no intention of playing chicken with you, Mister Milosh. We will talk again.' He headed towards the exit, stopping for a moment before opening the door. 'We didn't plan on killing you, Mister Milosh. If you aren't willing to part with the canister, that's fine. We'll just make sure nobody will ever be able to buy the secret from you. Think about it.'

The lights went out the moment the doors closed behind him, leaving Milosh in total darkness.

***

The man didn't show up again, not for the longest time. The room went dark, so Milosh took a nap, saving energy. Lights came on, accompanied by an annoying buzzer—seemingly seconds after he fell asleep. The buzzer kept droning on and off, a constant annoyance the merc strapped to a bed couldn't shake. Then lights went out, and the cycle repeated. Milosh was pretty sure they did so in irregular intervals, just to confuse him. Usually, he would have been able to check his HUD for the time, but they put an EMP bracer on his arm, disrupting all of his internal electronics. Milosh made a mental note to install EMP shielding in his augmentations at the next opportunity.

It was slow and elaborate, sapping Milosh's willpower. He endured it, just as he endured hunger and thirst. The only thing they didn't cut him off from was his pill cocktail.

Every now and again, a narrow slit opened in the doors, and a tray of freshly printed, white pills containing a mixture of drugs slid inside his cell. Good to know at the very least they wanted him alive, for now. Without the combination of immunosuppressants, boosters, and stims, he'd be dead meat by now.

Cybernetic augmentations gave Milosh an edge over the competition, making him stronger, faster, and more durable than any baseline human and most combat drones, but it came at a price. The drug cocktail kept his body from rejecting the implants, stopped the pain, and prevented infections from developing. His captors knew it. They also knew what specific combination Milosh was using. They must have reverse-engineered the supply in his autoinjector implant, now rendered as inert as his other augmentations, or tested his blood to recreate it. Either way, the pills were a power play.

Through them, Crowley bragged how much he knew about Milosh, and how he could kill him without even thinking about it—it would be a matter of a few days without the slit opening, and bam, you're gone, merc.

Happy thoughts like this helped Milosh bide the time, but he could only play a passive game for so long. Eventually, the time will come to bite the bullet and bust out of the cell. But first, he needed a plan.

Coming up with one wasn't really that much of a hassle—dealing with obstacles was always easier than taking initiative. There was only one weak point Milosh could use to try and escape. Disarming the brace without raising suspicion was the hardest part. Crowley, or whoever, surely monitored the cell around the clock. If his augmentations worked right, Milosh could just rip it off, and that'd be the end of it, but the EM pulses it sent made him weak as a baby—certainly not capable of any feats of strength or speed. His captors made damn sure to search and disarm him, but Milosh, as every good mercenary, had more than one trick up his sleeve.

In this case, literally.

Over the next couple of days, for lack of a better word, Milosh collected a supply of pills. He suspected they were feeding him more than needed, both to debilitate him with overdose and simulate more time passing than it actually had. He pretended to eat the pills like a responsible prisoner while pocketing them in his prison jumpsuit. He only took a dose when he felt the pain arising where the implants met his body. This tactic brought with it an additional benefit; he could measure the time.

The way things looked, he had spent over a month in this cell. And yet, he didn't feel hunger, nor did he remember eating. The captors likely injected him with sustenance while he slept, drugged-out through the vents probably. The whole situation stank and made little sense. He figured the only way out of this mess was figuring out what was going on.

If it had been over a month, the Querub wouldn't have hung around unless they knew for sure he was alive. If his crew left, the soldiers would have simply vented Milosh into space.

Suddenly, all the missing pieces clicked together, and Milosh knew for sure why he was being kept alive in the first place. As long as his crew lived, they were both witnesses and proof that PAC Navy hired mercenaries in pursuit of bioweapons, outlawed both by OSEE and the Council of Colonies.

The soldiers wanted to use Milosh as bait to lure the Querub into a kill zone or trade him for the mercs' silence.

Both Crowley and his commander knew Milosh wouldn't talk, which meant only one thing—they'll try to dupe him, maneuver him right into contacting his crew, and playing the game on a board set up just for them.

Wanna play games? Let's play a game, Milosh thought and made up his mind.

The next time pill arrived, Milosh pretended to take them, as usual, then squatted on his bedding as much as the straps allowed, facing the door. He forced his thumb into his left forearm; the lockpick multitool slowly slid out of a synthskin pocket.

Getting rid of the EMP brace was a matter of seconds, and soon Milosh felt his strength return. The straps tore like paper when he pulled at them with the power of synthetic muscles. For a moment, nothing happened, a second of uncertainty before the storm. He always felt weirdly calm before the action started, imagining himself as a quiet pocket of air in the eye of the cyclone. If he was wrong, the soldiers monitoring his cell will flood it with gas and take away the chance for freedom, but if he was right...

The cell door opened, letting in a young soldier in a teal navy uniform, rifle drawn. Milosh leaped, ramming the door with his massive body. The kid fell on the floor like a ragdoll without as much as a cry of surprise. Milosh glanced at the body while reaching for the gun. The boy's face was awash with blood from the broken nose, head bent at an unnatural angle. The coppery stench of blood spoiled the air's recycled sterility. 'Shit luck, kid. I hope you have life insurance.' He checked the gun, finding to his surprise that the safety light was green. Crowley isn't trying very hard, he thought.

A volley of bullets slammed into the frame where his head was a second ago with a loud thud. Milosh's overclocked reflexes and years of battlefield experience had saved him as he rolled on the floor, avoiding the next burst. He pushed himself off, flying up the corridor ceiling. The shooters stopped to correct their aim. 'That's more like it,' he said, returning fire and forcing the soldiers to retreat.

He ran down the hallways, chased by bullets—the soldiers couldn't keep up with him, despite Milosh going slow in unknown terrain. The soldiers were likely trying to funnel him somewhere—comm station, Milosh guessed. He let them do so for a while, until the nearest corner. He dashed into a small cabin—someone's personal space—and hid under a desk. Milosh didn't think the soldiers would run past him—he wasn't an idiot, and neither were they.

Nonetheless, they had to get inside the cabin to flush him out, and that was enough. The door slid open. A grenade rolled on the floor towards the desk. A loud bang sounded as soon as it stopped, releasing the cordite-smelling mist. The soldiers waited until the entire cabin filled with it before entering, immediately spreading into a wide formation, burst-firing into the smoke.

Milosh kicked off into a sprint, lifting the desk from the ground. He rammed into a pair of troopers, their pained groans accompanied by the awful crunch of breaking bones. He swung the table at the third, swiping him off his feet as if he weighed nothing. The fourth soldier stood paralyzed with shock. Milosh ripped the gas mask and comm headset from his head.

'Thanks, buddy,' he said in a friendly manner and tapped the soldier on the arm. The soldier's headset displayed augmented reality prompts, and directions suggested that the soldiers have been trying to push Milosh towards the comm relay.

Milosh headed towards the ship's engineering room instead, memorizing the hallway layout in the process. The light on his rifle changed to red without warning—the target wasn't following Crowley's plan, so he couldn't be allowed to shoot anymore. Milosh just smirked to himself and sped up. Keep your toys, Mister Crowley. Now that he knew where he was going, there was no reason to be slow. A pair of soldiers supported by a combat drone tried to set up a barricade on his way, but Milosh charged into the thick of it before they had a chance to raise their weapons. He couldn't shoot them, but the rifle was still pretty useful as a club.

One soldier fell before he had the time to react, head smashed in. Blood and teeth splattered on the wall. The woman raised her weapon to fire. Milosh swiped her off her feet with a kick and clubbed her in the back of the head. The drone reacted fast. Milosh kicked it into a maintenance shaft and closed the hatch behind it.

The engineering room was full of machinery and drones. Milosh had the advantage of surprise, but that wouldn't last. He needed a good weapon and a diversion. He rummaged through the shelves, tossing tools carelessly behind until he found two plasma torches. Milosh hastily strapped them onto his forearms with industrial-strength duct tape, with firing mechanisms inside his palms. He squeezed the triggers, creating short bursts of blue-hot gas in front of him.

'This is gonna be fun,' he muttered and turned towards the door. One place to go—the shuttle bay. Groups of soldiers and combat drones

tried to cut him off, forcing Milosh to head towards the comm station
—he appreciated the dedication but had other plans entirely. Each time
the soldiers appeared, Milosh doubled back down the corridors and
tried to approach through a different deck. There were only so many
corridors he could try. Every moment spent trying to get past them
meant the noose tightened around his neck.

Milosh rushed towards the last deck leading to the shuttle bay.
Stinging pain tore when bullets hitting his body, but Milosh didn't
stop until he was in range to fire the plasma cutters. The remaining
grunts scattered before the black smoke of burned flesh raised into the
air. Milosh shook the trooper's corpse off his hands and headed towards the bay. He was glad he couldn't smell the carnage—the gas mask
protecting him from the odor of death and burned flesh just as well
as it did from the toxins in the air. He sped up, gray, empty corridors
turning into a blur as he did.

Milosh felt his pace fall to a limp when the adrenaline pump stopped
drowning his nervous system in combat stims. Pain and fatigue slowly
crept in to replace the fight-or-flight instinct with apathy. The soldiers
were using shock rounds, non-lethal, but gradually taking effect. If he
weren't operating in a frenzied state, Milosh would have been captured
by now. The torches' flame badly burnt the synthskin on his forearms,
exposing armored graphene mesh and the synthetic muscle underneath.
Just a while longer, Milosh thought. Just get in the shuttle, that's it.

A mighty blow struck Milosh off his feet and onto the ground. He
tried to get up, moving as if in slow motion, ears ringing. Something
grabbed him by the forearm and shook violently, then dragged his body
on the floor. Sharp pain in the torn muscles brought him back to his
senses. Milosh fired the torch on his other arm and thrust it into the
object, burning through the metallic armor, raising a cascade of sparks
and black smoke. It let go with a high-pitched howl of pain. He jumped
on his feet, nearly slipping on the bloody smear marking the floor—
his blood.

The object was a drone, shaped like a canine with a small head,
mounted on a gyroscopic neck. The body was elongated and flat, with

magdrive trays where legs would be in a live creature. He couldn't force himself to take the eyes off the shining, titanium fangs. Almost hypnotic. The beast shook its head, sending the pieces of Milosh's graphene armor-mesh and the torch flying through the deck. It backed down the corridor, preparing to pounce. Milosh tensed. The entire world shrunk to him, the beast, and the hiss of the remaining torch.

A second one leaped from behind him, titanium fangs closing on the plasma cutter and ripping it off with synthskin and pieces of armor. Milosh howled furiously, swirled to face the new attacker. The first dog-drone slammed into his neck and back.

A sharp whistle tone cut the air, and the drone let go but stayed near the wounded merc splayed on the bloodied floor.

'Clever girls, aren't they?' asked Crowley in a conversational tone, when he entered the hallway escorted by two armed troopers.

Milosh didn't reply, beaten and barely conscious. He fought to catch a breath, the world reduced to the dull, gut-wrenching pain tearing through his body in hot waves.

Crowley gestured towards the soldiers, who stepped forward, grabbing Milosh and dragging him back towards the cell, leaving a trail of blood on the floor. The dog-drones followed them closely, sniffing the stains.

The cavalcade reached the cell, and soldiers tossed Milosh on the floor, grunting in exertion.

Crowley stood in the doorway, hand on the wall-mounted console. 'Too bad you didn't try and call your friends,' he said with a smirk. 'What were you trying to do? Escape a military fleet in a shuttle? Please.'

Milosh lifted his head from the floor, straining in pain. 'I was trying to find a pisser.'

'Ha. Amusing indeed, well said,' replied Crowley, unimpressed. 'Anyway, sadly, you're far too dangerous to be kept aboard, and you're of no use to us.'

'So what, you're gonna vent me?'

'I will do no such thing,' laughed Crowley. 'The last thing we want is to endure the... *Inconveniences*... Your crew would cause if we did. We're going to keep them busy, and you... Well, you'll see.'

Milosh tried to say something but faded into darkness.

12

The Yusan shook violently when the waystation's laser beam hit its solar sail, starting the deceleration. The mothership carried its crew through the Great Beyond for three long months, and now its journey was nearly over. The Yusan had made the journey nine times before, but as always, crossing the Heliopause and hundreds of AUs between the Solar System and the Oort Cloud were not without its dangers. Even the tiniest miscalculation in the NaviNet predictions at launch from Hydra could have resulted in the Helikaon Waystation missing the ship entirely, or even worse, hitting the hull instead of the solar sail. Either way, the results would be catastrophic, be it becoming lost forever in the Cloud or an instant death of everyone aboard the Yusan.

The Great Beyond itself was also not bereft of inherent dangers. While mostly made up of hundreds of AUs of empty interstellar space, it inspired an abundance of tales of freighter crews encountering haunted shipwrecks, pirate ambushes, unidentifiable vessels, stray asteroids on their plotted courses, and dying in catastrophic collisions. A spaceship sailing the void couldn't alter its course or decelerate, else it would become stranded in the Beyond with little hope of rescue.

The Yusan spun around its axis like a child's toy, carried on the laser beam from the Helikaon Waystation. The light fractured in the sail's prismatic fabric, making the mothership resemble a swan dancing on a rainbow bridge. Shao found it exceptionally beautiful.

She watched the deceleration from inside of her inertia pod, streamed by the outside cameras directly to the visor of her pressure mask.

Finally, the beam ceased, and the Yusan kickstarted its own engines. The deceleration created an uncomfortable two-g aboard the craft; tiring and stomach-twisting but safe.

Shao minimized the outside feed, bringing up her main HUD display menu. She commanded the pod to release her and shuddered at the unpleasant release of pressure accompanying the kinetic gel protecting her from the outside forces retracting into the pod's inner compartments. The liquid filling her lungs drained along with the tube into the mask, leaving behind a hot taste of rubber and licorice. She got out as soon as the hatch opened, cringing under the strain of gravity. Her knees buckled despite bracing, as the pressure proved too much for muscles after prolonged sensory deprivation of the chamber. Shao crawled back to her feet, grunting, using the pod's chassis for support. The cramps passed after a short massage from a service drone, though a slowly growing migraine marked the body's protest against such treatment.

According to Shao's HUD it was still at least an hour before they reached Helikaon. Early bird, she thought and got to work. The cabin released a flock of service biodrones in response to her commands. The squid-like bioengineered machines busied themselves instantly, packing all her belongings into vacuum-sealed bags and stacking them by the room exit. Watching her mementos, training materials, and clothes unceremoniously collected made Shao think of scavengers picking her life clean. She shuddered again, this time not because of gravity.

Shao considered messaging Mai and the rest but judged against it. She'll wait for them by the airlock, to avoid the crowds. She brought up a comm window onto her HUD and called Yuan Zhenya. He picked up immediately.

'Hi Dad. I see you're out of the pod too.'

Yuan's feed shook rhythmically, accompanied by a distant guzheng melody. 'Good to hear from you, Shao. Yes, I like to keep busy.'

'Hitting the gym at this time?'

'It's the best way to keep fit. Also, nobody bothers me, when they're all in pods waiting for the ship to stop—usually.'

Shao shook her head. 'Sorry, didn't mean to interrupt your schedule.'

'That's not what I meant. I'm glad you called.'

Shao resisted the urge to disconnect. 'Yeah. I called 'cause I'm leaving soon.'

'Yeah, I know. Are you coming to eat breakfast with me?'

'No, I know you're busy. I'm gonna go get to Seventeen before the crowds, you know.'

'Ah. I see. I wanted to wish you a safe journey before you go.'

'Thanks. Well, I gotta go.'

Shao felt as bad about the situation as her father probably did. She couldn't bring herself to approach it. One thing she could do, however, was being a perfect little corporate pilot.

Shao called off the drones and started packing her remaining belongings in the last bag despite the high deceleration drag. Physical activity keeps the mind from wandering. Moving all of her things from Yusan to Seventeen before everyone else will let her avoid the crowds, and show her father that she does treat the assignment seriously. They'll have time to talk when she comes back. To start over.

She traveled light, knowing that space on board the mining ship would be limited, so the entirety of her belongings outside of the Sōngshǔ fit neatly into three large bags. Shao looked back at the now empty room, immaculate and somehow ominous. Whatever semblance of personality her belonging gave it was gone without a trace as if she was never here. Only some trash and leftover personal items she didn't want, piled into a neat stack by the drones—ready to be incinerated. It's all we are, she thought. Useful for a while, cut to size, and recycled when no longer useful. A biodrone scurried out of the closet, carrying a leather jacket in its segmented tentacles, headed towards the trash stack. Shao nearly forgot about it, a memento of the last day of freedom, gone in an instant.

On an impulse, Shao dropped her bag and turned back. She retrieved the jacket and put it on. It smelled of old tobacco and really was too big—and yet somehow comforting. It inspired confidence, proving that she could take matters into her own hands. That she wasn't yet another cog in the great machine. She tied the jacket's belt down to make it fit a bit better and put the collar up. She imagined her father's face seeing her in an ill-fitting jacket won from some smuggler in a bar.

'Deal with it,' she said, steeled herself, picked up the bag, and headed down the decks towards the joint connecting the Yusan's rotating living modules with the stalk where the mining ships were docked. The mothership was still slowing down before its final approach towards the waystation's docking platform, so she didn't expect to stumble onto anyone. When she exited the elevator leading to the ship's core, however, she stumbled upon Green, also packed and ready to go.

He waved a cheerful greeting the moment he saw her. 'Hi! Didn't expect to see anyone here so early.'

'Yeah, I figured it'd be best to avoid crowds. Early bird gets the worm, right?'

'I don't think we're gonna run out of ships, but I know what you mean. Nice jacket, by the way... Though it looks a little too big for you.'

Shao shrugged, putting her hands in the jacket's pockets. 'I'm a slave of fashion, you know...' she started but paused when her hand touched something hard inside the pocket. The chip. She almost forgot about it too.

'I know now,' laughed Green, then frowned, seeing Shao's surprise. 'What's up? You seen a ghost or something?'

'I don't know,' she said, pulling out her hand and opening it.

'It's just a data chip. Shao, are you ok?'

Shao shrugged. 'No, yeah... It's not mine. I kinda won this jacket off this old pilot, some kind of smuggler, I guess. It's nothing.'

'Uh-oh, old smugglers, mysterious chips.' He laughed. 'I didn't know you from that side!'

The elevator door opened, letting in giggling Toft and Mai. 'See, told ya they'd be here before us,' said Mai, smiling impishly. 'Who wakes up that early anyway?'

Toft made a grandiose gesture, laughing uncontrollably. 'Our captain and future CEO must rise early to behold their domain.'

'Cut it out, dickwad,' Shao scolded him jokingly. 'Or you're fired.'

'From an airlock,' added Green. 'It's not like my dream is being a corporate officer, commanding some trash can for the rest of my life, picking up rocks for the Man.'

The group headed out to the airlock leading towards the Yusan's spine, where the mothership's computer readied white and gold jumpsuits for them.

'What is your dream then?' asked Mai while they were changing. Shao detected a hint of sadness in her voice.

The augmented reality overlay displayed a quick warning in Shao's HUD, and suddenly their cabin was set free in the vacuum tunnel placed along the cap's inner axis. The sudden change in gravity took them all off balance for a moment. Before they could compose themselves, they were knocked back into their seats. The stalk picked the cabin up, and the magnetic rails safely placed it in the zero-g environment of the mothership's hull.

'I hate this thing,' muttered Toft, green with nausea.

'It's kinda fun, like being a bowling pin,' laughed Mai, utterly unfazed by the experience. 'Whoosh, boom!'

'Easy for you to say, floater,' replied Toft. 'I never asked for this.'

'Yeah, me either,' said Green. 'I always wanted to be a freelance trader, just doing my thing. Away from all the red tape and etiquette. It was Pat's idea to sign up for mining operations.'

'Don't get me started.' Shao rolled her eyes. 'I'm already looking forward to half a year of "esteemed this" and "esteemed that." Ugh, it makes my blood curl.'

Mai lit her jumpsuit's point light under her face, her cybereyes shining bright red through the beam of light. 'First half a year, then the rest of your life,' she said and waved her arms around, making spooky sounds.

'Well, yeah, that's how it'll be,' said Shao grimly.

Toft finished checking his suit's systems. 'You're talking about it like it's a bad thing. My grandparents ran a bicycle rental shop on Earth. They worked hard for me to get the chance at a good life.'

'You're right, corp life isn't bad,' admitted Green. 'It's just... Boring.'

'Soulless,' added Mai.

'Preplanned from the cradle to the grave,' said Shao. 'March on, little robots, make the cred for papa.'

'Not like we have a choice,' shrugged Toft. 'What are you gonna do, drop everything and be a space hobo?'

Mai giggled at the thought but said nothing.

Shao shrugged. 'Doesn't mean I have to like it.'

'Let's go see our new ship, eh?' said Green with forced cheer. 'We're gonna have time for bitching and depressive thoughts later.'

They headed out of the cabin, magnetic clasps letting go as soon as they left, releasing the booth from its moors and back into the system.

The deck was dark and devoid of activity except for a couple of maintenance biodrones, silently moving their squid bodies along the maintenance shafts in search of malfunctions. Green commanded the ship's computer to display the route to Seventeen, and they followed the bright AR arrows to the correct bay. A cheerful voice played out a greeting message, together with safety instructions and product placement.

They entered the telescoping sleeve, connecting mining ships to the Yusan's external hull. The vessel powered up with a loud hum, lights coming online as soon as the crew entered the inner airlock. The Seventeen vibrated slightly, preparing for its virgin flight. Shao's HUD displayed a notification about network change, and the Yusan's news feed was replaced with rows of updates concerning the progress of the ship's systems waking up.

'That's gonna take a while,' stated Green, having read the same information as Shao did.

'We are early, after all,' replied Toft. 'We wanted to avoid lines at the bowling alley, now we have to wait for the lights to come on.'

'I bet the ice cream machine's broken,' added Mai cheekily.

'Fair enough,' said Shao. 'Wanna check the ship out while it's powering up?'

Green looked at her, surprised. 'That's against regulation.'

'I know, right?' Shao commanded her suit to seal. The thick collar of her suit opened, and a light, metallic hood extended from the compartment inside. The smart materials folded themselves into a helmet with a flat opaque faceplate. She opened comms to the others, placing the windows in the corners so that they didn't obstruct the view from the helmet's camera. 'So, you guys coming?'

Mai joined her immediately, followed by Green and a reluctant Toft. They traversed the sleeping ship's decks, discovering the white, neatly finished corridors. Mess hall, bridge, engineering, crew quarters, cargo hold, and mining drone tubes—all were sealed under plastic vacuum wraps, waiting for the life support to come online.

Soon enough, they had circled around the Seventeen and faced the airlock again.

'Well, that was enlightening,' said Toft. 'Adventure of a lifetime.'

'Give her a break, Lasse,' said Mai. 'You were gonna sit on your ass for an hour instead?'

'Fair enough.'

Green looked over his crew with concern. 'Hey, cut it out. No fighting. Wanna head back to the mothership, have something to eat?'

'Not me, I wanna see her wake up,' replied Shao. She touched the wall, feeling the vibration through the suit's glove.

Mai engaged her magboots with a click, locking herself to it. 'I'm with her.'

'Well, Seventeen's gonna be our home for the next few months,' nodded Green. 'What say you, Mister Toft?'

'Might as well, it's gonna finish booting before we get back to Yusan anyway.'

'So, anybody got cards?' asked Mai.

'Nope, left them in my other jumpsuit,' said Shao, smiling.

'So, we gonna watch the lights come on?'

'I think we can find something to do, Lasse,' said Green. 'Hey, Shao, wanna show us what's on that mystery chip of yours?'

'Sure, why not.'

Mai looked at Shao inquisitively. 'You didn't tell me about any mysterious chips.'

Shao looked away. 'I found it in the jacket pocket right after we left. The training ran us so hard I completely forgot about it.'

'The one from Styx?'

'The same.'

'Why don't you bring the rest of us in on the secret?' inquired Toft.

Shao shrugged, told the whole story of their escapade.

'... And then I fell right onto Dad and his guards, coming to rescue me.'

Toft grinned widely, 'Wish I was there to see it!'

'No, you don't' replied Mai. 'Shao's dad's scary when he's angry.'

'Not angry, just disappointed,' added Shao, mocking her father's tone. 'Anyway, wanna watch a movie?'

13

The recording ended, and the silence was almost palpable. The Seventeen's crew looked at each other, each of them shaken and visibly crunching the information.

'Yeah, I know,' Shao said finally. 'It's pretty ghastly.'

Green rubbed the chin of his helmet as if it were his face. 'You think there's something in that story?' he asked finally. 'It looked pretty real to me.'

'Let me run a scan on the files,' said Mai, reaching out for the chip. 'I'll check the authenticity.'

Shao handed her the chip. 'You do that. But... So what if it is?'

'I could do with a million credits,' said Toft. 'I always wanted my own house in some colony or the other.'

'More like your own fleet.' Green laughed. 'You can't sit on your ass on some moon watching sitcoms and drinking malibus.'

'Why not? It does sound fun.'

'For a week, maybe.' Mai shrugged absentmindedly. 'Then what?'

'Fair, fair,' admitted Toft. 'It's still nice to imagine.'

'Wait, what are we even talking about?' asked Shao. 'We have a mission roster, and our course isn't going to be anywhere near that quadrant.'

Green hung his head. 'Yeah, we do. Damn, and to think I couldn't wait to launch just a few weeks ago.'

'And now you don't?' asked Shao.

'You know I planned to do the tour with Pat. It won't be the same without him. Not to mention our entire plan got delayed at least five years now, if not more. I'm going to have to put my career on hold so he can get enough work hours to apply for the same ship. It'll put both of us in a bad light.'

'You're only an esteemed Mister Green as long as you follow the esteemed party line,' said Mai.

'What about you?' asked Toft. 'You have a glorious career ahead of you, what's a few months of boredom?'

Shao shook her head. 'A glorious career of compromise and fighting the establishment. You know they almost split Mai and me up like they did Jared and Pat.'

'Oh, are you two related?' asked Green innocently. 'But I thought...'

'No, we're not related,' replied Shao with a small smile, accompanied by Mai's giggle.

'The data checks out,' said Mai quickly. 'It's an authentic log on OSEE serials.'

'So the Deep Cloud really does drift somewhere in space,' said Toft thoughtfully.

'Not anymore it doesn't,' Shao pointed out. 'Silver and those floaters salvaged it.'

'Those pirates, you mean,' said Green. 'They're bound to be looking for the shuttle too.'

'We don't know if they're pirates,' protested Shao. 'Even if they were, what does it matter?'

'They'd come after us,' said Toft. 'We aren't really talking about—'

'We have that chip, and they don't,' interrupted Mai. 'They don't even know who we are, how would they even know where to look?'

'I bet they have the data downloaded somewhere,' argued Toft. 'And the original recorder, too. They must know where the shuttle is.'

'Besides, they probably took it already,' reasoned Green.

Shao realized this might be her best chance to make up for her screw-up with Mai's reassignment. If the thing is real and they recover it, both Mai and she will make their own rules. Screw the missing work hours, screw the tour.

'No, they didn't,' she said slowly. She needed to convince both men, not just Mai. 'The last entry is from November last year, and I got the jacket on Pluto, this March.'

'So what?'

'Don't you get it? The trip from the Oort Cloud to Pluto would take at least three months on a strong beam, and refitting a ship another month or two. Maybe longer. From Pluto to the Cloud it's another month if they can afford a strong beam like us. No way they claimed the shuttle already. They're probably still on Pluto.'

'So we could just go and check it out,' said Toft in a sudden realization.

'So what? We'd still be court-martialed.' Green shrugged. 'The corporation won't just let us go on vacation looking for treasure.'

'Even if we did find it, they'd just confiscate the crate, along with whatever's in it,' added Toft.

'Not if they don't know about it,' Shao said slyly. 'We could arrange for an accident to happen to us, grab the crate, sell it in the Solar System, and live free of the corp's nonsense.'

The other three friends looked at each other, warily.

'Now that's just crazy talk,' said Green finally. 'You'd have us just abandon everything we know, our families—'

'Not abandon,' interjected Shao. 'We'd just haul them out, hire some mercs to get them free from the corp. We'll have the funds for it. We could open our own freelance company, you'd be able to work with your brother, and nobody would tell you what to do.'

'That's just crazy talk,' repeated Green. 'How would you even get back to the System in the first place? In a mining ship? Zhenya will hold you up at the first waystation if we show up in a supposedly lost spacecraft.'

Shao smiled broadly, as always when she was two steps ahead of everyone else. 'We wouldn't show up in the Seventeen. We'll abandon it and take the Sōngshǔ. It's already installed instead of a lifeboat.'

'You won't cross the Beyond in a jumper ship, Shao,' opposed Toft. 'We'd starve. Even if the Sōngshǔ could withstand a waystation laser, its sail isn't meant to handle that kind of power.'

'Not to mention it would be stopped on the waystation anyway. It's registered as Seventeen's lifeboat.'

'We can work with that,' insisted Shao. 'A cargo hauler is leaving just after our mission starts. It's gonna drag the previous mission's finds to Earth via Jupiter. We could catch a ride on that.'

'You mean the Incitatus?' chuckled Toft in disbelief. 'That bucket's an inertia raft; it'll be thirty years before it reaches Jupiter!'

'Twenty years or so,' corrected Green. 'But I get your point. Crossing the Beyond on a hauler is almost as mad as with a jumper. It doesn't even have life support.'

Shao sighed. 'You're right. It's a pipe dream.'

'I guess it's back to being corporate drones then,' said Green. 'Too bad, the idea of becoming a freelancer started growing on me.'

'I was just about to say that,' added Toft.

The group sat in the darkness of the deck, each lost in their own thoughts.

The silence of a sleeping ship no longer seemed full of promise. Soon, the first lights activated, and the decks filled with the hum of life support systems pumping atmosphere into the ship and warming up the cold floors.

Shao's HUD filled up with icons and notifications informing her of the Seventeen's status. The NaviNet icon popped up last.

Synching with the navigation network allowing the interplanetary traffic to function required a multitude of other systems to be in place. Without it, the ship would have no way of knowing its position relative to other tagged objects in the Solar System and risk collision with other craft or being stranded in space without the option of calling for help. Not to mention, of course, that NaviNet link was essential in allowing the waystations to plot a ship's course, launch it with the solar laser on the right trajectory, as well as intercepting and safely decelerating incoming vessels.

Shao commanded her helmet to fold as soon as the atmosphere was breathable. The fresh, pine-scented air filled her lungs, almost causing a coughing fit, but she soon got used to it. Others did the same, except for Mai, who was too busy on her internal HUD display to notice the lights were on.

'Guys, I have an idea,' Shao said, breaking the silence and interrupting her crewmates' tasks. 'What if we didn't go all the way on the hauler.'

'What do you mean?' asked Toft.

'We want to get out of the Yusan's reach and jump to the Solar System, right?'

'No, we want to not spend the rest of our lives in jail and on welfare,' replied Green.

'Yeah, yeah, bear with me.' Shao waved him off impatiently. 'What if we hitchhiked on the Incitatus only for a week or two, then jump ship when it passed by the final waystation on the inner edge of the Cloud? What was it...' She commanded her HUD to display the list of waystations in the D Sector of the Oort Cloud. The display informed her that they were now in range of Helikaon refinery station, the last and outermost waystation in the Cloud. It was preceded by Hector and Agamemnon stations, backtracking over a hundred AUs to the Hellespont relay dedicated to rerouting ships to one of the other ports in the D Sector. 'See, we could ride the hauler until Hellespont and take off,' she said, streaming the chart to the others.

'And what would that accomplish?' asked Toft. 'We'd still be in the Cloud with the hot potato in our hands and your dad on our trail as soon as we log anywhere using the Sōngshǔ's ID.'

'Hellespont has a large docking station. Freighter crews use it to repair their ships before sailing through the Great Beyond.'

And we could easily sell them the Sōngshǔ,' supplied Green, rubbing his chin. 'We'd sell it for parts or something, or just leave it adrift and pay for the passage. I have some savings.'

Shao winced at the mention of selling the jumper but said nothing. As long as the guys agree, it's fine. She can always talk them out of the sale later.

'What? You're in on the idea, Jared?' asked Toft, surprised. 'Since when?'

'Since it looks like it just may work,' he replied. 'We could take a detour, look for the Deep Cloud's shuttle. If we find it, we could ride the Incitatus until the Hellespont station and then—'

'And then sell the crate on Jupiter,' interrupted Shao. 'The Colony authorities don't care about OSEE law.'

'Fuck, you're starting to get to me,' said Toft. 'Mai, you've been quiet all this time. What do you think?'

Mai's eyes switched from blue to green, and Shao imagined her moving icons and windows on her HUD so she could see the physical space. 'I think I just found the magnetic field the journal talks about,' she said.

14

Lederman watched his patroller dock to the Ranger Station's prison module from his shuttle's through the HUD display. The craft's external cameras caught the Europa's disk reflected in the positioning lights just as it entered the hangar bay's maw. His shuttle entered the station soon after, docking smoothly to the commissariat module.

The transitional period between docking to the station and clearing the last airlock was always Lederman's favorite. It only took about ten minutes, but it was like a month-long vacation for him—at least compared to the energy-draining nightmare that was his office on the station. No decisions to make, no urgent messages, or responsibilities, just the routine of entry procedures.

Lederman liked to think those liminal moments like slides, boiled down to their most important elements. The shuttle airlock filled with disinfectant smell, crossing the escalator sleeve between the bay and the transit cabin, waiting for it to match the velocity of the station's rotating module. The small thud with which the craft connected. Last seconds of elevator music-filled peace. The airlock doors open—last deep breath and he dove into the bustling tumult of the Ranger commissariat.

Lederman's senses involuntarily registered the surroundings—the pull of one-g rotation gravity on his body, the bright lights illuminating beige walls filled with augmented reality posters spewing laws and regulations at the stressed paper pushers and Rangers doing their best to ignore the tumult of constant activity.

He headed straight for his workspace, an empty cubicle where a comm screen turned on the moment its user logged onto the station's network. Lederman sighed heavily as if the almost unused chair and the drab office area drained the energy out of him. How I hate this place, he thought.

'You last logged in two hundred and forty sols ago, Captain Manuel W. Lederman. You have one hundred and twelve new messages,' the greeting screen informed him.

Lederman minimized the pop-up angrily. 'I'm here for five minutes, give me a break.'

'Talking to yourself, Manny?' asked someone behind him.

Lederman turned around and greeted David Adebisi, leaning over the semi-transparent plastic wall with a half-wrapped tardiburger in hand. 'At least I'm not chewing with my mouth open.'

'What's the problem, anyway?' Adebisi took another bite out of his meal.

'How can you eat that crap? It's made of mashed bugs.'

'Tardigrades, not bugs.' Adebisi shrugged. 'It's really good, just imagine you're eating a bunch of really tiny bears.'

'Like that's gonna help.'

Martin Cheng's round face rose over the thin barrier on the opposite side of the cubicle like a sweaty full moon. 'They're actually made of a gene-modded strain called fatigrade. I think the name's cute. They grow almost a thousand times as big as normal tardigrades, you know.'

'I don't give a fuck,' replied Lederman, angrily. 'Don't you two have anything better to do?'

'We just missed your cheery smile, Manny.' Adebisi chuckled.

Lederman's HUD added another notification, this one from his bio-monitor informing about cortisol levels rising above healthy values and asking for permission to release counteragents. He ignored it. 'I bet you did. Sitting on your asses all day got you starved for entertainment?'

'No, actually,' said Cheng. 'The boss sent you five messages calling you to his office, but you ignored them all. So he sent us.'

'Fuck. I didn't ignore them, they're just lost in that mess of... This.' Lederman motioned to his screen as if his colleagues could see the augmented reality icons on it.

Adebisi patted him on the back with compassion. 'Welcome to the office life. Be happy you're only here every few months.'

'Yeah, this is a nuthouse,' agreed Cheng. 'Can you believe that Sarah still steals coffee prints from the cafeteria? Still!'

'Didn't you get a platinum print chip two years ago?' asked Lederman, raising his eyebrow.

'Yeah, we did,' replied Cheng. 'And that bitch still sneaks out to steal the one-use chips.'

'She's a klepto,' added Adebisi. 'I heard it's because of her marriage issues, you know.'

'No, I don't know.'

'Maybe it's for the better,' consoled Adebisi. 'You don't want to know.'

'I didn't ask.'

'They all say that,' said Cheng. 'I got her phone number if you're interested.'

'Why would I be?' asked Lederman. 'We're not even on the first-name basis, and she's married.'

'Ah, you still got the hots for your gunner, eh?' asked Adebisi with a knowing smirk. 'What's her name? Kara?'

'It's Lara,' corrected Lederman. 'And it's none of your business, even if I did.'

'Oh, come on, Manny, old pal. Share some of the high-life with us. Tell us about all the things you do in those months alone in space, so romantic and all.'

'Working. We're working.' Lederman blushed against his will. 'Which is what you two should be doing, then maybe you'd get your own ship.'

'And miss out on all the hot rumors in the Central?' Cheng feigned outrage. 'Besides, I'm not cut out to fight pirates.'

'You're more like cast from a form, I'd say,' added Adebisi. 'Like a cake.'

'Say that to my face,' countered Cheng. 'I'll punch you in the nuts.'

'A pillow fight it is,' laughed Adebisi and pretended to duck the punch Cheng threw at the air.

'Cut it out, children,' intervened Lederman. 'You said Martins wanted to see me?'

'Oh yeah, he did,' replied Cheng. 'Something about your prisoner, I don't know.'

Lederman wearily got up from a chair. 'I'll better go see him then.'

Heading down the corridor, Lederman couldn't help but notice the state of general agitation everybody was in. The Ranger station was usually half empty; spaceship captains like himself were out in the Cloud, reserve staff was spread thinly across the stations, and the bookies filed data away in their cubicles, their work disrupted only by rumor-milling.

The Rangers weren't an army or police corp that needed to fill quotas and responsibilities placed on them by supervisors. They were a volunteer organization funded by corporations, prospectors, and free traders tasked with maintaining order in the Oort Cloud. On this frontier, no nation or corporation could—or even attempted to—establish the rule of law.

The vast expanses of space in the Cloud were littered with valuable raw materials and tempted prospectors with unimaginable wealth. Still, they were too far away from the Solar System to allow a quick response from it. The distances within the Cloud itself were, well, astronomical. There was nobody to help the crews marooned on some asteroid or attacked by pirates.

That's where the Rangers came in and did their best to maintain a semblance of order. They rented about a dozen stations refitted to function as a mix of docking stations, living modules, and temporary jails. It wasn't much, but it was all they could get to house and refuel their rag-tag fleet of scout ships, small corvettes, and raiders patrolling the Cloud.

Their staging point on Kerberos station allowed a resupply and disposal of prisoners, albeit with an up to five-month trip one way. Other than that, the Rangers had to do with whatever they could buy or barter in exchange for police services and responding to emergency calls. They were not a unified force prepared to react to any significant emergency, and yet the station seemed to be in the middle of just that.

Lederman stopped the nearest person, an unknown Outer woman hurrying somewhere with a stack of datachips. 'Where's the fire?' he asked. 'Everybody's running around like they gave away free donuts somewhere.'

'Didn't you hear?' she asked. 'We're moving all the prisoners.'

'What? Why?'

'I don't have time to debrief every clueless space jockey, go talk to the brass.' She hurried on before Lederman got the chance to reply.

'I see you didn't lose your charm,' a familiar voice said from behind him.

'Oh, you know my rough charisma. Not everyone's bag of tea.' He turned and found Tomasson grinning at him.

'It's a "cup of tea," cap.'

'Yeah, whatever. You made it here quickly. I thought the paperwork is gonna take you longer.'

'Me too, actually. And it would have, but the boss called me up to his office when you weren't responding. I left Dassler with the perp and hopped over here.'

'I lost the message in all this mess.'

'Yeah, somebody kick over an anthill or something?'

'No idea. I tried getting some information, but... You saw for yourself.'

When they arrived at Martins's office, he was already furious. 'Lederman! Where the fuck were you?' he yelled as soon as the two of them entered.

'Stuck in traffic, boss. I'd have bought you a hot dog on the way, but you know how it is.'

Martins got up from his majestic armchair and leaned over the desk like a gorilla. He was a large Outer man built like a truck, so he pulled off the look quite nicely, despite wearing round HUD glasses too small for his face. 'Do you think this is some kind of a joke?' he asked in a low growl.

'If it isn't, then I'm in the wrong circus,' replied Lederman. 'Cut the shit, boss; nobody's scared of you since we found out you sleep with a plushie.'

Martins sat down again, taken off guard by Lederman's words. 'Now that just hurt my feelings. And Mister Whiskers's feelings, too.'

'Sorry, boss, I'll buy you a happy meal.' Lederman shrugged. 'I had a shitty day so far.'

'Well, I'm gonna make it shittier, just for you. You're gonna regret ever joining the force.'

'Can you get to point?' interjected Tomasson. 'Or just get a room already?'

'Come on, Lara,' said Martins. 'Why can't you let two old grunts have their fun?'

'Yeah, that was uncalled for,' added Lederman and sat down. 'I'm gonna need therapy after your mean comments. So, Mike, what's up?'

Tomasson sighed and sat down on the other chair. 'The whole station's gone crazy or what?'

'Or what. Some slag from Callisto came here a few days ago with two transport ships and offered to take almost a hundred perps off our hands,' replied Martins. 'Cheaper than a penitentiary corp, too. How about a drink?'

'Hit us up, vodka tonic for me,' said Lederman. 'What slag?'

Martins waited until Tomasson opted for a martini and commanded the bar printer to produce the drinks. When the servitor drone delivered them to recipients, he took a sip of his whiskey before replying. 'She said her name's Delacroix. I ran the background check request by the central.'

'What did they say?' asked Tomasson.

'She's a transport manager working freelance, overseeing large-scale shipments to the System. Worked with Neutron Dynamics, Zhengdao, Callisto Transplanetary, even OSEE governments, like PAC and Pan-Europa. Clean as a whistle.'

'What the fuck does she need a hundred prisoners for?' asked Lederman. 'You sure she isn't working with some pirate lord?'

'No, but we didn't dig anything up. She only wanted those with a twenty-year sentence or longer, but no lifers.'

'That's a lot of people to move,' said Tomasson.

'And a lot of mouths we don't have to feed,' agreed Martins. 'We had to empty the brigs in three stations to fill the quota; hence the mess around here. We're the closest to Helikaon Waystation, so the whole damn chaos falls on my head.'

'I hope the cred's good, at least,' stated Lederman, sipping his drink. 'It'd be a shame for her to go through all the hubbub for peanuts.'

'The cred we gave her is enough to buy a small moon, but less than we'd pay to a penitentiary corp. And without all the fucking bureaucracy. We'll make it back on feeding and life support costs alone within five years. Not to mention the free space in the slammers to put new perps in.'

'Overcrowding hit some stations pretty bad, I heard,' admitted Lederman.

'Worth the cost of getting rid of the trash,' agreed Martins.

'So, is that why you called us over?' asked Lederman. 'So we can help you ferry a bunch of pirates?'

Tomasson chuckled over her drink. 'That'd be a sight. We'd have to cram them into a crate and haul it behind us on a chain. Europa is a raider, not a freighter.'

'As much as I'd like to see that, that's not the reason,' replied Martins. 'You did arrive in a madhouse, but at a very fortunate moment.'

'Is it your birthday, Mike?' asked Lederman. 'I knew I should have bought you that hot dog.'

Martins put down his drink and looked Lederman in the eyes. 'This is a high-pressure job, and we joke around, gotta vent somehow,' he said. 'But this is serious, so cut the crap.'

'I'm all ears.'

'Good. One of the perps we have here in the brig, a lifer, made a deal with us to reduce his sentence.'

'Let me guess, he wants to be one of the guys we ship away?' asked Tomasson.

'Exactly. Now, normally I wouldn't go for it,' admitted Martins. 'The perp's name is McNamarra, he's a smuggler we tagged in at least five shootouts with our people, and we know for a fact he's wanted in the System for at least five murders—probably fragged more people in the Cloud, the bounty doesn't say.'

Lederman brought up the data transmitted from the chief's desk onto his HUD. The mugshot showed a bald, bearded man with neon facial tattoos contrasting with dark brown skin and cybernetic eyes. The crime record listed next to the picture was pretty impressive. 'Why are you letting him go then?' he asked. 'Sounds like he should end up in a slammer for good.'

'Normally, yeah, he would,' agreed Martins.

Tomasson casually flicked a lock of blond hair that fell on her eyebrow. 'But he offered a deal too good to pass up?'

'Exactly. In exchange for reducing his sentence and shipping out with the rest of the perps, McNamarra spilled leads that could help us take down Captain Pam.'

Martins paused for effect, but if he was hoping for a reaction, he clearly misjudged his audience. Lederman stared at him blankly before giving Tomasson a puzzled look. She returned the gaze just as perplexed.

'Sorry boss, but who the hell is that?' asked Lederman eventually.

Martins sighed and motioned at the drone to bring them another round of drinks from the printer. 'Right, you've been out for the last six months,' he said. 'While Europa was dealing with the outer reaches of the Sector, we had some trouble here in the core.'

'Our job's like stopping a flood with a wet rag, isn't it?' said Tomasson without humor.

'Them's the breaks.' Martins shrugged. 'While you were away, we had a bit of a situation here. One of the old pirate barons, Savid Delgado, died recently. And by that, I mean he's been jettisoned out the airlock on a flyby next to our station.'

'That must have been fun,' said Lederman. 'Raiders keelhauling each other takes the problem of our hands, what's not to love?'

'Fair enough. Except he was killed by another pirate leader, known as Captain Pam.' Martins uploaded the mugshot to their HUDs.

Lederman examined the picture in detail, absorbing everything he could from it. The woman, Pamela Lebovsky, according to the bio, looked nothing like a Cloud bandit should. Round, chubby face with smiling blue eyes and a perky nose, hair so blond it was almost white. She looked like a secretary, not a pirate. And yet the list of raids and attacks connected to her was longer than most old pirate barons. 'That one's been busy,' said Lederman after reading through the bio.

'That was all before she took over after Delgado,' replied Martins. 'We heard rumors she's trying to create a fleet.'

'That's just awesome,' said Tomasson with distaste.

'So far we know of two ships. A modified freighter she "inherited" from Delgado, the Plunderer, and one other vessel we don't know much about. She took out three patrols with them. Needless to say, we won't be able to stop her without some serious support if she puts her paws on more boats.'

'And we'd want to avoid asking a corp for help,' added Lederman, nodding.

'We might not have a choice,' said Martins. 'We won't have the firepower to stop her.'

'Pirate fleets never last long,' said Tomasson. 'It'd be a matter of weeks before they get into a shooting match over loot or some other nonsense. Besides, they'd have nowhere to resupply and regroup.'

Lederman knew she was right. Pirate crews were usually made up of mutinied corp workers, mercenaries down on their luck, and common criminals. A single pirate ship could survive by looting prospectors and traders, sometimes by docking to resupply stations under forged IFF signatures and stealing. None of these things brought enough plunder to sustain a fleet of ships with large crews, and sneaking a large number of spaceships to a station without raising suspicion was exponentially more difficult. Not to mention staying hidden from Rangers and free-lance mercs hunting them for bounty.

'She's planning something big,' said Lederman. 'Do we know what it might be?'

'No idea. That's what makes her our number one priority.'

'Okay, I think we get it,' said Tomasson. 'So, what did our bird sing about her?'

Martins leaned over the desk confidentially, looking at them under a brow. 'Pam and her crew found a drifting OSEE ship. McNamarra dealt with her second in command. According to him, they smuggled two ships over the Hellespont Waystation—a junker corvette and an OSEE research ship. He said Pam wants to arm the find and bring it back to the Cloud.'

Lederman puckered his lips with distaste. 'And then she'll have three ships. That's just fucking dandy. What are we supposed to do about it, though?'

'We can't do anything about it,' admitted Martins. 'Except trying to catch them on their way back. That's not why I wanted to talk to you. McNamarra also told us where Pam's flagship, the Plunderer, sits, waiting until the rest of her fleet comes back. They're repairing damage from the last scuffle.'

'And you want us to take her in before that?' asked Lederman rhetorically.

'Exactly. Here are the coordinates, take Pam out while we're packing the perps onto the transport ships, and there will be a clean and empty brig waiting.'

Lederman looked over the uploaded coordinates with a smirk. 'Would you like some fries with that?'

15

Zhenya watched the mining ships' IFF trackers from an observation deck aboard the Yusan. The bulbous crafts traveled away from the mothership in waves of five, reminding him of slow-motion fireworks. He brought up the IFF ID's for each ship to his HUD, looking for ZMV Seventeen. It was one of the first ships to detach a week ago and now floated in the outlying ring, getting further and further from the others.

The trajectory will take them to one of the denser regions of the Oort Cloud, where they can expect a bountiful run. The ship's officer, Jared Green, has added some last-second changes to the flight path, extending the journey by two full months, which was unusual but not worrisome. The crew needed actual flight experience to improve their chances of a high-profile assignment in the future—especially since Mai Wren was reassigned to the ship, despite the expert system's recommendation. Extending the trip for her benefit proved Green had the potential to become a great officer.

Zhenya pondered what reasons his adjutant may have had to arrange the transfer, though he could see no obvious way it benefited him. Ambitious subordinates making moves to further their agendas was nothing new, but the thought of Sun using Zhenya's daughter in his machinations was worrisome. As if on cue, the augmented reality display informed Zhenya about the adjutant's arrival. The doors behind him opened with a hiss.

Zhenya turned with a polite smile. 'Esteemed adjutant, it's nice to see you. I hope all is well?'

Sun lowered his head in a deep nod, almost a bow. 'Esteemed captain, everything proceeding according to the schedule, the fleet is away, and the transponders are broadcasting. No technical issues.'

'I'm very glad to hear that, esteemed Mister Sun.' Zhenya observed his adjutant's face like a hawk but maintained a mask of polite disinterest. Politics are a never-ending game, he thought. The problem is, everyone plays by their own set of rules. 'Did you know Shao arranged for her friend's reassignment?'

'No, not at all,' said the adjutant without hesitation. His face remained calm, though he did raise an eyebrow in surprise. 'I can try and find out who is responsible for aiding her, esteemed captain.'

He knows I know he's lying, Zhenya thought. 'I don't think reassigning technician Mai Wren was a good idea. It will hurt the girl's career in the long run. But Shao didn't go against the regulations, only against me. Leave it be, please.'

Jin Sun bowed his head once more. 'I'm here to aid however I can, esteemed captain.'

'So I see. Thank you, dear adjutant,' replied Zhenya. 'Especially for your discretion in the matter.'

'Of course, esteemed captain.' Sun took the comment as his cue to leave, ensuring Zhenya he was correct. The adjutant was playing a game behind the scenes. Zhenya wondered why Sun bothered to report in person instead of sending a message. He turned his attention to the void of space once more, just in time to see the last ships disappear into the darkness. Something was off about Sun, Zhenya thought, not for the first time. The adjutant was naturally interested in taking over his boss's seat on the Zhengdao board. Who wouldn't be? But what did the adjutant hope to gain by getting involved in the tense situation between Yuan and his daughter?

When the Yusan's computer assigned Shao and her friend to different missions, Zhenya expected his daughter to be displeased, but

Shao's reaction was much more explosive than he imagined. He leaned towards staying the course and giving Shao time to breathe; the girl would understand in time. Sun's involvement undermined his authority as both a father and a captain. It wasn't the first time Sun took liberties in interpreting his job description, as any ambitious person would, but why this time *specifically*?

The obvious solution was that Sun hoped to present himself from the best side in the hopes of winning Shao over. He would be sorely disappointed if that were the case. Not only was Sun almost twice Shao's age, but his demeanor was everything Shao rebelled against. Zhenya considered the possible implications. He determined it's not a likely option, but made mental notes to make moves in the future that would protect Shao from Sun's advances and repercussions of rejection. His daughter's relationship with Mai Wren was far from platonic, and the potential for distraction was too great to allow Sun's interference.

What were the other options? Sun using his position as a confidante to gather dirt to be used at a later date was a given, but for what, Zhenya did not know. All he could do was speculate and keep his eyes open. As long as the adjutant was under scrutiny, there was little he could do, unless he took great care to mask his actions.

The stiff, corporate etiquette in social relations was a double-edged sword used by players to both communicate and obfuscate the underlying struggle for power and influence that never ceased for a moment. Zhengdao was a tank full of sharks; polite predators, but predators all the same. Jin Sun knew Zhenya's plans to retire his role as a chairman after this tour, perhaps even retire from the corporation altogether. The power vacuum it created would need filling and who would be a better fit than Yuan Zhenya's own daughter? Unless there was someone else better suited for the role... Perhaps the previous chairman's adjutant, already well-versed in all of the political agendas and ongoing matters? Especially if Shao Zhenya somehow discredited herself, proving her unsuited to bear the responsibility that came with power.

This must be it. Sun's ploy wasn't aimed at him, but Shao. There was still time to counteract it, but first, more data had to be gathered.

Leaving the observation deck, he quickly headed towards his quarters. He brought up his chief of security on a personal comm line.

Sarah Lowe's face appeared in a HUD window, semi-transparently taking up a corner of his vision. 'Greetings, esteemed captain. How may I be of assistance?'

'Greetings, Sarah. I have an... Informal request,' said Zhenya.

Lowe's expression didn't change, but she dropped the pleasantries without losing pace. 'Of course, what do you need?' she asked. 'Something to do with our destination?'

'Not exactly. It's about Shao. I want to make sure she's safe.'

'Yes, sir. She already left the Yusan, however. There's nothing we can do for her until she returns.'

'That's what I wanted to talk with you about. Please inform your assault team that from now on, they are under my personal direction. They are to prepare for a potential Kennedy scenario.'

Low raised her eyebrow in surprise. 'Is that so? Do we have a mole on board, or is there something else I need to know?'

'No, no such thing,' Zhenya assured her. 'It's merely a precaution, an exercise if you will.'

'Right, as you wish, captain,' replied Lowe with audible skepticism. 'Anything else?'

'Choose two of your most trustworthy people. I want them to be Shao's personal security at all times when she returns from her tour.'

'Done and done.'

'Also, put a discreet tap on Jin Sun's comms.' Zhenya paused, waiting for her reaction.

Lowe nodded with a shadow of a smirk. 'This request is of course completely unrelated to the previous one?'

'Naturally, why wouldn't it be?'

'Right. Is there anything else?'

'That'd be all, Miss Lowe.'

'If I may have a moment of your time, though, sir,' said Lowe and paused, waiting for approval. Zhenya nodded. 'I took the liberty of sending a stream to Helikaon refinery security, letting them know that we're coming. I also sent a stream to the Ranger Station in the sector, and asked for current intel.'

'That's very commendable. What's the news?'

'A lot of empty noise, but a couple of interesting facts. An OSEE explorer ship went missing last year. Helikaon station had a minor meltdown in one of the reactors. The Rangers sold off most of their long-term prisoners to someone, moving them elsewhere. A bunch of prospectors report seeing a radiation spike on Sedna. The usual number of foo fighters and disappearing planets stories.'

'Anything else?'

'Yeah, I left the best for last. Apparently, there's a new pirate king in town, organizing a fleet.'

'A fleet? He's bound to aim for something big, I bet.'

'It's a she, but yes, I think so. There are only three big targets in this sector of the Cloud, the—'

'Helikaon Waystation, our hauler ship, and the Yusan,' interrupted Zhenya.

'Or they may split up and hit our mining ships.'

'Of course, please alert the Rangers with our ships' courses.'

'Already done, sir.'

'I'll join the security training. I can't expect people to die for me unless I'm willing to do the same.'

'I wouldn't expect any less from you, captain. Your battlesuit is ready when you are.'

'I'll give it a spin when I have the time.'

'You still think it's excessive, sir?'

'I do. Sitting inside powered armor to deal with a pirate raiding party seems a bit much.'

'We all know your humility, captain. But since you insist on risking your life with the ground pounders, you need to be safe. The powered suit has all the functions you will need to command the battle and will keep you safe from harm. Not to mention the firepower to make a difference.'

'Yes, I heard it all before,' surrendered Zhenya. 'I will learn how to operate it.'

'Thank you, sir.'

'That'd be all, you tyrant,' said Zhenya with fake anger. 'And thank you.'

'I'm happy to order you around any time, captain. With all due respect.'

'Great. How about a dinner after the shift? I should be done with my duties by then.'

Lowe smiled brightly. 'It's a date. See you then.'

Zhenya disconnected the comm, sighed, and entered the transit tube to his quarters.

16

The station's massive, gothic silhouette dwarfed everything around it but still looked insignificant on the backdrop of the Milky Way. Tall spires of thermal exhausts and defensive laser turrets made the irregular core of the megafactory resemble a place of mad worship. Double rings surrounded it, rotating slowly around the station's body, their protruding docking stations busy with the commotion around a few dozen cargo vessels and freighters of various sizes. Small, defensive platforms in orbit around the refinery gleamed with armaments, watchful for any danger. Every now and again, a laser beam shot out into the void to intercept an asteroid or a piece of cosmic trash on a collision course.

A few thousand kilometers away, a Helikaon waystation hung in far orbit, its ring surrounded with an ecosystem of service platforms, refueling departing ships and providing essential commodities and venues—restaurants, medical clinics, bars, and gambling dens. Tiny, one-person vendor crafts swarmed around a line of ten or so freighters awaiting launch clearance like flies, each broadcasting loud and colorful ads to push their wares and services—from hot dogs to companionship.

The waystation's single-lens dish aligned with an invisible point in the vast darkness of space. The lens flickered as the station emptied its energy reserves to power the multi-megawatt laser, and a bright beam of light shot into the void. The station's computer tracked the data package it received from the Solar System months ago—a plotted course of an incoming vessel, sent from a waystation hundreds of AUs away. The beam shot towards the incoming vessel according to that data, and, if the calculations were correct, it would hit the open sail, slowing it down. If it didn't, the incoming ship would be lost in the Oort Cloud forever, if it even managed to slow down at all.

A few minutes after the beam ceased, a sleek, white corvette came to a halt inside the waystation's ring, its silvery solar sail tucking away inside its hull. Three short wings on its sides fired jets from the maneuver engines, and slowly, almost gently, the spaceship came to a halt relative to the waystation.

The waystation had only a skeleton crew, and no designated tower operator—each of the six crew members took turns checking in incoming traffic. Short-range radio dishes inside the ring turned towards the corvette, establishing the connection at the same time as the defense turrets locked onto it.

Dave Matthews, a short, stocky man wearing a blue t-shirt and teal cargo shorts, floated in zero-g through the comm room towards the computer terminal. His bare feet easily found footing on the floor as he pushed a few buttons. He sucked on the coffee tube, making sure to close the cap afterward, and combed through his short ginger mane. 'This is Cloud Waystation Twenty-Six, sector D, repeat, this is Twenty-Six D,' he said to the microphone mounted on the table. 'Incoming craft, state your business and broadcast the IFF, over.'

A few seconds passed before the response came through. 'This is the Flamingo, Captain Ned Ibolya speaking,' responded a deep, confident voice. 'We're carrying energy cells and a sentenced crew to the Helikaon station, on contract. Transmitting IFF and license now.'

Matthews looked through the data, checking it over with anti-forgery software. It seemed real enough. 'Aight, captain. Stand by for drone control, repeat, stand by for drone control.'

'Standing by, Twenty-Six D. You mind sending a couple of beers over while at it?'

'You can get chow and supply once you're through customs.' Damn truck drivers, he thought, smartasses and comedians, all of them.

He pushed another button, and a holographic projector displayed the footage from the drone. It was in a white cargo hold stacked full of crates. Two men in civilian-looking red jumpsuits stood in front of the camera. The taller of the men, pale-skinned and with a brown goatee, grinned inside his suit and showed the drone a middle finger. The other visibly sighed and displayed an augmented reality cargo manifest towards the sensor.

Matthews ran the data through the system, then examined each crate's contents. He scanned both the barcodes on the sides, then the contents themselves using various telemetric devices installed on the drone. Eventually, he was confident everything was in order. 'All right, Flamingo,' he said. 'You're cleared for ingress, see you on your way out.'

'Looking forward to it,' came the reply. 'Want something from the grocery store?'

'Nah, all good here, boss.' Matthews chuckled. 'I do have one more question, though.'

'Shoot'

'What the fuck's a flamingo?'

The only reply was a burst of hearty laughter as the comms channel closed.

'Figures.' Matthews watched on his display as the spiral coil at the back of the corvette spun with increasing velocity, gently pushing the ship forward until it was out of the ring, then launching ahead towards the refinery in the blink of an eye as soon as it was clear.

17

Milosh regained consciousness, his scream of terror muffled by the apparatus stuck in his throat. His body shook violently in a tube filled with inertia gel as the ship rapidly decelerated. His tattoo-covered body lost a lot of muscle mass during weeks of forced stay in a tub, but his augmented arms and legs retained all of their bulk—after all, graphene-polymer and artificial muscles don't need exercise. His head was shaved bald, along with facial hair. A tight, uncomfortable breathing mask sealed his mouth and nose as an intubation pipe delivered oxygen to his body. Various tubes were inserted under bright orange prison shorts to ensure hygiene; IVs stuck into his veins provided protein and sustenance during the long journey. He could barely make out transport tanks similar to his through the almost opaque, green gel. The hard, murky substance filling the tank pushing on his body caused a panic attack, which he fought to contain.

The last thing he remembered was those damn dogs, and the man, Crowley. Milosh had no idea where he was, but at least he wasn't dead. It's not much, but it's a start.

He fought to free himself, but the gel held him tight—electromagnetic pulses emitted from the braces mounted on his wrists and ankles prevented his limbs from exercising much force.

A sudden flash of light interrupted his struggle. Someone came to say hello, Milosh thought.

A slim silhouette entered the room. Milosh couldn't make out the details through the thick layer of goo. Definitely a woman, he guessed.

He was proven right when the person walked right next to his tank. His cybernetic eyes fought to focus the lenses and enhance the image with some degree of success.

The woman leaned in as if examining a specimen in a museum. Perhaps she was. Milosh saw she had platinum-blond hair tied in a tight ponytail, face with regular, biosculpted features, full lips, large eyes, and a straight nose. That face rang a bell. He tried to grin at the woman, a futile effort against the force of the breathing apparatus on his face. I remember you, he thought. I guess you aren't dead after all.

The woman flinched, catching his gaze, and spat on the floor with disgust. She stepped back and entered a command into the tank's mechanism. The last time Milosh saw her they were on Sedna, and the PAC Navy bagged her. Looks like they brought her back.

Milosh's tank shook and began sliding on the floor towards the exit. From the corner of his eye, he noticed that the other tanks followed suit.

They passed multiple closed cabin doors on their way until they reached a wide hall, where two men in jumpsuits overlooked a dozen drones unloading cargo crates. They wore no helmets, and Milosh could just about make out the faces of a young man with black hair and an older guy with a goatee and a shaved head. To his disappointment, their faces meant nothing to him.

The line of holding tanks passed through the cargo hold quickly and entered a broad, slightly curved hangar. Milosh saw a crew in brown jumpsuits operating magnetic forklifts, taking away the crates put on the floor by the drones. Some informative signs hung from the ceiling, high above them, but he was unable to move his head to read them. They looked graphical, so not the military. Where the hell...

Milosh considered his chances of busting out now, but not only was he utterly helpless in the tank, but he was also in unknown terrain surrounded by potential enemies. He decided it was better to wait. Wherever they were taking him, it was bound to offer more options.

The drone caravan passed a worn-looking airlock, then drove through a long, slightly curved corridor for at least half an hour. Milosh observed his environment as best he could. They passed many people going about their business, wearing all kinds of jumpsuits and regular clothes in what seemed to be about one-g.

We must be on some sort of space station, Milosh concluded. Not military, though, too messy.

The prisoner line took a cargo elevator down a few levels, to another large deck. There weren't any ships on this floor—only lines of cargo transports slowly moving towards round hatches in the wall opposite the elevators. Drones flew overhead, scanning the cargo, directing it to one of the dozen or so large hatches on the walls. There were maybe thirty people on the platform overall, seemingly from different crews, slowly processing through the customs.

Milosh saw various makes and colors of jumpsuits worn by regular humans as well as a large number of Outers and zeroes, whose bioengineered features and extravagant fashion distinguished them in the crowd, even through the thick gel. He didn't have much time for observation as the gel tank line he was at the lead of was scanned by a drone flying nearby and must have been directed to some sort of fast traffic lane.

He saw the woman again when they reached one of the hatches. She approached a zero in a brown uniform, exchanged a couple of words. The official scanned the tablet in her hands with a small device and came closer to examine the tanks. Milosh met his stare through the gel, not for the first time today, judging by the bored expression of the official's wide, bony face and lack of interest in his small, colorless eyes. The clerk made a vague gesture, and the whole line of containment tanks moved towards the hatch.

Milosh's tank was first up the ramp. The circular door opened sideways and the tank fell onto the side. He tried looking back into the cargo bay, but as soon as the drone carrying his tank left the compartment, the hatch closed again. He managed to see a small light above the door on the inside change from red to green, and the tank started moving upwards on a transmission line towards an unknown destination. I'm in a fucking airlock, he thought. The fuckers are gonna space me after all.

Suddenly, the pressure of a sudden acceleration pushed the gel into Milosh's body, and the pod launched into space.

Free-floating, he could see the station for the first time as his tank rotated in space. The station's outer ring slid clockwise away, multiple mass driver barrels like the one he was just ejected from sporadically spewed out crates towards the station itself. The refinery's enormous silhouette rose into view, sprawling multiple vents, turrets, spires, and hatches. The tank spun again, and he could see other pods floating in a wide line behind him. Definitely not in Kansas anymore.

Without warning, the tank spun back rapidly. The refinery station was once more the centerpiece of the stage, but this time Milosh realized where he was headed. The structure's inner ring was similar to the first, except it rotated in the other direction.

A couple of freighters docked to it, but most of the protruding docking stations were empty. A barrel-shaped transport ship zoomed past, maneuvering engines on its brightly colored sides bursting with flames as the craft headed out into the void.

As Milosh's tank drifted closer, the silhouette of a larger vessel docked to the ring slowly dawned from behind the station's body. Its hull was almost as long as the entire segment of the cylinder. The craft was massively armored, almost like a bunker, deeply concave along most of its length.

At first, he thought the ship was embracing the ring's cylinder, but he soon realized it was docked parallel to it. A swarm of drones, only visible thanks to their position lights flickering to and fro, worked on attaching large cisterns and containers to the side of a whole freighter in the concave space between the ship's boards.

The tank shot past a dozen smaller craft looking as if they were composed mostly of the engines and headed towards the silent behemoth. Just as he was only a few kilometers from his destination, he realized what bothered him about the giant ship—it had no visible drive system.

As soon as the containment cylinder entered the concave, eight segmented legs caught it, and the caretaker drone scurried between the containers in the canyon, maneuvering with ease among the chaos of chains and busy drones. Jet engine exhausts on each side of the hexagonal body of the machine ignited and fell cold, seemingly at random as the drone took twists and turns at high speed. Suddenly it rushed straight down towards the bottom of the concave and fell into an airlock. The drone's arms released the gel tank, and the machine rushed off into space to fetch the next item on its worklist.

The airlock closed, leaving the adrift tank in the dark confinement. Milosh barely had time to adjust his eyes to the darkness before the hatch on the other side opened, flooding the airlock with white light. A grapple shot slammed into the tank and hauled it inside the bay. Two armored men armed with rifles dragged it out before Milosh had an opportunity to look around and released the grapple.

Milosh's body slumped as the gel softened and retracted. He collapsed as long unused muscles immediately cramped in unison, only the lack of gravity prevented him from falling face-first onto the metal floor. He fought to compose himself and relax his muscles, but he didn't get the chance. All at once, the pipes and tubes were pulled out along with the breathing mask, causing Milosh to vomit violently. Then the IVs popped out, disconnecting him from the gel tank's system altogether. Gasping for air and fighting shock, Milosh didn't see the tubes aimed at him. A rush of cold, foamy liquid from valves on the ceiling flattened him on the white tiles, violently washing the grime and leftover gel away.

A bell rang somewhere, and the cabin door opened. A short, stocky Outer woman joined the guards, eyeing Milosh with a wry grin on her rubbery features. Her eyes ran up and down his naked body shaking next to the wall. The spasms continued, but Milosh's mind was elsewhere. He noted all the details, looking for a way to gain control of the situation.

The woman wore a blue uniform, with a large belt and knee-high magboots. Her jacket had a crested horse-head badge on her chest, right next to a pocket with a rolled notepad tablet and electronic metal pen, leather gloves tucked in behind the belt, keycard holder, and a pistol sheath on her hip.

'Welcome to the Incitatus, Stepan Milosh—or should I say *convict*,' she said, with a sarcastic smirk. 'I hope you enjoyed your shower after a long journey.'

Milosh tried to reply, but his numb tongue refused to form words, and all he managed was a grunt.

'Don't bother. This is not a conversation. My name is Delacroix, but you can call me god. From now on, I'm responsible for your rehabilitation and work on this ship. You'll be told more when you recover from decompression.'

Two guards entered the room behind her, followed by a four-legged walker drone equipped with bedding. The men grabbed Milosh and strapped him to the machine, then led it down the labyrinth of narrow, brown corridors. Their magnetic boots held them to the floor in zero-g, but the drone just floated behind them, using its long legs to push off the surface and keep up.

As they walked, the warden continued. 'You must be wondering what's gonna happen to you now. Well, you'll be serving a sentence of twenty years of labor onboard the Incitatus. As you can probably guess, it's a prison ship. It's bound to launch towards Jupiter and then to Earth.'

'A-a-a.' Milosh tried his best to reply.

'Aren't I afraid you and other lowlifes will do away with the ship and become pirates?' she asked melodramatically, exaggerating each word. 'No, no, I don't. The ship doesn't have any engines or defense measures. What's gonna happen is, we'll drag it out to the waystation, and shoot it towards the Solar System, letting inertia take you all the way there, slingshotting off of the gravity of planets and moons along the way like a rock skipping on water. You do know what rock skipping is, yes?' She paused as if waiting for a reply, and when that didn't come, she continued. 'It doesn't matter. Your journey is going to take years, but the waystation doesn't have enough power to move that kind of mass with normal speed. Even if it had, it would be too expensive. In any case, the ship has no steering, no weapons, no way to slow down, and practically no signature so nobody will find it. Space is big, you know. Even if somebody had found it, protector drones are more than capable of dealing with a pirate boarding party... Or a mutiny.'

She paused as if waiting for a reply, but it didn't come. Milosh's muscles itched as they slowly warmed up to obey him. He was still weak, and his augmented limbs were restrained, but he could move.

The woman continued to monologue as if she learned the lines by heart, and paid little attention to anything else. Very slowly, Milosh shifted into a different position. He hoped the guards zoned out, having heard the same speech many times before. He was right.

'H-h-h... How fun,' he said, managing words with difficulty at first. 'Listening to you talk is the torture part of the sentence, I take it?'

'How dare you?' gasped the warden. 'I'm taking my precious time to educate you as to the circumstances of your rehabilitation, sir!'

'Better just shoot me right now, please. Way more humanitarian.'

One of the guards couldn't help but snicker.

The warden's face grew black with a flush of anger. 'Convict scum,' she shrieked. 'Careful, you might just get what you wish for!' The woman stopped in her tracks, about to punch him. Bed-drone and guards stopped too, uncertain of what to do. 'You think you're so tough,' she ranted on. 'I could break you right now!'

'On our first date?' asked Milosh, gathering his strength.

The warden must have noticed a dangerous gleam in his eye or was simply a coward. She took a step back, her eyes widening. The guards glanced at each other.

Milosh pounced. The bed jumped as he launched himself upward, headbutting the warden. Her nose collapsed onto itself with a loud crack of a broken bone. The woman fell on top of the stretcher, dark crimson blood from a busted lip flowing out, bubbling before her face. She gasped for air, in shock.

Both guards instinctively jumped in to help their boss. One reached out to tug the warden into safety, away from the convict's strapped hands; the other reached for the baton at his belt.

Milosh twisted in his bed. Strapped by ankles and feet, he couldn't pull with force but still had enough to overturn a lightweight drone. The machine rotated, baton hitting the chassis with a hiss of electricity. The shock caused the locks to release. Milosh immediately pushed himself off the bed and wrestled the first guard into a wall. The man's helmet banged on the metal, protecting the wearer's face. Milosh twisted the baton from the victim's hand. Almost gently, he tapped the guard's face with the baton and bounced upwards towards the ceiling.

The guard thrashed uncontrollably, floating to the middle of the corridor, where the warden was desperately trying to gain footing. The second guard managed to shove the stretcher drone aside just in time to meet the charge head-on. The guard steadied himself on the ground to block the blow. Milosh pushed himself off the ceiling, flying above the man. He thrust the baton between the guard's shoulder blades. Electricity crackled, punctuating the guard's scream. The stench of ozone and sweat mixed with the air conditioning's clinical aroma. Milosh landed on his feet and swung his weapon like a bat, momentum pushing him away, back where they came from. Milosh landed on the wall like a cat, immediately pouncing. A small dart hit Milosh's back as he flew, and his muscles went limp. He hit the wall carried by momentum, pain caused by the blow radiating like a thousand little bolts of lightning.

Delacroix shot him again, just for good measure, and sheathed her held-out tranquilizer pistol. 'Must I do everything myself?' she asked the remaining guard, her voice guttural and shaky. She turned to face the security reinforcements as they emerged from around the corner. 'And you took your time, eh? Did you have to finish taking a dump?'

'No ma'am, sorry, ma'am,' they replied.

'Whatever.' She scowled. 'What was that moron even thinking, there is no way he can escape the ship.' Tough words failed to mask Delacroix's lips were shaking, and she looked about ready to start crying.

The first guard took off his helmet and swiped sweat from his gray forehead. Panic in the guard's black eyes turned to anger; he landed a kick on Milosh's paralyzed body, sending him flying towards the newcomers. 'Dunno, ma'am,' he said. 'Looks like he wanted to make a run for it before we depart.'

'Before the ship departs, you mean.' She grinned. 'I intend to take the commercial flight back to Pluto and cash in; don't know about you, Stan.'

'Of course,' Stan said. 'It was just a matter of speech.'

'I know, I know. You think I'm taking the role too far?' she asked and turned to the other two guards. 'Take that trash to the rest; I think I'll skip the rest of the meet and greets.'

'Of course, ma'am,' said the guards in unison, catching Milosh as he floated towards them.

'I'm going to freshen up and get off this damn death trap,' added the warden. 'Are you coming, Stanny? I think I need a drink. And someone to accompany me.'

'Um... Yes, ma'am,' answered Stan hesitantly. 'If you say so, ma'am.'

'I say so. Now come.'

The remaining security guards put electronic cuffs around Milosh's ankles and wrists, tying them together.

He watched angrily, still unable to move.

'Poor Stan,' said the first guard, shaking his head. 'I bet he wishes he got mauled to death by now.'

'You said it, Lee,' chuckled the other. 'What a cruel fate.'

Laughing, the two guards hauled their charge down the corridor casually, letting the lack of gravity do the work for them.

Once at their destination, they opened the holding cell door. Inside, a group of prisoners sat on benches, shackled to seats a meter apart. The group consisted of three Outers and an Earther in orange prison suits, tattooed and scarred.

'Ahoy there, mateys,' chuckled Lee. 'We brought company for you, pirate scum. Make him feel at home.'

'Yeah, he's the warden's special friend,' added the other guard. 'Very special.'

The prisoners glared at Milosh menacingly as the guards busied strapping him in the free spot on the end of the bench, right next to a huge Outer man. An elastic line stretched from Milosh's wrist cuffs behind the seat down to his ankles. He started to move and strain, the paralyzing agent's force subsiding. The giant sitting next to him growled menacingly. His red cyber eyes glowed, sharpened chrome teeth bared. His flat, scarred face bore the expression of pure hatred.

'Calm down, Otis,' Lee scolded him. 'You'll have plenty of time to get to know your new friend during the journey, don't worry.'

'Oh, we'll take good care of him,' said a skinny, almost skeletal-looking Outer, narrowing his slanted black eyes, his lips curled in a cruel smirk. 'Don't worry about that, good sir.'

'Oh, I'm not worried,' replied Lee happily. 'The warden would be furious if something were to happen to her boy toy. I'm sure you can respect that.'

'We sure can.' The dark-skinned Earther on the opposite end of the bench cackled. 'We'll throw him a real party.'

The guards left the holding cell, closing the hatch behind them. Prisoners waited in tense silence for a while, staring at Milosh. He stared back defiantly, in silence. Only his right hand was twitching and jerking in rapid motion, opening and closing his palm. The staring contest between Milosh and the remaining four became palpably intense. The men leaned forward in their benches to see him over Otis, whose giant body obstructed the view as he leaned over the smaller Earther.

'So, what did you do to piss off Delacroix so much?' asked the giant, Otis, in a surprisingly gentle, low baritone.

'Let's just say it wasn't love at first sight...' replied Milosh carefully, his hand still twitching rapidly as he tried to reach his skin pocket.

'You must have really stepped on her toes,' Otis said, raising his hairless eyebrow.

'Yeah, something like that,' agreed Stepan, shrugging.

'The guards sure did pull off a nice show,' interjected the last Outer. He had been silent so far; his small, almost child-like frame slumped in the far end where Milosh could barely see him. 'They think we're all a bunch of primitives.'

'Yeah, that's demeaning,' agreed the dark-skinned prisoner, rattling his manacles.

'To be honest, you're not making the best first impression,' stated Milosh. 'You might as well have gone with a yarr, shiver me timbers, and all that.'

The Earther laughed, and after a second, the other prisoners joined him in unison.

'Hah, t'was but a ruse, ye landlubber,' giggled the small Outer.

Milosh noticed a tattoo of a spider web on his rubbery lips stretching with his smile.

'You forgot the ahoys, Pie,' chuckled Otis.

'My bad,' apologized Pie. 'Ahoy.'

'Anyway, the name's Harvey Otis,' said the huge Outer. 'The skinny one's Sticks, the tattooed smartass is called Spider, but we call him Pie for short. The joker over there's Allison McNamarra.'

'I don't like that name, call me Al,' said the dark-skinned Earther seriously.

'Yeah, you best do that,' agreed Otis. 'Or he'll slit your throat in your sleep.'

'Do you think I'm a murderer, big guy?' asked McNamarra. 'A pirate without morals?'

'Not at all, I know you're a respectable businessman,' replied Otis. 'Just working the wages, moving wares from point A to B, and being imprisoned unlawfully.'

'So are we,' laughed Sticks. 'Except point A is a sucker's cargo hold, and point B is our pockets.'

'You don't even have any pockets,' argued Pie.

'But if I had, I'd keep my booty in them.'

'Keep your booty in your pants, pal,' chuckled McNamarra. 'Also shut up, and let our man introduce himself, god damn it.'

'Nice to meet you, gentlemen.' Milosh pretend-bowed, his hand constantly twitching. 'The name's Milosh.'

'All right, Milosh, come clean,' urged Otis. 'What did you do to the warden? And don't even bullshit me, security wouldn't throw you under the bus without reason.'

'Why not? They looked easily irritable,' replied Milosh with a smirk.

'That may be, but they're also in a hurry to get out of here,' said Pie. 'Spill it, or we really will give you a warm greeting.'

Milosh's smirk turned into a grin, 'Try me.'

The whole ship shook before anyone had the chance to answer. Prisoners in the holding cell felt the acceleration push them into the benches, the hull moaned and creaked, protesting such treatment. The shaking grew more potent, almost painful, forcing the breath out of their lungs. After what seemed like an eternity, the tremors subsided, but the pressure remained, steadily increasing.

'Looks like we're on our way.' Milosh stated the obvious. 'That should mean the warden and the guards are off this boat, right?'

'I guess so.' McNamarra shrugged. 'What does it matter? There's still combat drones on security detail.'

'Yeah, we're still in the shitter,' added Pie. 'And still tied to the wall.'

'They're gonna take us to the cells eventually,' said McNamarra.

'So what, who cares?' disagreed Pie. 'They'll keep us in the handcuffs all the way no matter what.'

'Quiet,' said Otis, silencing the argument. 'Enough stalling, oner. You're starting to piss me off.'

'Really? I was just starting to enjoy our little chat,' replied Milosh, rubbing his right forearm and wrist forcefully on the bench's edge.

'What did you do to the warden?' asked Otis, menacingly. 'And the fuck's wrong with your hand?'

Milosh rubbed the bottom of his forearm on the seat with long, careful motions. Almost got it, he thought.

'The answers to both your questions... Are connected...' he said through his teeth, straining visibly. 'You see...'

Milosh's final motions revealed a small, elongated item stuck deep in a hole right in the middle of his right palm. The opening didn't bleed, synthetic skin and muscle covering a cybernetic limb. Only some dark green liquid poured out as the object slowly peeked out of the pierced spot. When it was out, Milosh grabbed it with the left hand and presented with the gesture worthy of a magician producing a pigeon from a hat. 'I stole her pen,' he finished, grinning like a maniac.

18

The flock of guide ships ladened with additional fuel tanks carried the Incitatus away from the refinery, their engines straining to pull the massive prison craft behind them.

Assist vessels quickly burned through the deuterium tanks twice their own size attached to the hulls, detaching each tank as it depleted and leaving it behind to reduce mass. Behind the flock, the Incitatus floated majestically, its V-shaped hull seemingly bucking and rearing on invisible waves. Within hours of flight, the formation reached the waystation. The prison vessel was far too massive to fit inside the station's ring.

On cue, the escort ships released the links and kicked the thrusters to slow down. The leviathan passed them by, carried by the force of inertia towards the waystation. Freighters and other vessels cleared the area, letting the giant ship pass.

The escort crafts dropped their final deuterium tanks and detached their external modules around the waystation—each a massive laser fueled by a battery relay. Having dropped most of their bulk, they were no bigger than flies behind the massive hull of the transport craft. The Incitatus pushed on uncaringly, oblivious to the frantic activity behind it.

'Waystation Twenty-Six D, this is Remora One, we're in position,' communicated the assistant flock leader.

'Sure thing, Remora One, Twenty-Six D ready whenever. Don't get your panties in a twist,' replied Matthews, watching the spectacle from his control cabin on the waystation while sucking on a smoothie through a straw. The pink bathrobe he was wearing waved slowly around his body as he dodged out of the way to avoid a bubble of strawberry-flavored liquid hitting it—it landed on his shorts instead. Only one of the displays in the room was focused on the data regarding the Incitatus and the launch. Other terminals were showing a rerun of a talk show, in which a frantic Outer woman explained to the host excitedly how she married an alien and gave birth to baby Jesus.

'Copy that, Waystation Twenty-Six D,' signaled the flock leader. His immaculate uniform bore the horse head insignia. Telemetry and flight control instruments spaced neatly around the cockpit displayed a flood of data. He leaned into one of the screens. 'Waystation Twenty-Six D, can you run a scan on the hull for me,' he asked. 'My readings are slightly off.'

Matthews sighed and headed for the one screen showing data from the departing ship - the station's sensor arrays were much more powerful than anything a little ship like Remora could outfit. He was about to run diagnostics, but then the talk show host introduced another guest—a bearded man wearing a "Lone Gunman" t-shirt claiming vehemently that the Earth is flat and space travel is a hoax.

Ah well, fuck that noise, thought Matthews. The stiff just has a glitch anyway. Probably. 'Already did that, Charlie, my man,' he lied. 'Everything is five by five, no sweat.'

'Roger that, Waystation Twenty-Six D. Fire on your mark.'

The escort flock and the waystation fired the lasers, millions of megawatts hit the sail at the back of the Incitatus at the same time. Almost double the maximum waystation's power hit the sail, sending the behemoth on its long journey towards the Solar System. The station's maneuver engines kicked off to compensate for the forces involved, surrounding it in a halo of ejected fuel.

'Shit, spilled it all over myself,' exclaimed Matthews over the comms, forgetting they were online.

'Is there a problem, Waystation Twenty-Six D?'

'What?'

'Are you having difficulties there, buddy?'

'Yeah, no. Just a... Thing.'

'Roger that. Remora fleet over and out, we're heading back to base.'

'Okidoki. Don't forget to pick up your trash on your way back.'

The assist fleet pulled their lasers back, then kicked on the engines and flew back towards the distant Helikaon refinery. Traffic around the waystation slowly reorganized itself as the station technicians readied for the next launch. Matthews fought with tissue paper in zero-g, trying to clean himself up while the mother of an alien Jesus and the flat Earth preacher got into a fistfight, to the general rejoicing of the audience.

'Next on "Can You Believe It",' said the host with a wide smile, baring her pearl-white teeth. 'Our guest will be a man who made telepathic contact with the alien race living under the oceans of Callisto and a woman who gave birth to an egg—stay tuned!'

19

The Yusan slid through the void, dark except for an occasional flash of maneuver thrusters correcting its course. Its main engine was cold, having completed its job many weeks ago.

Inside, a fast-paced guzheng melody broke the silence of a simple square cabin, empty except for a bed in the center. Zhenya opened his eyes, immediately awake. His cybereyes HUD flashed a welcoming screen. Zhenya took care of the reminders and notifications during the morning routine, and left the bathroom. He put on a black jumpsuit with silver details waiting for him on the hanger instead of the white and gold captain uniform. Today he was a CEO, not an officer. The slow rotation of the living quarters created a pleasant half-g, allowing him to quickly push through the spherical pipe-like corridors criss-crossing the ship towards the command center located at the top of the dome. He moved with the grace and certainty of a man traversing the same route every day for years.

He was preoccupied entirely with the bright HUD displaying a constant stream of data about the ship's position and status. Performing a check-up on the way to his workstation was a long-standing routine, wasting no time on a commute that could be used for tasks not requiring his full attention.

Watching the diagnostics program flash in front of his eyes day after day was also terribly dull, and Zhenya had better things to do with his time. A small window in the corner of his HUD display played a rerun of an old sitcom. An Earther and an Outer sharing a cabin on a space station going through their lives, fighting about everything. In this episode, Clark, the oner, suspected his roommate, Alissa, tampered with the thermostat. They both blamed each other, but neither knew it was, in fact, the station manager's pet biodrone. Good times.

Zhenya entered the Yusan's command center with a well-practiced slide, hanging on to the round door frame for balance and launching straight into his chair. He gave a mental command, and the nearest screen turned towards him, displaying a conference stream on the AR screen. Zhenya saw a brightly lit room with a long, oval table, surrounded by chairs. The windows opened to a stylized render of the Milky Way seen from afar. The mining ship captains sat in the chairs, looking at him expectantly. Nineteen seats were taken, one empty. Zhenya couldn't help but notice the empty seat belonged to Jared Green, the officer aboard Seventeen. 'Good morning, crew,' began Zhenya cheerfully, waving off the worries for now. 'How are we all feeling today.'

'Very well, thank you, captain,' replied everyone in unison, the ship's computer timing the reply delays to minimize the laser stream's communication lag. Corporate protocol dictated the reports were to happen face to face—and so the crews did their best to pretend the teleconference happened in real-time.

Zhenya could see that the reply was more than just corporate protocol—the officers really were in good moods. That bode well for the mission progress. 'Glad to hear that, dear friends.' Zhenya highlighted the first crewmate in everyone's HUDs. 'How are matters, dear colleague Lei Chen?'

'Everything progresses according to estimates, captain,' answered the woman, bowing. Her eyes flashed yellow as her internal computer sent data straight to Zhenya's HUD. 'My prospector crew is almost done with their telemetry. The data is promising, and we should not only meet but exceed the projected results. If it keeps up, we'll fill our quota and then some by the end of the solar year.'

'I'm delighted to hear that.' The morning started with good news and was a good sign for the rest of the day, despite Green's absence.

Maybe they're suffering comm array problems. New ships tended to be glitchy. Zhenya selected the next officer in line. 'And how are you, dear colleague Hendricks?'

'We're having a bit of trouble with the local Ranger station in the sector, captain.' The officer's voice was full of shame—real or fake. 'They're still arguing our right to mine in the asteroid field, claiming an independent survey crew claimed the rocks first. But we will work around the issue. Already an inquiry has been made to local vagrants to arrange for a random pirate attack. That would free the field from any claims aside of our own.'

'I'm looking forward to hearing about your success and progress, dear colleague.' He finished reading the report and laid his eyes on the next chair in line. Green had struck him as a responsible young man, and he should have logged in by now. A small delay was acceptable, but Zhenya was getting seriously worried. He sighed heavily and paused his sitcom. 'Yusan to officer Jared Green, repeat, Yusan to officer Jared Green,' he hailed the missing officer twice, but the chair remained empty.

Zhenya looked over the other officers—some of them looked concerned, and rightfully so. A ship missing in the Cloud is always troublesome, to say the least. 'Has the Seventeen contacted any of you, dear colleagues?'

Jenny Kovalsky, the officer on Fifteen, raised her hand hesitantly. 'I was on comms with technician Mai Wren last week. She was asking about a magnetic anomaly in the quadrant near us.'

'What exactly did she want to know?'

'She said they changed their course to extend their tour,' replied Kovalsky. 'Their new route took them through a neighboring quadrant to our flight path. Mai just said they detected some magnetic anomaly and asked if we can confirm it.'

'And could you?'

'Well, yes. Our sensors did pick up an unusual magnetic field there, but we didn't investigate.'

'Could you please send me the coordinates, dear colleague?'

'Of course, esteemed captain,' replied Kovalsky and almost immediately sent the data over on a private comm stream. 'I took the liberty of packaging all the sensor data from the quadrant with comms between our ships.'

'Commendable forethought, thank you,' said Zhenya, before addressing the rest of the officers. 'I hope you forgive me for the schedule change, but I need to look into the matter.'

'Naturally, esteemed captain,' replied Kovalsky, and the others muttered an agreement. 'It would be understandable even if... Yeah,' she paused awkwardly.

Zhenya was amazed how the crews managed to gossip so much despite the distances between the mining ships. 'I will forward the call to my esteemed adjutant Jin Sun,' he said, filling the silence. 'Please continue your report as normal.'

The officers muttered an agreement again, looking at each other with concern. Getting to know your coworkers and forming attachments was unavoidable on a long flight like this, despite the stiff corporate protocol. Many of the trained crew members spent their free time in the company of the missing Seventeen's crew and were naturally worried.

Zhenya hid his face in his hands, rubbing the temples to fight the approaching migraine. Finally, he hailed Sarah Lowe. Despite the early hour, she was in full uniform when a comm window appeared on the screen.

'How can I help you, esteemed captain?' she asked seriously.

'The Seventeen didn't report in,' replied Zhenya. 'I need you to look into it.'

'Are you suspecting foul play, captain?'

'Not necessarily. Perhaps they suffered a comm malfunction too severe to fix with spare parts printed onboard.'

'But we need to cover all the angles anyway?'

'Naturally, we need to be certain all our crews are safe and accounted for.'

'Naturally,' said Lowe with a nod. 'Do we have any intel outside of their flight path?'

'Yes, we have a confirmed communication in this quadrant.' He uploaded the transcript from Fifteen. 'They went to investigate an anomaly there.'

'I'll gather a squad immediately. Should I tell Captain Powells too?'

Zhenya thought for a moment before replying. 'Let Edgar know, but don't engage the Jīnlóng in the search. Not yet, at least.'

'Very well, captain. I'll take the Zhengjiù then,' replied Lowe. 'I request permission to equip a laser buoy, esteemed captain.'

'Granted. Time is of the essence; you will need the boost on your way back.'

'I'll move out as soon as possible,' said Lowe and disconnected, leaving Zhenya alone with his fears.

20

J ared Green disconnected from the comms and got off the chair. He turned around, long legs barely fitting inside the shallow niche of the communication room.

Shao immediately got up from her station to meet him. 'So, how did it go? Did you get through?'

Green shook his head. 'No signal. I mean, there is a signal, but it's like we can't get through some interference.'

Mai and Toft entered the Seventeen's bridge carrying a box of tools. Mai looked at her crewmates, and her face sank. 'No luck?'

'None. It's like our comm laser is out of range,' replied Green.

'That's impossible,' Shao argued. 'We should be well in NaviNet's range. What gives?'

'No idea,' said Toft. 'We just did the maintenance check for the millionth time. Everything seems to be in order.'

'Except the sensors are trying to source more power to the laser than it's capable of sending,' added Mai.

'The guy on the science ship,' said Shao. 'Redding. He said the anomaly caused strain on the comms.'

'Yeah, I remember,' replied Mai impatiently. 'But we're not close enough for it to affect us, right?'

'If we assume Redding noticed it right away,' said Green. 'It could have been weeks before he spotted it.'

'Or whatever the scientists did to it made the interference stronger,' said Toft.

'Kovalsky detected it,' said Shao. 'And they just flew past the quadrant.'

'I guess we have no choice but to pick it up now,' said Green.

Mai shrugged and let go of her end of the box, forcing Toft to put it on the floor. 'I'm gonna keep working on isolating the interference,' she said and left for her cabin.

'She alright?' asked Green, looking at Shao.

'Yeah, she's just scared. I am too.'

'It was your idea to come here, looking for trouble.'

'Don't I know it?'

Toft raised his hands, walking between the two. 'Hey, hey, don't you give up now! We made it this far. Millions of credits just waiting to be plucked, remember?'

Shao looked down on her feet, hands crossed. 'What if there aren't any? What if the looters were wrong, and it's just junk?'

'Then we blow it up, shut down the interference, and get back to work,' replied Toft. 'We just gotta be able to reach a NaviNet buoy. Or the Yusan. Or whoever.'

'I guess you're right,' admitted Shao. 'It's been a long month, is all.'

'I get it; we're all stressed. But hey, don't you wanna be a freelancer anymore?'

'You know what, no, I don't,' replied Shao wearily. 'It was a dumb-fuck idea. But you are right; we have to find the source. If it is a treasure, we'll shut down the signal and give it to Dad. If it isn't, let's blow it up so we can get out of here.'

'Wait, wait, wait, hold on a minute,' blurted Toft. 'I get it, going freelance is stupid, but we can't just hand over the treasure.'

'Since when are you on board with all this?' asked Green. 'For the last few weeks it was nothing but "Oh, we gotta turn back. Let's not throw away our careers... Blah blah," and you're ok with it now?'

Toft looked away, trying to hide a sudden blush. 'You know, we're already here. Might as well get something good out of this mess.'

Shao looked Toft in the eyes, causing him to blush even further. 'So, we don't give it back to Dad. What then?'

'We could, I don't know,' muttered Toft. 'Go over his head and show it to the board?'

Shao was about to argue, but Green interrupted her before she even got out a word.

'That's actually not that stupid,' he said. 'Think about it. We bring it back to the Yusan, what do we get? A pat on the back. And the thing, whatever it is, sits on board for a full year, doing diddly squat, just emitting its magnetic field.'

'Putting everyone at risk of the pirates,' added Toft. 'Or whoever that was on the recording, coming back to get it.'

'They wouldn't attack the Yusan, come on,' opposed Shao.

'Maybe they wouldn't, maybe they would.' Green shrugged. 'But the box wouldn't make any money either way. We bring it back to the head office; there'll be a reward, we'd be heroes. And the corp can work on it in four months, everyone's happy.'

'Except my father will kill me,' said Shao. 'It was fun to joke around about running away, but I can't... We can't just go missing. Dad'll go nuts, start looking for us...'

'Not if we leave the Seventeen here, with a message,' noted Toft. 'Sure, he'll be angry, but before he can do anything, we'll already be talking with the board. And isn't your grandpa a founding member of it?'

Shao shook her head. 'He is, but so what? How do you intend to get to the Solar System without Seventeen? On the Sōngshǔ?'

'Well, yeah, actually. Your idea from back then was good,' replied Green. 'We can mod the mining laser to push the Sōngshǔ towards the Hellespont Waystation and hitch a ride there.'

'We won't get to the Hellespont on the Sōngshǔ from here. Its sail isn't made for beams that strong. Plus, we'll run out of power for life support.'

'Let's go with the original idea then,' said Toft. 'Hitch a ride on that barge, what was it?'

'The Incitatus,' said Green. 'We can hop on it and leave when we're in range of Hellespont.'

'You know what, that might work actually,' said Shao. 'Holy shit, Dad will be furious.'

'Does that mean you're back on?' asked Toft.

'I guess I am,' said Shao, looking up at him with a shadow of a smile.

The Seventeen's internal comms came online with a click, Mai's face showing in everyone's HUDs. 'That's good to hear, babe, cause I found the rock where our treasure is,' she said in a leisurely tone. 'I've started the landing sequences; it'd be a shame to lift off now.'

Shao brought up the positioning stats and the external camera feed onto her HUD. The mining ship was slowly preparing to attach itself to a lone asteroid nearby. Its hull opened like an umbrella, revealing servos and drills crowning the long segmented legs hidden under the living module's cap. Hydraulics pushed the segmented scales of the craft apart, forming a thin, but sturdy hood. The Seventeen was ready to embrace an asteroid tightly or swallow it whole if it was small enough. Shao switched the windows, bringing up a close-up on their destination visible in a separate window of the HUD—footage from the prospecting drone Mai sent while they were talking. It just looked like any other asteroid to her—an icy shell with a metallic core. It would make a decent strip-mining target in case the treasure is a dud, she thought.

Seventeen's main engine came to life, a long blaze of burned deuterium propelling it towards the distant rock. Shao and the rest of the crew hurried to their stations as the acceleration started to build up gravity on the ship. She managed to slip her body into the chair just as they reached one-g, and tightened her seat belt and cushions.

Soon, the asteroid was visible on external cameras, and the mining vessel recalled the drone. The rock was tiny compared to some of the Oort Cloud's rubble but still dwarfed the approaching ship like a mountain. Slowly, with arms spread almost horizontally in relation to the cabin, the Seventeen touched the icy surface in a spot designated by the onboard computers. Clouds of helium ice instantly evaporated in contact with metal, surrounding the ship in a quickly freezing mist. Clasps and drills pierced the rocky surface beneath, attaching the mining ship securely to the asteroid. When the arms were firmly in place, they flattened, and the thin hood's side stiffened, soon forming a tight and sealed dome on the rock's surface, with the crew section above it—a tiny bubble atop the mound.

Shao looked at the footage inside the perimeter, looking for any signs of human activity, but couldn't see anything. 'Mai, why did we park here? Are you sure you got the right spot?'

'Oh yeah, one hundred percent,' replied Mai over the comms. 'Check this out.'

Mai painted a red circle around a small icy rock near the middle of the screen. Shao zoomed in over the area, trying to see the object disguised in a mist of quickly freezing liquids.

Toft must have been trying to do the same, but instead of dabbling with the sensors, he sent a drone down to look at it up close.

'It's a shuttle,' said Shao. 'We found it. We found Redding's ship.'

'That we did,' agreed Toft. 'But I don't think anyone's home.'

The small craft was sunken meters below the asteroid's surface, sticking above it in a bubble of ice. The shuttle's rear hatch was wide open. There was no way anyone inside could be alive.

'Where is he? Where's the crate?' asked Shao.

'Sensors detect a hollow space right next to the shuttle,' said Mai. 'My best bet is that the crate's there.'

'And Redding?' asked Green. 'Did he leave?'

'Let's hope he did,' replied Toft. 'I'm punching it.'

The machinery under the Seventeen's hood detached and rotated, revealing the flat lens of a mining laser. Lights inside the ship flickered as it charged, then a bright-blue beam shot towards the surface. The rock instantly exploded, filling the inside of the dome with rubble. The crew module shook and reverberated as rocks pummeled it from below.

Warning icons popped up all over Shao's HUD, reporting a dozen malfunctions at the same time.

'Lasse, shut it off!' yelled Green, trying to be heard over the rocks banging on their hull. 'Shut it off now, god damn it!'

'Already did, dude,' replied Toft. 'Relax, Jared, sheesh.'

'What the hell happened?' asked Mai. 'Did we hit a bomb or something?'

'It's almost like the ground just blew up,' replied Green. 'I can't see anything there.'

'Hold on, I'll clear it out,' said Toft. 'Gently and steadily, don't you worry.'

The engineer entered a command and a swarm of drones launched from the arms of the ship. They flew back and forth, systematically scooping all of the material into the storage compartments, inflated slightly with the weight, but not nearly as much as Shao had expected.

'I thought there's going to be more rubble in this... Rubble,' Shao said.

'Beats me,' replied Toft. 'Maybe we hit a gas pocket, and it ripped?'

'So much for the treasure then...' Mai sighed.

'No, wait,' said Shao. 'There's something there!'

With the rubble now cleared, the cameras showed a crater under the dome, a few hundred meters deep, and very narrow. Toft slowly worked the collector drone down the shaft. Its sensors detected a solid object at the bottom of the shaft. The engineer maneuvered it carefully closer to illuminate the depths of the crevice. The spotlight caught a large crate near the bottom. The crate's door fast-froze ben into the crater wall a few meters further up. The drone hovered near it, casting light from the reflectors onto the metallic surface.

'Oh god, I can't look,' blurted Mai.

Shao instinctively leaned in to see up close even though the image was displayed directly onto her HUD. 'Oh no.'

The drone illuminated the broken figure of a man in a vacuum suit, crushed and melted into the wall. The helmet was broken, and the ice around was dark brown and bubbled.

'He must have stepped on the hole thinking it was solid,' said Green impassively. 'The crate must have torn up during the fall; the door ripped away and killed him.'

'What fall? There's zero-g on this rock,' said Mai.

'The fuck do you think happened then?' asked Green.

'I... I don't know.'

Toft drove the drone towards the crate without a word. Shao watched him pilot. Slowly and carefully, he illuminated the contents—a metallic object resembling a capsule. Its surface reflected the light with a golden gleam. Shao could see no hatches, or damage—it looked like a drop of liquid metal, less than two meters long.

'What is that?' asked Green. 'Get closer, Lasse...'

'Working on it, dude,' answered the engineer. 'Just gotta wiggle over that rock...'

'Is that a torpedo?' asked Mai. 'It looks like a torpedo.'

'You're a torpedo,' snapped Shao. 'It's what the guy was talking about, the treasure.'

'You're a treasure, bitch,' replied Mai. 'Wait, that didn't come out right...'

'Yeah, right,' cut in Toft. 'If you're done flirting, I'm gonna try to bring the thing up, hold your thumbs.'

They watched intently as the drone descended the tight shaft, trying to get near the mysterious object. Toft used the drone's sensors to scan the object making sure it was safe to approach. He ordered the machine to attach itself to the reflective surface with clamps. As soon as the drone attempted to lift it, Shao realized the capsule was very light, with barely any mass to it. Still, traversing the jagged tunnel upward was quite a challenge, and the drone almost crashed a few times on its way up towards the surface. Eventually, it was free and made its way back to the ship, delivering its cargo to the main hold of the mining vessel.

Shao and the rest of the crew immediately rushed down there, stopping only to don their white-gold vacuum suits, and gathered around the capsule. Released from the drone's grasp, it floated in the cargo hold, weightless and serene in zero-g.

Toft approached first, slowly circling it. 'How do you wanna go about it?' asked Toft hesitantly, careful now that his real body was potentially in danger.

'Dunno, maybe we should just leave it alone?' pondered Green, leaning in to inspect his image in the capsule's reflective surface.

'No way, we came all this way.' Shao's colorful hair flashed red under her suit's mask. 'We're opening that thing.' She made a step forward, reaching for the plasma cutter on her belt.

She made a step forward, reaching for the plasma cutter on her belt. 'Woah, woah, what are you...' Green moved to intercept her and in his rush touched the capsule's surface. It immediately became transparent, stopping everyone in their tracks. They stared in astonishment, petrified by the view.

'What the...' blurted Mai, her face suddenly pale.

'Is that...' Green gasped, then fell silent again.

Inside the capsule, curled in a fetal position, a dry and wrinkled mummy stared back at them with unseeing eyes. Light gray skin with darker spots was pockmarked with direct computer interface ports and other implants of unknown function. The body was humanoid but atrophied and disheveled, contrasting all the more with the massive head. The lack of any visible mouth or nose made the dark, bulging eyes stand out. But the most striking feature was a circular set of short, gold metal rods piercing the skin around the cerebellum like a crown.

'Did we just find an alien?' asked Toft.

'There are no aliens,' Mai snickered. 'But look at that cyber. What in the hell?' She pointed at the equipment implanted into the creature.

Toft scrutinized it, curiosity getting the better of his fear. 'No idea what it is, but it's gotta be worth a fortune.'

'Told ya,' said Shao, faking smugness to mask the tremor in her voice. 'Let's bag it and move; we have a train to catch!'

They scrambled to move the capsule carefully aboard the jumper ship attached to the Seventeen's core.

21

The last few days weren't the most exciting in Milosh's life, but they were certainly educational. The prison ship accelerated slowly over the next two days, forcing the prisoners to stay in their cells. Milosh removed the cuffs restraining him and the other inmates in no time, but there was little they could do in a small cell guarded by the electronic eye of a security camera. Eventually, the cell door opened, and a security drone led them out onto their new home's decks.

Milosh noted the lack of human wardens. It seemed like nobody was willing to take on a two-decade-long trip with the inmates. Understandable as it was, Milosh knew prison-corps employed well-paid specialists on the holding stations. The guards were compensated for their time and rotated by shuttles every few months. That was not the case here. The only other people here were inmates.

Numerous squid biodrones scuttered about, performing maintenance tasks, while security robots guarded the prisoners. The security drones themselves weren't top shelf either. Low-yield maglev repulsors kept the flattened dome of the main chassis afloat, sensor placement atop, and a stun baton arm and a centrally placed auto shotgun under it.

Cheap low-tier junk used to guard mining ships against boarding parties, five creds a dozen, Milosh decided. If this is a registered prison barge, then I'm a ballerina.

The drones led them to a large, mostly bare mess hall, laden with cheap tables and the same bottom-tier synthesized rations as they had in the cells. Milosh counted around eighty inmates total and maybe a hundred drones, not counting the servitor biodrones going about their business and ignoring the humans. He didn't see any passive security except for the monitoring cameras—no magnetic locks, no sentry guns, no wall turrets, no emergency seals on the decks, nothing.

They led the group towards the mess hall and left them to their own devices afterward, letting them line up for the meal. Milosh accepted his plate of vaguely chunky slush stoically and headed towards the tables, eyeing the inmates.

Otis, Stick, and Spider occupied a table with a crowd of Outers, already forming a few gangs among themselves. McNamarra sat with a group of freakishly muscular oners covered in tattoos, leaning down in a hushed conversation. A couple of other groups bunched up as well, as far away from others as it was possible in a confined space.

Milosh could count on at least some goodwill, having freed his cell-mates, but it was clear that they took their sides in a quickly stratifying environment. Soon most of the inmates will be free, and the low effort security wasn't going to hold out for long. Of course, none of them could escape the barge, so a mutiny will result in total anarchy.

Two men sat away from all the gangs: a red-haired Earther with a short beard and a chubby Outer with sealed induction plates on his palms. Milosh recognized them instantly.

'Muldoon, Chatty, I see you're guests of this fine locale too,' said Milosh, sitting next to them. 'I thought the Navy made you walk the plank.'

Muldoon shrugged over his plate. 'We thought they flushed you, too.'

'How nice of this Crowley fellow to rent us rooms in this cruise liner instead, no?'

'Yeah, he's a fuckin' blessing. You think they're still tracking us?'

'Depends,' said Milosh. 'Did you tell them anything?'

The silent Outer smiled instead of replying, but Muldoon chuckled. 'Oh yeah, we sang like birds, what do you think? Nah, Crowley can eat shit. I've been through worse than the PAC bullshit in my five years of marriage.'

'Any clues on their angle?' asked Milosh rhetorically. 'What do you think they want to score?'

'They wanna pin Querub down,' answered Muldoon without hesitation, confirming Milosh's thoughts. 'They can't frag us and get rid of witnesses until they silence the crew. Else the company is gonna make a stink around it.'

Chatty nodded and pointed his finger at Muldoon as a sign of agreement.

'I was thinking the same thing,' admitted Milosh. 'But what do we do about it?'

'Sit out the twenty-year flight hoping the others won't do anything stupid?'

'Yeah, about that. I helped my cellmates with their cuffs. I reckon we have a week tops before it's on.' Milosh lifted his handcuffs, showing the other two the disabled lock.

'What the hell did you do that for?' asked Muldoon in an exasperated voice.

'I didn't know you two are on board, for one. And also we could use their help escaping.'

'Start a riot, use the momentum to piss free, and grab the nearest comms?'

'Could work,' said Chatty, joining the conversation. 'Provided we don't get fragged in the fighting.'

'Pff, fat chance of that,' scoffed Muldoon loudly. 'Any of us alone could eat that sore band for breakfast.' The statement earned him a hostile glare for a couple of heavily augmented Outers sitting by the table over. 'The fuck you monkeys lookin' at?' he asked them. The Outers returned to their meals, keeping their heads down.

'Can you get a bearing on the Querub from here?' asked Milosh.

Chatty nodded. 'Lemon squeezy. As long as you get me to the comms before we drift too far away from the nearest waystation or beacon.'

'Need me to open your cuffs?'

Chatty shook his head, accompanied by Muldoon's hearty chuckle. 'Who do you think we are, amateurs? Wanna change our diapers too?'

Muldoon finished the meal with visible disgust and wiped his hands on the orange prison jumpsuit. 'Aight, fuck it. How long do we have?'

Chatty pretended to count on his fingers. 'I estimate about a month before we cross the Hellespont's range.'

'If we don't get the word out by then, we're shit out of luck anyway,' said Milosh.

'Better get to work then,' said Muldoon.

'If we send a comm too late, we can always bounce on a lifepod or something. Broadcast a tracker and hope the Querub takes a dip into the Beyond to pick us up,' said Milosh.

'If that can even has any lifepods,' said Chatty grimly.

Milosh would rather not ponder that alternative. 'It better. Either way, we can't call for help too soon, or the PAC jarheads will have time to zero in on the Querub. If they aren't listening to signals waiting for just that...'

'Then they're fuckin' idiots,' finished Muldoon.

Milosh shushed the conversation seeing the security drones coming towards them. 'Looks like the lunch break is over. Recon the grounds and see what we're working with.'

'Roger that.'

The drones corralled the inmates into groups of cellmates, leading Milosh back to Otis and the rest. It led them through the maze of corridors filled with hydraulics, pipes, and machinery, packed almost too tightly to cross. The squid-like figures of biodrones passed them by uncaring, busy on their schedules implanted into the animal brains by cybernetic subroutines.

'So, had fun at dinner?' asked Milosh casually as they walked.

'What's it to you, merc?' replied McNamarra.

'Oh, you know, I freed you, so I thought maybe we could be friends.'

'Thanks, but I already got me some friends,' said McNamarra.

'And your friends ain't our friends, buddy,' said Sticks. 'You're keepin' a lousy company.'

'Better watch your mouth, before I make your ass lousy,' threatened the pirate.

'You ain't my type, bruh,' mocked Sticks. 'And I don't bend over on a first date.'

'How about we keep the lid on it, for now, eh?' interrupted Milosh impatiently. 'Save it until after we break out of this can.'

'You're dreaming, buddy,' said Otis. 'You got us out of the chains, and thanks for that, but we're still stuck here.'

'It is what it is,' added McNamarra. 'We gotta make the best of it, cause it's gonna be a long ride.'

'So you'd rather divide the ship into gangs and beat each other over the head for twenty years than get the fuck out of here?' asked Milosh, feigning surprise.

'Got better ideas?' Sticks asked.

Milosh smiled broadly. 'I'm so glad you asked because, as a matter of fact, I do.'

22

Helikaon Waystation, or Cloud Twenty-Six, was the last beacon of human civilization in the Oort Cloud. It serviced the ships on the route connecting the Helikaon refinery to the Solar System. Beyond that, there was nothing else in the furthest quadrant of the D Sector. Nothing besides mining expeditions, pirates, and only the gods knew what else that could be hiding in the unexplored interstellar space. Lederman hated it. The station was too far to receive energy through the solasers, like the stations in the System. It had to rely on freighter crews exchanging energy cells for raw materials and spare parts, bartering like in the good old days. It wasn't that weird, come to think about it—the interplanetary credit currency was based on kilowatts of power after all. Lederman hated the mentality that this bartering brought with it, nonetheless.

Without the intermediary of cred, trading felt different somehow. Dirty. The disheveled state of the station itself didn't do much to alleviate his shady outlook. On the contrary, the living modules were damp and musky, with constantly malfunctioning lighting providing cover for throngs of grifters and petty criminals pushing their wares on drifters and prospectors alike. Even the neon colors of the supposedly decent restaurant looked sleazy.

The Outer receptionist—or maybe a bouncer—was a young woman using way too much makeup, looking like a theatrical mask on the backdrop of her chromaskin changing colors following its own logic. She looked up from her desk at Lederman and winced at the Ranger's brown duster coat, dripping wet. 'Hydraulics in the ceiling leaking again?' she asked.

Lederman shrugged. 'No, it's raining. What do you think?'

'Sheesh, another happy customer,' she said, fixing her neon-strand hair. 'Take that shit off before you enter; the cleaning drone's busted.'

Lederman took off his coat and hung it on the rack. 'This better be here when I get back.'

The receptionist scoffed. 'Like anyone would wanna steal that lice magnet.'

'Whatever,' replied Lederman and passed by her.

As soon as he entered the corridor, his HUD picked up an augmented reality beacon, pointing towards one of the private rooms on the second floor. Lederman headed toward the marked room, trying not to brush against the dirty walls.

'Is there a reason we couldn't meet at the port, Mister Matthews?' he asked as soon as he entered the room.

A short man sitting at the table lifted his goggles and straightened up. 'Hello to you too, Mister Lederman,' he said. 'And yes, there is a reason. Lunchtime.'

Lederman sat down, sighing heavily. 'Why can't you people just be normal?'

'Normal people don't take jobs in the far ass of the System,' replied Matthews happily. 'Anyway, it's on you.'

'Fine, I am kinda hungry. I hope the food here is decent, at least.'

They each ordered. Lederman decided on chicken wings, praying that what he receives had at least lied next to a chicken once, while Matthews settled for a tardiburger.

They chatted about sweet nothings until the food arrived. Matthews wasn't a model employee, but he knew his gig. Lederman was a good listener and learned a lot about the daily dramas of crews operating in this part of the sector over the years. Matthews was a good talker, and Lederman soon found out plenty about the captains and their troubles. Lederman let most of the chatter fly by, memorizing key phrases.

Captain Mdebe Ivanov of the Sun And Moon passenger freighter complained that his lucky charms—Zoroastrian magi and a Neo-Muslim imam—argued all the time, disturbing the passengers. Lisa Alexander from the Cordoba sat in the docking bay for months because of her feud against the dock workers who refused to unload her cargo. The Nightingale was put on auction when the captain, Xiao Swiney, suddenly died. John Silver and his Scallywag sat in port for the past week.

Then there was talk about the Zhengdao mothership sitting by the refinery while a bunch of mining ships scattered about the sector, prospecting. The few people who called Helikaon their permanent home were excited—the corporation just sent a giant hauler ship on a slow trajectory towards the System. The locals counted on new contracts from the corp soon—work like that was always an opportunity to get rich quickly. Contracts are sold to the lowest bidder, and the backstabbing was rampant. Lederman couldn't blame them; a gig that big was nothing to scoff at.

He nodded sagely when Matthews blabbered on about some slag moving a bunch of canned criminals through the station some time ago. He knew more about that mother than he cared to already, but there was no reason to let it be seen. Say what you want about barter or cash trade, information was a currency just the same, and Lederman wasn't about to give money for nothing, even if Matthews did.

A servitor drone arrived with their meals, and the two men ate in silence, sporadically interrupted by Matthews talking with his mouth full about this factoid or the other. They had a few beers, and the chit-chat fell to more esoteric topics. Matthews was a great believer in conspiracy theories of all kinds, and so Lederman had no choice but to get acquainted with the latest stories. The crew of STS Irmanda and a few other ships reported spotting foo fighters on the edges of their radar scan. Mysterious objects picked up one second, gone the next, nothing new. Ship crews reported them since the dawn of space flight, since Yuri Gagarin. Some joker long ago connected them with an old myth about UFOs made up back on Earth, and the story lived on, propagated by memetics. It was nothing but bored truckers talking; still, Matthews seemed to love it.

Lederman understood it very well; as all people spending most of their lives in space, he was more than a little superstitious. In fact, he came to enjoy the talk, almost against himself and didn't want to end it. Nonetheless, it was time to get to work. 'All right, it's getting late,' Lederman said eventually, between one beer and the next. 'Let's get to the point. I heard you know a thing or two about this new pirate, Pam?'

'Captain Pam, yeah,' admitted Matthews. 'I was gonna get to that.'

'Let's, then.'

'Fair enough. So yeah, there's talk about her starting to gather supporters, cutting a name for herself and the like.'

'I heard she's been separated from the other ship in her fleet, yeah?'

Matthews nodded energetically. 'You bet. Rumor mill has it she's sitting and waiting until she has a force to work with. Maybe she wants to hit the refinery?'

'That would sure suck,' said Lederman impassively. 'I bet you know someone who knows exactly where she's holed up?'

Matthews rubbed his chin as if thinking deeply.

Lederman sighed and wirelessly transferred a couple of thousand credits to Matthews's account. The Ranger station will reimburse it, he hoped. Even if not, the bounty will more than cover it.

As soon as the transfer was approved, Matthews's face brightened as if by magic. 'Yeah, I think I might have a clue,' he chirped. 'Silver. You remember, I told you about him. He just came back from the System. The word is, he has a bit of a smuggling operation going on.'

'What about it?'

'See, he knows who Pam's right hand is; they moved ships down the same route. Talk with him. I bet he knows where she'll be sitting.'

'I'll do just that then. Where did you say I can find him?'

'Go fess up the main lane. There's a watering hole on the mezzanine, the Rainbow Cat.'

'Quaint name, isn't it?'

'Not very creative, I'll give you that. But what can I say, we're simple folk.'

Lederman said his goodbyes and headed out, hoping to catch this Silver fellow with a bottle in his hand. Alcohol always made interrogations easy. When he reached the reception area, he realized somebody stole his coat from the hanger. 'I fucking hate this station.'

The receptionist looked up from above her desk, disinterested. 'Whachu said?'

'I asked, where's my coat?'

The receptionist shrugged. 'Lice carried it off.'

Lederman glared at her, having half a mind to do something drastic, but decided against it. 'Fuckin' keep it,' he said and left the building.

***

Matthews finished his meal before opening a commlink. The window showed nothing but a brim of a hat before Silver's smiling face came into focus.

'What up, brother?' asked the pirate, his voice slurry. 'Got news for me?'

'As a matter of fact, I do. Standard fee applies.'

'Sheesh, talk 'bout selflessness, and comradery between sailors.' Silver laughed but wired five hundred credits through.

Matthews grinned, seeing an augmented reality icon pop up in his HUD corner, informing him of the payment. 'Nothing's free,' he said. 'Anyway, there is a Ranger heading your way, grim fellow.'

'A Ranger? Fuck does he want?'

'He wants to talk with the someone who knows the man who ferried Pam's new ship to the System. He's looking for her, you know.'

Silver chuckled, showing the gold fillings in his teeth. 'The police man wants to arrest Pam? Bring her to well-deserved justice, no doubt. Well, it falls to me, as a law-abiding simple mariner, to make sure he knows exactly where to find her.'

'I thought you were just gonna frag him.'

'Hell nuh. Police types going missing all over the station brings nothing but trouble. It's seven years of bad luck, they say. Not to mention their fellow officers are bound to come calling, looking for them.'

'Right. And we don't want the rest of his crew investigating.'

'Exactly. It's on them to catch Pam unawares. If the luck is on their side, so be it. If not, they're out of my hair anyway.'

'Whatever you say, boss.' Matthews shrugged. 'And I bet it'd be a real shame if someone gave her a bit of a warning, eh?' Looks like Lederman's gonna have a bad day.

'What's the policeman's name?'

'Lederman, why are you asking?'

'So I can raise a toast for the eternal peace of his soul.'

23

Zhenya watched his fleet's position on the backdrop of the sector map: nineteen mining ships traversing the space in a loose ring. One beacon's absence burned like hot coals. His eyes clouded with gathering tears and the image distorted, the augmented reality doing its best to compensate. The cabin doors behind him opened with a hiss, and he straightened immediately, turning with a stern face.

Jin Sun entered the cabin hurriedly. 'Esteemed captain,' he said. 'The first reports arrived.'

'From the search and rescue party?' Zhenya did his best to sound neutral.

'Among others, yes,' replied Sun. 'Would you like to see it first?'

'Yes, Mister Sun, I would.'

'Naturally, esteemed captain.' Sun uploaded the data to Zhenya's HUD. 'I hope you won't find it presumptuous of me to ask how the search for your daughter is faring?'

Zhenya turned back towards his AR screen and displayed the report on it. 'Am I to understand you haven't read it?'

'Correct, esteemed captain,' replied Sun. 'I came here as soon as the data stream arrived.'

'You could have just rerouted it my way instead of interrupting your duties.' Zhenya shared the access with Sun. 'I'm sure you have your hands full.'

Sun nodded and leaned over the panel next to Zhenya. 'Apologies, esteemed captain,' he said quietly. 'I grew fond of your daughter, however, and wanted to be here when you receive the report.'

Zhenya looked at his adjutant, trying to wrestle Sun's real emotions from behind the corporate mask of politeness. Was the adjutant genuine in his worry, or did he have some sort of a ploy in the making? Zhenya worried he might be becoming too preoccupied with his own concerns to keep an eye on ambitious coworkers. He could see nothing in the man's face except polite compassion. He turned back towards the data, studying it carefully, and let go of suspicion towards the adjutant —for now. 'It seems that whatever magnetic anomaly was reported has passed,' said Zhenya finally. 'The shuttle is yet to find anything at all in the area.'

'Perhaps their sensors don't have enough power?' Sun wondered. 'If the Seventeen suffered a critical malfunction or stumbled onto pirates, the transponder wouldn't transmit the location.'

'If that was the case, Shao... And her crewmates... Could already be dead.'

'Or have limited supplies without functioning life support,' added Sun. 'It could be that time is of the essence. We can't take that risk.'

'I take it you have a suggestion?'

'Yes, esteemed captain,' admitted Sun with a polite nod. 'Perhaps the Jīnlóng's sensor arrays could speed up the search process.'

Zhenya rubbed his chin. 'We shouldn't leave the Yusan without an escort.'

'Do we have any choice? The Yusan is safe and sound, who would dare raid it here, next to the waystation?'

Zhenya considered what agendas could Sun be following that would require depraving the Yusan of its escort but found none. 'You are right, dear adjutant,' he agreed. 'Why did we drag the Jīnlóng here if not to protect our people?'

Sun's face brightened for a moment in a brief smile. Zhenya thought he saw a glint of triumph in his adjutant's eye but thought little of it.

Sun was always happy to have his way—a flaw of character to be sure, but he was right nonetheless. If it was a trap Zhenya just walked into, he's going to deal with it when it's sprung.

'I will take a shuttle to the Jīnlóng,' said Zhenya. 'Please let Captain Powells know of my arrival and arrange a cabin for me. Would you be so kind as to accompany me aboard the frigate?'

'Of course, esteemed captain,' replied Sun. 'Would you like your personal items and messages transferred to the frigate as well? I can arrange it with secretary Ljubek before we depart.'

'Unnecessary, dear adjutant. They can deal with any pressing matters themselves until we return. I will also have little need for trinkets while searching for Shao and her colleagues.'

'Yes, esteemed captain.'

Zhenya and Sun headed out towards the shuttle bay, where a sleek limousine waited, engines humming. He briefly wondered what it was Sun could be up to, but Lowe's intel didn't give him much to go on. No overt suspicious moves, and yet, everything about Sun's behavior was troubling... Zhenya pushed those futile considerations aside and shifted his focus to the Seventeen and Shao. Fortunately, the travel between the mothership and the frigate was brief and left little time for him to worry.

He needed to feel in control, needed to act. It was the only reason he was even out in the Oort Cloud instead of enjoying his position in the corporation from a luxury villa on one of Neptune's moons. And yet, right now, he could do nothing, and anxiety gnawed at his insides. Shao was lost somewhere in the vastness of barely charted space, and all he could do was look at the maps and guess where she might be.

He compiled the data from Seventeen's programmed route with the reported sightings and the magnetic anomaly's projected area. The resulting area of space was massive. Even with state-of-the-art sensor technology of the Jīnlóng, it would take decades to sift through it. Cross-referencing the areas already scouted by the recon team did little to narrow it down.

Sarah Lowe's expedition headed towards the projected center of the circle, outlining the anomaly. She assumed whatever it was that Seventeen was looking for would be at the core.

Zhenya overlaid the images on top of each other, creating an augmented reality diorama in front of him, and leaned back on the shuttle couch.

The acceleration gently pushed Zhenya into the seat, and he found himself drifting off into a half-sleep as he stared at the chart as if trying to will it into revealing its secrets. And then it hit him.

What if the anomaly isn't regular?

Typically a magnetic field would be made up of two regular bands, one for each pole, and whatever would be the source sits neatly in the middle. That is where Lowe was trying to locate the missing ship, where it was presumably heading. And yet, she didn't have complete data, only reports from the other ships.

He sat up in his chair, opened a calculating program in his HUD display, and got to work.

By the time the shuttle landed half an hour later, Zhenya was walking circles inside the shuttle's walkway, like a tiger trapped in a luxurious cage. As soon as the hatch opened and the HUD popup reported it was safe to depart, he pounced onto Jīnlóng's hangar deck and energetically headed towards the approaching group of uniformed soldiers.

The welcoming committee was spearheaded by a gray-haired and wrinkled man with a grim expression, Captain Powells. He stopped and saluted as soon as Zhenya neared him. 'Esteemed captain, it's a pleasure to have you aboard.'

'The pleasure is all mine, esteemed captain,' replied Zhenya. 'I assume my adjutant informed you of all the details?'

'Yes, sir, we're heading to look for a missing crew. I think you made the right decision, captain. For what it's worth.'

Zhenya smiled. 'Thank you, Edgar. It means a lot to have your support.'

Powells leaned in confidentially. 'You know I'd tell you if I thought it was stupid. I can't stand the corp kiss-assery.'

'Me too, old friend. More than you know.'

'So, where are we headed?' asked Powells as they headed towards the frigate's bridge. 'Are we joining the scouting party?'

'No, I think they headed to the wrong quadrant,' replied Zhenya. 'I extrapolated the data and concluded that the magnetic anomaly in question is oscillating.'

'That's why Lowe found nothing but space there. Makes sense.' Powells nodded.

'Exactly. It behaves less like a static field, more like a searchlight. I'll upload the coordinates to the Jīnlóng's computers directly; we need to make haste.'

'Don't worry, Yuan. We'll find your girl.'

24

Milosh tightened his grip on the wrench and pulled with feigned effort. The valve turned, and the hot water spray showering the tight corridor instantly ceased. He could have done the job with his bare hands easily without the tool, but the security drone watched his crew work. Milosh wasn't sure how advanced their software was. It didn't seem to be, but you never know. He thought it unlikely that the machine would be able to surmise that his augmented muscles worked at full power, but it cost nothing to pretend otherwise. His crew was sent over to fix blown hydraulic pumping coolant to somewhere or the other, one of many malfunctions on a ship this size. The hauler's long, indented hull was constantly bending under pressure caused by the strain on materials. Usually, the onboard detachment of squid-like biodrones was enough to maintain the decks, but a massive leak like that called for the prisoners. Or maybe it didn't, and the security drones were just programmed to keep the inmates busy; Milosh had no way of knowing.

What he did know was that this particular leak was far from accidental.

Hidden under one of the pipe intersections, jammed between the sensor lens and the water pressure reader, was a plastic card and the reason biodrones failed to show up here. Milosh quickly glanced around. McNamarra and Spider worked just around the bend, observed by a drone the same as he was. Spider must have felt his glance. He turned around, raising an eyebrow questioningly. Milosh soundlessly worded a plea for help. He wasn't sure Pie understood at first, but then the skinny Outer jumped up, lack of gravity carrying him towards the ceiling. 'Rat, oh god, I saw a rat; it was huge,' he yelled, pointing fingers at the floor. 'Al, kill it, kill it!'

McNamarra peered towards the direction Pie pointed at, then back at Spider. 'The fuck, man. There ain't no rats on this ship...'

Pie glared at McNamarra angrily, trying to communicate his intent through eyebrow movement, but kept yelling, 'It was an alien then, huge ass motherfucker! It's gonna suck out our brains!'

'Maybe mine,' said McNamarra, tapping his forehead. 'Cause it ain't gonna find shit in that crazy dome of yours.'

'No, Al, look, there is a rat-alien in there,' repeated Pie, frantically. 'It's huuuge.'

McNamarra's face brightened with understanding, and he leaned over the opening behind the pipes. 'Holy shit, man, you're right. There is something there. Lemme at it.' He pushed his hand inside the hole, held still for a moment, then shrieked in theatrically fake pain. 'Aaa, it got me. It fuckin' got me. Help!'

The security drone finally expressed an interest in the commotion and hovered towards Spider and McNamarra, leaving Milosh alone. Milosh quickly pulled the plastic card from its hiding place and hid it in the skin pouch on his forearm. He gave Pie an "ok" sign with his hand.

Spider immediately calmed down, smiling at the perplexed drone. 'I must have been seeing things, sorry, mister robot.'

Hearing that, McNamarra pulled his hand from the hole. 'I just had the worst cramp,' he said. 'But it's fine now.'

The machine hovered there, its software not able to make a decision.

Spider reached out to it with a calming gesture, talking to it like a scared animal. 'It's aight now, robot, we're going back to work, it's cool.'

'We're all done here, even,' added Milosh, approaching the group. 'It's all fixed; the squids are coming up to mop the place.' He pointed at a row of half a dozen biodrones, who entered the deck in a row before spreading out to catch the floating bubbles of liquid.

Milosh pointed at a row of half a dozen biodrones, who entered the deck in a row before spreading out to catch the floating bubbles of liquid. The security drone must have received instructions from Incitatus' computer system as it moved to corral the prisoners out of the hallway.

'Man, what I wouldn't do to get my hands on one of the little guys,' muttered Spider.

'What for?' asked Milosh casually. 'They don't look very tasty.'

McNamarra chuckled, but Spider was dauntless. 'I used to work as an operator on Perseus station,' he said. 'I ran drones for a prospecting outfit. Biodrones, too.'

'Really? I thought you were a pirate,' replied Milosh. 'You don't strike me as an honest citizen, Pie.'

'Bite a dong, merc,' McNamarra snickered. 'Nobody's born a pirate. You think anyone sane would choose to be a raider?'

'I wouldn't know. You seem to enjoy it good enough.'

'I'm a smuggler, man,' protested McNamarra. 'I didn't do anything to anyone.'

'Right, whatever.' And I'm a flower salesman, Milosh thought. 'What was it about the drones, Pie?'

Spider shrugged. 'What I was trying to say is that the service drones have access everywhere. If I could get my hands on one, I could hack it and get access to all the onboard systems.'

'Could be nice to get our hands on one, then,' replied Milosh.

'We could use a map of the ship, too. And some ice cream.' McNamarra chuckled. 'We ain't gettin' outta here. Merc boys' friends or not.'

'I wouldn't be so pessimistic,' said Milosh, looking around.

The group was lead towards a gym hall, where a bunch of other prisoners was busying themselves working out on zero-g appliances. The drone corralled Milosh, Spider, and McNamarra inside and left them alone.

'I ain't pessimistic, that's the truth,' said McNamarra. 'There ain't nothing we can do without a ship.'

'What if I had a ship, theoretically?' asked Milosh. 'And a map of the upper decks, including the comm room?'

McNamarra and Spider gathered closer, shielding Milosh from the security sensors as he pulled the plastic card from his skin pouch. A hasty drawn but detailed plan of the corridors laid out a large portion of Incitatus' upper decks, including a service docking bay, an infirmary, and the comm room.

'How did you get that?' asked Spider. 'Is that why you wanted me to make a scene?'

'Well, I just needed a distraction; the rest is on you.'

McNamarra chuckled, shaking his head and letting his dreadlocks float around. 'You almost had me thinkin' there was a real rat there, fucker.'

'Anyway, with that map, we can start the works,' said Milosh, getting everyone back on topic. 'If we get you the drone, can you get us to the comm room?'

'You betcha,' replied Spider. 'Easy as stealing a candy.'

'Good. I'll get that sorted.' Milosh nodded.

McNamarra smiled widely. 'You do that, merc. I'll go see if I'm not over somewhere else.'

Milosh shrugged and turned to look for Muldoon and Chatty, leaving Spider and McNamarra to their own devices. He found the two mercenaries in the corner of the gym, drinking foul-smelling moonshine away from the other prisoners. 'Where the hell did you get that shit?' Milosh asked instead of a greeting.

'Oh, you know, there was a malfunction in one of the water recyclers.' Muldoon laughed. 'Chatty and I went to fix it.'

'So you figured out how to dodge the tin cans?'

Chatty nodded, letting Muldoon reply, 'You bet. It turns out the bots don't have much in the way of brains, so Chatty's eye drone can bounce at any time. We scouted most of the upper decks, did you get the map?'

'Yeah, nice little sabotage you pulled to get it to me,' Milosh replied. 'How did you know we'll get sent to fix it?'

'Easy as one-two-three,' said Chatty, winking with his metallic drone-eye ostensibly. 'I kept a peeper on you and opened the valve when you were the closest team to us.'

'And you couldn't just wait to give it to me in person?'

Chatty just grinned in response and raised the mug in a toast.

Milosh smirked, shaking his head. He couldn't blame Chatty for enjoying a little conspiratorial fun. 'That's not all I'll need, though. One of my cellmates is a hacker. He can get us to the comm room, but we'll need a thing. One of the service biodrones, specifically.'

'So we're taking passengers with us, boss?' asked Muldoon.

'If he can get us out of this ship, yes. Is that a problem?'

'Not really. How about we drop you a squid in a locker, down the service bay?'

'Works just fine,' agreed Milosh. 'It's close to the med bay; we can get tools to open the baby up in there.'

'So, your hacker, is he the skinny Outer with face tattoos you were talking with earlier?' asked Chatty nonchalantly, sipping moonshine from a cup.

'Yeah, why?'

'You better turn around then,' said Chatty, pointing behind Milosh.

Spider stood right where Milosh had left him, awkwardly gesturing at a muscular, bald oner making demanding motions.

'Well, that's fucking great.' Milosh sighed and moved to intervene, followed by Muldoon and Chatty.

'Got a problem with my buddy, bitch?' asked Milosh as soon as they were within earshot of Pie and his adversary.

The oner turned to face them, grinning stupidly through a cracked lip. 'This little feller, your buddy?' he asked. 'Why dont'cha stick with ya own people instead of this gray?'

Milosh sighed heavily. 'Really, that's what your problem is? Why do you always have to step into a shit like that, Pie?'

Spider tried to answer, but the burly prisoner interrupted, 'Oi, don't talk to the gray when I'm talkin' to ya.'

'Make me, bitch.' Milosh shrugged, fully aware that Muldoon and Chatty were moving to the side. The goon smiled, misinterpreting their motion. He must have assumed Milosh's companions moved aside to show they're withdrawing from the confrontation, and he moved closer, throwing a surprise punch.

The guy was quick for an unaugmented human but to Milosh, his fist moved in full slow motion. He easily dodged it, grabbed the man's elbow, and pulled him forward, throwing the inmate off balance.

Before the falling man could react, Muldoon and Chatty struck his knees from the sides with downward kicks, putting their mass into it. Combined with the force of their magboots, pulling them to meet the deck, they exerted enough force to snap both kneecaps with a disgusting crunch. The howling man rolled on the ground, never to get up. Security bots reacted by swarming the gym, and opening fire before most inmates even realized what happened.

'Thanks, buddy,' Spider managed to say before the taser darts struck him down, shaking in agonizing pain.

25

The cabin's silence was broken only by quiet breathing. Shao focused on Sōngshǔ's full sensory interface controls, maneuvering between giant containers slowly bobbing inside their open space cargo hold. The ship's steering overlay replaced her organic vision with external camera feeds and system input. The jumper was barely a fifth of the size of each container, and even the smallest unpredictable motion could squash them like an insect. She couldn't wipe the sweat off her forehead, fearing a moment of lost focus can cost them their lives, even despite Mai's vigil in the jumper's neural interface. She was vaguely aware of Toft and Green watching the instruments. The engineer walked between panels carefully not to distract her and Mai, while the officer drummed his fingers loudly on a console.

'You're gonna break something like that, you know,' said Toft to interrupt the tense silence.

Green shrugged. 'The controls are locked. I'm just stressed out, is all.'

'Don't worry, buddy. Just look at the girls; they're having fun.'

Shao didn't think Toft knew they can hear him through the jumper's full sensory interface.

'I envy their calm. I can't stop thinking about what they'll do to us if we get caught.'

'I know, but you're not helping yourself or anyone else with that. We made the step, now we have to follow through.'

'Repeat it one more time, and I'm turning this boat around,' threatened Green jokingly.

'Bet you fifty you won't.'

'Fifty credits? After we get the coffin to central, I won't get out of bed for less than a million.'

'That's the spirit...' started Toft, but was interrupted by a tremor and grabbed the chair in sudden panic. The diagnostics routine had finished and displayed the report on Shao's HUD. Everything checked out. She gave a final look through the external cameras. The thin, tadpole-like shape of their ship grasped the dark hull of the larger vessel, four limbs armed with electromagnetic trays firmly attached.

Shao disconnected the sensory interface and smiled. 'All right. Sōngshǔ is docked tight. We can go out.'

Green immediately got up from his seat. 'Finally! I need to stretch my legs. I'll start working on the door.'

Toft squeezed his body between the seats and entered the airlock cabin. Shao watched him put on the jumpsuit and toolbelt, struggling to reach the plasma cutter from the tool closet. He then turned upside down awkwardly in zero-g and opened the floor hatch. Bright blue plasma flame lit the cabin as he started cutting the hull underneath them.

'Aight girls, playtime's over,' said Green, poking Shao and Mai in the arms. 'Back to reality with you.'

Mai opened her eyes, cybernetic retinas rapidly shifting until they adjusted to the light. Implants flashed once and went dark, when they broke the connection.

'Playtime's over,' repeated Toft, grinning widely. 'We're here.'

'We weren't playing-'

'Flying's not a-' Shao and Mai started at the same time, blushing fiercely. Mai's cybereyes turned bright pink.

'Sheesh, calm down,' Green pretend-scolded. 'We're not in the corp anymore, you can enjoy your jobs.'

'Yeah, you're right,' agreed Mai quickly. 'It was fun.'

'And now it's over,' said Toft. 'We're heading out.'

They all got up and joined Toft in the airlock. The engineer had finished his work; the cutter neatly placed back on its place in the tool cabinet. The small cabin was filled with various equipment and vacuum jumpsuits hanging on racks alongside the walls. They hastily put on the vacuum-sealed masks and white-gold suits and dove into the hatch. Shao put her leather jacket on top of the spacesuit—it fit pretty well over the bulky overalls. Shao followed Mai down the airlock, admiring her smooth agility in zero-g. She could never hope to match it, but there was no danger of tearing the suit.

Toft's cut was neat and precise, all sharp edges on the barge's hull smoothed out meticulously. They had no problem getting out, and soon enough, Shao looked around curiously—they were apparently in some sort of maintenance corridor intersection: pipes, valves, and narrow catwalks leading in all directions. The pathways were dark and lit only by the crew's helmet visors illuminating the way ahead.

'You sure this is a safe spot, Shao?' asked Green. 'What if the crew find us here?'

'No way,' she replied, smiling smugly. 'I made a list, and I checked it twice, it's a fully autonomous vessel. No naughty kids are coming 'round the corner.'

'Damn, too bad.' Mai giggled. 'I hope there's some good news, though.'

'You like bad boys then?' asked Toft with a smirk.

'She didn't mean bad at life, loser,' cut in Shao sharply.

'What did I ever do to you?' Toft scowled.

'Cut it out, you two,' interrupted Green. 'We gotta keep our wits about us; this is not a vacation.'

'You're right, sorry, buddy,' agreed Toft. 'I'll send the drones out, find someplace to lay low.' He jumped up back to the ship and logged onto the Sōngshǔ's central computer, bringing up the ship's system onto their HUDs. The signal flickered and vanished. 'Hold up, there's a glitch in the system,' he said, logging back in. 'It's like the system received a mirrored login along with ours and booted us. I'm gonna need to retry.'

He had to attempt a couple of times, directing multiple subroutines to ensure the connection stayed up. Eventually, a dozen tiny, hexagonal drones armed with camera lenses on each side of their tiny hulls jetted down the intersections.

Toft grinned with satisfaction. 'Got it.'

The machines scattered throughout the decks, mapping the labyrinth of corridors for the Sōngshǔ's crew. Shao observed the progress in the camera feeds on their HUDs and mask displays, learning the layout of cabins and corridors in real-time as the drones explored the vessel. She quickly realized their intersection was hidden in a maze of columns and tunnels surrounding the hydraulics responsible for releasing and unloading the cargo of hundreds of ship-sized containers and canisters once the ship arrived at its destination. Barring some extremely unlikely malfunctions, there wasn't a reason why any of the ship's service drones would come here. The scout drones located one of the ship's ration stockpiles and weapon closets. 'Why the hell does an automated hauler have ration stockpiles? And guns?' muttered Toft, more to himself than anyone in particular.

'Maybe it's feed for their biodrones?' suggested Shao.

Toft shook his head. 'No way, look. It's marked as mycoproteins, synthmeat, tardipaste, that's not dummy feed.'

Green rubbed his chin, forgetting about the mask. 'Maybe they were going to have a crew, but changed plans?'

'Doesn't make sense,' disagreed Shao. 'The haulers are dropped on a ballistic course to the Solar System; they aren't built to hold a crew.'

'Maybe someone screwed up on Helikaon,' said Green. 'These things happen, lucky for us. Let's watch on.'

The food reserve was further than they would like, but Mai managed to quickly hack the hatches and the warehouse manifesto, allowing Toft to set up a drone from their own ship to steal food and water unnoticed by the maintenance system. Shao followed another scout drone to a tool shed equipped with emergency repair supplies. She imagined multiple sheds like that were placed in case of catastrophic malfunctions of the leviathan ship.

'I think I found a cozier place to nap than the Sōngshǔ,' she said. 'Not much cozier, mind you.'

Green joined her after a minute. 'Yeah, it'll do.'

When Toft and Mai agreed that the cabin suits them perfectly, Shao and Green moved the necessities, and set up a mobile airlock at the door. The compartment was relatively spacious; especially when they removed the heavy tools from their beddings and put sleeping bags into their ports, to serve as separate bedrooms. The cabin was nearby the water exchange valve and decontamination showers since it was meant for use during an emergency while the ship was still under construction. They scrambled to gather up sleeping bags, portable tablets, tools, and whatever else they could think of from the jumper but leaving the capsule behind.

'Let's take a sample from the mummy,' Shao said. 'See, there's an infirmary right here' she pinged the location on the map made by drones.

'I don't know,' argued Green. 'It's quite a trip. And what if the mummy's contagious?'

'Contagious with what?' Asked Mai. 'The scans didn't show anything.'

'Plus, if it is carrying something, that's all the more reason to scan it,' added Shao.

'The question is, why an uncrewed ship has an infirmary,' wondered Mai.

Toft nodded vigorously, 'I was just about to say. Maybe it's a leftover from the construction, like the decomp.'

Mai shook her head. 'Nah, it looks makeshift.'

'The whole thing seems off somehow,' said Shao. 'The construction crew would need those supplies and systems, but why stock guns?'

Finally, they left. Green sealed the hole in the Incitatus' hull with the plasma torch yet again, and they headed out to their new home away from home.

'Goodbye, little squirrel,' whispered Mai, looking back, pale in the blue light emitted by her eyes. 'See you soon.'

'Like hell, you are,' Toft said. 'That ship's not bound to reach Titan for twenty years.'

'We aren't staying on it the whole way,' argued Mai. 'Only a month, 'till we're in Hellespont range. Then we'll jump right off and catch a ride to Styx on some freighter.'

'That's no reason to get sentimental,' started Shao, but changed her mind halfway. 'Fine, I'll miss the Sōngshǔ too. It came a long way with us.'

'Watch it, or I'll get sentimental on your can,' threatened Mai. 'What's your deal anyway?'

'Sorry, it's hard for me too,' admitted Shao. 'To be honest, I'm terrified.'

Mai embraced her, somewhat awkwardly in the vacuum suit. 'Yeah, I get it,' she said. 'We'll make it alright, don't worry.'

'Sure as daylight,' interjected Toft, turning around to face them, walking backward. The road ahead displayed on his mask HUD. 'We'll hop off this wreck soon, get to Titan, sell the alien to the board, and none the wiser. We're all living happily ever after on a beach sipping vodka martinis. And I'm sure your old man will forgive you, he gets what it means to be ambitious.'

'Pff, like anyone's ever gonna sell you alcohol,' Shao teased him, sticking her tongue out.

'I'll buy a bar and make them sell it to me.' Toft shrugged. 'We'll be rich.'

'Fellow billionaires,' said Green, stopping and pointing at the hatch leading to the tool shed. 'Welcome to your new mansions.'

26

Shao woke up tired and miserable. She couldn't get any sleep; the tight confines of the closet closed in around her like a coffin. It was also freezing cold, despite the thermal blanket taken from the Sōngshǔ. She crawled out of the compartment with relief. There was no light in the cabin, so she had to use her mask's mounted flashlight to see anything—not that there was a lot to look at. The compartment was messy, filled with tools lying around everywhere between their personal items brought from the jumper. The sleeping bag filled most of the space, along with the leather jacket Shao used as a pillow. She forgot to close the personal hygiene bag and now various bottles and brushes floated everywhere as if they had minds of their own. The scent of chems mixed with the scent of machine oil and copper wiring.

Shao felt alone and lost. It was easy to boast about deserting the corp, abandoning her father, and escaping to the Solar System. Now that it was too late to turn back, she felt tears gathering in her eyes. She fought the feeling until it passed, then brought up Mai's comm window on her HUD. 'Hey, are you asleep?'

Mai's face showed up in the window almost immediately. 'Can't. This place is awful.'

'Got you. Wanna head out and do something?'

'Like what? Paint the roof pink?'

Shao thought about it for a minute. 'We could stick around here before the guys wake up. Or go check out that shower.'

Mai smiled at the thought. 'Lemme grab a towel.'

They returned half an hour later, holding hands. Shao looked around the cabin. It was exactly as they left it. 'Looks like they're sleeping in.'

Mai shrugged, disabled the magboots, and pirouetted onto the sleeping bag sticking out of the open closet.

She is so graceful, Shao thought. And so beautiful, even in this ugly jumpsuit. We should go dancing when we're out of this mess. 'Wanna stay here or take the sample and scans to that medlab Toft found?' she asked finally.

'Sure, let's go. Beats sitting here like frozen groceries,' replied Mai.

'Let's sneak out and let the guys clean this mess up,' said Shao, smiling. 'We'll be back before they get anxious.'

The cabin doors opened before Mai had a chance to reply. Green and Toft entered, carrying bags of supplies from their jumper. They also decided to abandon full spacesuits for more comfortable undersuits.

'Oh, you guys are awake already?' asked Green. 'Had a good night, I hope? We slept like shit.'

Toft nodded in agreement. 'Yeah. We figured we'd go and bring our food from the Sōngshǔ, so we don't have to haul it from the barge's storage.'

'If it even is storage,' added Green. 'Might just be a computer error. We saw plenty of lights flickering on the way.'

Mai shrugged. 'They don't build these haulers to last, you know. Things are bound to go haywire.'

'Word. At least we won't have to pump the airlock, looks like there's pressure and atmosphere all over the ship,' said Green. 'Unless something's gonna rupture on us.'

He's growing into the captain's shoes, Shao thought. Worrying in advance.

'And what are you two up to?' asked Green. 'We're not interrupting anything, I hope?'

Shao shook her head. 'Nah, we thought you two are still asleep,' she said, hiding her disappointment. She had hoped to be able to spend more time with Mai, just the two of them. 'We were just going to check out the sample in this whole medlab. You don't have to go with us.'

Green's long face immediately lit up with interest. 'No, no, we'll go,' he said. 'Curiosity eats me alive, to be honest. I almost woke you up two hours ago to see if you wanna check.'

'There is another service bay right around the corner from the medlab,' interjected Toft. 'We can get some tools from there, fix this place up a bit.'

Mai clapped and hopped off the mattress, engaging her magboots. 'Damn yes. I can't spend another night cooped up like a chicken.'

'It's settled then,' said Green, dropping the supply bags and marching back out decisively.

Shao and Mai glanced at each other, giggled, then followed their captain through the dark corridors. Shao looked around nervously, examining the weirdly organic piping of rust-smelling decks. She would never say it out loud but was glad the guys came along. This ship gave her the creeps.

The group marched through the halls devoid of gravity. The Incitatus' narrow corridors turned and twisted without warning. The hauler had a computer system, but whenever Mai tried to link them in to display an augmented reality map, it almost immediately crashed, leaving them directionless. The lights were flickering in and out, forcing them to activate their headlamps. Mai ran an overlay bot marking objects in their way with a blue grid; otherwise, they'd be tripping and falling, which would be dangerous in zero-g.

They forged ahead using the 3D map charted by Toft's scout drones, but they could only rely on those up to a point. Toft had lost contact with his toys during the night and received no new data, so they couldn't know if there were passages that the machines missed along the way.

At one of the junctions, Shao saw a squid-like biodrone hovering in circles under the corridor ceiling. The machine seemed fritzed, erratically circling a vent with its tentacles waving around without purpose. She didn't stop to take a closer look, unsure what would happen if the drone spotted them.

They finally arrived at their destination.

Green looked at it without much hope. 'This it? It doesn't seem to be any different from other hatches.'

Toft shrugged. 'Mapping drones assigned the names from the hauler's system, what do I know?'

'The same system that keeps crashing?' asked Mai sarcastically.

Shao stepped forward. 'There's only one way to find out.' She approached the door, expecting it to automatically open, but to her dismay, it remained closed. 'It's locked.'

'Why would you lock doors on a crewless ship?' asked Toft.

'Maybe they're afraid of ghost burglars,' said Mai, leaning over the terminal by the doorframe. She dismantled it quickly and worked on the cables for a moment before the hatch slid open with a hiss. 'Open, sesame,' she said. 'Here you go, all done.'

The group entered the room, noting with some surprise it really was a medbay. Rows of glazed closets along the walls hid shelves full of basic medical equipment and medicine, a couple of robust industrial drug printers stood in a corner, together with biotech scanners and centrifuges. A large autodoc bed in the center of the room lit up with augmented reality windows the moment Shao drew near.

'Anybody else starting to think something is not right on this ship?' asked Shao, leaning over the red autodoc bed.

'You mean like food stores and medbays on a barge with no living soul aboard?' Toft posed a rhetorical question.

Mai giggled nervously. 'Maybe there are dead souls on board.'

'Don't even joke like that,' said Green. 'Hey, this machine here looks like a DNA scanner, wanna plug it?'

Shao nodded and inserted the sample into the machine. The HUD interface wasn't working, so she inputted a command manually, and the machine whirred into motion, analyzing the data. She turned back to the others. 'I think the autodoc can display the scans for us. Mai, wanna kick-start the bot?'

'You bet.'

The program started activating a voiceover routine, greeting them with a chipper female voice, but Mai shut it down immediately. It took a moment for the autodoc to translate the data made with prospecting hand scanners and simple medipack readers the Seventeen had onboard.

First, it displayed a list of chemical components present: oxygen, carbon, hydrogen, nitrogen, and so on. Nothing out of the ordinary, to Shao's disappointment. There were some unexpected materials—gold, synthetic resins, metaplastics, graphene, titanium. Shao guessed that's what the implanted crown was made of.

The autodoc started displaying 3D imaginings of the body next, as soon as the machine's software translated the data and extrapolated the missing bits.

The creature had long, fragile bones with circular joints in its elbows, knees, and fingers—it must have been able to bend its limbs in all directions. Shao wasn't a biologist, but she was quite sure there was no way for it to withstand even one-g without suffering trauma.

The autodoc moved on to the being's delicate head now, displaying layer after layer of projections and data. The corpse had a roughly human-looking skull, albeit very thin and fragile. Eye sockets were large and spacious, while the rest of the bone structure atrophied. The implantations didn't end with the crown-like instrument either. The machine extended through most of the brain and spinal cord in a complex, almost synapse-like structure.

'That's the freakiest thing I ever saw,' said Mai, instinctively touching her cybernetic implants.

Toft stared at the imagining with awe. 'We're gonna be millionaires,' he said. 'First people to ever encounter an alien...'

'Sorry to break your bubble, Lasse,' said Green behind them. 'But the DNA sequencer just finished, and this thing is one-hundred-percent human.'

'No way,' exclaimed Toft. 'Have you seen this model?'

Green shrugged dispassionately. 'Yeah, it's a very heavily augmented dude. By the looks of it, he followed the Outer line of thought and pushed the boundary along a mile or two, but he's still human.'

'So much for the glory, then,' said Shao quietly. 'Might as well turn back, no?'

'Our coffin boy might be human, but these implants are some magical stuff,' said Toft, doing his best to zoom in and make sense of the approximate images created by the autodoc.

'What do you mean?' asked Mai, immediately interested. 'Let me have a look.'

'See, here?' asked Toft, pointing at a complex crystalline structure lodged in the mummy's brain. 'I think those are neural links; hard to say though.'

'There is no way someone put so much hardware in the guy's noggin without killing him,' argued Mai. 'The bot must have misread the data. Maybe parts of the brain are fossilized and...'

'No, look here,' interrupted Toft. 'See how those structures here go from the crown to the back of the head? And then back to, what is that part in the middle of the brain called?'

'Temporal lobe,' said Shao, fascinated. 'And the back of the head is the parietal lobe.'

Toft nodded hastily. 'Thanks. Yeah, those two. Check the wiring, it turns counterclockwise on the right hemisphere, but clockwise on the left.'

Mai leaned back, disbelief on her face. 'It's mirrored. That's unbelievable.'

'Why? What's so special about a neural interface?' asked Shao, not understanding what Toft and Mai meant.

'It means the autodoc didn't just read corrupted data,' explained Toft. 'It made a model based on an accurate scan. It's not very good quality, but it's an image of an actual implant or an entire series of them.'

'And it's not an implant we can identify,' added Mai. 'Not with the data taken by the hand scanners. We gotta bring the coffin here.'

The lights flickered as if to underline Mai's words, and the autodoc's software crashed, distorting the mummy's image in a series of lagging error screens.

Green clapped and got up from a chair. 'All right, let's take this as a reminder we're not in a lab, but on a derelict ship heading nowhere fast.'

'We're heading nowhere slowly, you mean,' corrected Shao. 'But yeah, I get you. We need some accommodations.'

'So, we're still going to the corporate HQ?' asked Toft hesitantly.

'I don't think there's a point,' said Green. 'We should just take the coffin to the Yusan.'

'Great, Dad's gonna love it,' said Shao. 'I'm gonna be grounded until I'm fifty.'

Mai put her hand on Shao's shoulder. 'We still need to stick around until we reach Hellespont. Sōngshǔ doesn't have the power to reach a waystation on its own or to get back to Seventeen.'

'The bay it is, then,' decided Green, leading them back into the ship's bowels.

'Since when is he so bossy?' asked Mai.

They headed back into the labyrinthine network of maintenance corridors, towards the nearby docking bay. They moved quietly, the excitement from a few minutes ago replaced by disappointed silence. The vision of accolades replaced with the grim reality of having to face the consequences for abandoning their ship and duty didn't invite conversation.

As they were approaching the intersection where the docking bay was located, Green suddenly raised his hand and stopped. 'Hold on, everyone,' he messaged them, text only. 'I hear something.'

Shao moved closer, taking cover behind a bend.

Fortunately for them, the lights in this part of the ship were permanently fritzed, drowning the intersection in darkness. Then, she heard it—hushed voices, closing in. Shao could make out an annoyed-sounding man, scolding someone.

'Hold onto that thing, god damn it,' the voice said. 'It bit me!'

Harsh laughter ensued, followed by another voice. 'Don't be a fuckin' baby. It barely even drew blood.'

'Hold it and shut the fuck up,' replied the first voice.

'Relax, mate. The cans never get as far as this deck, what the hell for?'

'What if there are sensors in the walls? Just follow the damn SOP and keep your mouth shut.'

Shao saw two men emerge from behind the corner, carrying something oblong and struggling, covered in orange cloth. Both wore jumpsuits in the same bright color. One of them, an athletic red-haired Earther with a goatee and a ponytail, stripped down to a white undershirt. The other, a large Outer with a dark hole where his left eye should be, struggled to keep the package still.

'Be on the lookout for my eye, at least,' said the Outer in a hushed tone. 'It's gotta be here somewhere.'

The ginger man nodded. 'Fuckin' thing had to lose signal right now of all times, eh?'

'When it rains, it pours.'

The men passed Shao's hideout and moved along behind the corner. She heard the hiss of an opening airlock, and more hushed voices, too distant to make out the meaning.

Green gave her a startled look. 'I thought this barge had no crew?' he whispered.

'That's what I thought, too,' replied Shao. 'Haulers never have any crew, what the hell?'

'Maybe they're barnacles. Stowed away, like us?'

'That's not good, not good at all.'

'Let's wait and see; gotta learn more.'

It took almost fifteen minutes before they heard the airlock open again. The men came back, absent the package. They were walking fast, heading straight towards the intersection.

Shao realized they are going to enter the corridor where she and Green were hiding, but it was too late to withdraw. Frozen by a sudden panic, her thoughts raced, scrambling for a solution.

The strangers were a few meters away from her when the Outer man stopped, putting his muscular arm on his companion's arm. 'Yo, Muldoon. Hold on,' he said.

The red-haired man turned around. 'Something happen?'

The Outer nodded, making a vague motion with his hand. 'I think I got the eyebot signal. Got some visuals, too, but it keeps crashing.'

'Well, where is it then?'

'Stupid thing is stuck in a vent, 'bout a hundred meters that way,' replied the Outer, waving towards the corridor to their right.

'Go get it then; you look like an idiot without it.'

'Yeah, yeah, love you too. I'll see you back at the cell.'

Muldoon put his thumb up in agreement. 'Keep an eye out for the tin cans, mate. You know, the other one.'

'Oh, fuck you.'

The Outer man headed into the dark corridor, accompanied by Muldoon's laughter. A moment later, the red-haired man shrugged and headed back the way he initially came from, to the left of Shao's hideout.

'That was close,' said Green, sweating profusely. 'Let's go before the Outer comes back.'

They scrambled through the intersection and into the round airlock.

Mai quickly forced the lock to open with a hiss of hydraulics that sounded dangerously loud to Shao. The hatch slid open in slow motion, driving Shao to the edge of panic. She expected the men to return at any moment—and do who knows what. They certainly weren't Zhengdao employees, and she couldn't recognize the orange jumpsuits.

The airlock opened eventually, despite getting stuck halfway for a moment, and Shao followed the others inside. The outer hatch opened just as slow, but soon enough, they entered the docking bay.

The area was rather shallow, but wide and tall, with no ceiling— the walls led straight up into the darkness of open space. The floor was stacked with multi-floor racks, full of autonomous forklift drones, dark and quiet. Rows of tool cabinets ran along the wall on the far side, in the middle of the wide dark-red stripe painted on the walls. Higher still, the paint ended, exposing dark, pockmarked metal plating.

Shao looked around cautiously. 'Looks like this is it. We can get all the tools we need in here,' she said on the comms.

Mai nodded, her slumped posture betraying her fear. Shao couldn't tell whether the anxiety was caused by the gaping darkness above them or the possibility of being discovered.

Toft moved past, heading towards the cabinets. 'I don't think we'll need a forklift, guys,' he said. 'Let's take what we came for and go.'

The group spread out, rummaging through the shelves, looking for anything useful: power tools, plasma torches, isolating spray bottles. Shao quickly gathered as many tools as she could fit in her belt and hands, not paying attention to what they were.

'Hey, check this out,' Toft cried out. He leaned over a red toolbox, holding a nail gun in one hand and a stack of soft floor isolation plates under his armpit.

Someone had scratched a wide letter X across the toolbox lid, but otherwise, it seemed much like the others. Suddenly the box rattled and jumped, lifting off the floor.

Toft put his foot on the lid and pushed it back to the floor. 'I wonder what's inside,' he said.

'Maybe those guys left a drill on or something,' guessed Green.

'I'm gonna check.' Toft reached out to open the lid before anyone could stop him.

The top opened slowly, revealing an orange cloth, pressed tightly into the box.

Toft poked it with the nail gun carefully. 'Isn't it that dude's jacket?' Suddenly, the jacket exploded upwards, revealing a mass of pale tentacles shooting towards his face. Toft twitched, and the nail gun fired.

27

C hatty's confidence waned with every step through the dark corridor. The deck he was on was full of floating rubble—pieces of
hard to identify trash, ranging in size from dust particles to a human
head. The lights flickered just often enough to disorient him, making
the way more difficult than it would be in total darkness.

After violently smacking his forehead on a corner of a weightless
crate, he settled on using his hands to navigate his way through the
labyrinth of clutter filling the corridor. It seemed to be some half-
finished maintenance way—probably a side result of the hauler's hasty
retrofit to support life. At least some of the floating bubbles of goop
seemed to be moldy protein paste.

Chatty wiped the gunk off his face with disgust, muttering curses. If
not for a faint signal indicating where his ocular drone was, he would
have turned back and called it a day.

The transmission was weak as if blocked by something. It was
enough to indicate that the drone was near, stuck in a vent. Chatty's
command console built into his eyes socket barely had enough bandwidth to receive the signal stream, it was much larger than it should be.
He reckoned whatever was causing the interference also cluttered the
drone's locator beacon.

Chatty squeezed himself past two crates, almost completely blocking the passage, and found himself in a round room stacked floor to
ceiling with dimly lit pods, each about half a meter long. Thick cables
and piping connected every one of them to a large cylinder in the

center of the room. Chatty recoiled instantly at the putrid stench of it all and heaved.

Something scuttled in the darkness, the quiet clicking enough to cause Chatty's flight-or-fight instinct to kick in. He forgot about the foul odor and readied a shank. Whatever hid in the darkness, it wasn't a security drone. The bulky machine would be sticking out here like an ass in a pineapple farm, Chatty thought.

He slowly moved to the canister and carefully leaned to peak out the side. An oblong biodrone floated past him; its segmented tentacles clicking as it turned and drifted away, pushed by the waving magnetic repulsors on its sides.

Chatty let out a sigh of relief. 'You scared me, you little fucker.'

He followed the machine, staying just enough away not to disturb it. The squid-like biorobot hovered into the nearest crate, emerging after a moment with a white canister in its tentacles. It slid through the air, navigating its way to the top of the cistern, where it stuck the package into a large valve.

Chatty followed one of the thick pipes coming from the tank to the nearest pod. The plexi dome was covered in dust, so he wiped it with his sleeve. Inside, another biodrone lay curled, connected to a cluster of transparent cables. He could make out a dense liquid moving inside. 'It's a biodrone recharge station,' he muttered. 'Fuck me, what a mess. No wonder those things are so creepy.'

What would it mean for the prisoners' long-term survival if the biodrone fuel got contaminated with some bug? It could explain the lights fritzing out and subsystems failing in the last few days. Biodrones not doing their job right due to some infection could paralyze the entire ship soon. 'All the more reason to get the fuck outta here,' he said out loud. 'Just gonna get my eye back...'

There were several large vents in the upper section of the room. Based on the snippets of footage he received from the ocular drone, he surmised it must be stuck in one of them. The biodrone pods must have interfered with the signal somehow, but it should be there. One of the vents had a hole in the lid's grate, probably made by the ocular drone's laser cutter. The vent hatch wasn't much more robust than the pipes, that's for sure.

He began climbing the pods, careful not to dislodge them from the wall. The last thing he needed was to be covered in whatever goo was inside them. Disabling the magboots, he kicked himself gently off the capsule, heading towards the vent, making sure he had a grip on something along the way.

As soon as he had a grip on the vent grate, Chatty pushed his body downwards, feet touching the wall. He turned the boots back on, firmly attaching himself to the wall, and pulled on the grill. Chatty groaned with effort, straining to push the damaged lid open. Eventually, it let go, and he allowed it to float away.

Chatty crawled inside the tightly fitting tunnel. He could barely move, but there was just enough room to crawl forward, using a small finger-flashlight to make the way. Something clicked in the darkness, and a black eyeball approached, using eight thin, segmented legs to walk in an arachnid fashion. 'Here you are, little guy,' he said, smiling. 'Come to papa. I missed you. And I missed the depth of view, you know.'

The drone hesitated, as if fearful, then skittered back into the darkness.

'No, no, don't run, baby, come to papa,' pleaded Chatty, feeling like an idiot. He still couldn't get a connection going, so the drone operated under its rudimentary autopilot. Chatty crawled further, only his legs sticking out of the vent now.

The eyebot neared him again, shyly dancing in place. Chatty lured it. 'Your batteries must be drained, come recharge.'

The drone's legs clicked on the vent's inner surface as it approached.

'Here you go, that's right,' encouraged Chatty.

Hesitantly at first, then faster, the drone climbed on Chatty's face, feeling its way on his gray face towards the empty eye socket. It positioned itself as if to enter its rightful place, but instead of lodging itself into the control station implanted in Chatty's bones, it opened the laser cutter.

'No, no, no!' Chatty desperately tried shuffling backward, but it was too late. The searing heat carved the inside of his empty eye socket, burning through the charging station and the thin bone behind it, into the brain. Chatty screamed in agony, kicking and punching the vent walls. He tried calling Muldoon, but words turned into a wet gurgle in his throat.

28

The Incitatus' massive frame drifted majestically through the darkness. The triangular vessel took its first step on its long fall towards the sun but didn't leave the Oort Cloud—it was yet to pass the line of no return before the Great Beyond when the unwilling crew would lose all hope of escape. Under the watchful and ever-present eyes of cameras and security drones, the prisoners spent their days following an unchanging routine.

The day opened with drones herding the inmates in the cantina, where they were fed a colorless goo of barely edible substance Milosh suspected was some low-grade mycoprotein.

After breakfast, Milosh's group was sentenced to six hours of watching edustreams, implanting them with maintenance and repair skills mixed with propaganda and a mind-numbing stream of subliminal messaging conditioning them to be docile and curb aggressive tendencies.

Milosh's cybereyes served him well, filtering away invisible laser beams carrying the impulses, so all he had to endure was boredom. Otis proved vulnerable to conditioning, getting more and more complacent every day. At least Spider and McNamarra had found a way to keep lucid, so Milosh was not entirely on his own.

After the conditioning, the drones herded the prisoners towards various tasks onboard the enormous vessel, usually requiring a lot of time to finish, and not much in the way of actual skill. Milosh wasn't a mechanic, but even he noticed the barge's systems suffered some sort of cascading breakdown. Various subsystems glitched every day, often escalating into major malfunctions making entire sections of the ship uninhabitable. Last night a glitch caused the workspace attire charging system to fritz, rendering support equipment, most magboots included, unusable.

The prisoners stumbled on open shelves in supply cabins in the dark, claustrophobic labyrinth of scarcely lit corridors. Tools and food rations missing, equipment in disarray causing the biodrones to run amok trying to deal with the unexpected. Their squid brains were more adaptive than the simplistic programming of the security machines, but they lacked the abstract thought required to come up with solutions to complex problems, so the prisoners were often called in to clean up.

Milosh managed alright, though some prisoners had trouble moving in zero-g without help. The drones would not let them return to their cells before the job was done, and slackers had to endure bolts of electric charge from their stun guns.

Milosh's group had work aplenty. There was always something leaking and cracking on the decks, lights went out without warning, doors, and airlocks jammed halfway without a visible cause. The maintenance biodrones fluttered here and there on their segmented squid tentacles as they went about their business, but they acted erratically and didn't seem to fix anything. Milosh fully expected to wake up one day to the roar of air escaping the hull because of some rupture—they had to get out of here fast.

Milosh spent every moment free from labor planning and thinking—security drones followed the prisoners everywhere, their simple programming preventing any deviation. The metal guards followed the gang, their mag-drives allowing them to quickly get everywhere onboard to poke the crew with their shock batons and threaten with assault shotguns on any sign of delay or defiance.

Unlike the smart and adaptive biodrones, the security machines' programming was far from complex: don't let the prisoners out of sight and keep them moving so they never get the chance to scheme. Together with the manacles taking away the prisoners' freedom of movement, it was a pretty foolproof system, Milosh was forced to admit.

If they hadn't dealt with this particular issue, the drones would present sufficient threat to keep the prisoners in line. As it was, a couple of them were already destroyed in small riots that erupted between inmates. Security drones and turrets hanging from rails in the ceiling quickly overpowered fighting prisoners. They had a sparse few options to change that dynamic since their contact with other work gangs were limited to meals in the mess hall, where the atmosphere was already tense. Bands formed early and were already antagonistic to each other. Now, after weeks of isolation, the hostility turned into outright violence in the halls. Nobody gave the mercs any trouble, most of the inmates were small-time pirates and bruisers. They kept their distance so far, but it was only a matter of time.

Milosh waited for a sign from Muldoon and Chatty with rising impatience, feeling the pressure rise on all sides. McNamarra had started organizing his gang of oners into what he called a Terran Brotherhood, trying to secure a turf close to the restricted zone with security lockers. The brotherhood waited for a good moment to break free, take over the ship from their machine wardens, and take out other gangs. The ensuing chaos would endanger any hope Milosh had of contacting the Querub and getting out of the predicament.

Milosh knew he had to escape, and soon. If the prison barge crosses the line from the Cloud to the Great Beyond before they reach out to the Querub, they will be too far for rescue and stuck with the doomed inmates.

He came up with and rejected dozens of ideas, each one more outlandish than the last as the days passed. All of them broke apart over Muldoon and Chatty's disappearance. Milosh always considered himself a smart guy, but he was honest enough to admit creative planning wasn't his strongest suit. He was a mercenary: he got paid, got the mission objectives from the client, then got the job done. The prison routine was getting on his nerves, but he needed a prompt to work off.

After a breakfast of disgusting ooze and flat water, Milosh's crew readied for their re-education. A security drone hovered towards them, the low buzzing of the magnetic drive announced its approach. The drone's broad, triangular body stopped right before Milosh. An array of cameras and sensors stared at the mercenary with its dead gaze.

Milosh stared at the machine menacingly; his distorted mirror-image reflected in the machine's visor. His mustache had grown back, but he took to shaving his head bald to avoid the lice somehow spreading between the ship's passengers like wildfire.

Manacles held his cybernetically enhanced arms in front of his chest to fool the machine's dog-brain. Milosh fought the urge to slam the heavy shackles into the drone's chassis.

The rest of his gang, consisting of Otis, Sticks, and Spider, followed in line closed by another hovering machine. The prisoners slowly headed towards today's task, each taking a toolbox from the maintenance cabin.

The party crossed many dark and narrow corridors. Milosh soon realized they were headed towards a rarely visited area of the ship, the higher decks near the cargo holds. The prisoner cells nested near the bow of the barge, and they rarely ventured far.

As far as Milosh could gather, the majority of the ship's mass, aside from the cargo, was the bulky hull full of hydraulics and support rails, intended to keep the barge in one piece during its long journey. Maintenance corridors and cabins were relatively scarce in the area. The prisoners had no business there unless something severely out of the ordinary had happened—as it seemed now to be the case.

The drone led the gang up towards the craft's starboard gunnel, to a small hangar filled with forklift drones—their robust frames, dark and inert, not intended to activate again until the end of the spaceship's journey. The bay opened upwards, directly into open space.

Milosh immediately realized why they were led there. Tools and spare parts floated haphazardly in the open space, filled the bay with garbage. Open tool chests and cabinets flapped loosely in the void, but the magnetic lock lights on the doors shone brightly, indicating they haven't malfunctioned.

Squid-like biodrones flurried back and forth in that mess, metallic tentacles grabbing multiple tools at the same time, placing them back on the shelves. The magnetic surface should have held the equipment in place once the doors opened, but the locks indicated that they were still locked.

Biodrones could not disbelieve the input from the locks and just gathered more tools to put on the shelves—stuck in a loop of repetition. Several of them glitched and spun out of control, bouncing off the shelves and other drones, creating more chaos.

Security machines displayed the command to clean up the hangar onto the inmates' HUDs augmented reality filters, and the prisoners set to work. Milosh kicked himself off the airlock frame, floating towards the center of the tool vortex. With a few practiced maneuvers, he reached his destination with ease, despite the manacles. The mercenary looked carefully around the bay as he floated, passing a flock of confused biodrone bodies collecting the tools.

One of the items floating near the far wall attracted his attention. An orange prison jumpsuit jacket floated between spanners, proudly displaying a crudely drawn winged knight on a horse. Muldoon's jacket. Milosh kicked himself off a drone rack and headed away from it, towards the open space, followed by Otis.

The two gathered the tools closer and closer to the open ceiling until the security drones focused most of their attention on them. Their programming commanding to prevent escape.

Milosh gestured towards Spider on the other side of the hangar bay. 'Yo, Pie. Check the third closet from the port; I think I see something that needs your attention there,' he said, confident that his comrade would understand the hint while the drone's programming wouldn't see anything wrong with his words.

Spider followed his notion, immediately spotting the jacket. 'Aye, aye, baws,' he replied, mock saluting to an extent allowed by the manacles. The Outer headed towards the locker, snatching the jacket as he drifted. Pie looked inside the shelf, first pushing his toolbox inside to keep it from floating away.

Milosh saw Spider pushing something into the chest and covering it with the jacket before he went back to organizing the mess. After a few minutes of work, Spider removed his kit and closed the shelf, with some difficulty. He grinned widely, lifting his thumb towards Milosh. 'Nothing there, nothing interesting at all,' he said. 'Just some rags, baws.'

'Got it, well done,' replied the merc. He returned the Outer's gesture and returned to gathering the tools before the drone poked him with a shock baton.

The gang worked slower than they should; there was no hurry. If they finished the job here quickly, the drones would assign them some other pointless task. The biodrones weren't smart enough to solve a complex problem themselves, but once they saw the humans deal with the situation, they could replicate the results and learned to lock the shelves. The work went much faster than Milosh and the gang would have wished.

Once the hangar bay was cleaned, the security drones corralled the workers again, waiting only to let them take their toolboxes before leaving the bay. With some surprise, Milosh noticed that the service drones remained in the bay, their tentacles scanning the walls and hatches with short laser bursts. He didn't have a lot of time to take a good look at what they were doing. Security drones had shoved him out to the corridor and led the whole group away. Instead of taking them to another place of labor, however, the machines herded every-one back to their cells and left, locking the hatch after them.

The prisoners were left alone; the drones didn't even take the time to make them put away their kits.

'Well, that's new,' said Otis, breaking the silence. 'Think it was something I said?'

'Maybe you offended its mother, or perhaps it's the body odor?' suggested Sticks, scratching his bald gray head in feigned wonder.

Milosh shrugged it off. 'Everything on this piece of junk fritzes.'

'It was something else,' said Spider. 'That mess... That was no mal-function. I can tell a hacked terminal when I see one.'

'Muldoon's not a hacker, neither is Chatty,' stated Milosh. 'Where are those two anyway?'

'So that's what bothers you?' asked Sticks. 'I could tell your mind is off your game.'

'Yeah, you almost got shivved twice today,' added Otis.

'Have I?'

'Yeah, once by me and the second time by Sticks here.' Otis laughed.

Milosh smirked and shook his head. 'Oh, fuck off. I'm serious. They were supposed to report back yesterday.'

'We should sneak out and look for them, then,' said Spider. 'Seeing as we have some free time, it seems.'

'Damn right, Pie,' agreed Milosh. 'We may not have much of it though. Did you get it?'

'Sure did, baws.'

'Get what? What's going on?' Sticks nervously twitched and snapped his fingers. 'I don't like this whole business. Smells fishy.'

'Oh, that's just my toolbox.' Pie giggled. He opened the chest and lifted the orange jacket. The nauseating stench of rotten eggs and burnt plastic spread through the air.

A biodrone floated into view; its elongated body motionless, seg-mented metal tentacles tightly bent in an agony-like state. Its sensor array bulbs were dim, with no sign of usual activity. The light-gray chassis' artificial skin was broken by a long construction nail piercing it across the entire width, dug deep into the drone's body, almost all the way through. Thick, oily blood gathered around the wound in an irregular bubble.

Otis hopped up in surprise, floating up to the cell's ceiling. 'Damn you, man,' he exclaimed. 'Warn me next time, I almost soiled myself!'

'And almost flew away, compadre.' Sticks laughed, catching the Outer and dragging him back down. 'Good thing the window's closed, or we'd have to catch you on a lasso.'

'Cut it out, people,' barked Milosh, focusing their attention. 'We don't know when they will come for us so stop screwing around and pay attention. Pie, can you get this thing back online and reprogram it?'

'Should be easy enough. It's not badly damaged; it looks like it just turned off, so it doesn't bleed out all over the place.'

'How did it get spiked is the real question,' said Milosh, looking at the drone up close. 'Muldoon and Chatty wouldn't damage the goods that way.'

'Maybe it got damaged in the locker? Or spiked itself?' wondered Otis.

'Yeah, those things bug out all over the place,' said Sticks. 'I saw one try to weld a hole through the outer hull just yesterday.'

'Questions will have to wait. Pie, get on it, Sticks, stand watch. Help me with that panel, Otis.'

Milosh turned around and gestured to the sides of the bunk. The mercenary then grabbed hold of the frame and strained his arms to lift it. Artificial muscles did their job. Slowly, the two-story double bed lifted from the ground with a loud creak of abused metal. The floor panel bent and released from its bedding, floating slowly upward. Milosh and Otis pushed it to the side of the cell where it stayed. The ripped floor panel revealed a crawlspace, leading into the darkness of a maintenance shaft.

Meanwhile, Spider opened the biodrone's chassis, revealing the gelatinous muscles and meat of the creature inside. The squid's eyes and parts of the cartilaginous head capsule had been surgically removed, wires connected the sensor arrays to nerve endings in the empty eye sockets. The creature's brain was covered with a metallic alloy dome. He gently lifted the thin shielding, revealing a lobotomized, living brain connected to sophisticated computer—processors and microchips cooled by the drone's blood flow.

Sticks spat with disgust, the saliva immediately forming a floating bubble. 'I fucking hate biodrones,' he said. 'I mean, look at this fuckin' thing.'

Pie ignored him and reached to his temples, where the tattoos going upwards from his mouth ended. He scratched the rubbery skin, revealing a cleverly hidden cap, the size of his fingernail. He pulled on it and released the end of a nanofiber cable, tugging it gently until half a meter snaked out from his skull, then plugged himself into the biodrone's revealed CPU. His eyes rolled upwards.

'That's just nasty,' commented Sticks.

Spider didn't reply, his mind jacked into the computer, fingers twitching randomly to the rhythm of electrical impulses.

Milosh watched with a mixture of awe and disgust as the squid drone's metallic tentacles joined the dance, man and machine connected through a neural interface into one being.

'Hurry up, boys,' Sticks ushered them, his hands laid flat on the hatch. 'I feel vibrations; the tin can's coming back.'

'Almost... Done, just... Need a minute,' Spider said, his voice breaking from exhaustion.

'We don't have a minute, for fuck's sake!'

'We need to put everything as it was, quickly,' cried Otis with exasperation, pulling down on the bed.

'What's the plan? What's the plan?' panicked Sticks. 'Do we have an emergency plan?'

The hatch opened suddenly, sliding aside to reveal the smooth angular body of a security drone. Its sensor array's glass eye scanned the cell, assessing the situation. The machine's shock batons immediately sparkled with electricity. The thick barrel of an assault shotgun targeted Spider, and the machine's magdrive buzzed as it charged to eliminate the threat of mutiny.

Milosh launched himself, pushing off of the cell wall with both legs. He ripped off his shackles and swung them at the drone. It parried with a shock baton, the electric discharge flashed like sudden lightning. The shotgun turned towards Milosh and roared. A rapid barrage of flak shards rained on the merc's unarmored body. His skin peeled, revealing the armor mesh, bloody mist whirled in the air.

Otis slammed the bunk into the machine's chassis with a loud bang. It spun violently.

The bombardment continued, supersonic flak shards cutting the bed into shreds in seconds. The thunder of autofire drowned the prisoners' screams. The air filled with coppery stench, bubbles of thick blood spread everywhere in a sticky mist.

Milosh grabbed hold of the drone and slammed his fingers into the sensor. He gritted his teeth with effort and strained, piercing the plastic cover and tearing the electronics with his bare hands.

Shock batons stabbed into Milosh's gut with a flash of light. A cloud of thick smoke stinking of burnt flesh added to the chaos. His body shook and flew away violently, slamming into the wall. The drone stabilized its flight and aimed at Milosh.

Before it could fire, Sticks's thin body hit the machine from the side.

'Just die already, you piece of shit!' he yelled, smashing the armored chassis repeatedly with a wrench.

The drone fired, drowning Sticks's shouts in the roar of autofire. His chest exploded into a bloody pulp, muscle, and bones strewn all over the cell, bouncing like pebbles off the walls before floating away.

Milosh rammed into the machine from below, once more destabilizing its flight. He kicked away from the drone, desperately trying to avoid the deadly stream of shards. Tangled together, they spun around the ceiling.

Otis tore a metal bar from the bunk bed and slammed it into the drone, bending the armored plates, sending them flying into a wall. Otis followed it with a furious roar. He held the bar in both hands and mauled the machine like an angry gorilla.

The chassis bent more and more every time a hit landed with a loud, metallic bang. Eventually, it cracked, revealing the mechanism inside.

Milosh grabbed the edge of the crack with his left hand, surrounded the chassis with his legs, and punched directly into the blinded drone's circuitry.

Something exploded inside with a thud and sparks. The damaged drone fell silent, inert. Black smoke whirled above it like a funerary pyre.

Otis let go of his improvised weapon, blood flowing from his shredded arm surrounding him in a crimson most of bubbles. 'Our emergency plan was real shitty,' he said, breaking the deafening silence.

'Tell me about it,' agreed Milosh, wincing in pain. His side was aching and bleeding, wounded by the flak from the shotgun. Right arm was unresponsive, electronics probably damaged by the shock, if not worse. He felt nothing from it. Eyes and ears were bleeding, and he could barely hear Otis over the high-pitched ringing. 'Could be worse though,' he said finally, tongue and lips numb. 'That thing almost did us in real good, am I right, Pie?'

When Spider didn't reply, Milosh turned to the hacker. Spider was drifting aimlessly amidst the bloody mess, holding the gore that was Sticks in his arms. Paying no heed to the bodily fluids staining his orange jumpsuit, Pie cradled the corpse, tears mixing with the floating blood.

'Shit, man...' started Milosh, but fell silent, at a loss for words.

'He's gone, Pie,' said Otis gently. 'There's nothing we can do.'

Spider unplugged the cable, letting it pull itself back into his skull. The biodrone activated its engine again, spike still in the wound, but no more blood flowing.

The Outer hacker blinked a few times through the tears, as his senses adjusted to the vision shift.

'We gotta go, Pie,' repeated Otis, putting his large hand on Spider's shoulder. 'Before another one shows up.'

'There'll probably be more than one,' added Milosh. 'Come on, Pie. We need you.'

When the Outer didn't react, Milosh and Otis gently wrestled Sticks from his embrace and led him down the maintenance shaft. Milosh gave the cell one last look before heading down. Sticks's mutilated remains hovered in the cell, spinning slowly. Blood, gore, the security drone's motionless wreck, and the debris revolved around them. He didn't know the skinny smuggler well but realized with some surprise that the man's death weighed on him—perhaps because of Spider's reaction. I'm getting too soft for this job, he thought.

The prisoners crawled through the tight ducts, following Spider's drone leading them to the ship's gunnel. Narrow pathways filled with pipes and sharp edges tore at their prison suits; naked feet and hands soon bled from multiple cuts and scratches.

After what seemed like hours, the biodrone stopped in front of a ventilation crate. Its segmented tentacles quickly disassembled the lock, and the gang floated into the hangar bay. Forklifts were still secure in their charging racks, but all the biodrones were gone, and the hall was dark, silent, and cold.

'Aight, Pie, Otis, get us some power tools,' commanded Milosh. 'We need some weapons, at least.'

'Are we gonna take on the drones, baws?' asked Spider in a hollow tone, when the men left to wrench the drawers open.

'Not unless we have to,' replied Milosh. 'Send your pet to let Al know it's time to bounce, and we're gonna look around. Gotta find Muldoon and Chatty. Then we head to the comm room, aight?'

Otis drifted to join them, hauling a couple of sets of nail guns and plasma cutters. 'Why wait for McNamarra? Or stop to look for your buddies? If they got lost, too bad.'

'First of all, without them, we'd have no chance to leave this place,' said Milosh.

'They helped us, and thanks for that,' argued Otis. 'But now, fuck'em. We gotta get the shit outta this can.'

'The baws is right, you know,' said Pie in support. 'We find them and get outta here together, or Sticks died for nothing.'

'What about McNamarra and those idiots he hangs out with?' Otis wasn't convinced.

'We grab Al and whoever fits on board of whatever Milosh can call to pick us up,' replied Spider calmly. 'Sticks would want that.'

Before anyone could argue any further, they heard the hangar airlock's outer hatch open, red light signaling the passage is open and the countdown is ongoing.

'Quick, bounce!' Milosh urged them. 'The drones found us!'

'It's too late. We can't get back into the shaft,' whispered Otis.

Milosh kicked himself off towards the lock. 'Shit, hide then, over there!' He took cover behind the airlock frame, high-pressure nail gun in hand. He managed just in time, too. The red light turned bright green, and the door slid open. A dark shape drifted into the hangar bay, slowly and carefully.

In a split second, Milosh grabbed the edge of the airlock frame, pushed himself onto the intruder with force, and repeatedly fired his nail gun. To his surprise, the shape cried out in a high-pitched, female voice in a burst of pain and terror. The copper scent of blood filled the room. Milosh lit the nail gun's beam and looked right into the still, black eyes of a young girl drifting away from him, mouth open in shock.

29

The Europa decelerated rapidly, its flat, saucer-shaped hull shivering from the strain caused by the main drive fighting against the velocity. Helikaon Waystation's laser had propelled the corvette towards the target nine sols ago, but it was up to its engines to slow down.

Inside the corvette, Lederman lied submerged in a kinetic gel tank, waiting for a green light to exit the pod. His breathing mask's visor displayed the Europa's trajectory and speed, among other useful information.

Judging by the energy spikes whenever the corvette's point defense lasers fired to push away space trash on a collision course, he surmised they were nearing an asteroid and a quite sizable one at that.

The ship's augmented reality informed that the ship had slowed down to safe levels, and Lederman immediately began the exit procedure. As soon as the gel was drained, he emerged, almost kicking the pod open.

By the time the other crew members opened their pods, he had showered and dressed—a brown armored jumpsuit and a new duster coat with ablative plating bought to replace the stolen one. 'Come on, people, move it,' he commanded sharply. 'We have a job to do!'

Fabian Van Alst, the Europa's pilot, snickered while wiping the green gel particles from his face's rubbery skin. 'Someone's in a battle mood,' he said.

Tomasson laughed and slipped to the showers, playfully shoving the Outer pilot out of the way.

'The captain caught the scent of blood I see,' said Dassler, reaching for a towel. 'You know ten minutes won't make a difference, right? The ship's on autopilot, and we can drive it from wherever.'

Lederman shrugged. 'Laugh all you want, but I won't be caught dead in my underwear.'

'Fair enough,' admitted Dassler. 'Fabian, what's our status?'

Van Alst didn't waste time on getting dressed and was already on his way to the Europa's bridge. He sat down, plugged the neural interface cables into slots in his wrists and temples, and took manual command of the craft. 'We're nominal. All systems green, five thousand kay away from the target and nearing,' he reported.

'How about you go near yourself to a pair of pants?' asked Lederman, heading towards the bridge.

'I don't mind getting caught dead in underwear, cap,' replied the pilot. 'My shorts are glorious.'

Lederman glanced at Van Alst's vintage SpongeBob boxers and said nothing.

Dassler passed him by and sat down in his station, taking a mug of coffee delivered to his desk by a drone. 'We'll see if your informer was on point, cap,' he said, taking a sip.

'He better fucking be,' replied Lederman. 'The intel wasn't cheap.'

Tomasson joined them on the bridge, carrying a coffee mug as well. 'How's the sitrep? Did we die yet, cap?' she asked.

'Yes, and we're in hell,' Lederman replied. 'At least I am. How's the cruise, Fabian?'

'We should be reaching the target in a jiffy, just relax, captain,' said the pilot. 'Watch a movie, maybe? You're stressing me out.'

Lederman sighed and brought up the charts onto his HUD. He was always nervous before action; it just couldn't be helped. Of course, the crew knew this, so they acted extra relaxed just to give him something to get annoyed at. The little ritual worked for them for years.

The Europa neared an unnamed asteroid, marked only by a number and a prospector report flagging it as an ice rock. Ladar and comm scans showed no signs of activity. Lederman wondered if the smuggler had lied to him. It wasn't unheard of for informants to give false information, hoping to grab the upfront cred and dash the sector, knowing they won't be getting the second part of the reward.

'Make a flyby around the rock,' said Tomasson. 'Maybe there's something on the other side.'

'Aye, aye, sir,' replied Van Alst and entered the course.

'Wait, don't slingshot,' added Tomasson. 'Flathat the surface, just in case.'

'Okidoki, anything else?' asked Van Alst. 'Want me to do a little window shopping for you while I'm at it?'

Lederman took his eyes off the sensor readings. 'Yeah, strap in the pods before we go in,' he said. 'And launch decoys on a course for the optimal slingshot maneuver.'

'Fuck me, boss,' complained Dassler instantly. 'We just got out of those things.'

Lederman shrugged. 'I trust Lara's instincts. Do it.'

'Fine, whatever,' agreed Dassler. 'You're the captain.'

'See, I knew there was no point getting dressed,' teased Van Alst.

The Europa approached the icy rock, its saucer frame turning to match the asteroid's curvature. The corvette's engine fell silent as it slid only a few kilometers above the surface, except for a rare maneuver burst from underside dishes. The discharge heat raised flares of exploding ice carving a track of instantly freezing mist behind it, like a manta ray swimming just above the ocean floor. When the vessel reached the asteroid's dark side, it discharged a cloud of tiny drones emitting radio and heat noise, parodying the bigger craft's signature.

A volley of missiles cut through the darkness of space without warning, leaving behind a thin wispy trail of smoke. Deadly nuclear warheads surrounded by flaming halos charged towards the decoys and exploded in an inferno, instantly vaporizing the machines. Onboard the

Europa, dozens of holographic consoles displayed alerts, warning the crew of the nearby blast and radiation exceeding the shield tolerance.

'Somebody shut that fucking noise down!' shouted Lederman.

The Europa's engines came back online, and the corvette jetted away from the asteroid. 'Where did those missiles come from?'

'No idea, cap,' reported Tomasson.

'Seriously, disconnect that crap,' yelled Dassler. 'It's giving me a migraine.'

'On it. The missiles came from above us by the way,' replied Van Alst, silencing the alerts. 'Damn pirates, firing at people before second coffee.'

'Yeah, speaking of, another barrage comes our way,' reported Dassler. 'Maybe shoot those things down, will ya?'

'On it, boss, engaging evasive maneuvers,' said Van Alst. 'Take care of those rockets, Lara.'

'I'm on it,' Tomasson said, engaging the ship's long-range weaponry. 'Told ya not to slingshot.'

'Yeah, yeah, lucky guess,' replied Van Alst. 'They didn't wait on the other side, so you were still wrong.'

'They must have been sitting in stealth above it,' noticed Tomasson. 'I can see their ship clear as day on the sensors now.'

'And we drove right into an ambush,' said Van Alst. 'Like amateurs. Thanks again, cap.'

'Come on, you two!' roared Lederman. 'The missiles!'

'Oh, yeah,' retorted Tomasson, winking.

'Like gods-damned children. Fabian, evasive maneuvers!'

Van Alst didn't reply, too focused on his job in the full sensory interface. Lederman knew he was heard, and that was enough.

The ship trembled when the main engines kicked in unison with the port thrusters. The corvette's flat hull rotated under the twin flames of nuclear fusion, forcing it to slow down and fight the inertia that pushed it right in the path of the missiles, still minutes away from reaching their target. If not for the inertia gel pods, the crew would have been crushed into a paste by the pull's force.

After what seemed an eternity of hanging in the balance, the thrust won against the craft's mass, and the corvette jutted forth. Laser batteries sent short bursts toward the distant missiles. A flower of nuclear explosion rose in the blackness of space once more—enormous balls of fire and radiation barely tiny flickers from a distance.

'Got them, captain,' said Lara Tomasson calmly. 'Piece of cake. No idea why they even bothered with the second salvo.'

'Doesn't matter,' replied Lederman. 'Fabian, get the engines rolling and get close enough to board.'

'Aye, aye, sir,' replied the pilot. 'So, we're taking them alive?'

Lederman ignored the question. 'Give me comms, Das.' He began speaking as soon as the navigator gave the thumbs up. 'This is the Ranger corvette IRC Europa, Captain Manuel W. Lederman speaking. Unregistered vessel, broadcast your IFF and prepare to be boarded.'

The captain repeated the call two more times, but no reply came.

'All right, the hard way it is,' he concluded. 'You know what to do, Fabian.'

The pilot didn't respond, but the Europa gained velocity rapidly and charged towards the pirate ship. Flak bursts exploded in fiery flowers, creating a screen against the enemy missiles, turrets pincushioned the pirate vessel with surgical laser bursts.

The enemy craft dwarfed the Europa—a bulky freighter jury-rigged with missile and mass driver turrets firing volleys of ordnance at the corvette closing in rapidly. The Ranger craft veered and pirouetted like a leaf in the wind, avoiding the deadly cascade with a dancer's grace.

The freighter tried to move out of the way of the laser bombardment from the smaller assailant, to no avail. The barrage was relentless, and soon the pirates were firing completely blind, bursts of white-hot projectiles bristling in space. Within half an hour, the saucer-shaped ship flew over the pirates at a short distance of merely a few hundred kilometers, launching volleys of EM ordnance at the blinded foe. The blasts covered the freighter's hull in bright electromagnetic flashes. The Europa's rapid-fire railguns blasted holes in the pirate's engine modules and ripped the turrets into molten shrapnel, now spiraling away into the void. The hull's integrity gave out, and the large freighter dented like an imploding tin can amidst the quickly freezing spray of escaping oxygen.

The Europa sped up and went into a tight noose turn around the inert pirate vessel. A small, tear-shaped boarding shuttle launched from the corvette and attached to the larger craft's starboard like a leech. Inside it, six rotund combat drones cut a path through the meta-material armored plates, plasma-torches extended on segmented arms, melting the thick protective plate with an intense blue flame. Cutting the breach took but a few minutes, and soon the atmospheric pressure exploded from the freighter in a momentary rush of air. Drones rolled inside the corridor, laying down suppressive fire and forcing a couple of men wearing mismatched armored jumpsuits to withdraw behind the corner.

Lederman, Tomasson, and Dassler followed behind them, wearing dark blue protective jumpsuits, each armed with a heavy rifle and a solid shield for mobile cover. Their magnetically charged boots stuck securely to the deck, despite gravity being close to non-existent inside the crippled spacecraft.

'Fire in the hole,' Dassler said matter-of-factly before launching a small grenade after the retreating crew.

An oblong explosive bounced off the wall, following the heat signatures, using its small magnetic drive. The concussive blast of air shook the deck after a few seconds, and the three Rangers moved in to secure the unconscious ruffians protected by drones rolling in front of them, ready to fire at anything that moved.

'Aight, bag 'em,' commanded Lederman. 'We gotta move. Which way's the bridge?'

'That'd be... Forward and the second left,' replied Dassler, looking at a scan result displayed on his visor's HUD.

'Roger, head out, people,' confirmed Lederman, and all three proceeded down the hull.

Lederman marched with the team through the dilapidated decks, noting the walls covered in vulgar graffiti over apparent signs of a gunfight that must have taken place at least a few months ago. Damaged decks bent inwards, full of various trash—plastic bags, food packaging, drops of oil and water floating through the hallways. Lederman couldn't tell whether the destruction was due to the pummeling the freighter took from Europa or general negligence. They crossed multiple sections reinforced with rebars and beams, holes patched up with sheets of mismatched armor plating, pipes passing the sections without apparent reason—the freighter has clearly been repurposed for combat outside of drydock and has seen numerous skirmishes.

The deck shook with gunfire, railgun slammed into the crumbling hull. Drones ran into hostiles, though Lederman and picked up the pace.

The attack caught the pirates off-guard. A dozen disorganized floaters were busy trying to patch up a gaping hole left in the hull by the Europa's flyby bombardment when the drone formation crashed into them, almost instantly dropping three of them.

Tomasson left them no chance to surrender or orient in the situation—she opened fire. A barrage of supersonic pellets hit the enemy's shins and knees, knocking them off balance. Tomasson stepped forward, calmly aiming at drifting enemies, shooting them right in the solar plexus one by one with a short burst. Plastic rounds designed to flatten for maximum impact kicked the air and will to fight out of them instantly. The incapacitated pirates spiraled towards the ceiling. Like birthday balloons, Lederman thought.

Dassler rushed to disarm and tie the unlucky marauders together with magnetic cuffs, making sure they're out of the fight for good. The entire band was bagged in less than a minute before any of them had the chance to reach for weapons, let alone open fire. The Rangers moved like a well-oiled machine, not giving the pirates a chance to peep.

Lederman ordered half of the drones to take the prisoners to the Europa's brig and moved deeper into the pirate vessel. They encountered no resistance until the bridge, where a hastily built barricade composed of various computer parts, chairs, locker doors, and similar junk blocked the boarding party's advance. Pirates clad in metal plates attached to their patched jumpsuits with wiring and plastic straps immediately opened fire at them, railguns destroying two of the drones with the first salvo.

As soon as the rotund machines exploded in a rain of sparks and shrapnel, the Rangers retreated behind the corner. The next salvo of magnetically propelled spikes rumbled on the deck wall, piercing the rusty pipe and drowning the corridor in a hot mist of recycled water. The haze quickly solidified into glimmering crystals sticking to the surfaces until the next barrage of covering fire tore through the ice and metal, blasting hot drops into the vacuum again.

Lederman pressed his back to the wall, hiding his figure from the shooters. 'Let me guess; it's the only way to the bridge?' he asked rhetorically.

'Sure looks like it,' Tomasson confirmed, firing another concussion grenade around the corner.

The rush of oxygen expanding in the tight quarters ruptured the thin atmosphere. Another salvo of rails thundered on the deck in response, followed by a frag grenade. The explosion of shrapnel shook the deck, and red-hot metal shards filled it with deadly splinters. The pirates almost got the Rangers by surprise. Lederman scrambled to cover Tomasson from the blast, closing his eyes instinctively as he braced for the pain. It didn't come—Dassler drove a drone on top of the exploding grenade at the last moment. The machine got torn to pieces but deflected most of the shrapnel.

'Dassler, report,' commanded Lederman. 'Your vitals are dropping.'

'Yup, got me good,' replied Dassler, trying to sound calm. 'Pretty sure they don't like us, cap.'

'Get back to the ship,' ordered Lederman. 'Take three drones with you, just in case. Fabian, can you do something about them?'

'I'm on it, hold tight,' replied Van Alst over the comms. 'Lemme put my shorts on.'

Lederman saw Dassler scowling on the comm window. 'Did you take a shower just now?' he asked. 'We're fighting for our lives here, for fuck's sake. Das is wounded!'

'I know, I know,' replied Van Alst, 'What do you want me to do about it?'

'Your fuckin' job, maybe?' Lederman asked angrily, a spittle of saliva dropping onto the helmet faceplate.

'Calm down, boss. I'm already in their network,' said Van Alst with exaggerated exasperation. 'Have some faith.'

' Another barrage of gunfire cut the corridor, tearing into the Rangers' hideout. Tomasson shot a couple of bursts from her rifle at the barricade in reply, using the wrecked drone as cover. Suddenly, the freighter's ceiling's anti-fire systems came alive, flooding the deck with a thick, non-flammable foam. The chemical solidified instantly, pressing down on them like a heavy blanket.

'Maybe that will cool you off, boss?' asked Van Alst over the comms with a chuckle.

Lederman punched an opening in the foam with a rifle and climbed out, followed by Tomasson and the remaining drones. The Rangers charged towards the barricade. Pirates clambered out of the foam as well and raised their railguns to open fire at them. They pulled the triggers, to no avail. Lederman realized their weapons were jammed. Before the ruffians had a chance to understand what was wrong, the Rangers crossed the blockade. The defending ruffians reached for their knives, stumbling suddenly—Van Alst must have hacked their visors, concluded Lederman.

The two Rangers had no real difficulty incapacitating the defenders. After a quick exchange of blows, they all floated in the air with their hands and ankles tied together behind their backs. Lederman ordered the drones to cut down the closed hatch leading to the bridge. As soon as the plasma torch created an opening, the Rangers burst into the cabin, weapons ready to fire.

The bridge was dark, filled with machinery in varying degrees of disrepair. Many panels had been stripped, likely recently. A vortex of assorted trash slowly rotating in the cabin had been disrupted by the Rangers taking a position in the center of the cabin, ready for an ambush. No attack came, however, and the only person outside of them was sitting motionlessly in a captain's chair, hands raised in surrender.

The obese woman, wearing a jumpsuit with skull insignia, had a scarred face, clearly visible thanks to light inside her helmet. Blond hair fell on her face, over a perky nose and cybernetic eyes looking at the Ranger party with evident disdain. 'Fine, fine, I surrender. Jesus, talk about overreacting.' she said snarkily.

The Rangers approached her with caution.

'Lay down your weapons and disable the ship's AI,' ordered Lederman. 'You're under arrest for piracy and attempted murder of the crew of MV Gloria.'

'Yeah, yeah, I know. Been there, good times,' replied the pirate captain dismissively. 'I already said I surrender, are you deaf?'

'I was just stating that for the protocol, gotta file the paperwork,' replied Lederman and immediately scolded himself for engaging in a discussion.

'Yeah, fucking bureaucracy,' snorted the pirate captain. 'It's eating our lives away.'

'I know, right?' agreed Lederman unwittingly before collecting himself and resuming the formal tone. He wasn't used to people held at gunpoint acting like they were in a shopping mall complaining about the weather. The woman's attitude distracted him, and he felt his resolve fade. 'We're gonna haul you to the station,' he said harshly, 'and leave a buoy so somebody can come to pick the ship up.'

'Thanks, wouldn't want anyone to steal it.' The pirate rose from her chair, paying the Rangers no mind despite the guns trained at her chest. 'Let's get on with it. The name's Pam, by the way.'

'You're not the one giving the orders here, Pam,' Lederman scolded.

'Ok, what do you want to do then, boss?' asked Pam ironically, putting her hands on her hips. Lederman stared at her in annoyance, red-faced.

Tomasson snorted quietly.

'Oh, just shut up,' said Lederman exasperated. 'And tell me, how did you even know we're coming?'

'Which is it, then?' chuckled the pirate.

'Both!' growled Lederman angrily.

Pam chuckled again. 'Well, obviously a little bird told me.'

Tomasson switched to a secure line. 'Looks like your informant may have had an agenda,' she said.

'We'll take care of it later,' replied Lederman. 'Let's bag this bitch and get outta here.'

'Bad news, boss,' said Van Alst. 'Das just got to the shuttle; it doesn't look good if the autodoc is anything to go by.'

'Fuck. Will he make it?'

'Yeah, if we get him some medical attention. We don't have the tech on the Europa.'

Lederman looked over the wrecked cabin where Tomasson was restraining the pirate captain. He gritted his teeth. 'We're gonna have to take our prisoners to Helikaon before heading back to the station. I have a few words for Mister Matthews anyway.'

30

Zhenya breathed out, his eyes closed. He stepped slowly forward, sword raised, bare feet gently touching the cold floor. Guzheng music washed over his ears, blood pulsing to the rhythm of a quiet drum in the background. He let the darkness envelop him, breathing deeply, meditating in motion, swapping from one tai-chi pose to the next with fluid grace.

The attack came without warning, from both sides at once. Blades swung with lightning speed aimed toward Zhenya's neck and waist. Without opening his eyes or losing the rhythm of his meditation, he parried both blades. His inhuman reflexes augmented with state-of-the-art combat chems made the attacking men's perfectly honed technique look clumsy. In a swift, dance-like motion, Zhenya leaped into the air, pushing himself off an opponent's thigh with a kick. Cracked bone sounded like a gunshot amid the zither's rapid crescendo. He swirled in the air, cutting down with force forcing the opponent to parry the swing and step back. His curved blade swung in a quick riposte. Zhenya bent his back towards the floor as he landed. His foe's blade cut millimeters away from Yuan's face, but the attacker had no chance to cut downwards. Yuan's foot kicked under the man's kneecap, cracking it with a loud, gut-wrenching noise.

He jumped back on his feet, assuming the final tai-chi pose, and opened his eyes. 'Good training, esteemed colleagues,' he said. 'Please, feel free to visit the infirmary.'

'Thank you, captain,' replied the men in unison, allowing the medical drone to lift them. Both were sweating profusely from the strain as well as the effort of hiding their pain.

Zhenya paid no more attention to either of them. He sheathed his sword and left the training room, headed towards the showers. Just as he left the room, however, a message notification popped up in his vision. Without slowing down, the captain displayed it on his cybereyes' HUD. He lowered his eyes in a quick nod of greeting. 'How can I help you, dear adjutant?'

'Esteemed captain, forgive the intrusion on your daily schedule,' said Sun. 'We have arrived at Seventeen's landing site.'

'Very well, dear colleague, thank you,' replied Yuan. 'I assume you hailed the crew already?'

'Of course, esteemed captain. There is no answer. It would appear to be abandoned.'

Zhenya hesitated but showed no emotion. 'Interesting. I will join you presently and lead the contact team.'

Sun's face expressed nothing but concern. 'Are you certain that is wise, captain?'

'Please refrain from questioning my orders, dear colleague.' Zhenya's quiet answer was leveled and polite, but it electrified the adjutant immediately.

'Of course, esteemed captain, my apologies,' Sun said, bowing deeply.

'None needed, dear adjutant, none needed,' replied Zhenya, closing the connection. One must always keep the underlings on their toes, lest they walk all over you, he thought.

Sun was growing bold as of late, reaching beyond his responsibilities. He still showed no obvious inclination to undermine his boss, but it was apparent Sun was working towards something.

After a short visit to the gym's locker room, Zhenya quickly headed towards the Jīnlóng's hangar bay, sending directives to Captain Powells and his security entourage.

White corridors passed before his eyes, virtual arrows pointing towards the destination, even though Zhenya knew the way by heart and paid no attention to the ship's systems' attempts to aid him.

Within minutes, Zhenya emerged from the elevator in the ship's cavernous hangar bay. A squad of ten troopers led by Sarah Lowe awaited his arrival in front of the shuttle. The soldiers carried railguns and wore white-gold jumpsuits with ablative armor to protect against laser fire and kinetic damage.

To his surprise, Zhenya also saw Jin Sun commanding a group of the Jīnlóng's engineers who operated a flock of drones loading a suit of powered armor onto the shuttle. 'What is the meaning of this, adjutant?' asked Zhenya loudly, over the ruckus of activity.

Sun patted the suit's armored frame, smiling. 'I thought you would like to take your command suit for the mission, esteemed captain.'

Zhenya eyed the massive frame with distrust. The armor, painted corporate white and gold, of course, was enormous, almost the size of Zhengdao storm drones. He examined the battery with a laser sail panel on the armor's back and the armored limbs. The suit reminded Zhenya of early 20th-century space suits used back in the day. The resemblance was uncanny, except those ancient space suits were not two-and-a-half-meter-tall armored monsters armed with missile batteries and lasers.

The suit's charging drone—a human-sized spider armed with a microwave laser battery, that stood on six thick, segmented legs—was already inside the shuttle. The powered armor suit is an unstoppable weapon, Zhenya thought. A bit of an overkill for a meeting with one's daughter. 'Isn't this a little too much, dear adjutant?'

Sun bowed respectfully, somehow managing to make the gesture seem like a dismissive shrug. 'It's the protocol, esteemed captain,' he said.

Zhenya narrowed his eyes, seeing the gesture for what it was. The suit's HUD's red light gave his face a sinister look, contrasting the immaculate white of his vacuum suit. 'It's a mining ship crewed by children, not a pirate corvette armed to the teeth,' said Zhenya. 'I'd sooner drop dead than go to greet my daughter wearing this nonsense.'

'I'm sorry, esteemed captain,' interjected Sarah Lowe, saluting briefly. 'I believe your adjutant is correct to worry for your safety.'

Sun bowed again, this time in thanks.

Zhenya furrowed his brow, feeling rising irritation. 'Is that so?' he asked, confounded by Lowe's stance. She hated Sun's guts.

'Yes, sir. Your daughter and the rest of the crew disappeared in the line of duty. They're either mutineers, who might have taken Shao hostage, or victims. Either way, your safety is our priority. If you insist on accompanying us, I must insist you're well protected.'

'Well said, dear colleague,' agreed Sun at once.

'It could have been an accident,' said Zhenya. 'A comm array failure. Life support glitch. Maybe they're on a prospecting trip or racing around in their jumper.'

Lowe crossed her arms stubbornly. 'Or maybe they fell victim to pirates, or one of them is a mole from another company. I can't take the chance.'

Zhenya exhaled through his nose with annoyance and gave up. 'If that's the only way we can move on with the mission, then so be it.'

The harness inside the suit tightened itself around Zhenya the moment he stepped in. The servomotors whirred quietly as they adjusted to his body. The suit's systems came online one by one, replacing his HUD with a complex array of windows informing the wearer about the suit, ammunition, and comm relays between the commander and the ship as well as squad channels and links to each soldier separately. Energy level scales, tactical maps triangulated by the armor's sensors, Seventeen's schematics, and camera feeds from the shuttle and soldiers overwhelmed Zhenya's vision for a moment before he adjusted and minimized unwanted panels. 'I feel a little overdressed for the party,' said Zhenya finally through the command suit's comm channels.

'The protocol is there for a reason,' stated Sun impassionately. 'I simply presumed it would be unwise to seem as if the code of conduct can be treated as a guideline instead of law, especially in front of the crew and the board of directors.'

'Very well, dear adjutant Sun,' the captain conceded with a sigh. 'Let's head out with the entire execution platoon, nuke them from orbit while at it, why don't we?'

31

J in Sun watched Zhenya lead the squad into the shuttle calmly, struggling to hold the smile of triumph at bay before following them into the craft. As soon as everyone was on board, the assault shuttle rotated on a platform to face the opening hangar bay. The vessel's white and gold armor contrasted with the darkness of space, juxtaposing the bright holographic Zhengdao Corp. logo with the black void and the clean hull.

Magnetic rails on which the boarding ship rested powered up and shone with a red of warning lights for a few seconds. As soon as it reached full power, the mass accelerator released the charge, and the shuttle disappeared into space in the blink of an eye. Sun watched the coolant drown the white-hot rails in gel, dissipating excess heat, before being sucked back into the filtration system.

He opened the comm channel to Captain Powells, whose face appeared almost immediately in the HUD's window. 'Can I help you, adjutant Sun?'

The old man's eyes pierced Sun's soul, as always. 'Indeed you may, esteemed Captain Powell,' replied Sun. 'I worry that our dear Captain Zhenya might be overcome with sorrow over his daughter's disappearance.'

Powell blinked twice, but let no other sign of internal turmoil show. 'Is that so, adjutant?'

'I believe he came to think Miss Zhenya declared a personal war on him.'

'Miss Shao? That hardly seems possible,' replied Powell with disbelief. 'I spoke with Captain Zhenya a few hours ago, and he expressed nothing but concern for her daughter's well-being and that of the crew.'

'And yet, not only did he take a squad of marines to meet her,' said Sun. 'He also took the mobile command powered armor.'

Powell exhaled through his nose. 'He hates that bloody tin can.'

'He does indeed.'

'I'll have a chat with the good captain when he comes back from Seventeen,' said Powells after a pause. Sun didn't for a second think Powells was planning on doing so. No matter, he thought. The records will show Sun's concern during any potential investigation in the future.

'Perhaps you should,' agreed Sun. 'Meanwhile, I would like to use Jīnlóng's long-range communication to send a message to the board of directors.'

Powell furrowed his brow but nodded. 'You may use the beacon, adjutant. Is that all?'

'Yes, esteemed captain, that is all,' said Sun with a polite smile.

32

Despite its enormous velocity, it still took the shuttle over an hour before it docked to the asteroid where the Seventeen was located. Zhenya stood in the shuttle's boarding bay, comfortable in his armored suit. The soldiers on both sides were submerged in inertia gel tanks, protecting them from the rapid acceleration. Zhenya's body was also protected from the conditions—the inside of the suit was an inertia gel capsule as well. The suit's armor rivaled that of the shuttle but guaranteed better protection, due to the powered armor's smaller frame.

Zhenya silently listened to the soldiers' nervous chatter. The troops were tense, as always before boarding a potentially hostile vessel. He had no reason to share their anxiety, but his own nagging worries more than made up for it. He brought up the comm systems for the tenth time, trying to reach the Seventeen. It didn't respond. Zhenya hoped against hope that the ship suffered a major malfunction of its computer network, and the crew was just trapped inside. He suspected the truth was much worse. Meditation didn't help, and for once Zhenya was thankful for the powered suit's support - it hid his trembling knees from the soldiers.

The mining craft sat quietly on the rock's irregular surface.

'Esteemed captain, we're sitting tight,' reported Lowe. 'We're ready to cut through to the living quarters.'

'No need, squad leader,' replied Zhenya. 'The airlock will do fine.'

'Very well, esteemed captain,' acknowledged Lowe. 'You heard the captain, soldiers. Get ready to knock on the door.' Zhenya detected a hint of disappointment in her voice. Lowe was a soldier first and foremost, and she always looked forward to some action—even if the gung-ho approach was redundant and out of place.

The soldiers waited in silence as the airlock cycled. As soon as the hatch opened, Lowe released a dozen round scout drones, which immediately dispersed searching every nook and cranny of the mining ship, while the squad set up a defensive perimeter. Zhenya stepped onto the deck, followed by his charger drone. He watched the video footage and atmospheric sensor readings fed onto his HUD by the drones flurrying about.

'It seems the entire ship is empty,' reported Lowe as the soldiers took position on the main deck. 'No life forms, no active frequencies, nothing.'

The drones finished their run over the vessel, reporting no activity whatsoever and only the nominal power levels of a ship on standby. Zhenya observed footage from the squad's cameras as they confirmed the results, searching cabin by cabin. The entire crew was gone.

'They took the time to clean up the cabins and move the unpro-cessed mycoprotein tanks,' noticed Zhenya. 'Nothing points out to the ship being looted.'

'Agreed, esteemed captain,' replied Lowe. 'It would appear they left, except there are no signs of another craft landing here.'

'Check the lifepod bay. Make sure the jumper is gone.' Zhenya got out of the command suit. 'See, no pirates.'

Lowe shrugged. 'There could have been.'

'I almost wish there were,' admitted Zhenya. 'We would free Shao... The crew, and be done with it.'

'If wishes were credits, esteemed captain.'

'Then everyone would be rich,' he finished.

Lowe switched comms to her squad, leaving Zhenya alone with his thoughts. Empty corridors and decks of the mining vessel were aban-doned, but not in a rush. Someone took their time stripping the ship of any supplies but didn't salvage the electronics or half-full cargo hold, all the drones except for one were also in place, sitting in their charging racks. Where did everybody go? And why?

The squad comm window appeared again. Lowe's face expressed concern. 'Esteemed captain, the jumper craft is missing,' she reported. 'But there is something else.'

'What is it, squad leader?' urged Zhenya.

'It seems that the crew dug a hole under the ship,' replied Lowe bluntly.

Not knowing what to make of it, Zhenya headed towards the Seventeen's docking bay, under the living module's cap. Lowe and four soldiers gathered around a narrow well, dug into the ice of the asteroid floor. Zhenya's eyes hung on a single loader drone erratically spinning above the fissure. 'What's that one doing?' he asked.

Michaels, one of the security troopers, replied, 'It's been doing that since we came here, esteemed captain. It broadcasts gibberish, too. Seems broken.'

Zhenya nodded and faced the opening.

Lowe stood next to him, also looking down the dark, narrow tunnel. 'The ice sheet around the hole seems blasted open, but the tunnel itself is smooth, cut.'

'Interesting. Have you found anything else?'

'Yes, esteemed captain. We broke open the black box and accessed the surveillance logs.'

Zhenya nodded but didn't lift his eyes off the opening. It was hypnotic; he could almost understand the drone's fixation on it.

Lowe took the gesture as approval and continued. 'It seems the crew came here looking for something and found it in the opening. The vid feed is completely corrupted by magnetic interference, and the audio's pretty bad. We did get the gist of it, though. It seems they found an object and headed towards the Solar System, to corporate HQ.'

Zhenya looked at Lowe, surprised. 'Corporate HQ? How the hell do they plan on getting there in a jumper?'

'It seems they want to catch a ride on a hauler headed towards the Hellespont station.'

Lowe uploaded the recording, allowing Zhenya to listen to the footage. 'We're going back to the Jīnlóng, squad leader,' he said after the recording ended. 'There is nothing left for us here.'

'Should I prepare a statement for the board?' asked Lowe. 'Since your adjutant isn't here, and the chairpersons would love to hear the report from a witness.'

Zhenya nodded again and headed towards the shuttle. Mutiny and desertion of duty couldn't be hidden from the board, the breach of contract was too serious and the costs too great. Shao's insubordination and escape will put her career in jeopardy—unless the board never hears about it. 'Do that. It is a great shame the magnetic interference destroyed the surveillance feed.'

Lowe's eyes widened, and she opened her mouth to protest. 'Yes, sir, completely destroyed,' she said instead, seeing Zhenya's tortured expression. 'Unintelligible and corrupted. I'll purge the file immediately.'

'Such a great shame,' said Zhenya. 'Please inform Captain Powells that the Jīnlóng will head on an intercept course with the Incitatus post-haste. And please tell Edgar to keep it off the records.'

33

A bloody bubble drifted above the girl's still body. Her torso turned in a slow spin, face frozen in an expression of shock, eyes wide open. Milosh stood over her for what seemed like forever, nail gun still in his hand. Suddenly, another silhouette rushed through the airlock, speeding towards the body. Milosh raised the gun ready to fire, his honed reflexes instinctively following the new target before his conscious mind could make a decision.

'Woah, woah, woah, dude, stop!' cried a young man in a brown jumpsuit floating in through the hatch. Milosh registered sweat on his pale skin, panic in his eyes. 'Don't shoot, man, please!'

'Hands where I can see them,' he commanded, aiming between the two newcomers. The other person was also a young floater woman, maybe twenty-years-old, her brown jumpsuit staining with blood as she held the unmoving body in a desperate embrace. The girl's eyes cast a deep purple glow, illuminating her features, contorted in what must have been wailing; no sound came through the comms, however. Holy shit, I shot a kid, thought Milosh frantically. What are they even doing here?

'Yeah, yeah, yeah, man, got my hands up, see?' The boy complied, raising his hands. Panic made his voice high and squeaky.

'What have we got there, baws?' asked Spider, pushing himself off the ceiling to drift closer.

'Fuck if I know,' replied Milosh. 'They aren't prisoners, that's for sure.'

Otis emerged from behind his cover on the other side of the hatch. 'I suggest telling us who you are, boy,' he said, passing the two girls and putting his giant hand on the young man's shoulder.

'Yeah, yeah, yeah, just don't kill her... I mean us,' repeated the boy. 'I'm Lasse Toft, and these are Shao and Mai.'

'Great, that's a start,' said Pie. 'I'm Pie, the big guy's Otis, and the angry gorilla here is Milosh. He will kill you if you don't tell us what the fuck you're doing here. Capisce?'

'I might just kill you anyway,' growled Milosh, covering his confusion with aggression.

'We just stowed away for a few kliks; we didn't do anything, I swear,' replied Toft. 'We're just barnacles, man. Please let us help Shao. Mai, how is she?'

The girl moved her lips soundlessly inside the helmet, horror on her face, speaking through tears.

'Get your audio on,' said Pie, shaking his head.

'She's alive, but barely. Help her, you fucking bastards!'

'Why would we do that?' asked Milosh, training the nail gun at Mai. 'For all I care, you're just a small complication. Let's go, leave them to the drones.'

'You'd just leave them like that?' asked Otis, crossing his massive arms on his chest.

'Yes, I would. We gotta find Muldoon, get a hold of McNamarra, and find the comm room. No other way off this joint.'

'Um, we have a ship,' said Toft sheepishly. 'Help Shao; we'll make a deal.'

Milosh turned the gun's barrel at the young man's face, pushing it to the transparent faceplate. His cybernetically augmented arms strained. The boy's eyes focused on small cracks crawling on the helmet's surface as it slowly caved under the pressure.

'Or you can just tell me where your ship is so that I won't shoot you in the face,' he said slowly. He wasn't that keen on solving his problem with shooting—that's what got him into this mess in the first place.

Nonetheless, years of mercenary work taught him that the best way to deal with chaotic situations is to take control by force and worry later.

Toft's face grew even paler, he looked as if he's about to pass out, but he clenched his jaw and stood firmly. 'You shoot me, you never find the ship,' he said. 'Help Shao.'

'Come on, baws,' said Spider. 'We can call up Al from the infirmary. Don't be a dick.'

Milosh hesitated. The kids didn't seem like a threat, and there wasn't much point in antagonizing the Outer hacker. Without Spider, Milosh could kiss his escape goodbye anyway. 'Fine, grab her and let's go,' he said aloud. 'We'll patch her up; then, you tell us where your boat is.'

The stowaways took the wounded girl and followed Milosh and Spider out of the hangar bay through the ship's claustrophobic corridors. Otis lagged behind, making sure that the unexpected company didn't bolt. Pie's biodrone led the way to the nearest medical storage unit. The door was locked, but the floater girl quickly short-circuited the electronics and broke the seal. Too quickly, Milosh decided. The kids have been snooping around here before.

Mai and Toft carried Shao inside and worked to cut her free of her jumpsuit while Pie hacked and activated one of the medidrones stored in a charging rack. They placed the still unconscious Shao on the surgery table as soon as it unfolded.

The biodrone plugged into the medical robot's interface, and Pie input a set of commands through it. Multiple telescopic arms tipped with various tools and scanners protruded from the drone's boxy chassis located under the table. An opaque dome of the medical tent closed over her head. Scanner lights and quick bursts of laser light flashed through the plastic.

'Okay, your friend's taken care of,' he said frowning. 'Now, where's your ship?'

Toft and Mai quickly exchanged glances and turned to him. 'It's well hidden, but we'll take you to it when Shao gets better,' replied the girl, eyes turning to a pale, green glow.

'Fuck that noise, take us there now,' said Milosh, raising his nail gun.

'She's the only one who knows the launch codes,' interjected Toft quickly.

'You think I'm an idiot?'

'Kay, wait a minute,' said Otis, walking between Milosh and the kids, his hands raised. 'You aren't stalling, are you? Cause that's a terrible idea right now.'

Milosh didn't wait for an answer. 'Are there any more of you?'

'No, sir, just us,' quickly said Mai, eyes flashing repeatedly. 'We just want our friend to be okay, that's it.'

'One more question,' said Milosh. 'Have you seen an Outer without an eye and a ginger dude, Earther, walking like a soldier?'

Toft shook his head almost instantly, but Mai hesitated, and her eyes blinked in colors again.

They're lying, Milosh thought. But why?

'We gotta hit up Al anyway, and quick,' interjected Spider, worried. His gray skin was paler than usual—switching between neural interfaces, loss, and stress had taken their toll. The biodrone was plugged into the medical robot still and flashing with red, green, and blue lights under the semi-transparent dome.

'Why the hurry?' asked Milosh.

'Well, according to the network info, we'll be approaching Hellespont Waystation in less than seventy hours. If we don't catch a ride out of this junker by then, we're in for the long haul, comm station or not.'

'Sounds pretty arbitrary. What's the deal?' asked Otis.

'Well, it is. If we don't get outta here before we're out of reach, it's nothing but hundreds of AUs of the Great Beyond before we reach Heliopause. Decades of nothing except nothing and more nothing.'

'Just get the comms on, Pie,' said Milosh. He still held the young hostages at gunpoint, but his attention diverted towards the next problem already. 'Catch Al and get us some visual of the decks. Look for the comm station and our friends' ship too.'

'Good thinking, baws.'

Spider's drone left the medical table and plugged into a terminal on the wall. The console glitched, displaying a dizzying array of colors and numbers through the augmented reality. Despite that, Spider faded into the neural interface again, almond-shaped eyes oscillating under heavy eyelids.

A few seconds later, the holographic display on the wall opened, and a tridimensional map of the Incitatus shone with green lines, dotted by multicolored signatures moving rapidly.

'The blues are biodrones, I got them all under me now,' explained Pie. 'Straightforward system. They didn't think anyone was gonna try to fuck with it.'

'Or they just figured it doesn't matter if someone does.' Milosh shrugged. 'It's not like they thought we could get out of the ship.'

'What's with the other dots?' asked Otis.

'The greens are security drones, and reds are us, the prisoners. See those three over here? That's us in the medbay. The barnacles here aren't in the system.'

Otis leaned in, pointing at the intertwined groups of dots. 'I'll be damned, it looks like they're fighting.'

'Looks like we're winning, too,' noticed Milosh. 'The ship is ours.'

Red dots were grouped around the remaining greens on the main deck, and one by one, the security drones checked out and disappeared. Many crimson dots faded out as well, but they had superior numbers and simply overwhelmed the opposition. The prisoners watched the events playing out in silence, fascinated by the simplistic representation of the battle. Eventually, the last green dot in the room was extinguished, and the red dots dispersed through the decks chaotically.

Scavenging, Milosh thought. No discipline at all. 'Get me Al on the comms, Pie,' he commanded. 'There's no time to waste.'

'Sure thing, gimme a minute.'

Spider logged back into the mainframe, displaying the contents through augmented reality so that everyone could see. Milosh wasn't a computer expert, but even he noticed the onboard operating system really was simplistic. For sure, the Incitatus wasn't the most complex vessel in the Solar System.

A quick browse of available functions and drones near the vessel's main deck revealed the list of biodrones and cameras nearby. Many were destroyed and devastated, but the mutinous convicts couldn't possibly have found them all. It took a bit of searching, but Spider soon found a set of biodrones close enough to the leading group of prisoners and remote-controlled them closer. He ordered a group of six drones to form a circle and fly straight at the group.

The biodrone's squid eyes spotted McNamarra surrounded by a few of his Terran Brotherhood buddies. All were buff and many had cybernetic enhancements visible, despite their orange jumpsuits. Their attention turned from fighting the drones to engaging in a hit-and-run melee against an equally large gang of Outers. Other prisoners nearby kept their distance and approached the brawl with respect, if at all.

Milosh gauged the cantina with a trained eye. He noticed the entire main deck was devastated—dinner tables and chairs were ripped from the floors, apparently used as improvised weapons and protection. Most of the illumination was gone—lamps destroyed by autofire or blunt force. Over twenty dead and dying men were adrift through-out the deck, their bodies burned by electricity and ripped to shreds with security drones' autofire. The machines also took heavy losses—wreckage in various states of destruction littered the air, strung about and spiraling everywhere. Must have been a hell of a battle, Milosh thought. Glad I wasn't there for it.

There were many more green dots scattered throughout the ship. Milosh figured they're no threat for now. They'll be consolidating their force before striking back. Milosh wished Pie could take control of them as well, but the terminal he was using had no access to the drones' software. McNamarra noticed the approaching biodrone and swung a metal pipe at it.

Spider opened the channel on the craft's PA system. 'Yo, Al, buddy,' he started. 'Don't hurt my eyes and ears, man.'

McNamarra lowered the pipe, functioning magnetic boots they found somewhere held them on the ground among the floating wreckage.

Other convicts looked around in a panic, startled by the sudden voice from nowhere, but Spider ignored them. 'I see you got things under control here, eh?' asked Spider through the loudspeakers.

'You bet your ass I do,' replied McNamarra, grinning widely over the bushy black beard he grew in his time onboard the Incitatus. 'We took down all of those fuckers; the ship is ours.'

'Sure did,' agreed Pie, apparently deciding it was wiser to not mention the other gangs. 'We got out too, and we got access to the mainframe.'

'Sounds peachy. We'll get the weapon lockers open and head your way.'

'That's the plan... We have a bit of a complication, though.'

'Oh yeah?' asked McNamarra in surprise. 'Well, spill it.'

'I'd rather you see for yourself, mate.'

'Fair enough. Lemme just get a hold of the lads I sent to get the guns, and we'll head your way.'

One of the convicts joined McNamarra's group, bouncing and leaping in zero-g. His arm was bloodied, hair tied in dreadlocks floated wildly around his brown face.

'What the hell, Cortez?' McNamarra turned to him angrily. 'Where's the rest of the crew? The fuck's our guns at?'

'The Russians turned on us, Al,' answered Cortez, breathing heavily. 'Fuckers waited 'til we pried the emergency locker open and ganged up on us. They took out Scuzz and the rest, they got all the guns now.'

One of the Outers booed mockingly hearing that. A few inmates joined him.

'I'm glad you just announced it to everyone,' said McNamarra. 'Good thinking.' McNamarra's moved back to close ranks with his oner pals, but found no shelter in camaraderie. The inmates closed rank on the Brotherhood, improvised weapons poised to strike. One Brotherhood goon dropped his weapon and bolted to escape the closing circle, another two followed. Someone threw a chair into the group, and the Terran Brotherhood dispersed, leaving the stash of loot for the scavengers.

'Well, fuck,' Al stated stoically.

34

The augmented goon slammed his fist into the console with a curse, breaking it apart. Mai shuddered and instinctively looked at the whirring medical table, where the drone performed the surgery. All systems normal, Shao was safe. That's the important part. Trembling, Mai turned to Toft, but his presence was of little comfort. The bloodshed and the aggression completely broke him, and Toft was curled in a corner of the medbay. Mai's stomach twisted into a knot, but she held back the panic. Shao was defenseless and had nobody to keep her safe but Mai. She turned her attention to the captors, arguing among themselves. Maybe there's an angle she can play. Something. The skinny Outer with a tattooed face waved his hands desperately, pleadingly.

'No, baws, we have to go help.'

The large goon with a shaved head and a handlebar mustache shook his head. 'Forget it, Pie. I was on board taking McNamarra with us, but he's done and gone. He and his brotherhood of idiots made their bed, now they gotta sleep in it.'

'So what, you're gonna just let Al die? Die like Sticks?'

Mai didn't know who Sticks was, but the name didn't seem to make much of an impression on the goon. He crossed his arms in refusal, dark, metallic mesh peering through the wounds on his forearms.

'I said forget it. I'm not risking our lives on an off chance he's alive. You know damn well he wouldn't lift a finger to help you.'

A third prisoner, massively muscular Outer leaning back so far, joined the discussion, his voice surprisingly pleasant.

'That is without a doubt true, Milosh,' he started. 'The real question is, would you lift a finger if any of us was in peril? Cause right now I fuckin' doubt it.'

The goon, Milosh, threw his hands up in exasperation. 'Fine, Otis, you win. Let's go find McNamarra. Just don't cry if you get shanked. Pie, keep an eye on our birds.'

Milosh left with Otis, leaving them alone with the tattooed inmate. He looked away awkwardly when Mai met his gaze and focused on a squid biodrone.

'What's going to happen to us?' Mai asked quietly.

Pie shrugged without turning. 'I've no idea. I don't Milosh's gonna gank you if that's what you're asking.'

'He shot Shao.'

'Pretty sure it was an accident,' replied Pie, but there was no certainty in his voice.

Mai wanted to shake him and... She didn't know. Something. She had a hundred things to say, but words didn't come out.

'What are we going to do?' commed her Toft from his corner. Mai glanced at the Outer, but Pie didn't seem to realize they had a direct comm line open.

'Any ideas?' she replied.

'I... I don't know. We have to run.'

'And leave Shao?'

'No. I don't know. Mai, what are we going to do?'

Thoughts were racing through Mai's head. Toft was a wreck, he's not gonna be of much help, he was completely out of his depth. So am I, she thought, and didn't reply.

Milosh came back sometime later, his orange uniform torn and covered in blood. Mai didn't think it was his. Otis entered a moment later, followed by two newcomers—both oners, a wounded man with brown dreadlocks led by the other, almost as muscular as the giant Outer.

'You didn't tell me we have guests,' said the last one, eyeing Mai with hungry eyes.

'Leave them alone, McNamarra,' replied Milosh. 'They're just barnacles.'

McNamarra grinned in response. 'So what? Doesn't mean we can't have fun.'

Milosh stepped in between Mai and the goon. 'I said leave them the fuck alone.' The two men stared at each other until McNamarra folded and looked away. Mai felt irrationally grateful for a moment.

The wounded newcomer collapsed on the floor, getting the captors' attention.

'Put Cortez on the autodoc,' said McNamarra in a commanding tone.

'It's taken, Al,' said Pie. 'A barnacle chick is in there.'

'I don't care, toss the bitch out and put Cortez in.'

'He'll be fine,' replied Milosh. 'It's just blood loss, patch him up with a stim.'

'Is that how it is? You care more about some ass than your buddies, merc?'

'Cortez is not my buddy and neither are you, Allison,' said Milosh, spitting the name out like an insult. 'I saved your ass because of Pie, and that's it.'

'Baws, Al, come on,' interjected Pie. 'Give it a break, we already lost Sticks, and we're not out of the woods.'

Milosh stared McNamarra down. 'Pie's right. We need muscle to get to the comm station, you're muscle. Either help or get the fuck out of my way.'

'Fine, I'm with you. Doesn't mean I'm taking orders from you, merc.'

'Whatever. Now that it's settled we gotta get to the comm station.' Milosh glanced at Mai and Toft. She felt a cold shiver and slumped unwittingly.

'Pie, I need you and McNamarra with me,' continued Milosh. 'We'll take the girl with us, so she doesn't try anything. Otis, stay with Cortez and the one in the autodoc. Lock the door.'

Mai noticed Milosh didn't mention Toft, who remained curled and trembling—he probably doesn't consider him enough of a threat to bother watching. She didn't have time to consider it, as McNamarra lifted her by the neck and shoved brutally out of the medbay. Mai struggled to get free. McNamarra's fist came out of nowhere, hitting her in the side of the head. The lights dimmed, pain exploding like a supernova inside Mai's skull.

She came to momentarily, gagging and vomiting. Her skull seemed to be made of sharp glass, knees weirdly weak. She felt a sharp tug and her body slumped against the wall.

'Jesus, the bitch barfed on me,' she heard McNamarra's voice through the ringing in her ear.

'Shoulda thought about it before you knocked her out,' replied Milosh from somewhere unseen. 'Maybe you wouldn't have to carry her. Wipe yourself and pick her up.'

Mai struggled to get up and run, away from the inmates and back to Shao. Where is Shao, she thought frantically. Where am I? The corridor was dark, lights blinking online sporadically only to spazz out again with a flash. Mai thought she saw a movement behind them, but before she got a chance to look closer strong arms lifted her up and she stared right into McNamarra's furious face.

'You walk now, birdie, get it? And please, try running again, make my day.'

The inmate shoved her onward, and she followed, watching Pie and Milosh float ahead in the corridor—only she and McNamarra had magboots. They turned a corner, walking right into a group of half a dozen other inmates: all lean, but muscular floaters in orange jumpsuits doing little to hide cybernetic augmentations. They were busy taking apart a group of some sort of drones, Mai wasn't sure. Milosh said something to them in a commanding tone, but it didn't seem to have much of an effect—one of the inmates, maybe their leader, chuckled menacingly.

Only a fragment of the conversation reached Mai's still ringing ears: 'Make me, Earther.'

Mai wouldn't believe someone can move so fast if she hasn't seen it. Milosh pounced forward like a hungry predator, kicking and firing the nail gun before the others had a chance to react. Blood burst from their wounds. Two inmates flew to the sides like ragdolls, the others jumped Milosh without hesitation. Mai thought she saw metallic gleams in their hands—knives. She glanced at McNamarra, expecting him to go aid the merc—but he just stood there, calculating smirk on his face. Another convict slammed into the deck, his leg sticking out at a weird angle. The remaining gangers fled, bouncing off the walls as they floated down the corridor. Milosh returned a moment later, fresh cuts and bruisers marking his face.

'Thanks for the help, Al,' he said.

McNamarra grinned widely, baring his discolored teeth like a snarling animal. 'Anytime, friend.'

Mai was pushed onward and they resumed the journey through the labyrinth of decks as before, though she noticed McNamarra's gait changed, became more cautious. He underestimated the mercenary, she thought. Now he's planning something. Whatever it was, couldn't be good for her and Shao—at the moment, Milosh was the only thing standing between them and McNamarra. The thought of that changing made her shudder and almost fall when the bruiser shoved her onward.

Half-stunned Mai stumbled and the grueling road began anew. Her face ached, with the dull pain of a broken tooth and a slowly swelling cheek. Mai tried bringing Toft back into the comms but didn't have much luck. Something glitched in the comms, interfering with the feed; she got nothing except white noise filled with incoherent gibberish. Neither could she get any hold of Green—he was just behind them when Shao was shot; what the hell happened to him?

'Can you open it?' she heard Milosh ask just as McNamarra shoved her back, stopping her from bumping into the merc ahead. They reached a reinforced hatch of some sort.

Pie nodded and stepped forward, his biodrone pet attached a segmented arm to a magnetic lock. 'Don't worry about it, baws.'

'At least nobody got here before us,' noticed McNamarra. 'Would be a shame if someone looted the station.'

'Here, it's open.' Pie's drone disconnected, and the hatch slid open with a quiet hiss. A rush of decompressing air hit Mai's face, carrying with it the plastic stench of a stale server room air conditioning. It felt weirdly comforting, reminding Mai of Titan's Crown and the time spent fixing NaviNet relays and components. The station's maintenance terminal smelled the same as the comm array on the barge.

Mai's thoughts drifted away back to the good times. Back to the first time she met Shao, all fluttered and happy with her new jumper and wanting to spruce it up for racing. Mai thought about their work together, about fixing the Sōngshǔ up and boosting the engines, about Titan's dark-green surface slowly turning under them. About the first time...

'Gods damn it!' Milosh's harsh voice ruptured Mai's seconds of comforting memories. She tried to focus on what he was saying over the ringing in her ears.

'Nothing I can do, baws,' apologized Pie, connected to a dark terminal. 'It's screwed up, some sort of interference. And it got the drone all weird, too.' Mai followed the Outer's gesture—the squid biodrone looked stunned, its tentacles dancing on the deck.

'We need this to work, Pie,' insisted Milosh. His face flared with anger, he looked about ready to punch the Outer. This might be it, the chance, Mai thought. Her throat convulsed as she struggled to utter words through the suddenly dry lips.

'I can fix it,' she managed a hoarse whisper. She repeated it louder. The three arguing convicts fell silent and turned to her.

'What did you say?' asked Milosh. Mai shrunk into her suit, wishing she never opened her mouth.

'I can fix it... If you promise you won't hurt Shao,' she said, trembling. 'And won't leave us here.'

McNamarra frowned, punching into his open hand. 'Fuck that. Fix it, or I'll bash your brains out.'

'And then who's gonna do it?' she replied.

Milosh nodded. 'Fine. Fix the comms, and I'll make sure nobody's gonna touch Shao or you. You hear me, McNamarra?'

'Yeah, whatever.'

Mai approached the dark terminal. She reached for a cap in her wrist, pulling the full sensory interface cable from its port. Connecting to the machine was like stepping into a cool waterfall. The pain and exhaustion washed away in an instant, leaving only the data.

The Incitatus' rudimentary computer system wasn't designed for FSI connection and didn't provide sensory input except for audio. And yet the chaotic mess felt like hundreds of fingers, probing, pushing on her mind. Something was severely wrong with the network—the usually clear strings of code were distorted into three-dimensional geometric patterns. Math crystals, thought Mai, making herself chuckle. She hoped the laugh didn't translate into her body in the meatspace. If it did, the convicts might think she's screwing with them.

Right, the convicts. The code was all screwed up as if a complete amateur tried to re-write. It asynchronously looped on itself, distorting the commands and subroutines, causing them to crash and reboot. No wonder everything on this ship glitches, she thought. She brought up the system backlog—it seemed the error was a recent development. Maybe one of the inmates tried to hack it. Restoring the backup wouldn't do any good, it'd take too much time. She could teach the computers to work with the glitch instead. The distorted code proved to be very adaptable—as soon as she started optimizing the network to read the code, a cascade of feedback rushed through the system. It's fixing itself, realized Mai. In a split second, she saw the entire network clear as day.

The cameras showed rioting prisoners taking out the remaining security drones. Suddenly the machines consolidated their efforts, working in unison across the decks to isolate and eliminate the mutineers. Doors closed, cutting off the prisoners' escape and splitting large mobs into parts. Lights shut off to blind them. The disorganized defense shifted into meticulously precise counteraction in an instant. The Incitatus fought back.

Mai scrolled through the available options—life support, medbays, drones, and maintenance, even the previously separate security drone sub-network fell in line with the distorted code. Even the Sōngshǔ. Mai tried redirecting the security drones to take out the prisoners in the medbay and the comm array, but she couldn't get the system to accept a command—well, the network *accepted* it, but didn't respond. Maybe it's for the best, she thought. I wouldn't want them to frag Shao. Or Toft.

She brought up the comm array and scanned the area—she found the Hellespont Waystation beacon shining like a star among smaller dots—other ships, mostly private freighters. A few had transponders running in hidden mode, but the array detected them without issue—the broken code caused their comms to malfunction as the heavy string of data hit them. Mai browsed quickly through the IFF signal details. She didn't know to whom belonged the corvette marked as the Querub and didn't want to interact with the hidden PAC Navy fleet scanning the subsector. What got her attention was a clear ID signal of a Zheng-dao frigate docked to the Hellespont. Holding her breath, she sent an emergency signal to the Jīnlóng. Now, all she could do was hope they receive it.

Mai disconnected from the comm array system, pain returning threefold, causing her to slump on the floor.

'Did you get it?' asked Milosh insistently. Mai couldn't bring herself to move. Fortunately, she didn't have to.

'Yeah, she got it online,' said Pie, logging in. 'It's weird, but it works.'

'Good. Signal the Querub.'

35

Lederman took the last puff of smoke from his narcostick and put it out in the tray.

'That shit'll kill you, you know?' said Captain Pam from the cell. Lederman gave her an unsympathetic look. She sat on a metal bench, her orange prison jumpsuit unzipped to the waist. Underneath, she wore a white tank top, showing off fluorescent arm tattoos snaking about in a psychedelic pattern. 'I'm serious,' she added. 'They're banned for a reason, you know.'

'Like you care about the law, scum,' replied Lederman.

'Hey, watch that potty mouth, you don't want your scout license revoked.'

'And what about you, warning me of the dangers of smoking? Gonna start selling cookies now?'

'I just care about your health, is all.' She grinned.

'Oh, shut up.'

They arrived at Helikaon station a few sols ago, immediately placing Dassler in the station's medical facilities. Much to Lederman's chagrin, they were stuck in the dock ever since, as the Europa suffered significant damage in the altercation with the pirate freighter and wasn't fit to fly. Suspecting the station's manager had a hand in tipping Pam off about their approach, Lederman tried to get a hold of the Ranger station. He made no progress in organizing transport out of the station.

The brig door slid open, letting in Tomasson accompanied by Matthews wearing slacks and sandals, beer can in his hand.

'The station manager is here, cap,' she said, shoving her companion forward gently. Her expression didn't betray much, but Lederman knew her well enough to be certain she shared his suspicion.

'Hi, there, Mister Lederman, good to see you again,' said Matthews, reaching out to shake hands. Lederman left him hanging, and eventually, Matthews dropped his palm awkwardly. 'Right, sorry I couldn't see you sooner,' he uttered. 'Been busy and all.'

'Whatever. Did you get in touch with central?' asked Lederman.

'Yeah, see there's a problem... We didn't get a confirmation yet from Ranger HQ on Pluto see... So we can't really... Ah... Give you an emergency transfer.'

Lederman calmly reached for his pocket printer producing another narcostick and lit it. Matthews was stalling, no doubt about it. Lederman fought to resist the urge to knock the station manager's teeth out. 'You don't need confirmation, imbecile,' he said, slowly and deliberately. 'We showed you our certificate, just give us a ship.'

'Yeah, man, stop being a dick!' shouted Captain Pam from her cell. 'The man can't stress like that; it's unhealthy!'

'Would you just shut the hell up?' snapped Lederman.

Pam laughed, clapping her knees. 'See? He's a bucket of nerves, give him a break!'

'Cut the crap, Pam,' Tomasson scolded. 'Mister Matthews... Dan, we really need to get moving. Give us the go-ahead, and we're history.'

'The name's Dave. And as I said,' replied Matthews. 'I can't let a damaged ship through the hoop, and I don't have a temp to lend you. Not without the emergency request confirmation from Pluto.'

'We're transporting a goddamn criminal, you idiot!' yelled Lederman. 'Who knows how many contacts she has in the sector!'

'I resent that accusation,' said Pam. 'I'm a political prisoner!'

'You're a goddamn pirate!'

'Poteito, potahto.'

'Time is of the essence, boy.' Lederman ignored the prisoner and turned towards Matthews again. 'The longer we stay in the sector, the more at risk we are.'

'I get it, captain, but I can't let your ship out with a damaged sail, and I can't give you a ship.' He shrugged. 'Won't be no good to anyone if you get lost in space, would it? Besides, you don't think the pirate has cronies on the waystation, do you?'

'We're not suggesting anything like that,' said Tomasson reassuringly. 'But we do need to get a move on.'

'That's exactly what I'm suggesting,' growled Lederman. 'They knew we were coming for them, and I sure as hell didn't send them a memo!' Even if Matthews didn't warn Pam of the incoming Rangers, he knew who did, Lederman was sure of it.

'I guess I can check the departure schedule, and you can talk with the freighter crews, see if they'll take you along.'

'Please do,' said Tomasson at the same time as Lederman growled: 'Get on it!'

Matthews unrolled a tablet from his wrist and pressed a few buttons. Shortlist of ship names shone on the plastic surface. Matthews pushed it in front of the Lederman's face. Lederman felt his annoyance grow—only two ships leaving within the next forty hours. 'So yeah, there's the Flamingo, but they're headed deeper into the Cloud, and then you have the Scallywag headed for Pluto shipyard for refitting. I could ask the captain if he'd take you along?'

'I love the name. Can we go on the Scallywag, oh captain, my captain?' asked Pam excitedly, clapping her hands.

Lederman was tempted to say no just out of spite, but he was sure that's just what the pirate really wanted. Annoy him enough to stay, and give Matthews and her cronies the time to hit the Rangers and free her. 'Sure, why not. I'll go talk to their captain.' He shrugged. 'It's that Silver fellow, was it? Tomasson, stay with the prisoner.'

'Yes, sir,' saluted Lara. 'Now, don't give me any crap, Pam, or I'll tranq you.'

Pam touched her chest in feigned shock and offense. 'Me? I would never.'

The hatch slid shut behind him, and Lederman didn't hear his officer's response.

Matthews led him through the station's corridors and elevator system towards the hangar bays. The station's inner decks were clean and well maintained—unlike the commercial modules. Though they could use some repairs, he noticed. The paint job was lousy on some decks, and the lighting had seen better days—some lamps were flickering, others were utterly dead, drowning the decks in shade and darkness. Lederman and Matthews crossed the mostly empty habitation modules, hundreds of rows of barren locales, lights out in most of the windows.

Only a few residents loitered about, mostly Outers in civilian clothing, jeans, t-shirts, lumberjack jackets, and sweatpants. Some mothers watched their kids chase a ball on the main deck, a couple of elderly retired space jockeys sitting on a bench were passing a bottle of amber liquid. Now and again they passed a drone slowly going about its business cleaning the decks or patching up some damage. Plasma torches glowed bright blue, surrounded by lights flickering red and yellow to warn the pedestrians away. Mixed groups of Earther and Outer kids amused themselves throwing rocks at robots or spray-painting obscenities on their chassis.

They took a ride in one of the many shuttles without having to wait in a queue. Lederman stared Matthews down without a word, too angry to break the uncomfortable silence. Matthews didn't seem like a traitor, just a slacker in a shitty job in the middle of nowhere. Lederman fought to resist the temptation to break his nose. After less than half an hour, they emerged into the outer ring, with all of its commotion and dirt.

The sound of electro-country mixed with other music coming from a few streets further away, and a change in the crowd let Lederman know they were near the hangar bay section of the outer ring.

"Happy Hour Harbor," said the neon hologram displaying a repeated animation of an ancient galleon sailing in a whiskey bottle. The mixed stench of booze, cigarette smoke, hallucinogenic drugs, and sweat stunned Lederman like a blow with a hammer. The establishment was dimly lit, visibility made even worse by the clouds of faux fog. A scantily-clad Outer girl with fluid, fluorescent tattoos danced on a small stage, the only well-lit element of the hall. Her chromatattoos snaked about, accenting her body as she danced. She was pretty good, judged Lederman. The few clients didn't pay much attention to the dancer, however, busy with their bottles and their worries.

Matthews led them past the stage and into an alcove, where a dark-skinned man in a cowboy hat waited with a bottle of rum and three cups. Lederman recognized the guy. Silver—another crooked lowlife, the same who sold them the intel on Pam's whereabouts. Lederman considered warning him about Matthew's double-cross, but there wasn't much point. Smugglers are used to dealing with criminals, and Pam's going away for a long time. When they approached the table, Silver wiped his narrow mustache with the back of his palm and stood to greet the guests. 'Morning, friends,' he said with a thick accent. 'Good to see you again, Policeman. Mister Matthews tells me you need a good transport outta the sector, no?'

'Yes, Mister Silver, we need to transport a dangerous prisoner to Pluto,' replied Lederman, sitting down. 'Unfortunately, our own craft has sustained damage, and we can't requisition a temp, according to Mister Matthews here.'

'Diagnostics don't lie, Captain Lederman,' stated Matthews matter-of-factly. 'Your sail is busted, not our fault.'

'Be that as it may, we need to rent a freight to the Ranger station, and I hear you're going that way?'

'So you want to rent this here sailor's ship for your escapade? The Scallywag is the bes' damn boat this side of the macarena galaxy. We ain't cheap. And we already have a passenger.'

Lederman sighed. 'I am aware of that, yes. Ranger Central is going to reimburse the costs, I'm sure.'

John Silver smiled broadly. 'Let's get to business then. I'm sure the good Mister Redding won't mind.'

Lederman pricked his ears, not surprised in the least in a sudden change of tone. Silver kept up too many appearances for someone who was just a simple freighter captain. His behavior only assured him the man was a smuggler. Not my problem, he thought.

'I may take passengers on board,' continued Silver. 'But the Scally-wag is a small boat, it has room and supplies for ten people. My crew counts five heads, plus the passenger. I can't be takin' any firin' squads aboard, see?'

'That's understandable.' Lederman nodded. 'In that case, you can count three passengers—me, my officer, and the prisoner. The rest of my crew can follow us in a few days when our ship is fixed.' Lederman noticed Matthew's expression but didn't think to come forth with information. Silver didn't need to know Dassler is in no condition to go anywhere for weeks.

'Sounds good to me, captain, as long as you won't disturb our guest. Let's talk cred, then.'

'There's nothing to talk about, just write us a bill, and Ranger HQ will cover it.'

Captain Silver grinned widely and greedily like a shark. His chromed and gilded teeth shone in the dim light of the alcove. 'Your words are music to my ears, friend,' he said. 'Head to dock seventeen whenever you're ready. My crew and I will await you with open arms.'

'Then we have a deal, captain,' announced Lederman, getting up. 'I'll head right back to the brig and get us packing. We don't want to delay your endeavor. Which is what, if I may ask?'

'The Scallywag carries good Mister Redding to Pluto, friend. Along with some ice in the cargo 'old along for the ride. Can't afford empty trips, you know how it is.'

'I'd think they have plenty of ice down at Pluto.'

'Ah well, who am I to tell people what to buy?' said Silver apologetically, spreading his arms. Multiple silvery rings and chains on his fingers and forearms sounded quietly as he did so. 'It's such a shame you can't stay for a drink, friend.'

You can smuggle a freaking Loch Ness monster for all I care, thought Lederman. 'Sadly, I don't drink. Are you coming along, Mister Matthews?'

'I'll stay awhile and have a drink with the good captain, don't want to cause offense.'

'Suit yourself,' said Lederman and left the bar, immediately adjusting to his "policeman strut" once more, taking note of people and events around him in a slide show. Seemingly casual, his mind was entirely focused on the surrounding area.

On the way back to the station's holding cells, he sent directives to Van Alst and Tomasson, ordering them to get the prisoner ready for transfer. He brought up Silver on his HUD to confirm the departure time and the Scallywag's bay number.

Tomasson and the drone carrying the prisoner in an opaque cabin met them halfway; together, they headed towards the rented vessel, civilians and criminals alike parting before them.

Before they reached the hangar bays, however, Lederman's HUD brightened with an incoming transmission icon from the Europa. Lederman responded in a text message. 'Talk to me, Fabian.'

'We received an emergency broadcast, sir,' transmitted the pilot.

Lederman almost smiled. 'Our papers from Pluto. Finally.'

'Sorry, captain, but no such luck. It's a relay comm from central, an emergency call.'

'Bummer, but what does that have to do with us?' Lederman shrugged involuntarily, causing Tomasson, who didn't hear the conversation to raise an eyebrow.

'The message was bounced through the central station, but the emergency is here in Sector D. We're apparently the only squad that can react in time. There's a mass cargo freighter on a slow haul to the System in trouble. Apparently, the prisoners Martins sold off ended up there, and now the contact is lost.'

'So what? Who gives a damn?' messaged Lederman. 'Those things have no drive; they aren't going anywhere.'

'Yup, I read you. But the owner is on the line, and Martins wants us to check it out. Get it under control if there's a breakout.'

'I don't give a shit what he wants; we can't just leave our prisoner here!'

'It's a direct order from the brass. The owner, this Delacroix woman? She's breathing down Martins's neck and he doesn't want any shit getting traced back to him,' said Van Alst. 'We may not like it, but we gotta go give it a look. Here are the coordinates.'

'Jesus fucking Christ, what else?' said Lederman out loud, gaining a startled look from a passerby.

'What's up, cap?' asked Lara.

'We gotta go take a look at a barge full of rocks and prisoners, falling towards the System a second before it falls in the void, why do you ask?' said Lederman sarcastically.

Before Tomasson could reply, Silver emerged from the crowd, escorted by two short zeroes in mismatched armor. 'I thought I'd do my good deed for the day and stop by to back you up, policeman friend,' he said cordially. 'We wouldn't want your dastardly prisoner to bounce, right?'

'I'm glad you did,' replied Lederman. 'Not only because I appreciate the gesture.'

'Ah, you decided to grab a drink with me afta' all?' smiled Silver and almost immediately found a flat cantine in his coat pocket.

Lederman shook his head. 'We'll have time for that later. I do need to ask you for one more favor, for now.'

Silver shrugged and took a swig from the canteen anyway.

Lederman gave him a stern stare. 'Captain Silver,' he said frankly. 'I'm afraid I must ask if you'd be willing to adjust the course for us?'

Silver immediately protested, forgetting about the dialect. 'It's not possible, my boat only takes so many supplies...'

'I understand, but it's an emergency.'

'Even bigger emergency? Hoo, busy day you got there!'

'So it would seem,' agreed Lederman. 'I must insist however that you'd be so kind and make a short jump within the sector. Central will, of course, reimburse and reward you for the aid given to Rangers.'

'Reward you say, captain? That sounds more agreeable. The Scally-wag can be at your disposal within an hour, as long as we return to the station to resupply before resuming our journey.'

'Perfect,' replied Lederman. If Martins wants us to run around like dogs, he thought, at least he'll have to pay for it.

36

Green relived the same moment over and over. Every time he closed his eyes, he watched the convicts drag his friends to the infirmary from a hole behind the pipes. He wanted to jump in and help. Rescue them. Instead, he hid behind a hydraulics junction, curled in the darkness until everything went quiet. He saw the trail of blood twirling in the corridors after they left, and was beside himself with fear and panic. The convicts took Toft and Mai hostage, and Shao was dead. Shao. Dead.

He disconnected the cord linking him to the Sōngshǔ's systems, kicked the chair away, and got up, drifting into the middle of the cabin. Green hid his face in his hands and let out a dimmed howl like a wounded animal, rotating in the small space.

Eventually, he got a hold of himself and pushed off the ceiling back into the command chair. 'Think, fool,' he said to himself. 'What are your options?'

He looked around the cabin. Half a dozen chairs behind him, four inertia gel tanks in the back stacked one on another. All were empty except the one holding the mummy. He moved towards it, opened the silvery casket. Nothing looked like a weapon to him. The shriveled corpse was naked, dried skin stretched on fragile-looking bones. Maybe he could trade it for his friends? He rejected the idea. The mutineers had no use for the corpse, and if they did, they could just take it from him.

What else was there? Control panels, spare jumpsuits, some tools, comm systems, and drives. Nothing useful. Green's thoughts scattered as he tried to figure out what to do. Murderous thugs took his friends, and there was nothing he could do.

Why didn't the corporate officer training prepare him for that? Why didn't the ship have any weapons besides the standard point defense systems? What was he supposed to do, fly the Sōngshǔ into the hauler? Why was the barge so poorly equipped to deal with takeover situations, he asked himself over and over.

But he knew the answer. Zhengdao didn't arm the haulers because it didn't matter if some barnacles stowed away. The barge will arrive at its destination, and nothing could change that. Sure, someone can jump onto the barge and steal some materials, but how are they gonna leave the Great Beyond without a waystation? Pirates aren't known for having access to high-tech drives and buoys.

Green didn't have the training for combat. Normally, their best chance of survival in case of a pirate takeover was to call for backup and cooperate with the hostiles. That is what Mai and Toft were doing, following the protocol and cooperating with the convicts so that they wouldn't get killed... Like Shao... Who was dead...

Green fought off another panic attack before he lost it again. Hot tears poured around his face, and he shook them off. Mai and Toft followed the procedures, cooperated, and bought time, but what could he do? He'd make for a poor excuse of a rescue party; the convicts would overpower him with ease. Maybe someone else then? Sōngshǔ had comms, and they didn't yet reach the Great Beyond—that means the hauler will still pass by the last waystation, the Hellespont. After all, that is where Shao planned for them to jump the ship. They still can.

Green grabbed the cable floating nearby and plugged himself back in the ship's interface. He felt an unexpected jolt of electricity burn his temple when the plug touched his implanted adapter port. The interface displayed before his eyes normally, so he ignored the glitch and brought up the comm systems.

He activated the jumper's comm array, scanning the void for transponder signals. It was a long shot, but maybe he could at least find a buoy to relay his call for help?

The Sōngshǔ's laser array expanded in the rear of the ship and sent hundreds of short microwave laser bursts in a wide arc. Chances of catching a return signal were small, but Green set the maximum power output to the array and hoped for the best.

A weak return signal less than a second after the ladar pulse caused Green to jump in his seat. He ran a scan again, trying to locate it.

'What?' he whispered. 'It's coming from inside the barge? How...'

The computer reported that the scan was received and bounced by the Sōngshǔ itself before being rerouted to another system. Green figured it's some kind of glitch, but diagnostics showed no malfunctions and no other receivers in the ship's chassis.

'Great, perfect bloody timing,' he muttered to himself and gave the panel a good smack. Another jolt of electricity hit Green's temples, and the entire HUD turned into a mess of pixels. The interface cleared up after a moment, and Green resent the signal. This time the comms got return signals from the Hellespont Waystation a couple of million klicks ahead of the Incitatus, and much to Green's surprise, a fleet signal bearing the codes of the Zhengdao corporation.

Before Green thought to stop it, the Sōngshǔ automatically sent a greeting signal to the corporate fleet and received a return message a few minutes later.

The ship identified itself as the Jīnlóng, a Zhengdao Defence Force interception frigate, and it was heading right at them. Green suppressed the third outburst of fear breathing fast into joined hands. He forced himself to stay calm and focus, weighing his options. The frigate was headed for the Incitatus and would reach it within a few days, regardless of what he did. There was on off-chance that the Sōngshǔ's signal went unnoticed, but the Jīnlóng surely had better sensor arrays than the small jumper craft.

In any case, whatever reprimand he would receive from the corporate court beats seeing Toft and Mai murdered, like the prisoners murdered Shao. Green sighed heavily and opened the channel. 'This is the Sōngshǔ, hailing the Jīnlóng,' he said. 'This is an emergency distress call; please respond.'

'Sōngshǔ, this is Captain Yuan Zhenya. I was just about to hail you, Mister Green. I take it your little escapade has fallen into ill luck?'

Green hesitated, hearing the one voice he prayed not to. 'I guess so, esteemed captain,' replied Green, swallowing hard. 'This whole thing was a mistake. I admit and surrender to your authority.'

'Of course. I take it you got bored of sitting on the hauler and will come quietly? Be so kind and tell Shao I want to speak with her.'

'Captain... Shao and the rest have been taken captive—'

The reply didn't come, and the connection was broken. A couple of minutes passed, leaving Green staring at his HUD in astounded silence. He had not expected Zhenya to just hang up on him like that. Gloating, punishment, and threats of repercussion, sure, but not that. An incoming message made him jump in his chair. Green looked at the new comm confused. It was coming from the frigate, but on a different, coded, frequency.

'Taken captive by whom?' growled Zhenya as soon as the line was established. 'If one hair falls from my daughter's head, I'll skin you alive!'

'Esteemed captain, please listen,' replied Green. 'The convicts took over the hauler. They have the rest... They have Shao—'

'What convicts? What the hell are you talking about, moron?'

'The ones on the ship, sir?'

'She didn't... That bitch... But of course, she did, how else would she get the cred...'

'I don't understand, esteemed commander?'

'Don't *esteem* me, you idiot. This is a private channel. Tell me everything. Is Shao alright?'

'She's wounded, maybe... Maybe dead.'

'Stop crying, you pathetic coward, and speak!'

'They went scavenging for supplies because the computers on Sōng-shǔ fritzed, and we needed them to... To be able to tell when to jump ship. So we could hit the Hellespont and disappear with...'

'Disappear with what? Never mind that, tell me where they are now.'

Green sent the scan map of the Incitatus to Zhenya, marking the emergency medbay's location where his friends were kept. Zhenya cut the comms as soon as the upload was completed, and Green was left in silence. He unplugged himself from the jumper craft's systems and opened his eyes when the HUD disappeared into afterglows obscuring the cabin in splashes of light. He wiped his eyes with the back of his palm, getting rid of the sweat and tears, and blinked a few times. His vision cleared.

A couple of centimeters away from his face floated a biodrone, staring at him with its cold, cybernetic eyes.

37

'ut I told you, Shao is the only person who has the access codes,
and we can't go until she's up and running,' replied Mai, raising
from her usual seat by the medical drone, watching over Shao inside
the surgery dome.

'With all due respect,' interrupted Milosh, clearly meaning no respect at all. 'If we don't get outta here, we'll be out beyond the point of
no return. No comms, no rescue, nothing.'

'We won't need rescue, we can all leave on our ship and go our own
way, no harm, no foul,' said Toft somewhat sheepishly. He recovered
somewhat from his stupor, but still trembled whenever any of the
convicts looked at him.

'We tried your way, boss,' added McNamarra mockingly. 'We sent
the signal, and look how much that gave us.'

'We're not close enough for the Querub to pick us up before we
drop out of waystation range, true,' replied Milosh calmly. That calm
terrified Mai more than his outburst of anger a few days ago. 'But if we
move to the jumper and hop off, they'll be able to intercept.

'But we can't move the girl yet...' started Otis, looking at the drone's
display.

'The hell we can't,' interrupted Milosh. 'Hit her with a stim and drag
her ass to the ship. Hold on the transponder codes, Pie, and let's move.'

'Aye, Pie. Hold on to them, we'll get a nice little split of nothing
after Stepan's friends come rescue us,' said McNamarra.

'Give me a break, Al,' sighed Milosh. 'We've been over this. Hussars can haul this entire tin can away, and we can split the loot evenly.'

'Sure we can,' agreed McNamarra. 'Your buddies in corvettes and raiders armed toes to tits will split with us fiddy-fiddy. Fair and square.'

'That's right. Now pack a stimpack in that lass, and let's go.'

'Whatever you say, boss,' McNamarra got up and started rummaging through the shelves looking for a medkit.

'But... Shao can't be moved, she'll bleed out. You promised,' protested Mai, standing in front of the medical drone.

Milosh shoved her aside. 'I promised I won't let anyone touch you, and kept my word. If your friend bleeds out, then she'll bleed out,' he said. 'She's as good as dead if she stays here. Or would you rather we leave her with Al's pals?'

The girl shot a glance at McNamarra. Most of his lackeys were gone, and Cortez wasn't in the medbay with them, but she remembered their hungry stares well. The thought of staying on the barge with the convicts even worse than these two curdled her blood. How long were the inmates isolated? Too long, she thought.

'Stop scaring her,' interjected Otis and turned to Mai. 'We'll put your friend in a tightsuit, and keep an eye on her. Once on your ship, she'll be plugged in a medbay right quick.'

'It's not like you have a say in the matter,' said McNamarra. 'You can stay if you wanna. Maybe I'll even stay to keep you company for a while.'

Mai crumbled under the weight of the pirate's dark stare, her conviction falling apart. Her eyes turned pale yellow, and she hung her head down in defeat.

'That's a good girl,' said McNamarra, approaching the drone with a medkit.

Without a word, Spider gave the dome a quick set of commands, and it opened with a hiss.

Shao was stretched naked on the bedding, connected to dozens of cables and IVs pumping the oxygen and fluids through her body.

The gaping wound in her stomach was closed and sealed with a few hundred stitches, but she was still unconscious. The drone initiated a disconnect procedure, and the tubes slid out of her orifices back into the machine.

Mai grabbed a blanket and covered Shao quickly, staring down the inmates with eyes glowing a furious crimson. Grinning McNamarra gave her a mocking curtsy. Toft made a move as if he wanted to join his friend, but Pie sat him down forcefully.

'Fuck off, Allison,' blurted Milosh and stood between the women and the rest of the inmates. 'Get your shit together or I shove that grin up your ass.'

McNamarra averted his eyes eventually and stepped back. 'I bet you'd like to,' he muttered. 'There'll be shoving aplenty once we're out of this hole.'

'Help your friend get dressed,' commanded Milosh. 'The gang and I will be waiting outside.'

One by one, the inmates left the medbay, taking Toft with them. Left alone with the still unconscious Shao, Mai let out a long sigh. She waited in silence.

After what seemed like an eternity, Shao gasped for air and opened her eyes.

'Shh-sh, it's okay, it's okay,' whispered Mai, hugging her gently.

'W-what? My head's killing me. What happened?' asked Shao weakly. 'I can't see anything... Why is it so dark?'

'You were out for a few days; it's normal.'

'What happened? Did we have an accident?'

'What's the last thing you remember?'

'We were going to the bay to clean up Toft's screw-up. So the drones don't find us?'

'Yeah, so about that. You got shot in the gut with a nail gun and almost died.'

Shao blinked in surprise. 'Wow, thanks for letting me down easy.'

She got dressed carefully with Mai's help, putting on the medical nanoweb over her wound and then donning an orange inmate jumpsuit from the shelf. The suit adjusted its size with a quiet hiss. Mai replaced the suit's sedative load with painkillers and meds, and a few seconds later, the pain in Shaos eyes gave way to numbness.

'So yeah, that's not the end of the good news.'

'Oh, great.'

'I'm serious, Shao. We're in deep shit. The guys who shot you are mutineers, pirates, and we're gonna have to take them on board of the Sōngshǔ or they'll kill us.'

'Please tell me you're joking.'

'She's not joking, lass,' said Milosh, opening the door and entering the medbay, nail gun in hand. 'I see you're dressed, so let's get moving.'

Shao froze instantly, shock and fear clearly visible on her face.

'Yeah, yeah, princess, get over it,' said Milosh. He made a motion with his weapon's barrel, prompting the women out of the medbay.

Shao looked at the group of inmates, intimidated. McNamarra and his bruiser Cortez took up most of the room, dwarfing Stepan and the other convicts. 'But you can't all fit in the Sōngshǔ, it's just a small jumper...' she started.

'Oh really,' said McNamarra menacingly. 'That's not what your friends here said.'

'She's still out of it,' interjected Toft quickly. 'Doesn't know what she's saying.'

'Interesting,' said McNamarra, exchanging quick glances with Otis and Spider. 'We'll burn that bridge when we get there. You heard the boss; we're moving out, lads.'

The group of convicts led their hostages through the corridors. Lights were glitching out, changing brightness, or going out completely all of a sudden, changing their weightless march into an ordeal.

Mai could see pretty well in the darkness thanks to her cybernetic eyes and saw silhouettes skittering about everywhere they went. Bio-drones, she thought. Spider, the thin Outer hacker, caught her eyes and nodded. He must have seen them too. Restarting the comms brought a new life into the ship. It was eerie from the get-go, but now it was downright terrifying. Mai remembered the sudden change that overcame the security drones once she fixed the glitch. She didn't tell the others, but at least Pie noticed.

Some corridors have been vented into the void; others had hatches jammed shut. Spider had to either hack them or find a different route. Multiple times they saw rogue security drones skulking about in the darkness, but they managed to avoid fighting. They moved slowly, traversing the familiar corridors as if it were unknown terrain, further slowed by the wounded Shao. At least McNamarra wasn't around to shove her, Mai thought. The convict was talking quietly with Otis in the back of the group.

Eventually, they managed to reach the main cargo hold service airlock. Spider's biodrone wasted no time, and the door slid open. The expansive vault ahead of them sprawled seemingly forever; kilometer after kilometer of neatly stacked containers the size of a freighter tied together with miles of cable and chain keeping them from drifting away upwards into the open void of outer space, black and empty. Each container in the hold weighed many tons, rectangular, bulky, and swaying gently on its leash, responding to the tensions flowing through the rows.

'We're here,' said Milosh after a moment of almost reverent silence. 'Where to now?'

Toft and Mai looked at each other, then at Shao.

'The Sōngshǔ is hidden on the outer hull, some few hundred meters forward, on the starboard side,' Shao said.

'Thanks,' said Milosh. 'Now we can all just get the hell outta this pile of junk.'

'Yeah, about that,' interjected McNamarra, raising his rifle. 'I don't think I want to share the booty with you and your mercs, after all, boss.'

Otis and Cortez raised their weapons without hesitation, floating away from Milosh, Spider, and the hostages, setting themselves up for crossfire. Spider looked surprised but had enough presence of mind to move aside.

'Sorry, boss, you know how it is,' continued McNamarra. 'Besides, the girl said there's not much room on their ship anyway. Your fat asses wouldn't fit.'

'Yeah, Al, let's go and leave them to rot,' said Cortez.

'The hacker bitch comes with us, though,' continued McNamarra. 'We gotta have some entertainment on the road, no?'

'Come on, Al,' said Otis. 'Just leave the kid, we don't need her. Pie can hack the ship.'

'Don't be a wuss, big man,' laughed McNamarra. 'We'll vent her when we're done.'

Before Otis could say something else, a bright explosion behind the container nearest to them flashed, and the massive load swayed towards the inmates. The momentum pushed it from its normal range, and it headed straight for the group, threatening to crush them. McNamarra froze for a moment, but Milosh did not; lightning-fast, he bore his nail gun and fired at Cortez. Blood and pieces of Cortez's flesh exploded in all directions.

McNamarra started yelling something. Otis fired at Milosh, or rather at the empty space where Milosh used to be.

The merc's augmented limbs propelled him with inhuman speed as he bounced off the crashing container and launched towards the airlock. Pirates fired bursts after him. Ricochets bounced off the hull's reinforced metamaterial armor harmlessly. Milosh rammed into Otis like a missile, cracking bones and damaging the Outer's suit. Before anyone could react, Milosh bashed the stunned inmate's helmet in with a nail gun stock. Rapidly released oxygen exploded into an icy mist. Milosh pushed himself off the Outer's body and into the crashing container.

McNamarra scattered out of the way of the cargo and fired towards the fleeing mercenary. Otis moved in the wrong direction, right into the container wall. His huge body bounced off of it like a ball and hit the neighboring container.

Mai had only a second to register Milosh swinging by, grabbing Shao from her grip, and carrying her towards the airlock. The next thing she saw was a blinding flash of McNamarra's scattered burst following the merc with a bright yellow arc of deadly metal. She barely had time to notice the danger before she was shoved to the side by a strong push.

'Noooo!' cried Toft, shoving Mai out of the way. His chest suddenly became a mass of shattered bone and innards, his body tossed to the side by the impact's force.

Mai spiraled wildly, carried by the force of the blow, causing her body to drift towards the outer space above the shivering rows of containers. She felt peace overcome her, certain that was the end. At least I can see the stars one last time before I die, she thought. The thought gave her pause. There weren't any stars in sight a moment ago. Those aren't stars, she realized. Those are drop pods. On her body's next rotation, she zoomed in on her HUD. She was right. The stars were, in fact, elongated hulls of the Zhengdao Corp's boarding drone capsules, falling onto the Incitatus like steel rain of retribution.

Occasional laser flashes and matter bursts of the Incitatus' point defense system scorched bright marks on the falling pods. Still, the hauler's turrets were built to protect it from random space junk and asteroids, not a full-scale military drone bombardment. It was pretty clear that the sporadic blasts wouldn't destroy a single pod.

The Jīnlóng received her signal. Mai swirled, trying to stabilize her drift and get a hold of something. All she had to do now was to hide long enough for the corporate forces to find her. Screw it, I'll get sentenced for mutiny, but at least Shao will be fine. She took hold of a piece of debris from the container clash and pushed herself off it towards the Incitatus' hull. A few more meters and she would be safe, holed up somewhere until she could reach out to the corporate boarding party. Suddenly, she felt a sharp tug on her foot. She looked down and saw McNamarra's hands and the grinning face behind them.

'Not so fast, little girl,' he said. 'You're coming with me!'

She tried to kick herself free, but the mutineer anchored his feet on the wall and twisted his body, slamming the girl into the container wall. The lights in her cybereyes went out.

38

Zhenya's feet clad in powered armor touched the deck as he walked out into the dark cargo hold, followed closely by his reloading drone, the adjutant, and a squad of ten elite soldiers in white and gold combat armors. The reinforced version of Zhengdao standard spacesuits came with exoware reinforcing speed and strength, ablative armor, and additional sensors mounted on their straight, rectangular faceplates, relying entirely on their HUDs for visual input. The troops spread out in a fan to secure every angle—a futile task between rows of swaying containers and the open space above them, offering countless entry points. The security measures were protocol; their effectiveness was a secondary matter. Zhengdao combat drones had already scoured the area and secured it, uncontested, making sure it was safe for the field commander.

Zhenya reviewed the data provided by his armor's sensor array. He strained to keep his breath slow and methodical—the pods registered a firefight beneath them. There were casualties. Please, don't let it be Shao, thought Zhenya, addressing the prayer to nobody in particular. One of the containers was scorched and bent. It bore damage from crashing into the neighboring one. Both were stained with blood, pieces of equipment, and meat mangled beyond recognition. Three corpses drifted in clouds of gore, two men in orange convict jumpsuits, and one in Zhengdao fatigues—part of the Seventeen's crew, as evidenced by his serial number on Zhenya's HUD by the dead boy's RFID transmitter.

'Lasse Toft, the engineer,' said Zhenya, hiding relief. It wasn't Shao's body. Maybe she is still alive. She must be.

'Yes, esteemed captain,' confirmed Jin Sun. 'It would seem so.'

'Any sign of my... Of the other crew members?'

'It would seem they scattered or perished during the scuffle, esteemed captain.'

Zhenya fought to stop himself from screaming in his adjutant's face. 'That's very unfortunate. What about Green?'

Sun shrugged. 'Missing, I'm afraid. It would seem he disappeared. Once more, failing to uphold his word.'

'Order the men to hack into the mainframe,' commanded Zhenya, ignoring the unspoken "I told you so" in his second-in-command's voice. He had no time for political games right now. If Sun imagines he scored some points against him, so be it.

Two soldiers headed inside the ship, quickly disassembled the airlock controls, and added their suits into its control network. Before long, the footage from the cargo hold cameras was made available for the command suit.

'Send the drones after the mutineers,' he said after silently watching the footage. Two silhouettes in the firefight were smaller—women. They could only be Mai Wren and Shao. There was no telling which one was Zhenya's daughter. It would appear one was taken back into the ship, while the other carried away into the forest of containers. Zhenya watched a bulkier figure slam his victim into the container wall. A coppery taste of blood filled his mouth, and Zhenya realized he was biting his lip. 'Our first priority is to recover Zhengdao citizens. Recover my daughter. I want half the assets after the man who escaped into the ship.'

Zhenya wasn't sure the silhouette was Shao. The other convict dragged his victim into the labyrinth of crates and will be easy to find at their leisure, as there were fewer hideouts there.

'Of course, esteemed captain,' agreed Sun. 'If you think that's the wisest course of action.'

'I do think so, dear adjutant,' replied Zhenya. 'Commit the rest of the force to containment efforts. The pirates have clearly taken over the Incitatus, and therefore by law, it's salvage to be reclaimed as Zhengdao Corp property. All of it.'

'I... I see, captain,' replied Sun. 'Of course. I just thought your priority would be to recover Shao safe and sound.'

Don't tell me how to protect my family, Zhenya wanted to yell. 'It is, indeed, dear adjutant,' he said instead. 'Nonetheless, Zhengdao's greater good is also of the essence,' said Zhenya. 'I'm sure half of our forces is enough to recover her. Make sure they are aware she must not be harmed. And get me Green, flush him from whatever honorless hole he hid in.'

The commander disconnected the line and considered his orders for a moment. Seizing the ship and the cargo could be difficult to defend in court under the circumstances, but he wasn't about to let Delacroix pull one over him. Especially after the conversation he and Captain Powells had on the way here. Sun had played his hand, and he played it well, but too hastily.

Seizing the hauler put all the cargo in Zhenya's hands. Delacroix will have a hard time defending her rights to the raw materials, especially since it was her decision to change the craft into a prison on top of all things. The clients won't be pleased with losing their cargo and will probably get their part back, at a symbolic cost, but it was still a bonus to the bottom line. Enough to disarm any arguments Sun might forward to the board about Zhenya wasting company resources in pursuit of private agendas, for sure. But just in case... 'When you're done with relaying my orders, dear adjutant,' added Zhenya, 'be so kind and make yourself available. I want to run a message to the clients by you—since I value your council so much.'

Sun raised an eyebrow, surprised for once. 'Um, naturally, esteemed captain.'

Zhenya smiled and dismissed him. He'll deal with the adjutant as soon as they return to the frigate with Shao safe and sound. Powells assured of his support for the disciplinary action against Sun in the same breath as he informed Zhenya of Sun's scheming. The adjutant overestimated the ambition of the old captain, assuming probably everyone is as willing to grasp at straws for power as he is. He did not yet know the power of loyalty and honor—but that'll change soon.

For the next few hours, Zhengdao military drones scouting the giant hauler's corridors met hesitant resistance from the convicts. The mutineers armed themselves with the craft's emergency small arms powerful enough to take down small security drones. The hulking, heavily armored combat machines deployed by Zhenya simply obliterated any opposition.

Leaving the weapon lockers full was yet another failing on Delacroix's part, Zhenya thought. Her lack of foresight will serve me well. He watched on his HUD as yet another gang of inmates in orange jumpsuits rained projectiles onto the drone's bulky rear. The machine's magnetic engines flickered, the toad-like chassis rotated to face the prisoners. Its sensor array tracked the scattering prisoners as they rushed to cover, their hunched silhouettes clearly visible through the corridor walls on the x-ray scanner. Once the targets were locked, the drone launched a small proximity mine down the corridor. Within seconds, the ball of plasma melted the entire deck, instantly vaporizing three of the prisoners. The remaining men tried to flee in a mad dash to get away from the deadly machine, but precision lasers cut them down, short pulses severing their spinal cords with surgical precision.

The entire fight was over in less than ten seconds—no longer than other bursts of activity elsewhere in the ship. Before the molten metal that used to be the corridor junction solidified, the biodrones began buzzing about, examining the damages. Some approached the corpses; others extended their sensors towards the combat drone, ignored by the hulking machine cooling down its laser arrays. The lights in the junction flickered as yet another glitch rolled through the decks.

Zhenya's HUD went dark for a second, then came back online. The captain cut the video link, surprised. Zhengdao tech usually ran flawlessly. He ran a diagnostics check, but the systems were fine—the command grid link was fully operational, and all the icons of soldiers and combat drones shone green. For some reason, the link between his suit and the frigate was now relayed through an unknown host, but Zhenya assumed it was just the Incitatus' systems rerouting the connection to prevent lag. He made a mental note to notify the engineering team back at the mothership to run a full diagnostics when they returned and resumed tracking the progress in pacifying the mutineers.

He flicked through the tactical feeds, checking up on each squad's pace. The pacification force was spread thin, combat drones operating solo or in twin tag teams, scouring the corridors and cabins, flushing out the prisoners. Interestingly, some of the Incitatus' own security measures were still in place, and the combat drones engaged in dogfights with them sporadically. Cheap machines armed with small caliber autoguns weren't a threat to the military-grade counterparts, though. Zhenya didn't think it was necessary to have them hacked, particularly since some ignored aor even joined the Zhengdao force of their own accord.

Once he was sure the crowd control proceeded unimpeded, Zhenya switched to the feed that was of most interest to him—the five soldiers looking for his daughter.

The commando team had strategically placed the combat drones in main corridor arteries, isolating sections where the Zhengdao tactical computer suggested the hostage might have been taken. Heavily armed robotic sentries continuously scanned the gangways and hatches, making sure nobody could leave the locked-down areas.

Zhenya observed the soldiers spreading out. They divided the task among themselves. Soldiers wearing powered combat suits and high-volume needlers would normally work in pairs, but their sergeant decided it was unnecessary since the opposition could not possibly be armed with anything capable of taking down a Zhengdao commando, even with numerical advantage and surprise on their side.

Zhenya didn't take kindly to undue arrogance, especially when the soldiers looked for his daughter. He had to admit that a gang of prisoners armed in improvised armaments posed little threat to a soldier wearing state-of-the-art armor, even if they did hack the guard drones.

The squad quickly scanned room after room, maintaining radio silence except for an occasional quick report.

'Sarge, I got activity in sector yīng, looks like some sort of short-wave radio signal.' reported one of the soldiers.

Zhenya quickly muted the remaining comm traffic, focusing his attention on the trooper.

'Can you trace the source, Liu?' asked the sergeant.

Zhenya stifled the urge to join the comms and demand details. There was nothing he can do to make the situation better, and his presence can only disrupt the soldiers. Knowing it was one thing, holding an instinct to jump in to protect Shao was another.

'Affirmative. Just two cabins over, in one of the small hangar bays,' replied Liu. 'I'll head over and investigate. Should I jam the signal?'

'Proceed.'

'Belay that order, trooper,' cut in Zhenya, joining the channel before the order could be carried out. 'Radio signals travel slow, and we're very far from traffic. Whoever sent the signal clearly intended it for someone on the Incitatus. Their line is probably open by now, and the only thing we're gaining by jamming them is revealing that we're aware of the transmission.'

'Of course, esteemed captain,' acknowledged Liu, turning towards the bay.

Lights in the corridors were glitching in and out, repeatedly drowning the deck in darkness and sporadic flashes of halogen light. The technician on duty remotely hacked and opened the bay's inner airlock for Liu in advance, allowing him easy access into the bay. Once the lock was open, Liu entered the compartment, and the suit's sensor array scanned the area. The cabin held multiple rows of drone forklifts attached to their racks, waiting for the moment of unloading cargo. Swarms of biodrones flocked around the dormant machines, their tentacles waving in the air in unison with the pulsating lights of their magnetic drives. 'It's as if they're looking for something...' whispered Liu.

'Never mind that,' said Zhenya. He scolded himself quietly for letting stress show in his voice. 'The sensors indicate there is organic material a few meters to your left, check it.'

The soldier turned as commanded. A beam of light from his suit illuminated a swirling mist of dark brown substance.

'It looks like a bubble of coagulated oil, esteemed captain. Or something like that.' The soldier carefully approached the bubble. 'The puddle, it's blood,' he added. 'Looks like a few days old. At least.'

'Ignore it then, head to the source of transmission,' said Zhenya impatiently. 'And shut off the lamp, they'll see you.'

'Yes, esteemed captain.' Liu turned off the illumination and headed towards the outer bay hatch. The airlock leading into open space was completely dark, but the signal was clearly coming from there. 'Got them trapped in the 'lock, esteemed captain,' reported Liu. 'Bioscanner confirms organic heat signature inside. Nowhere to run.'

'Approach,' ordered the sergeant.

Zhenya didn't oppose it, allowing the professionals to do their jobs.

The airlock's round hatch was closed. A red light on the side panel indicated the outer doors were open. All airlocks had a built-in system preventing both hatches from being open at the same time. There was no way to get inside without hacking the door.

Liu inserted the universal interface adapters located on his suit's forearm into the port on the airlock door panel. It only took a couple of seconds for the Zhengdao engineer waiting in the shuttle to crack through meager security remotely. The door opened halfway, glitching and stopping every couple of centimeters, then froze halfway through. Liu sighed and approached it. The round, spirally opening hatch wasn't open enough to let him through, but the suit's built-in exoware's servomotors supported his natural muscles with inhuman strength, allowing the soldier to pry the hatch open. Without delay, Liu stepped inside.

A biodrone floated near the ceiling; its tentacles were holding a round shape, small eyes focused on the soldier.

'Esteemed captain,' said Liu. 'The signal is broadcasted by a drone, I'm afraid.' A bright light filled the airlock, casting the soldier's hulking shadow onto the gray walls. 'I'm going to go near and see what it's holding.'

'Capture it and let our analyst decipher the signal,' commanded Zhenya. 'And turn off that damn lamp, soldier!'

Liu reached out and retrieved the object from the drone's grasp. 'I... I didn't activate it, esteemed captain,' he said.

Zhenya watched Liu turn around slowly.

The forklift drone's barrel shape hung behind him; it's powerful reflectors obscuring the silhouette and turning it into a dark shadow in the airlock maw.

'Oh, it's just a...' managed Liu before the drone charged forward. Its twin blades smashed into his chest. They didn't pierce the armor, the drone had nowhere near enough mass and velocity for that, but they did hit with enough force to dislodge his magnetic shoes from the deck floor, sending him flying into space. Liu activated his suit's maneuver engines, trying to fly back into the airlock, but the drone pushed out-wards, and the airlock's external hatch closed slowly. The forklift kept on its course, pushing Liu further and further from the Incitatus.

Liu let go of the object held in his hands, screaming. It floated before the camera, and Zhenya watched in horror—it was a head of an Outer with a missing eye. The wound was torn with viciousness and force, burned all the way to the back of the skull. 'Order all soldiers to regroup, sergeant,' commanded Zhenya. 'They are being led further into an ambush. Our opponent is craftier than we gave them credit. Jin Sun, order the Jīnlóng to intercept trooper Liu before he's out of range and take command in my stead. I'll lead the search personally.'

39

Mai had stopped struggling a while ago. She had tried to set herself free at first, kicking and screaming at every opportunity, but McNamarra's fists beat her down every time. Now, she allowed herself to be dragged along, saving her strength and waiting for the right moment. McNamarra headed into the depths of Incitatus' cargo hold, among the massive containers.

Spider used his tamed biodrone to scout ahead, staying away from the Zhengdao forces and the hauler's own drone swarms, staying just out of reach. 'Aight, I think we're in the clear, Al' said Pie, emerging from the cybernetic interface back to the real world.

'Good business, friend.' McNamarra smiled, his breath fogging up the helmet display from the inside. 'Now it's time for you, little birdie, to show us where your nest is.'

Mai didn't answer fast enough, and the convict's foot armed in a magnetic boot crashed under her ribs. The impact shook her to the core and pushed the air from her lungs. Mai felt acid coming up from her bowels and soiled the faceplate with vomit. She tried to answer before the next strike landed, but she couldn't, gasping for air. She saw Spider turn his face away and braced herself. The next minutes were nothing but flashes of pain and nausea when the hits landed. It took a moment after the beating stopped before she realized it was over.

McNamarra's voice slowly got through the ringing in her ears. 'I'm gonna ask one more time,' he said calmly. 'Tell me where your ship is, or I'll break your legs.'

Mai nodded in agreement, trying not to cry. She swallowed the blood gathering in the back of her throat and displayed the Sōngshǔ's locator beacon frequency into their HUDs.

'Now, was that so hard, little bird?' said McNamarra. 'We're gonna be right and cozy in a few minutes. Then we can get out of those suits and have some real fun, no?'

Mai shuddered, but before she formed a response of any kind, McNamarra landed a kick on her face, smacking the girl's head into a container. Mai's left cybereye sizzled and went out, causing the other to shift between colors madly.

The convict grabbed her by the arm and pushed her floating aimlessly onward. 'Come on, Pie, let's get a move on.'

'Yeah, sure thing, Al' replied Spider meekly and sent his biodrone ahead of them.

Mai phased in and out of consciousness between bouts of panic and overwhelming pain. She tried to stay focused on the path she was pushed through, but the monotonous rows of containers quickly turned into a spinning gray and brown chaos as her eyes tried to reboot themselves. She heard snippets of the convicts' conversation washing over her.

'You really don't have to beat her up like that.'

'Oh, but I want to,' replied McNamarra. 'She'll get what's coming to her.'

Mai retched and tried to struggle, but the McNamarra paid no attention to her now.

'Hold on, I got something on the scanner,' said Spider, attempting to change the subject.

'Like what?'

'Hard to say, Al. Looks like one of the soldiers, but...'

'Alone? Let's check it out. I could use a real gun!'

McNamarra pushed Mai violently forward and sent her spinning. The containers they passed were scorched. Eventually, she saw what the two men were heading towards - a white and gold suited silhouette covered by a mass of biodrones. Their agitated sinusoid forms hung on the still soldier like locust, tentacles sticking to the white surface. They're trying to get inside his suit, Mai thought, seeing the blue flashes of plasma cutters erupt under the writhing mass of biological robots. She recoiled in disgust and saw Spider halt mid-jump as the realization struck him as well.

McNamarra paid no heed to the horror before him. 'Shoo, little fuckers,' he yelled, charging the swarm. He flailed his nail gun at the drones, which dispersed, but didn't go far. The robots hung around them in a circle, like a flock of vultures.

Mai realized the soldier is still alive. He was trying to reach his forearm, where a half-open slot was.

McNamarra had none of that. He swooped in, placed the nail gun exhaust to the soldier's faceplate, and pulled the trigger. Nails bounced off and scattered in a wild spray, not strong enough to penetrate the hardened shell. 'Oh, well. Fuck you then,' said McNamarra. 'I'll just take this and be on my way.' He dislodged the soldier's rifle from its sling and pried the forearm plate from the armor, peeling a high-yield grenade from the slot. He aimed the gun at the drone swarm, but before he could fire, the robots dispersed, disappearing between containers. 'Clever fuckers. Time to go, friend.'

He aimed the gun at the soldier's head; the looted rifle's trigger clicked, and the green status light turned red. McNamarra cursed, when the weapon systems locked because of the unauthorized use, and discarded the rifle with disgust.

'Those drones were acting weird,' said Spider as they moved on. 'They're maintenance bots; they shouldn't be trying to kill anyone. It's just not in their programming.'

'Who gives a shit?' McNamarra shrugged. 'Your toy works well, right?'

'I think so, yeah,' said Spider. 'I programmed the route to the beacon, and it follows. Wonder what would happen if I told it to do something else—'

'Keep wondering, nerd,' interrupted McNamarra. 'Whatever got into them, doesn't matter. We're getting on the little bird's boat and getting the fuck outta here. You can sit and think all day then.'

The group dragged on, following the biodrone's lead, dependent on its lights. Mai watched the drone intently. The hacker may ignore the warning signs all he wants, but if the drones were bugged, chances were she could use it to her advantage. The squid-like construct floated with certainty, but stopped every couple of containers, spreading its tentacles and antennae widely. It's listening for something, she thought. But for what?

Suddenly, Spider let out a muted cry of surprise, and the biodrone surged forward, flashing quickly out of sight, light disappearing behind the corner.

'What the shit, Pie,' cried McNamarra in the sudden darkness.

'I didn't do anything.'

Both men lit up their faceplates, thin streaks of light carving the darkness. The containers swayed slightly to the rhythm of Incitatus' internal pressure. They looked around in confusion.

'Call it back, for fuck's sake!' yelled McNamarra.

'I'm trying, it's not responding!'

McNamarra trained his nail gun at Spider, who froze mid-motion, with hands on the tablet.

'Al, no!' he protested.

'Call back the drone, or you're of no use to me, Pie,' said McNamarra. 'I'll put you down like a bitch.'

'But I didn't even,' started Spider. 'Wait, wait, wait, I got a signal again!'

'How fucking convenient,' said McNamarra. 'Don't try that bullshit again, Pie, last warning.'

'I didn't... Fuck you. It's right around the corner,' replied Spider. 'You'd geek me over a glitch, sheesh.'

'I killed for less. Move it!'

McNamarra pushed Mai off into the darkness and gestured for Pie to follow her.

She floated through the void. Mai's body crossed the unseen event horizon and was suddenly awash with blue illumination. She saw the cargo hold's mid-section support column emerging from the icy fog, and under it, the Sōngshǔ.

The small craft was right where they had left it. The jumper's lean silhouette hunched over the maintenance duct as if it were a squirrel hugging a tree branch. The Sōngshǔ's bulbous cabin gleamed, surrounded by a mist of ice crystals, illuminated from below by a flock of hundreds of blue lights floating around the column in unison. Mai reached out to catch one of the frozen drops as she flew by it, and blinked with surprise when she realized the crystal was a deep crimson. Her cybereyes adjusted the contrast, the mechanism in her left eye socket moved visibly, the external lens missing. It's blood, she realized suddenly and flung the shard away with aversion.

She floated through the cloud and touched a column just in time to see a mangled corpse in a familiar jumpsuit ascend into a slow orbit above the jumper craft. Biodrones were swarming all over it, plasma cutters at the tips of their tentacles busy dissecting the person inside. The man's skull was cut open, and Mai could see brain matter under the drone busily cutting into it, and another attaching glistening wires to something inside.

The man's face was surprisingly intact and clean. She let out a cry of terror, realizing she was looking at Green's remains. She watched in sheer horror as the dead face of her friend slowly drifted above her, his brown eyes staring straight at her - dead and unseeing.

Green blinked, and his eyes focused directly at her. A biodrone crawled out of Green's mangled chest, its tentacles slowly and carefully finding their way between his ribs, exposed and forced open like grotesque wings. The drone's sensor arrays moved as it scanned the column. Mai shrunk inside her suit, wishing she could just crawl away but was too terrified to move.

McNamarra landed right next to her, his legs spread wide. He trained the nail gun at the drone and pulled the trigger.

Green's face disappeared in a vortex of gore and tissue, his head and the two biodrones pierced by high-velocity nails. The corpse was flung violently off its orbit and drifted into the void of space above them. Swarms of drones rushed at them from all directions, cut down by McNamarra. The drones flailed, pierced by nails - and then the nail gun ran out of ammo.

Spider landed almost right on top of Mai, frantically inputting commands into his tablet. Some drones reacted to his commands and crashed into each other, causing a chain reaction, slowing the entire swarm down.

'You got this, Pie, keep at it!' yelled McNamarra, swinging the nail gun like a club at the drones. 'We take those little shits out, and the ticket out is ours!'

'I'm trying, but...' started Spider. 'But something is overriding my commands.'

Mai tried to crawl away from the pandemonium, instinctively heading towards the Sōngshǔ. I can make it, she thought. Just gotta get there and close the hatch, and it's all over... She paid no attention to the desperate fight around her; the two prisoners fighting for their lives amidst hundreds of attacking drones might as well have been just a dream. Just a moment longer and I'll be safe... One more push, she thought, desperately clawing up the column. Mai's hands touched on the Sōngshǔ's hatch. Her jumpsuit connected with the jumper's interface and the airlock opened, letting out a cloud of frozen oxygen particles. The girl rushed inside, lodged herself safely in the tiny cabin, and punched the keypad inside. 'Come on, you piece of junk,' she cried, punching the panel repeatedly. 'Close, god damn it!'

The hatch started to close, slowly. Mai watched as the biodrones swarmed around Pie. He was desperately trying to fight them off using his tablet as a weapon, but the machines were already attaching them-selves to his suit.

'Faster, faster!' yelled Mai, the hatch almost halfway down.

Suddenly, McNamarra's large body dove through the closing door-way, stopping it midway. The sensors detected motion and paused the procedure. 'Where's the hurry, little bird,' he said, shoving the girl away from the hatch panel. 'You didn't try to leave me behind, did you?'

Mai didn't respond. McNamarra threw her against the airlock's inner door window, and she could see what awaited them inside the Sōngshǔ.

The canister they had picked up from the asteroid was open; the mummified body inside was gone. It took her a moment to find it; the corpse's gray skin blended with the dark interior. But there it was, sprawled on the jumper's control panel, thin limbs floating aimlessly in the air. The creature's large head faced upwards, half a dozen biodrones tirelessly working around it. The crown-like apparatus implanted in its skull extended its rods at full length, piercing the cabin's walls and panels like a golden aureole. The spikes were growing into the Sōng-shǔ's computers like thorns.

'Move over, little bird,' said McNamarra, pushing her aside once more. 'Daddy comes in first...' He paused for a moment, looking inside the jumper's cabin with astonishment.

That moment was enough for Mai, and she took her chance. She reached out to his belt and hit the activator button on the thermal grenade.

Still shocked by the grotesque scene inside, McNamarra reacted slowly. He turned around, trying to catch her, but Mai moved with a speed born from desperation.

She kicked herself off McNamarra's torso and flung towards the closing hatch, just barely making it and squeezing through the opening. The cover began to lift once more. McNamarra tossed the charge away onto a wall and kicked at the door with force, trying to pry his way out of the airlock. Mai didn't care, she pushed herself off the Sōngshǔ's hull as hard as she could. She needed to get away from it, it didn't matter where.

She twisted herself around to look back at the craft. McNamarra had almost squeezed his body through the hatch, and then the grenade inside the airlock sprung to life behind him in a crimson bloom. The explosion's force was directed outwards through the open airlock, and the devastating blast swallowed the convict whole, tearing him apart and sucking him back into the Sōngshǔ.

Mai sighed with relief, safe at last... And then a pair of strong arms enveloped her in a steel embrace.

40

Lederman shuddered when the Scallywag's shuttle touched the deck. He couldn't shake the feeling of unease the entire trip, but couldn't put his finger on why. Silver and his crew of five floaters looked like any other rag-tag band of smugglers, and so did their ship. The Scallywag was aptly named—a saucer-shaped, dull-green freighter looking like a derelict from the outside turned out to be in much better shape inside. It was far from the standards Lederman was used to; lack of discipline among the crew was clearly visible from dusty interiors, unsecured tools lying around, and the general feel of neglect. Nonetheless, neither Silver nor the crew bothered Tomasson and Lederman much, nor did they bother the captive pirate captain locked in her cabin on board—as far as he could tell. Redding, Silver's other passenger, didn't leave his cabin either.

The crew complained about the extended journey, but it was only a couple sols over their original plan, and the promise of reward turned their frowns upside down.

And yet, even as they landed the shuttle in the Incitatus' forward bay, Lederman couldn't help but feel the hair on the back of his neck rise in anticipation.

John Silver came up behind him and placed his hand heavily on Lederman's shoulder. 'We're here, policeman,' he said. 'Lookin' forward to see how you sort this mess out.'

'It does seem a tad more than can be handled,' admitted Lederman.

'No shit, friend,' laughed Silver. 'Don't get yourself killed before we settle the bill bamba ya, aye?'

'Don't worry about it; just be here when we're done.'

'My boat and I aren't going anywhere, at least for now.'

'We shouldn't be gone long,' said Lederman. 'Tomasson, how's the ETA on the recon?'

Lara Tomasson looked up from her tablet. A dozen round drones armed with small needlers and impressive sensor arrays hovered in a tight formation behind her, their magdrives buzzing and blue warning lights flashing. 'Should be about good to go.'

'Aight, let's scan the decks, see what's what,' said Lederman. 'I don't like the looks of that corp frigate nearby. Let's recon the area and scramble.'

'You're all sexy when you talk like that, cap,' laughed Silver. 'Have fun, children; I'll clap in the shuttle and bunk mi res.' With that, Silver turned and left the shuttle's airlock, leaving the two Rangers alone in the dimly lit bay.

Lederman looked after the Scallywag's captain, waiting until the hatch closed behind the man. 'I don't like him,' he said.

'Is it because he called his ship the Scallywag?' replied Tomasson, smiling. 'Or because you're out of your comfort zone?'

'Both, to be honest,' said Lederman. 'And I don't like the thought of our prisoner unsupervised in that piece of junk.'

'Silver's crew will keep an eye on her,' said Tomasson. 'She's locked up tight; it doesn't take an army to keep her there. We'll get this sorted and get right back on track before we're too deep in the Beyond, don't worry.'

'Let's send the scouts first, see what we're up against.'

Tomasson finished inputting the commands, and the entire flock of drones rushed out of the airlock. The Rangers watched them disperse and explore the giant craft's corridors on their HUDs. It wasn't long before the drones encountered their first marks.

A group of half a dozen convicts was exchanging fire with unknown assailants in the dark hallways ahead. The lights flickered on and off, blinding the men. Two of them drifted, wounded or dying nearby. A streak of laser fire cut deep into the bodies, raising a mist of fresh blood over them as their cells exploded.

Other drones relayed similar scenes all over the hull section; groups of convicts desperately trying to hold off a relentless assault. They tried to flee, but a hatch slid itself closed, blocking their escape. It seemed there was more than one faction at play here; various groups of prisoners seemed hostile to each other, wary at best.

Some of the attackers were standard issue security drones armed with ballistic weaponry; others were white bulky monsters, lighting up the halls with laser fire. Soldiers in similar white armors were present, though those seemed to be targeted by the drones as much, if not more than the convicts. Lederman recognized the colors and the insignia—Zhengdao, a mining outfit from the System.

'The hell's happening here...' said Lederman eventually, watching the drones reveal more and more of the chaos.

'No idea, but it looks like the craft's systems are compromised,' replied Tomasson. 'Look at the lights.'

It was as if the ship itself were alive and working to remove the humans from its bowels. 'What the hell,' said Lederman. 'We're dealing with a psycho-hacker or something...'

'Very unlikely.' Tomasson shook her head. 'I've cracked the system... It's idle, and no active programs are running except for basic life support and maintenance.'

'What then?'

'I don't know,' she admitted. 'Something weird. Wait a minute. What...'

Lederman looked at the display his officer was distracted by. It took him a moment to realize what made her go silent in mid-sentence. A couple of the scout drones were coming back. 'What are you doing, Lara?' he asked.

'Nothing, they should be scouting the ship. Shit, now the rest of them turned back.'

'They're brand new drones, right?' asked Lederman carefully. 'Maybe the software glitched?'

'Doesn't look like it. It didn't freeze, and the driver bot says the drones are still moving away.'

'Well, that one sure isn't,' said Lederman, pointing at the bay gates.

The first scout drone skulked through the open hatch, carefully like a cat. The machine's sensor arrays wiggled about, curiously investigating the shuttle bay. Slowly, it lurched forward, hopping up and down as its magdrive switched on and off.

'What's it doing, Lara?'

'I... I have no idea. I guess it's scanning the room, but I'm not getting a readout from it.'

More scout drones flew inside, spreading around and exploring. One flew close to the shuttle, its single central lens focusing on the two Rangers standing next to the shuttle hatch.

They returned the gaze, puzzled.

It wasn't until a moment later when a hulking, bulbous silhouette of the Zhengdao combat drone slid into the bay like a small moon surrounded by the Incitatus' security robots before he realized what was happening. Lederman threw himself at Tomasson in a heartbeat, and both Rangers bounced off the inner shuttle wall painfully as the streak of laser pulses cut the air where they had just stood. 'Lara! Open the hatch, now!' cried Lederman, pushing himself off the wall to take cover behind the charging racks. He reached for a rifle and fired a salvo into the bay without aiming.

'I can't,' replied Tomasson. 'My control is overridden from the cockpit.'

'Silver! What the hell, man!' yelled Lederman into the comms.

'Sorry 'bout that, policeman' replied Silver. 'Don't be too mad at a simple sailor. Old John Silver is weak to the allure of gold, that's all there is to it.'

'What the hell are you on about?' asked Tomasson angrily, still trying to open the shuttle hatch through her tablet.

'Simple. Old pyaka Silver done you in real good. Your cred is good, but the grace of admiral Pam a cache of gold on this old dragon, headed down the gravity well, that are nothin' to sneeze at.'

'I knew I shouldn't have trusted you,' growled Lederman, crouching behind the charging rack, pinned by bursts of laser fire and flak.

'An' yet you did,' said Silver with contempt. 'Cry me a river, Captain Lederman.'

The shuttle's drive began heating as Silver prepared to leave, abandoning the Rangers.

Lederman looked around frantically, trying to find a better piece of cover. The moment Silver ignites the engines, Lederman and Tomasson will fry, incinerated by the fission drive's exhaust.

There was no other cover available—security drones spread out across the bay, covering all angles except the shuttle's direct vicinity, and the combat drone hovered in the middle of the bay. Its turrets relentlessly rained laser pulses onto the Rangers' positions.

Charging racks sheltering them bent and melted. Burned circuitry fizzled, showering them both with sparks. Suddenly, the shuttle's engines stalled and stopped; the vibration cut off instantly.

'The fuck is this nonsense,' yelled Silver over the comms again. 'What did you do, Lederman?'

'We didn't do anything,' replied Tomasson. 'It's the ship!'

'What do you mean it's the ship, lagga head?'

'Let us in the shuttle, and we'll tell you,' said Lederman.

'You think I'm stupid?' laughed Silver. 'Stay there and fry, for all I care. I'm outta here, shuttle or no shuttle.'

Lederman didn't answer. One of the security drones took advantage of his momentary distraction and flanked his position. A rail shot from Tomasson's rifle hit the machine's chassis before Lederman could react, and the drone spiraled away, damaged. Two more security drones swarmed Tomasson's back. Lederman raised his weapon, knowing full well that he could not possibly be fast enough to take them both out in time.

He watched as if in slow motion, Tomasson started turning around, fear dawning on her face. Security drones aimed their rapid-fire shotguns at her from up close... And froze mid-motion, momentum pulling them away from her.

And then the entire deck shook violently, tossing them about like ragdolls.

41

Powells sat in the Jīnlóng's command chair, waiting for the return comm from the Yusan. Sun's latest attempt at intrigue didn't exactly faze the old commander. Powells had seen more young, ambitious execs willing to backstab their boss than mornings on Titan, where he was stationed for twenty years during his tour of duty in the OSEE navy. They were all the same—sleek, sharp, and polite, up until the moment they cut your throat.

Sun should have known better than to hope for the old officer's support and discretion. Powells was never his friend, not even an acquaintance, while they shared a decade-long friendship with Yuan Zhenya. It should have been obvious to the young adjutant that the first thing Powells would do was to inform Zhenya as soon as they returned from the voyage to recover the Seventeen, which was now safely stored aboard the Jīnlóng.

Sun was no fool, and whatever intrigue he weaved, he made no rookie mistakes while at it, which meant by telling Zhenya about it, Powells had likely played right into Sun's hand.

A command console came online, displaying an incoming emergency comm augmented reality icon above it. Powells gave a mental command to accept the call. A blond-haired, blue-eyed face of a man in Zhengdao security armor on the footage didn't ring a bell in Powells' head, so he summoned a crew roster and ran a facial recognition protocol. The Jīnlóng was a huge ship, crewed by fifty people, not counting the security detail, and Powells didn't remember all of the crew's names.

Still, he liked to at least make an effort to call his underlings by name when he could. 'Trooper Thompson, is it?' he said when the matching result showed up. Henry Thompson was a part of Zhenya personal security under Sarah Lowe's command. Whatever the matter was, it had to be important

'Yes, sir, esteemed captain, sir.'

Powells waved dismissively. 'Spare me the etiquette, trooper. I assume you're on my comms with an important matter, not just to bore your superior officer with pleasantries.'

Thompson relaxed, but his face remained tense. 'Yes sir, we have a situation. One of the boarding party soldiers has been vented into space. Captain Zhenya ordered me to relay a request to intercept him, before—'

'Before he drifts away, yeah,' interrupted Powells. 'Send me the coordinates and trajectory, and the Jīnlóng will take care of it right away.'

'Thank you, sir. Here's the upload.'

Powells looked through the data. It appeared trooper Liu got himself jettisoned with some force, but not so fast enough he couldn't be intercepted. He relayed the coordinates and a set of orders to the crew, and before long, a shuttle was dispatched to retrieve the hapless soldier.

The augmented reality display painted the trajectories in the air in front of Powell's face, lines closing in on each other in neat parabolas, until finally, they met. A video feed window popped up, displaying trooper Liu drifting through space with a dozen squid-like biodrones grasping his white-gold armored spacesuit with their tentacles.

The shuttle hit maneuver thrusters and carefully piloted them to get the man inside the open hatch. The shuttle crew sent a quick comm informing that the package is safe in the hold, and they're on the way back.

Soon they will all be safe and sound back aboard the Jīnlóng. Powells thought he wouldn't want to be in Liu's skin; the soldier will never live it down, tossed overboard by a bunch of tiny maintenance drones.

The moment the shuttle touched down, Powells was on the comms with his aide waiting in the bay: Naida Clarke, a young woman from Earth, Tanzania, or somewhere around those parts. A serious, dedicated professional, just the way Powells liked his subordinates to be. None of Sun's backstabbing and double the ambition.

'What's the situation down there, Clarke?' he asked. 'I hope the poor bastard's unharmed?'

'Affirmative, captain,' she said. 'His vitals are normal. The drones tried to cut their way into his suit, but didn't make it.'

'They tried to cut their way in? That's not a programmed behavior.'

'No, sir. We think they malfunctioned.'

'You think?' asked Powells. 'I would say that's highly irregular. Have the science officers look at them, will you?'

Clarke shook her head. 'No, sir, can't do. The moment shuttle doors opened, the drones bolted.'

'Bolted where?'

'Some hid on the Seventeen,' said Clarke, pointing at the mining ship one bay over. 'Some scattered on the deck. The shuttle crew is already trying to round them up.'

'Put me on the vid with them.'

A dozen or so personal HUD feed windows opened up in the air before Powells's face. The augmented reality display became cluttered, and it took some arranging to get a clear view of it all.

Powells magnified one of the windows with technician Morozov chasing a drone in the mining ship's empty corridors. After a short chase, the man was already winded, breathing heavily and trying to fit his body into nooks and crannies after the agile biodrone. Powells made a mental note to make sure technician Morozov signs up for the fitness program aboard the Yusan when they return.

Finally, Morozov cornered his victim in the Seventeen's drone bay, where eleven mining drones rested in racks. One rack was empty;

its usual inhabitant was partially disassembled on a workshop bench nearby. Technicians were still working on it, trying to find the malfunction in its programming. 'Come here, little buddy,' said Morozov with a strong, Slavic accent, slowly approaching the cornered biodrone with arms spread wide. 'I'm not gonna hurt you, I just wanna give you a hug, that's it.'

The machine spread its segmented tentacles threateningly and baring its sets of tools and cutters like fangs, backing further away until its oblong torso hit the wall. It behaves just like a wild animal, Powells thought with amusement.

'You have nowhere to go, buddy, just come with me. And don't bite.'

Suddenly, the mining drones came online, their control lights flashing like predatory eyes in the storage bay's total darkness. Morozov turned around, startled, then sighed with relief. 'Ha, ha very funny, O'Connell. You got me very funny,' he said, his voice shaking. 'You almost gave me a heart attack with this one.'

Another technician came online. 'What do you mean, Lex? I didn't do anything.'

Morozov turned back towards the wall, where the biodrone was, only to see an empty deck. 'Central, I lost it,' he said.

An oblong shape fell on his face with a shriek; tentacles spread wide, sharp tools and plasma cutters aimed right at Morozov's unprotected eyes and throat.

Powells jumped up in surprise at the sight. 'Clarke, get security down there, shut down those drones!'

'I'm trying, sir, but I can't reach them,' replied Clarke. 'Oh god, the drones...'

She looked at the Seventeen where a row of eleven mining drones exited the open hatch left by Morozov. One of the technicians froze at sight, just for a moment, but it was enough for one of the machines to cut at her neck with a rock drill. Blood splatter flew through the cabin, hitting Clarke in the face. The woman opened her mouth to scream, but before she made a sound, the comm line closed abruptly.

Powells immediately opened a ship-wide emergency broadcast. 'Security, isolate shuttle bay five, full quarantine!'

There was no response. Powells checked if the line was open, everything worked just fine, but nobody replied. He started switching between comm channels, finding the same ominous silence on all lines. That's just great, Powells thought. The best moment for a comm malfunction. He got up from his chair and determined to contain the situation, even if he had to yell at his crew face to face. Then the lights went out, drowning the Jīnlóng's bridge in total darkness. 'What the,' started Powells, but never finished. He felt his feet lift off the ground. The bridge module stopped rotating, he realized. We're in zero-g.

He reached out to grab something and propel himself onwards, but couldn't reach anything, and didn't know which way he was even facing in the total darkness. Just as he started panicking, he felt his body slowly drift backward, and his feet touched the floor. Powells let out a sigh of relief. 'All right, looks like the carousel is back online,' he said to himself. 'No, that's not it...' The old captain realized what he felt was not actually spin gravity. 'We're moving.'

42

Shao struggled, desperately trying to set herself free, but her captor didn't even notice her efforts. Finally, after what seemed like an eternity of torturous pain in her wounded belly, Milosh dragged her into a small cabin and sat her down on a tool bench.

'Sheesh, you almost broke my rib,' he said, letting her go. 'Calm down, idiot.'

'Let me go, you—' started Shao.

'Fine, go, get killed,' he interrupted. 'It's not like I saved your ass from McNamarra.'

'Saved me?' she shouted. 'You took us hostage! You shot me!'

'What's a bullet or two between friends?' replied Milosh with a grin.

The absurdity of it all finally kicked in, and Shao burst into panic-induced laughter.

'I'd say that's more like it, but to be honest, you're freaking me out now,' said Milosh.

'Fuck you,' said Shao, between breaths. 'If you're gonna kill me, just do it.'

'If I wanted you dead, I'd just leave without you.'

'What do you want, then?' asked Shao, composing herself. She dropped her head as if in resignation, concealing a quick glance around the shed. Tools shoved off the bench floated nearby. I'll be damned if I go down without a fight, she thought.

'I already told you,' said Milosh calmly. 'I want to get the hell off this barge.'

'You already know where the jumper is,' replied Shao and made a gesture as if she wanted to push herself off the wall. Milosh reacted instinctively and moved to intercept. Instead of pushing herself, however, Shao grabbed a plasma torch drifting beside her and activated it. A vicious streak of plasma instantly hit the side of Milosh's helmet, frying the electronics and blinding the man.

Without hesitation, Shao kicked herself off the wall and plunged down the hallway. She didn't know where she was or where the corridor led, but it didn't matter. Hurrying across the deck amidst flickering lights, she kicked and vaulted herself off the pipes and panels, as far away from her captor as possible. Time for planning and decisions will come later when she's far away and safe from immediate harm. She almost didn't notice the biodrone reaching out towards her with tentacles.

Having caught the movement with the corner of her eye, Shao flashed the torch at the construct. Superheated plasma melted through the metallic carapace and the squid-body, vaporizing the drone's blood and circuitry instantly. She held onto a pipe and activated her mag-boots, clinging upside down to a ceiling. More biodrones were crawling through between the pipes. The torch in her hands was enough to take out one or two of them, but there were dozens.

She rushed towards the hatch leading into the next deck, waving the lit torch around, but just as she made the first step, the heavy door-way started to close, and lights flickered. The deck was now lit only by toxic blue bursts of light from the torch. She could just barely make out the swarming bodies of the biodrones, tentacles slowly crawling towards her from all sides, sensor arrays, and carapaces glistening with reflected flashes.

The torch choked and died, and the darkness fell onto the deck, devouring it whole.

Shao dashed desperately towards the closing hatch. She knew there was no way she could make it in time or that it would keep her safe. Suddenly she tripped and lunged forward. I stepped on a drone, she thought. Fighting for balance in the darkness, Shao felt the other boot's magnet failing, and she fell into the darkness.

Flashes in the distance lit the corridor, Shao caught glimpses of hydraulics teeming with biodrones. The flashes repeated regularly, again and again. Shao saw drones reaching out from the darkness, segmented arms slithering to grab her. With each flash, a machine exploded into a chaos of tissue and metal. The swarm's magnetic drives came to life, and the squid-like machines scattered about in unison, turning towards the hallway from which the girl first ran. Shao looked back, expecting the worst.

In another series of flashes, she saw Milosh steadily pushing himself towards her with a rifle aimed down the corridor. Each time the rifle's muzzle flashed, another biodrone next to her exploded—the crippled swarm dispersed and disappeared between pipes in an instant. The force of each shot pushed Milosh spinning backward, but the merc just pushed himself against nearby walls, shooting time after time. Shao tried to get away, but she was floating in the middle of the passage, well out of reach to the nearest solid surface. All she could do was watch helplessly as the man approached.

Once he was right next to her, Milosh reached out with the rifle's red-hot barrel and stopped Shao's motion. Her suit sizzled but didn't rupture. 'Are you done?' he asked. 'Cause we have places to be. McNamarra has a ton of head start by now.'

'Just like that, eh?' said Shao. 'I'm not gonna get away from you unless I give you what you want?'

'Now you're getting it,' grinned Milosh. 'And hey, maybe we can rescue your girlfriend on the way if we hurry.'

'You'd do that?' asked Shao, surprised. 'But why?'

'Don't look a gift horse in the mouth, lass.'

'Sorry if I'm having difficulties trusting you, you almost killed me. Twice!'

'The day's not over,' laughed Milosh. 'Besides, three times the charm, no?'

'Listen, asshat,' said Shao. 'If you think I'll do what you want just because you dangle Mai's safety in front of me...'

'Then I'm absolutely correct,' interrupted her Milosh. 'Besides, you're more likely to come along quietly if we get her back, and I want out of this fucking boat. Do you need me to draw you a picture?'

'No, I get it.'

'Good. Do what I say, and we'll all just leave this boat peacefully, then say goodbye at the nearest opportunity. And I won't even bring up how you didn't even ask if we could grab your other friend while we're going.'

Shao quietly followed Milosh through the tangled labyrinth of the Incitatus' corridors. The merc moved with certainty and predatory grace, though Shao noticed he was just as exhausted as she was, if not more so. His arms were pockmarked with burns and cuts, armored net peeked from under the skin. Milosh was clearly running on determination and adrenaline if his erratic behavior was anything to go by. Shao could only hope he was going to keep his word.

Avoiding any signs of activity, human or otherwise, slowed them down considerably. Some hatches, previously open, were now inaccessible due to the ship's aberrant behavior, others, while open, were protected by the wild drones. She caught a glimpse of white-clad silhouettes in the far decks, sniping at the drones. Friends or foes; they didn't stick around to get a closer look. Shao soon saw her involuntary companion grow more and more frustrated. He chose passages seemingly on a whim.

'Do you even know where we're going?'

'Yeah, around all the crap between us and the cargo,' he replied. 'I just can't find an open passage. I'm starting to think the only way through is by force.'

'Oh, that's a great idea,' said Shao. 'I'm sure you can take them all on. Go, I'll watch.'

'I think I'll have to,' replied Milosh after a short pause. 'Come on; we're gonna get some supplies and take them down.'

'What? You can't be serious!'

'Got a better idea? If we don't get out soon, we're stuck here.'

'Hold on, damn it, give me a moment...' Shao stopped and leaned on the wall. Milosh turned around, gave her an annoyed grimace, but didn't reply.

Shao shook her head, trying to clear it. 'So, we can't get to the cargo through an airlock...' She started when her pain eased.

'Yeah, I noticed, thanks.'

'Oh, shut up. What I mean is all our ways to the Sōngshǔ inside the ship are closed. What if we went outside?'

'Shit, that could work,' said Milosh, suddenly excited. 'I'd need a new suit, thanks for that, by the way, but it could work. And a working pair of magboots. We just need to find the nearest bay and...'

'And we can spacewalk to the Sōngshǔ, yeah.'

They headed straight towards the small drone bay where Toft first damaged a biodrone so long ago. Meandering corridors quickly confused Shao, but Milosh had learned the ship's layout quite well in his time as a convict, so they quickly got through to the bay. The airlock mouth gaped ajar, but it started to close as soon as they neared it.

Shao and Milosh burst into a sprint to squeeze between the closing doorway before their last chance at success closed for good. The airlock hatch wasn't designed for fast motion, and they made it inside with a good moment to spare. Milosh immediately started undressing, intent on changing the damaged jumpsuit for one of the brown emergency suits. And in good time, too, because the moment the internal hatch closed, the external vacuum seal opened, and the airlock instantly vented in a rush of escaping air.

'It's almost as if the ship tried to stop us...' said Shao when Milosh logged back on their comms.

'Probably Spider and his shenanigans,' replied Milosh, shrugging. 'It wouldn't be above Al to tell him to keep an eye on us and stall.'

'I'm not sure. Things were going haywire the whole time...'

'Doesn't matter,' decided Milosh. 'We're gonna get off that joint before...'

'Before what?'

'Before we're stuck on it. Get moving.' Milosh headed out into the bay, and Shao had no choice but to follow.

They scrambled out of the airlock and into the open hold, jumping towards the ceiling above. Shao floated upwards lightly, drifting effortlessly in zero gravity next to Milosh. The forklift drones neatly stacked in the charging racks came to life as they passed them; lights turning on and engines warming up. Luckily for them, the drones weren't designed for a quick startup, and both managed to float almost to the black rectangular opening bordering the deck and the open space.

Milosh initiated his magboots as soon as his feet touched the hull. The man brought his rifle to bear and shot down the first forklifts detaching from the racks. Shao hurried to crawl over the border and onto the outer hull of the hauler.

After a few more flashes of discharge, Milosh joined her. 'Go, go, go,' he yelled. 'Move it before they swarm us!'

The pair ran across the outer hull of the Incitatus' gray metamaterial surface, glistening like ceramic and pockmarked with small craters left by micro meteors. They moved as fast as the situation allowed, magboots preventing them from floating off into the dark void, but there was only so fast they could press on without their feet losing connection to the hull. A flock of forklifts emerged behind them and dispersed into a wide fan.

Suddenly, Shao missed a step and felt herself spinning, her legs moving away from the Incitatus as she slowly turned upside down. Milosh grabbed her hand at the last moment and pulled her down into a crevice between two armored plates, under a communication dish panel. 'Hold still,' he said. 'We have to wait them out, no way we can outrun them.'

Shao didn't reply, suddenly staring up with wide eyes. Milosh followed her gaze and froze.

A long, blindingly white spindle of a military frigate loomed above them like a sword. The craft's engines shone like small stars at its rear as the spaceship accelerated towards them. The spaceship seemed giant, less than ten kilometers above their heads, and quickly closing in. Astonished, Shao recognized the Yusan's escort ship—the Jīnlóng.

Before they had a chance to react at all, the ship rammed into the Incitatus' distant starboard like a lance. The frigate's white hull collapsed like a harmonica, small explosions reverberating throughout its length. The hauler's armored carapace rippled and broke when the shockwave carried through it.

Amazingly, the ramming craft's engines remained online for minutes, despite the ship itself being ripped apart by powerful forces and fused with the barge. Shao slammed violently into the hull when the shockwave reached them and crashed into the dish above her. The comm array broke off, and she bounced horizontally back towards the carapace, coughing up blood into her helmet. New flashes of burning pain shook her body as the stitches tore. She barely felt it when Milosh's body hit hers, darkness veiled her eyes, and she couldn't feel anything anymore.

43

Mai dreamed she was swimming in a warm, dense sea of inertia gel, floating effortlessly on the green surface. She happily watched the clouds swim above her, shaped like various animals she never saw but read about in children's stories. This cloud looked like a sheep, the other like a wolf, and this one, just above her, resembled a coiled snake. The snake hissed and bit her in the face, sparks cascading from its metallic, venomous fangs. It bit her and bit her again, but she couldn't move.

Just when she thought this nightmare would go on forever, Mai woke up with a startled gasp. She was surrounded by complete darkness, numb, and cold. She tried looking around, but she couldn't move, her body felt heavy and unresponsive. At first, she thought the odd hissing was nothing but a memory of her nightmare, but then something poked her right in the eye, and she felt hot drops fall on her cheeks. She tried to scream, but couldn't open her mouth.

'Calm down, Mai,' she heard a familiar voice next to her ear. 'It's just me, Lasse. Don't try to move, please. I'll be done in a moment.'

Mai recoiled at the sound of his voice and speech pattern. Toft talked like a machine, in a steady, almost mechanical manner. She tried to calm down and relax, slowly losing her composure as panic set in. And then, without warning, she was flooded with light, blinding her instantly.

'Oh, sorry.'

The light dimmed, revealing an array of six lamps, a metal-gray ceiling, and a blur that soon focused, becoming Toft's face. He looked horrible—his cheeks were pale and gaunt, and the cheery light in his brown eyes was gone, replaced with dark determination. He clenched his jaws, visibly in pain. 'Here you are, good as new,' said Toft. 'Well, kinda. I fixed your eye up as best as I could.'

'Lasse... What...'

'I couldn't get the lens to change colors though,' he droned on monotonously. 'I don't have the equipment here for that. You're just gonna have to live without.'

'Lens? I don't care about...' started Mai, then took a deep breath. 'What happened?'

'Oh, I just dragged you here from the Sōngshǔ before they caught you.'

'Who caught me? What do you mean dragged? Where is here?'

'The drones, Mai,' replied Toft. 'They'd get you like they got Green... They'd... Do the same to you.'

'I saw you get shot! How are you even alive?'

'Oh, yeah, been there. Didn't get the t-shirt though. They must have run out.'

'Stop it! Just tell me what happened!'

'Well, I saw the big guy aim at you, I guess I must have jumped,' explained Toft slowly. 'Next thing I know, I woke up in the medbay where the convicts kept us before, remember?'

'Yeah, I remember.'

'So yeah. The stims in my suit must have kicked in. I was losing a lot of blood, but I crawled to the med station. The same one you're lying in now, sorry. The drone did sterilize the bed, though. I got the thing to stitch me up and went after you. I figured McNamarra would go straight for our ship, so it wasn't that hard to catch up. I got there just in time for the explosion, so I pulled you away before the drones swarmed you. I took you to the medbay, got you on stims, got myself fixed. You were out for hours, so I figured I'd fix your eye. Happy birthday, Hanukkah, or whatever.' Toft shrugged and made a vague gesture with a mini welder he held in his hands.

Mai realized how awful he looked. The semi-transparent medical tightsuit revealed massive, gaping wounds in his torso, patched with gray artificial skin and rows upon rows of metallic stitches. The patches didn't stick to the edges of the wound properly. Inflamed flaps of skin were duct-taped to the skin of Toft's chest, but she could still see the nanite paste bubbling under the skin. The stench of blood and puss was almost overwhelming, even despite the odor of chemicals. His shirt was cut off, but long strands of fabric were sewn into the wound, and stitching went off into healthy tissue, following some bizarre pattern cut into Toft's tissue. 'Holy crap, what did you use?' she gasped. 'A drunk monkey with a sewing machine?'

'Nope, though I wish I had,' replied Toft. 'Something's wrong with the drone; it went off drawing pictures on me instead of patching me up. I had to do it myself. That's why I did your eye manually, too.'

Mai shuddered, imagining what the autodoc would have done to her face. 'Good call,' she said weakly and sat up, holding the edge of the bed to stop the dizziness. She looked around the room, only now noticing the state it was in. The place was wrecked; all the tools and tables except the massive medical drone were shoved to the wall. The deck was filthy with blood and pieces of burned equipment. A stack of a dozen or so dead bodies in orange jumpsuits were shoved into the empty space.

'Oh yeah, the decor here is amazing,' said Toft, seeing Mai's shock. 'Five stars. Looks like Zhengdao dropped off the downed prisoners here. For autopsy or some shit. Or they just don't wanna look at them.'

'I don't wanna look at them either,' she replied, gasping for air. 'Can we get out of here?'

'Yeah, sure, it's safe here, though. Drones never look in here, and the soldiers just drop the bodies off and leave. Actually, I haven't seen any Zhengdao guys in hours.'

'Wait, Zhengdao soldiers?' she asked, getting off the table and floating up.

'Yeah, they showed up some hours ago,' said Toft, just as unfazed about the topic as he was about the dead bodies. 'Haven't seen any since the ship shook. Maybe the drones got them.'

The memories of what happened started coming back to her. The escape, the drop pods, McNamarra. Green. She shuddered and forced herself not to think about it. 'Wait, if they're here, they must have come in a shuttle. We can get in touch with them and get out!' said Mai enthusiastically and kicked herself off the medical drone towards the hatch.

Toft followed her hesitantly. 'I don't know; they probably won't be very happy to see us.'

'Too fucking bad.' Mai shrugged. 'They won't execute us on the spot or anything. Old Zhenya will want to know where Shao is. I want to know too, in fact.'

'I have no idea,' replied Toft. 'Last I saw her was... Well, you know.'

'That other goon took her, Milosh.'

'We need to find her then.' Toft rushed forth and opened the hatch.

The corridor in front of them was dark and empty. Trash, ammo casings, blots of floating blood, and other detritus floated about, but nothing indicated a presence of any kind.

'What's the hurry?' asked Mai, trying to keep up after her companion, hastily scrambling through the corridor.

'We can't just leave Shao behind,' he said as if that explained his sudden change of mind.

'You took your sweet-ass time reaching that conclusion,' Mai mocked him.

'I thought she was dead... Or worse. Besides, I was busy saving you.'

'I know, thank you. And sorry, I guess I'm just jealous. Weird in a situation like that, eh?'

'Don't worry about it.'

'We both want to rescue her, okay? But don't run around like that, you're barely holding together. You wanna die before we even find her?'

'Right, find her,' agreed Toft. 'We need a functional terminal, maybe hack a feed from cameras. If they're even on anymore.'

'Sure beats running along the corridors and hoping we stumble on them,' agreed Mai.

The pair turned back to the medbay. Mai shuddered at the sight of the dead, but Toft just passed them as if they were furniture. 'Come on,' he said. 'They won't bite.'

Mai looked at Toft as if she saw him for the first time. 'That's cold, man.'

'Well, what can I say.' He shrugged. 'It's been a rough day.'

Mai realized Toft was barely holding on—he must have been drugged up to the teeth. It was just a matter of time before the stims' effect stops and the he collapsed in a heap. She wasn't sure if Toft was gonna live through the next few hours. She wanted to tell him Green was dead. She wanted to say something. Every time she opened her mouth to say it, tears swelled in her eyes and burning pain in the wounds from the haphazard surgery immediately exploded. How could this have happened? How could she even begin telling him? 'Lasse, I gotta tell you something. Jared...' she started.

Toft shook his head. 'I told you I saw it,' he replied in a hollow voice and turned around.

He did tell me, Mai thought, fighting against the fog of pain and exhaustion in her head. How could I forget? My brain must be fritzed just like the ship.

They got to work on the terminal and disassembled the cover quickly. Mai adjusted the full sensory interface cable installed in her wrist and plugged it into the slot. Her back arched, and she went limp. Within seconds, the virtual landscape of the Incitatus' computer system sprawled before her. It didn't change since the last time—the glitch didn't clear. If anything, the crystalline formations of code became more complex than before. Security measures blocked her access, but Mai's bots cut through them with ease. Not only were they not what she would call a bleeding edge of network security, but the firewall software also glitched and lagged considerably. She didn't even need to upload a virus to slow them down; the latency with which the electronic countermeasures reacted to her moves and attacks made dealing with them a child's play.

The ship's computers fought as best they could, spawning more and more defense bots, but soon enough, the entire network reached capacity and froze in a loop, trying to reboot crashed programs. Soon she was free to roam through the systems.

The architecture was very basic, and the system accepted her commands well enough. For some reason, the subsystems slipped out of control after a few seconds, as if they were forgetting given tasks. Same story as with the drones earlier. Frustrated, Mai opened the task manager panel, which materialized in augmented reality in front of her as a square panel with functions and programs listed in plain English text. Most of the CPU's computing power was free and unused, yet somehow whatever task she opened just disappeared after a second or two. It made no sense.

Mai commanded the ship's computer to display history. Looking back a few hours, there was an unusual spike of activity in the Incitatus' navigation subsystems, which made no sense for a ship without a drive and also thousands of tasks opened and closed, going on for weeks. Come to think of it, the glitch did seem to have started around...

'Lasse, when did we land on this barge exactly?'

'About two and a half weeks ago, May 20th, I think,' he messaged back. 'Why, what's up?'

'Cause a day or two after that, the entire system went the way of the dodo.'

'Like, extinct?'

'Oh, weren't dodos the ones that went crazy?'

'No, Mai, they went extinct.'

'Sucks to be them. I meant the system went crazy, anyway.'

'How?'

'Systems were coming off and on, randomly rebooting, restarting. I've no idea what is happening. Can't hold onto a program before it closes on me.'

'You have to try harder,' urged her Toft.

'No shit,' messaged Mai and closed the comms.

She needed to focus. She duplicated her icon and started opening multiple cameras feeds at the same time, hoping to catch at least a glimpse of Shao before the view died; narrowing down the search area was all she could hope for. She saw the convict gangs here and there, playing cat and mouse on multiple decks against swarms of drones, Zhengdao soldiers going against both the groups and, for some reason, against their own robotic support. They were losing that battle, too.

The Zhengdao shuttle in the main cargo bay was surrounded by an ever-shrinking perimeter of soldiers, slowly retreating towards the craft, intersection by intersection. They didn't give ground easily, but their fight got more and more desperate every minute.

A few decks below, she saw another shuttle, old and scrappy looking, surrounded by at least a dozen Zhengdao drones and a big swarm of others, which, judging by the fireworks, were trying to breach the hull.

Two more people were skulking around the corridors towards the upper decks—a blonde, tall woman, and a stocky-looking man, both wearing black armored jumpsuits. Mai wondered what their deal was, but the cameras flickered and shut down, forcing her over to further feeds.

External cameras showed nothing but frame after frame of the dark gray, pockmarked hull on the black background, the monotony broken by airlock hatches, comm arrays, and point defense system's turrets. She saw the wreckage of the Jīnlóng in the rear of the giant hauler, sticking out like a bright iceberg in the sea of gray. The frigate was irreparably damaged, crushed, and bent, its hull ripped open like a tin can. On the next frame, she saw two people under one of the arrays: a small, unmoving silhouette in the shadow and a man in a brown space suit hovering over it.

'Got them, Lasse,' she messaged and logged off.

'Awesome, let's go!'

'Yeah, they're outside of the ship,' she said. 'We need to spacewalk to get them.'

'Doesn't matter, my suit is sealed,' replied Toft.

'Let's go then. I don't know which array they're under; we're gonna have to sweep the hull.'

'Peachy. I hope we find them before that damn coffin falls out of the Cloud.'

'Yeah, I wouldn't prep the balloons yet.'

'What do you mean?'

'By the look of things, we left the Oort Cloud way back.'

'Fuck. How can you tell?'

'I was in the network,' she scoffed, annoyed. 'I saw the navigation feed.'

Toft sighed and headed out of the medbay without a word.

Guided by Mai's electronic recon, the two quickly made their way through the decks and corridors towards the nearest airlock. Not all snippets of camera feed she saw were accurate, and some hatches were closed shut by the glitching system, so sometimes they had to crawl through ventilation ducts to avoid obstacles. The dark corridors filled with rubble and hydraulics going haywire were a small nightmare to navigate—pipes were spraying a hot mist of used coolant onto the decks, making the trek on slippery ground harder. Mai took the lead now, Toft comfortably slipping into the role of a follower as soon as she took charge to lead them away from the fighting. The engineer's wounds were causing him visible distress, and Mai had to adjust the pace so that he could keep up. They stumbled upon traces of human activity, but not a living soul until they reached the airlock.

When Mai short-circuited the interface, the inner door slid open. The air contained in the deck burst open into space when they vented the airlock, immediately freezing into condensed crystal fog. The gust of escaping air dragged the weakened Toft with it, but Mai engaged her magboots and stabilized his body.

The two climbed out into the cargo hold—the same one in which Shao was wounded, and the same one in which Toft left the damaged biodrone seemingly so long ago. Mai couldn't believe it hadn't even been a month.

All of the forklift drone racks were empty now, for some reason, and Mai used them for stability as she helped Toft up. Climbing in total darkness illuminated only by Mai's suit helmet took forever. Without warning a beam of light centered on them from below.

A short burst from an automatic slug thrower bounced off the nearest rack, casting a rain of molten sparks of metal in front of them and stopping Mai and Toft in their tracks. She looked down, but was blinded by the sharp light—her cyber eyes adjusted, focusing on the stocky man with a rifle trained straight at them and a tall woman with a computer panel in her hands. Mai's HUD displayed a laser comm contact request.

'Stay right where you are,' she heard the man's harsh and commanding voice. 'You're under arrest.'

'What am I under arrest for?' replied Mai. 'Lollygagging?'

'Don't get snippy with me, missy,' said the man.

'Give her a break, Lederman,' interjected the tall woman. 'Hi, we're not gonna hurt you two, we just need to talk.'

'You have an interesting way of chatting people up,' said Toft grimly.

'Sorry for that,' answered the woman apologetically. 'It's been a rough day.'

'Tell me about it.'

'All right, we can talk,' said Mai. 'Just don't try anything.'

'Girl, if we wanted to hurt you, you'd be dead.'

'Aight, we're coming up,' said the woman and jumped towards them. 'My name's Tomasson, by the way, Lara Tomasson. And Mister Gruff is Lederman. We're with the Rangers.'

'I'm Mai Wren, and this is Lasse Toft. We're... Hitchhikers.'

'You didn't pick the express bus, did you?' said Tomasson, landing next to Mai on a rack. Lederman's jump carried him one rack below them, rifle hanging freely from a strap on his shoulder.

Mai stifled an instinct to run. The Rangers, if that's who they were, didn't seem threatening.

'All right, boys and girls,' said Lederman. 'Let's start over, okay?'

'Whatever you say, big guy,' replied Toft.

'Exactly, whatever I say. So, we dunked on this here craft due to a priority message claiming it's been overtaken by pirates and—'

'Pirates?' interrupted Mai. 'This ship's a prison barge!'

'Not according to the paperwork, it isn't,' said Lederman. 'It's a raw material hauler designated to Jupiter for use in the megaconstruction.'

'It is that,' said Toft. 'But there's also a bunch of guys in fancy orange outfits.'

Lederman exchanged looks with the other Ranger.

'So they aren't pirates?' asked Tomasson.

'Maybe they are,' said Mai. 'But they've been here for weeks.'

'You've been here all that time?' asked Lederman. 'Can you prove that this wasn't a pirate raid?'

'Oh yeah, totally.' Toft nodded. 'We've been stowed here all the time. Saw them in cells, and there were armed sec drones and all the prison getups.'

'But do you have proof?' inquired Lederman.

'Well, I have cybereyes with a recorder unit,' said Mai hesitantly. 'I could hand it over, but what's in it for us?'

'Fuckin' kids nowadays,' scoffed Lederman. 'No sense of duty, no respect. Hand over the data, delete the originals, and you won't get in trouble, what else do you want?'

'How about protection from desertion charges by our mother corp?' asked Mai quickly. 'As witnesses and all that?'

'So that's how it is?'

'That's how it is,' said Mai. Rescuing Shao was a priority, but she needed to take care of their futures too.

The Rangers gave each other a long look. Lederman shrugged, finally. 'Fine, have it your way,' he said. 'Tomasson will get your recording and testimony, but first, we gotta get out of here.'

'We were going up to hijack a comm array,' said Tomasson after making sure the recording was copied and purged from Mai's HUD memory. 'We have to send a distress call to the nearest beacon.'

'We're going up 'cause our friend is held hostage,' said Toft. 'We need to free her.'

'Freeing hostages is our specialty, kid,' said Lederman. 'Let's get moving.'

The four of them got through the cargo bay. The Rangers made sure that Toft kept up and didn't hurt himself further. They quickly scrambled onto the outer hull.

The group traveled mostly in silence except for basic communication; the scarred hull of the giant hauler was not easy terrain by any means. Lederman's grappling hook came very much in handy, shooting a long rope ten meters forward towards the nearest extruding element of the hull, then rappelling them onwards using the gun's motor to cover the ground with great speed. They reached the comm array within minutes, towering above the hull majestically, yet still dwarfed by the white-hot wreckage of the frigate in the distance.

'Hold up,' commanded Lederman, stopping the whole group. 'I have a visual on the bogey under the dish.'

'Are you sure?' asked Tomasson. 'I can't see anything.'

'Yeah, I got the bastard in my sights,' replied Lederman and trained his rifle at the dish. 'I'm gonna take him out, so we can approach the relay.'

'No wait,' interjected Toft. 'What if you hurt Shao?'

'Tough luck, kid.'

'Hold up, cap,' said Tomasson. 'What if you damage the array?'

'Shit, good point,' answered Lederman. 'I'm not looking forward to negotiating his surrender under fire...'

'Maybe we won't have to,' joined in Mai. 'If Shao is with him, they must be on the same comms. I'll scan for her frequency, and we can join in on their channel.'

'Fine, but take cover first, everyone,' agreed Lederman. 'If he tries anything, I'll pop his ass. There are other relays on this boat.'

Mai scanned the area for comm frequencies; however, the disturbing signal present in the Incitatus' network was interfering with her attempts. 'Can't get a hold of it,' she complained. 'Some noise is buggering the feed. The same thing happened when I tried to ride the cameras, everything just fritzes after a moment.'

'Let me help,' said Tomasson. 'I'll try to isolate the commlink and drown that noise.'

'Hurry up, ladies,' Lederman urged. 'We don't have all day.'

Mai connected her suit's network to Tomasson's and watched Lara work through her HUD. The Ranger woman tried to approach the task from a mechanical angle, rewriting the comm software to adjust and drown out the noise, but it persisted. It seemed to shift and mutate, adjusting to whatever cleanup routines Tomasson tried.

'Hold on, maybe try to enhance?' suggested Mai.

'Might work...' agreed Tomasson and adjusted to clear up the background noise. 'What is that, sounds like whispers?'

'Like some jackass chanting something, maybe?'

'I'm gonna enhance it further,' said Tomasson. 'Maybe if we bring it out of the background...'

'No, wait, don't!' exclaimed Mai. 'We saw a recording from a guy... Redding, I think, from where they found it. He mentioned comm problems, what if it's the same thing scrambling all the tech here?'

'Found what?' asked Lederman. 'Wait, you said: Redding?'

'I've been in the system, through IFS, and it's all weird. Like it's rewriting itself over and... Changing...' trailed off Mai, too busy to pay attention to Lederman's other question.

'That doesn't sound right. You sure you don't have a concussion? That bruise on your face looks nasty...'

'Trust me. The code is corrupted somehow.'

'Right, I'd have to let it in our system to clear it up...'

'And then it's goodbye, Las Vegas,' finished Mai.

'Maybe I'll try to kill it with a counter signal; it's just a radio noise after all.'

'Yeah, mess with it the way it messes with us...'

'This should only take a moment.'

Tomasson and Mai tinkered for a while, isolating themselves in a full sensory interface for speed, while Lederman and Toft stood watch, covering the relay. Soon, they had it: a program automatically adjusting to broadcast signals canceling the pervasive noise, adjusting and compensating for any changes and variables along the way.

Mai tried it out, exhaling with relief when the two signals canceled each other out entirely. She scanned the local frequencies and soon found a two-way comm-relay using Shao's code. 'Shao? Are you there?' she asked cautiously.

'Shao can't pick up the phone right now,' answered a man's voice. 'But you can leave a message.'

'That's the con, Milosh,' said Mai. 'He shot Shao and kept us hostage for days...'

'I can hear you. Don't talk about me like I'm not here.'

'Listen here, shitstain,' growled Lederman. 'I have you in my sights, so come up with your hands up, or I'll shoot your ass off right now!'

'Good bluff, chief, five points,' replied Milosh. 'But why do you think I showed myself to you? I got you right where I want you. I rigged the panels you're cowering behind with enough homemade thermite to make you wish it was Tuesday.'

'You couldn't know we're coming,' uttered Lederman, but doubt showed in his voice.

'I was expecting the tin cans to come knocking; not you,' Milosh agreed. 'But that doesn't mean I won't blow you.'

'You wanna try your luck, go for it,' hissed Lederman angrily. 'Don't think I won't blast your head off on my way out, though.'

'Good grief, either kiss or stop flirting,' interjected Tomasson.

Milosh chuckled all of a sudden with a deep, hearty laugh of a man running on fumes for way too long.

'Is Shao all right?' asked Mai. 'I wanna talk to her if she's alive.'

'Shao's fine,' replied Milosh. 'She's just unconscious, knocked her head real bad when that crazy son of a bitch rammed us. We could use some help, actually.'

'Why the hell would we help you?' asked Toft.

'Well, for one, we all want out of here, no?' asked Milosh. 'Besides, my boots are damaged again, and I can't get out from under this dish even if I wanted to, or Shao will float away into space.'

'All right, here's the deal,' reassessed Lederman. 'Let us get to the dish, and we'll help you and your friend out. We're Rangers, investigating your unlawful imprisonment on this ship; we don't have to be enemies.'

'Shao isn't his friend,' argued Toft, but Mai shushed him.

'Oh goodie, I'll happily testify and all,' said Milosh. 'But we gotta get out of that ship, or we're going to have to wait two decades to do that. My associates are coming to get me, but we have to be in drive range, or they won't be able to pick us up.'

'We'll get that sorted, just disarm the charges and let us come closer.'

'Yeah, yeah, *mi casa es su casa*; come over.'

'What about the charges?'

'There are no charges, chief.' Milosh laughed. 'I'm stuck here. Besides, I left the bombs in my other pants anyway.'

'Right, I thought as much. Had to be sure, though.'

'Hey, I get it. Been in an outfit myself. Still am.'

'So, you're not just a pirate, then?' asked Tomasson.

'Far from it, actually.' Milosh smiled and feigned a salute. 'Captain Stepan Milosh of the Hussaria Inc. mercenary company.'

'I've heard about you guys,' said Lederman. 'How did you end up in this sorry mess?'

'Long story short, I thought I was smart when I was stupid. But that ain't gonna happen again.'

'Great, I'm glad you guys are getting to know each other and stuff,' interjected Toft. 'But we gotta get out of here!'

'I know,' said Lederman. 'Lara, send a distress beacon.'

'Yes, sir!' Tomasson saluted and got to work on the array.

'It's not gonna help us,' said Mai sullenly. 'I've seen the charts; we're already in the Beyond. We're gonna be out of reach of any craft way before anyone manages even to put on their shoes, let alone pick us up.'

'That's where you're wrong, kiddo,' said Milosh. 'My associates should already be on the job as we speak. All we need to do is make sure we're within range of a pickup; they won't mind spending a couple of days paddling through the Beyond to get me. But we need to be in the direct area and broadcast our location as far as we can. We have to get your ship. That's where Shao and I were going before the wreckage over there decided to ram us.'

'Why did they do it anyway?' wondered Lederman. 'A malfunction, you think?'

'No way to know for sure,' stated Tomasson bluntly, her hands busy disassembling the comm array's outer panels.

'We can't take the Sōngshǔ,' said Mai quietly, almost a whisper. 'Whatever causes the drones to malfunction must have originated there. All the frenzied bots flock to the column where we left our jumper.'

'You think... You think we brought it with us?' asked Toft. 'Could it be the mummy?'

'What mummy?' asked Lederman.

'Shao found a set of coordinates on Pluto station, recorded by the Redding I mentioned earlier,' said Mai. 'He said it's for a buried cache of tech, worth a big chunk of cred.'

'We talked our officer, Green, into picking it up and deserting,' added Toft. 'We were sick of living under Zhengdao boot.'

'Sick of the old Zhenya pushing us around,' said Mai. 'Figured we'd run away to Venus and farm broccoli.'

'They don't farm broccoli on Venus,' said Milosh. 'Also, I don't believe you.'

'It's mostly true.' A new voice joined the conversation.

'Shao! You're awake.' Toft burst with joy and moved to help his friend up, but Mai cut him off and hugged her, holding her as tight as she could.

'I'm so glad you're okay!' said Mai. 'I thought... I mean, I was afraid that...'

'I know, Mai, I know,' replied Shao quietly. 'I'm fine, we're fine. And it's all going to be alright.'

'I was so worried...'

'Me too.'

'Charming. Anyway, that's the short and sticky of it?' asked Lederman. 'Anything else you wanna spill?'

'Yeah, we gotta come clean, Mai,' said Shao, then turned to the others. 'I convinced Jared and Lasse to defect, because Mai and I thought we could make a deal with the corporate HQ for a good pension.'

'Where is this Jared?' asked Lederman.

'Dead,' replied Toft, then fell silent. He took a step away from the group and stared at the charred frigate.

Shao looked after him for a second, processing the news, then continued. 'I don't think we have the time for a long tale,' she said. 'So I'll just get to the point. We found a coffin with a mummified corpse. Brought it with us. We stowed away on what we thought is an empty raw material hauler, we had no idea there'd be people on board.'

'And you noticed anything going haywire since then?' asked Tomasson. 'Doors opening on their own, lights flickering?'

'Yeah, we thought the ship was just shitty,' replied Shao. 'You really think it was the mummy?'

'Come on,' scoffed Milosh. 'Don't tell me a ghost story now!'

'I'm not. The body had cyber... Some sort of antennae or whatever. Maybe it had a virus?'

'Or worse,' said Lederman grimly. 'Maybe it worked exactly as intended.'

'Any idea what could it be?' asked Mai.

'Fuck no.' Lederman shook his head. 'But we can't take your ship, that's for sure. Whatever is causing the glitches is probably worse on your craft.'

'Not to mention we don't have the firepower to take on a drone army,' added Milosh.

'We could try to get our shuttle,' said Tomasson. 'But we'd have to take on a bunch of drones too.'

'Zhengdao,' blurted Shao. 'We can go to my father and just sur-render.'

'Their frigate is blown,' said Lederman.

'The Jīnlóng,' added Mai. 'We know... Knew... A lot of the guys on the ship.'

'Yeah... But they had to have landed in a shuttle,' agreed Shao. 'It's our only choice.'

44

Zhenya looked over at the containers behind him. Their dull-gray surface was pockmarked and slightly molten from the barrage of automatic fire the security drones rained on the Zhengdao commando party. They had been ambushed while searching the main cargo hold, hoping to find whatever it was the convicts were looking for.

Twenty security drones had emerged from behind the crates and opened fire from three flanks, not entirely surprising the well-trained group of a dozen soldiers, but catching them in the open. If not for the sudden violent tremor that tossed the Incitatus' deck a moment ago, the soldiers would have been in trouble.

The shake tossed the drones about like paper dolls, and Zhenya took the chance. His powered suit of armor withstood the violent turbulence with ease, even though his soldiers were debilitated by it. He launched forward, cutting the drones to pieces with his shoulder-mounted laser canon and the ceremonial sword. Lightly armored and scattered in disarray, the drones had no chance.

Zhenya had disposed of six before they regrouped, and by that time, the soldiers had regained composure as well. They finished the job quickly, dispatching the enemy. He watched in silence as Sarah Lowe commanded the troops, while a reloading drone fed his suit with power. The microwave laser glare surrounded the suit as it charged, adding radiancy and dignity to Zhenya's silhouette.

'Nicely fought,' said Lowe on private comms, relieved. 'We might not have been able to take them out without serious casualties otherwise.'

'Those machines are an inferior foe,' replied Zhenya, humbly. He made no mention of the fact that, unlike the commando's carapace armor, his power suit was pretty much impervious to the machines' weaponry.

'We sustained no casualties. Mostly thanks to your bravery,' continued Lowe. 'But everyone's tired and hurt. We should pause the search before it's too late.'

'We can't abandon Shao,' replied Zhenya. 'Not now when our drones fell prey to that virus, or whatever it is.'

'But, esteemed captain... Yuan.'

'Enough of that,' scolded her Zhenya. 'We will continue. Order the troops to take stimulants, and let's proceed.' He was determined not to turn back without Shao, especially as the situation developed in a worrying direction.

'I must formally protest,' insisted Lowe. 'There is no indication that—'

'Do you have children?'

'No.'

'Do you have anyone dear to your heart?'

Lowe stared deadpan into Zhenya's eyes through the comm window.

Unfazed, he continued. 'Sarah, we're here to find my daughter, before something happens to her. If... If it hasn't already.'

'I understand.' Lowe bowed her head, earning a couple of questioning looks from her squad, not privy to their officers' conversation. 'We're moving out, boys,' said Lowe, switching to a squad-wide band. 'Leng, ping adjutant Jin Sun, we need to run a radar sweep of the cargo hold.'

'Of course, sergeant!' replied soldiers in unison, raising their hands in a salute.

'Esteemed sergeant, ma'am?' Leng said a moment later. 'I can't get a hold of the adjutant. I'm getting a connection, but there's only static... And...'

'Well, spit it out!' commanded Lowe. 'Static and what?'

'Um, whispers, sergeant,' finished Leng. 'Like someone talking in the distance, but I can't make anything out.'

'Patch me through,' said Zhenya. 'I want to hear it.'

The soldier connected the line to the squad-wide band, and the entire group could now hear it. The typical static of a deadline was mixed with something, barely audible and vaguely resembling garbled human speech.

'What the hell...' gasped Lowe, startled.

'It sounds as if someone was talking in code... Or some alien language,' said Leng.

'Or backward,' added another soldier.

'I'll boost the signal, maybe it becomes clearer,' said Leng and got to work.

'No, wait...' started Zhenya on an impulse, but it was too late.

The static dissipated, and they could now clearly hear the unearthly chant. Shifting up and down the vocal scale, sometimes low and guttural, sometimes high pitched and thin, the voice mumbled incomprehensible syllables in an emotionless monotone.

'What is that?' whispered the troopers, confused.

'Whatever it is, my readings are off the scale,' said Zhenya. 'Shut it down; it's causing our systems to malfunction.'

Nobody replied or acknowledged the captain with a gesture. Zhenya repeated the command angrily. Nobody heeded him, the soldiers just stood there, silent, gesticulating, and waving their hands.

Zhenya tried to stomp his foot, annoyed, but the suit didn't react to his movements. 'Hey!' he shouted. 'Turn off the signal!' Nobody replied, and Zhenya suddenly felt trapped in his armored command center. He was tightly strapped and enclosed in a web of sensors intended to carry his muscle movement to the suit's powerful servomotors, but they didn't react at all, just pressed against him like a tight coffin. 'Computer, run diagnostics,' he said, but nothing happened. Zhenya breathed deeply and slowly, trying to contain the encroaching panic attack. He realized that other soldiers' gear also malfunctioned.

Lowe was waving a hand in front of her visor, Leng slapped the side of his helmet repeatedly. One of the commandos even walked into a container wall, as if blind. Another soldier pushed his fists where his ears were under the helmet, and dropped to his knees, visibly in pain. His magboots disengaged, and the soldier drifted above the deck, shaking in agony. Zhenya strained once more to move, but the powered armor weighed more than a ton; he might as well have tried to lift a shuttle.

Suddenly, the suit's systems came back online.

'Oh gods, it's back on,' he said relieved, but nobody answered.

The suit's targeting systems switched on, and red rectangles displayed around each soldier. Zhenya fought desperately to move or exert some control over his command station, but he could only watch as the suit tracked and locked onto every one of his subordinates.

The commandos were still completely unaware of their surroundings; Zhenya saw Lowe struggling to take off her helmet.

The suit's arm-mounted turret opened fire, and an invisible laser pulse cut a neat hole in the drifting soldier's faceplate. Blood and molten armor exploded in a swirling cloud. The suit moved to the next soldier, who was still comically trying to find his way around the container with his hands. The laser pulse cut his spine neatly down the middle and moved on to kill Leng and the other soldiers.

It moved slowly, methodically, as if on autopilot, but the troopers stood no chance, utterly oblivious to the mortal danger. Finally, Lowe managed to wrestle her helmet off, and quickly put on an emergency mask detaching from her suit's collar. She took a deep breath of relief and opened her eyes as soon as the cover insulated her face. Zhenya saw her fright as the carnage dawned on her. She raised her eyes at him just as the sword-wielding arm came down, cutting her in half. Zhenya watched the sergeant's corpse fly upwards into open space, guts, and blood trailing behind the torso. Lowe's face was frozen forever in an expression of shock and disbelief.

Yuan Zhenya screamed and cried, but couldn't move a finger. His cries could almost drown the insane, unearthly chant rising and falling in his comms—but not quite. Zhenya's armored command center kicked off the deck and walked away.

45

Milosh scouted ahead to make sure the way to the main cargo hold is clear. The Rangers sent out a distress call, hopefully letting both Ranger central and Milosh's company on the Querub know how things were. The mission ahead of them was now as simple as it gets. Get out of the Incitatus and hang on until help comes. Then they can regroup, and double back for Muldoon and Chatty, if they're still alive. All they needed to do was reach the Zhengdao forces and surrender—nothing easier.

Milosh's magboots were shot to hell by the shockwave, when the frigate crashed. The impact also busted his internal biomed printer, and he was running low on meds and stims. Soon, the pain and exhaustion will catch up to him, and that'll be all she wrote. He'll be at the mercy of the Rangers; for what it's worth, they seemed like an honest bunch. Their company sure beats the convicts and drones. But if they don't get out of the hauler soon, even that won't be a problem. The moment Milosh's meds stop streaming into the bloodstream, his augments will cause a slow, agonizing death as his body rejects the implants.

He was glad to roam ahead, at least the rest of them won't see his weakness. He didn't really enjoy being a part of a civilian group anyway, and he didn't have to worry the kids will screw something up, or the Rangers get in the way of what needs to be done.

Milosh used the Rangers' grappling gun to quickly traverse the rugged valley of the Incitatus' hull, pulling himself on the rope efficiently and rapidly, only ever touching down to the hull to push himself off again. The main cargo hold's canyon was just ahead of them, a dark chasm full of unknown terrors. The whole situation reminded him of the last time he was involved in that kind of a mess. The asteroid, Sedna, was ice, of course, not metal, but Milosh couldn't shake the feeling of synchronicity. He half expected to see a ladder leading down to the bowels of the chasm when he reached the edge. Nothing of the sort, though. The edge led straight down multiple stories of cargo containers. At least twenty floors down, thought Milosh. It should be a breeze. What's the worst that could happen.

The rest of the party tagged along within minutes, moving slower because of the wounded Lasse Toft and Shao.

Lederman joined Milosh at the edge first, looking down carefully. 'Are you sure it's here?' he asked. 'Looks like any old hole to me.'

'That's because you're vanilla,' replied Milosh with a smile, pointing at his cybereyes. 'I see heat signatures at the bottom, checks out with the shuttle engine warming up.'

'If you say so.' He shrugged. 'I'd rather stick to binoculars and vision mags than get my eyeballs replaced, to be honest.'

'Shame you don't have any with you, no? Don't sweat it, chief—the augmentation squad has your back.'

Milosh raised his hand to high-five Mai, but she ignored him, looking through the merc as if he weren't there. Fuck it, he thought. I made an effort. 'If you're done getting old,' he said out loud. 'Let's hike; we're losing daylight.'

Pointing at a completely black void of space above them, he turned around and vaulted towards the bottom. He fired a grapple towards the nearest container and slung downward in a wide arc. The others followed slowly, using magboots to walk down the slope.

Rows of cargo containers chained together slowly waved to the rhythm of internal strains torturing the giant spaceship, more visibly now. Giant crates heaved and leaned, often brushing and smacking into each other. The Jīnlóng crashing into the hull caused many chains to break, sending the cargo into an erratic dance. Anything caught between two containers slamming into each other would be ground into a fine paste.

That's just peachy, thought Milosh. Walk in the park. He vaulted in and out from between the containers, scouting ahead of the group to make sure they didn't encounter sudden problems. A couple of bio-drones hovered about, but they dashed away before he could aim.

Somewhere far below, at the bottom of the hold, Milosh could read heat signatures; the Zhengdao shuttle was heating up, and smaller bursts of heat erupted around it irregularly.

Firefight.

'We have to hurry,' said Milosh over the comms. 'Looks like the party turned sour for the corp, and they're preparing to dust off.'

'Bullshit, my father would never leave without me,' replied Shao.

'Unless he's not in command,' said Tomasson. 'We have no idea what went down.'

'Listen to Lara, kids,' said Lederman. 'It's only ten more floors; you can do it. Move out.'

'Wait, what's that over there?' asked Mai, but Milosh couldn't hear any replies.

The cargo containers above his head waved violently as if a giant fish had swam through reeds. Milosh saw discharges of automatic weapons in the darkness above, and brighter, blinding pulses of laser fire. He quickly disconnected the grapple, and shot again, upwards this time. He vaulted over the crates, somersaulting between the moving blocks and shooting grapple after grapple without landing once. A container on a collision course almost crushed him, but Milosh pushed himself off with all the strength of his augmented muscles and walked on his palms to the edge. Get your shit together, he thought. Focus or the meds running out will be the least of your worries. When was the last time I slept, he wondered.

Quickly shooting another grapple, he flung himself over the last obstacle to the slope, where the rest of the group was. On the hullside, a white powered armor suit fired lasers in all directions, holding onto the hull with its legs and one arm. Shoulder-mounted turrets sent pulses of laser light all over, trying to take out the humans.

The Rangers spread out, taking cover behind containers on opposite sides of the monstrous machine and firing at it sporadically. Their attacks made no significant impact, but they did keep the suit busy while Mai and Shao desperately struggled to drag Toft into a thermal exhaust on the outer hull's slope.

Milosh acted without hesitation, shot a grapple straight at the powered suit, and heaved himself off the cargo crate with full force. The machine immediately noticed and turned to intercept him with its arms, while the turret continued to rain fire. Only then, did he see the long, sharp sword in its armored hands. 'You've got to be kidding me,' he said and veered into a pirouette, dodging the blade by a hair. 'Tell me this is a joke!'

'Wish I could,' said Tomasson. 'We don't have the ordnance to take that bastard down.'

'Yeah, we're about tightly fucked,' agreed Lederman. 'Who knew Zhengdao landed with a freaking monster on top of the war drones!'

Milosh dodged another wide swipe of the blade that cut the cable he was attached with, but the merc fired another grapple at the suit's leg, then dived down, pulling the cable in at full speed. He kicked the suit with both legs at full force right in the armored ankle. The kick's momentum was enhanced further by the velocity of his dive, and the suit went spinning clockwise to the site. It continued to try and skewer the merc, but Milosh danced around it at full speed of his enhanced reflexes. He tried to maneuver the suit away from the vent where Mai and Toft were hiding, noting with surprise Shao isn't with them. She slowly crept on the hullside, nearing the fight. *What is that crazy girl doing?* Milosh thought but didn't have the time to dwell on it.

'Haven't had so much fun since Sedna,' he said, but couldn't hide the heavy breathing. 'That guy's gonna tire me out pretty soon, gotta say. The prison cuisine didn't do my stamina any favors.'

'What do you mean, guy?' said Mai from the relative safety of the thermal exhaust shaft.

'That's not a drone,' replied Milosh. 'I can see the hatch; there's a pilot inside!'

'Why does he want to kill us?' asked Tomasson. 'Maybe he thinks we're convicts trying to break the blockade?'

'Why don't you ask him?' snarked Milosh.

The suit started maneuvering engines in its arms. The blast singed Milosh, tearing off the brown fabric of his suit. The emergency seal closed the tear before too much pressure was lost, but the shock and pain caused him to miss a step. A thrust of the curved sword connected, chopping two of Milosh's fingers, severed neatly at the core. Milosh dove under the suit again then crawled onto its back. Lederman fired a burst into its head. The rails ricocheted harmlessly.

A sudden burst of heat struck Milosh right between the shoulder blades, melting away his spacesuit and peeling the skin off his back like paper. He cried out in pain and lost his grip, floating away in a cloud of escaped oxygen.

A spidery charger drone climbed onto a cargo container, aiming its wide array at him. Milosh could do little to stop it; not while trying to grasp the emergency mask on his belt with the wounded hand.

The charger array shone stronger with every second.

'It's gonna fry me like a grilled chicken, do something!'

The comm response was an angry, high-pitched shriek. Milosh realized it was Shao. The girl pushed herself away from the shaft, bearing a handheld plasma cutter like a dagger. Her frail body slammed heavily into the charger drone, knocking it off balance. The machine shook like a wet dog, trying to get rid of the intruder, but Shao cut straight into its chassis with the cutter. The toxic-blue flame dug deep into the unarmored hull, raising geysers of sparks and metal droplets. The cutter went through the machine's innards like a hot knife through butter. With a heavy, almost animal-like sigh, the drone shut down.

Milosh finally managed to grasp the mask, slippery with his own blood, and put it on. The rebreather's intelligent weave closed itself around the man's head, forming a provisory helmet.

'Now we're even,' said Shao, breathing heavily. Her face was pallid and coated with thick sweat.

Milosh could bet her wound opened when she hit the machine. 'Not even close, I saved your ass at least two...' started Milosh, then noticed Shao's suddenly mortified expression. He swirled around his axis just as the giant sword swooshed past his head. 'Ok, we're even.'

'I got the connection,' said Tomasson. 'But all I get is that damn interference!'

'Can you isolate it?' asked Lederman. 'Like the last time?'

Before Lara could answer, a continuous laser beam from below cut into her container, its bright light melting the outer layer of metal and digging deep into the ice and rock inside it.

'They're shooting at us from the shuttle!' Mai shouted. 'What the fuck!'

'They must think we're convicts fighting the drones, or worse,' said Tomasson. 'I'll upload the signal jammer onto a stick, think you can catch it, Milosh?'

'We'll never know till you try!' he replied and kicked himself off the suit's back. He held onto the turret at the machine's arm with both hands and flipped over, landing his feet squarely. Milosh's suit's top was torn into rags and exposed to vacuum. The armored webbing implanted under his skin shone like fish scales, reflecting the beam from below. It wasn't designed to be space-proof, but it did its job for now.

'I'll try to contact the shuttle and tell them to hold their fire!' said Mai and got to work on the comms.

Tomasson dashed out of her cover and tossed the black puck of the memory stick towards the powered suit. The cannon's bright beam chewing through her cover must have hit something volatile, and the entire cargo crate suddenly exploded in a cloud of ice and rock, ripping itself apart and taking the woman with it.

'No!' cried Lederman and dashed from his cover towards the cloud of rubble drifting away, ignoring the danger. 'Lara! Say something!'

The powered armor's turret turned to aim at the Ranger, but Milosh slammed into it with force, causing it to lose the mark. A laser pulse cut the container millimeters away from Lederman's neck. Milosh caught the stick with his bloodied hand and ducked before the armored suit rammed into the Incitatus' hull, attempting to crush him. He engaged the drive's magnetic plate and slapped it onto a comm array sticking out of the suit's helmet just as the arm turret aimed straight at him. Milosh tensed, half expecting to be cut in half by a laser pulse, but nothing happened.

'Oh gods, oh gods, please make it stop.' They heard a man's voice over the comms. 'Please, can anybody hear me, I'm not the one doing it, please, make it stop...'

'Dad?' said Shao.

'Oh gods,' replied Zhenya. 'Shao, is that really you?'

'Yes, it's me,' she said. 'Please, stop!'

'I'm not controlling the suit,' said Zhenya. 'The signal, it must have hijacked it... Shao, it killed them all...'

'Killed who?'

'Sarah and Leng, and Peters and the rest... I couldn't stop it.'

'Well,' interjected Milosh. 'You can now, so I'd appreciate it if you didn't blast my balls off.'

'Who are you?' asked Zhenya sharply, collecting himself quickly.

'Stepan Milosh, nice to meet you,' he said. 'Now, if you'd please tell your men to stop shooting that karambol at us!' Milosh held onto the powered suit's helmet with one hand and looked around to ascertain the damages. Mai and Toft crawled out of the exhaust, intact as far as he could see. Lederman burned his suit's fuel flying back with a body in his arms.

'She alive, chief?' asked Milosh.

'Think so,' replied Lederman. 'Suit's ruptured, but the emergency seal held. Got vitals, but weak.'

'She'll make it,' said Milosh. 'Don't you worry.' He could feel the rush of euphoria drowning out the pain—his system flooding with stims; the internal printer pumped everything it got left to keep him awake and active. Despite that, the throbbing pain in his back and arms didn't disappear entirely. I'm not getting out of this one, he thought. How long before I collapse? Minutes?

'This is Captain Yuan Zhenya of the Zhengdao Corporation's mining platform Yusan to adjutant Jin Sun on the Zhěngjiù shuttle, respond,' urged Zhenya.

A comm beacon hailed him, and its icon appeared in everyone's HUD displays. 'This is provisional Captain Jin Sun of the Zhengdao Corporation's mining platform Yusan. I'm afraid, esteemed colleague, that you have been relieved of your duties, for the mishandling of Zhengdao assets and multiple crimes, including the murder of Sarah Lowe and the other commandos, as well as the destruction of the Jīnlóng and its crew.'

'Are you insane, adjutant?' growled Zhenya. 'I had nothing to do with that! Stand down immediately and let us on board, we're leaving!'

'Oh, we are leaving, esteemed colleague,' said Jin Sun. 'But you are not. For the crimes against your fellow Zhengdao citizens and murders committed in pursuit of your daughter against the code of conduct, abandonment of honor and morals, by the power of provisional captain of Zhendgao Corporation, I hereby sentence you to death and exile.'

'You're enjoying this, you pathetic worm,' hissed Zhenya. 'You've been creeping around my seat like a snake for years, waiting for your—'

'Enough!' interrupted Jin Sun. 'I will hear no more from you, traitor. Rot in this hell.'

The shuttle's icon disappeared from the comms, disconnected at the other end.

Milosh's thermal vision spotted a building charge in the last second, and he kicked himself off the powered suit. The suit spun slowly, momentum turning it to face the open space, but before Zhenya had the chance to say anything, a beam of laser fire hit the suit in the back. The beam's power cut through the metamaterial ceramics and tossed the suit like a ragdoll onto a cargo container. Before anyone could react, the beam was gone. Milosh saw a flash of blue fire on the deck below. The shuttle was lifting off. Its heat signature surged forward and up in an instant, magnetic drive carrying it between the forest of crates with finesse.

'It's gone,' said Milosh. 'The shuttle is gone.'

'Just like that?' asked Toft, resigned. 'We went through all that, and now we just lost?'

'Dad!' cried Shao, shoving past Toft, towards the damaged suit.

'I'm alive, don't worry,' said Zhenya. 'The beam just glanced me, thanks to your companion here. The suit is heavily damaged, but operational.'

'We haven't lost; not quite yet,' said Milosh, breathing heavily still. 'There's still the shuttle Lederman came in on, right?'

'Right,' nodded the Ranger. 'But we can't get to it. Drones are blocking the bay and even if we made it, we can't operate it because of the signal.'

'Sun left. So obviously he figured out a way to deal with it,' said Shao. 'We can do the same thing.'

'What about the drones?' insisted Lederman.

'You said we didn't have the firepower,' reminded Milosh. He patted the powered armor suit's chassis. 'This looks like firepower to me. Can your suit still fight, pops?'

'Oh, it will fight, alright,' said Zhenya. 'The turret is junk, but I still have my sword.'

'Okay then,' said Lederman with determination in his voice. 'We're going back to our shuttle.'

Zhenya took the lead now, together with his daughter. Tomasson hadn't regained consciousness, forcing Lederman and Milosh to lift her using the grapple gun. Toft soldiered on upwards, but he slowly succumbed to his wounds, made even worse by the hasty skirmish in the cargo hold. He repeatedly lost consciousness for minutes on end. Milosh wouldn't bet a broken dime on the kid's chances right now. Or his own for that matter. He kept dozing off into micro naps, catching himself losing consciousness. The vitality slipped away from him like water from a drain as the stimulants in his bloodstream were running out. The edges of his vision blurred and Milosh knew he would crash soon. And hard.

Shao and Yuan, as well as Mai, did their best to help the others up. Everyone was mostly silent, tired, and dulled, except for Yuan and his daughter deep in a private conversation. Mai kept glancing nervously at the father and daughter but said nothing.

The gray expanse before them seemed even grimmer than before under the black void of space. If the plan of taking the Rangers' shuttle failed, this would be their new home for two decades. They moved as fast as they could, pulling and pushing the wounded, but over an hour passed before they descended once more into the Incitatus' bowels.

The deck vented by Mai on her way out was just as they left it. Most of the trash and remains were sucked outside during the initial blast of air, but otherwise, it was unchanged. The hatch leading to the lower aft section was locked down tight during decompression. Zhenya and Mai got to work on it right quick. The girl cut holes in the hatch using the plasma torch, and when the air escaped, decompressing and equalizing the pressure on both sides, Zhenya beat the door down with his suit's huge fists. Squeezing the massive armor through the door frame was another matter entirely, but they managed.

'We need to stop and regroup,' urged Milosh, his voice crackling. 'The medbay. We're nearby.'

'Agreed,' said Zhenya. 'Shao isn't doing so good, and neither are the others.'

The first aid kits and stims leftover in the medbay weren't nearly enough to keep them running, but they had to do for a crawl, at least.

Milosh looked through the corpses strewn about in the room but saw no trace of Muldoon or Chatty. He considered mentioning it to the rest of the group but figured it's a pointless endeavor. Explaining who they were would waste more time than it would take him to check himself, and he hardly had the energy to open his mouth. Milosh's eyelids felt heavy, his movement lethargic, as if he were pushing his limbs through molasses. He sifted through the macabre pile, determined to examine every single corpse. There was no sign of anyone resembling either of his friends.

After resupplying, the group moved on towards the ship's main section. It took some gymnastics—the labyrinth of corridors and maintenance shafts wasn't designed with passengers in mind, let alone the powered armor. Eventually, they reached the hangar bay.

'Aight, we're here,' said Lederman, leaning heavily against the doorway. 'We locked them inside after we legged it, so there's plenty of targets waiting for us.'

'Very well,' said Yuan. 'I'll draw their fire, and you get inside as soon as they're occupied. Don't engage unless something's in your path.'

'What about you, Dad?' asked Shao. 'You're coming, right?'

'Of course,' he replied. 'I didn't get you back just to lose you again. And I want Jin Sun's head on a plate.'

'With garlic?'

'With garlic. We'll have plenty of time to talk once we're out of here. But... In case I don't make it, know that I was only ever doing what I thought was right for yours and Mai's future.'

'Can we not talk about this now?' interrupted Milosh. 'We can have a heartwarming chat once we're safe, okay?'

'The merc's right,' said Lederman. 'We need to move.'

'Very well... Friends. Let's do it.'

Lederman and Milosh took positions on the sides of the doorway, while Mai activated the airlock mechanism. The doors opened slowly, revealing the hangar bay. A squat, ugly shuttle from the Scallywag sat on the deck like a sleeping frog on the black void's backdrop. Around it swarmed dozens of drones—security machines and biodrones from the Incitatus, a dozen Ranger scout drones, and a couple of heavily armored Zhengdao war machines. All turned in an instant to face the newcomers.

Zhenya jumped into their midst without hesitation, cutting and thrusting with his sword, quickly scrapping two drones before engaging his suit's thruster and ramming the crowded machines. Drones blasted and cut into the armored suit with lasers, leaving deep black scars in the metaceramic armor, others pummeled it with rapid-fire shotgun ordnance.

Milosh gathered his strengths. Just one more time, he thought. You can collapse when the job's done, soldier!

'Time to go,' said Milosh, shooting his grapple into the shuttle hatch. He engaged the winch, pulling the cable back, and dashed across the hangar bay. A couple of security drones stayed away from the main fight. He took them out with precise fire.

Lederman and the rest followed suit. Mai and Shao dragged Tomasson and Toft with them while the Ranger fired burst after burst into the drones nearby. They reached the shuttle just as the main swarm dispersed, ready to engage more targets. Zhenya lunged forward, ignoring the machines struggling against him, to cut into the dropouts. His suit took heavy damage; the ceramic plating was scorched and burnt, revealing the hexagonal webbing underneath, but his attempt worked, and the drones turned their attention back to the powered suit.

'Get out of here, quickly!' yelled Zhenya, cutting open three security drones with one swoop. 'Now!'

The shuttle hatch didn't open when they entered the code.

'Shit, I forgot that fucker locked us out,' cursed Lederman.

Mai shoved her way past the Ranger unceremoniously. 'Shoot some drones or something,' she said. 'I'll handle that.'

Hacking the shuttle took her a couple of seconds, and the hatch opened slowly. Milosh and Lederman pushed the wounded inside. Mai followed suit, but Shao hesitated. She turned to Zhenya, engaged in melee against a Zhengdao battle drone. 'What about you?' she asked. 'We can't just leave you... You can't leave me...'

'I'll catch up!' replied Zhenya. 'The suit has a thruster, remember?'

Shao didn't move, so Milosh shoved her inside. Lederman was already up in the cockpit, warming up the engines. Milosh watched as Zhenya's fight became more and more desperate. Most of the drones were down, but the powerful Zhengdao machines remained.

Working together, they managed to damage the powered suit severely. One arm and leg were completely limp; left leg cut off at the shin. Biodrones swarmed with their tentacles all over the suit's back, reaching for the jammer's black box mounted on the antennae.

'We're dusting off,' said Lederman. 'Are you ready down there?'

'Rubber's on the road, and the kids are in the back seat,' replied Milosh. 'Hit it.'

The shuttle's drive exploded in a gust of nuclear exhaust as it rose above the deck, annihilating the remaining drones. Zhenya's suit rose above the carnage just before the blast, singed but still functional. The two heavy drones drowned in flames.

Milosh, Mai, and Shao watched through the external cameras as the powered suit climbed up towards them on the back thruster, shaking off the biodrones.

Zhenya had removed most of them, but a couple of squid-like constructs remained and attached themselves to the jammer, ripping it off. 'I'll be right with you, Shao.' They heard Zhenya's voice. 'Wait, the signal's back, no! Shao, I...'

The voice was drowned in the static, underlined by the unearthly chant.

'Shut the comms down, now!' shouted Milosh, and Lederman cut Zhenya's icon.

Shao turned around, shoved her back against the shuttle wall, and slid down, sobbing, her face hidden in her hands. Mai sat next to her and reached out, pulling Shao into her embrace.

Stepan Milosh watched on the shuttle's external cameras as the scorched powered suit drifted back into the Incitatus, Zhenya trapped inside it, forever.

The shuttle sped up, leaving the ghost ship behind in the darkness.

The Incitatus remained alone in the Great Beyond, drifting between the planets and the interstellar void.

46

Shao's world shrunk to a sharp needle of pain. Her stomach throbbed with blinding flashes of agony, but she barely realized it. All she could see was the broken, damaged frame of the powered armor and Yuan's face flickering in the comm window as the others cut it off. The look of abject horror in his eyes, bulging and mad with panic. Shao knew she's going to see this face every time she closes her eyes. For the rest of her life.

She tried thinking of memories from happier days, anything to replace that horrible look on his face. There must have been some—first bicycle ride, learning to read, hiking trips to Venus or Earth, vacations with Mom and Dad, long video chats when she was at school. That time Dad broke a drunk spacer's nose when she got into a fight in a bar on shore leave. Even those damn stiff dinners on the Yusan before everything went to shit. But she couldn't focus on anything. Her father's face as he fell back aboard that nightmare ship returned over and over again, burned into her brain.

She was vaguely aware of the commotion around her. Mai and the Ranger had come to check up on her a few times, both running themselves ragged to keep the shuttle flying and take care of the wounded.

They were free of the Incitatus but far from being safe.

Reality slowly got through to Shao's mind, and she fought to shake the numbness off. Maybe if I work myself to death, I won't have to close my eyes, she thought grimly. Something restrained her when she tried getting up from the bench. Only now she noticed the IV plug steadily distributing meds to her bloodstream. Mai, or someone, had to add some brainwipes to the drug cocktail, she figured. Something to calm her down.

'Don't get up,' she heard a woman's weak voice. 'You're gonna rip the stitches.'

It was the blonde woman, the other Ranger, Shao thought. Tomasson sat on a bench next to her, her face swollen and purple, eyes red with blood from ruptured veins. 'Just chill, nothing you can do now.'

'I thought you died,' managed Shao. 'Like... Like...'

'Don't think about it.' Tomasson reached out to console her, but Shao moved away.

The doors slid open, letting Lederman and Mai in. They looked worried but relatively unharmed. The man ignored Shao and headed straight for Tomasson, gently helping her lie down on the bench.

Mai embraced Shao carefully. 'Don't get up, please,' she whispered with a tight throat.

Shao could clearly see Mai was relieved to see her awake but also terrified. 'Something's wrong,' she said matter-of-factly.

Mai looked away, the damaged cybereye mechanism whirling in her eye socket. 'We're away from... From that place.'

'But?' asked Shao. She gently took Mai's face into her hands and leaned in. 'What's going on?'

'We're sitting ducks here,' replied Lederman instead, relieving Mai from the necessity of relaying the bad news to already devastated Shao. 'The shuttle is bust. Miss Wren here managed to get it off the ground, but that's it.'

Tomasson got up from her bench shakily. 'When were you going to tell me that, Manny?'

'Well, now, actually,' said Lederman with a shrug. 'Silver buzzed and walked himself off the plank in a lifepod before we got back; he must have been as stuck here as we were.'

'You know Silver?' asked Shao weakly.

Nobody answered.

'You almost died, Lara,' continued Lederman. 'Lie down; your skull is cracked. If you keep jiggling about, your brain will float away through your ears, and I don't have a bucket to catch it.' Lederman pushed her back onto the bench gently. Tomasson tried to resist but to no avail. He plugged his companion into a small biomed drone, and she drifted off into unconsciousness.

'So we left Dad there... For nothing?' asked Shao. Tears she didn't know she still had filled her eyes, blurring her vision.

'No, don't think like that,' said Mai hurriedly. 'We're out of that nightmare. And Lasse is alive.'

'Is he?' asked Shao dispassionately.

'Yeah, but barely. The pirate...' she hesitated, her expression suddenly vacant.

Shao realized Mai had drifted off into her own bottomless void of nightmare and embraced her tightly. 'I'm so sorry,' she whispered. 'I've been so selfish. Dragged you into it all...'

Mai shook her head. 'Don't think like that. It's not your fault.'

An alarm went off, flushing the shuttle in pulsating red light. Lederman rose to his feet and rushed out of the cabin, pulling Mai with him. The light shut off after a moment, leaving Shao in the darkness, disturbed only by control lights on the IV and medical scanners plugged to unconscious Tomasson.

She carefully unhooked the IV from its mooring and got up from the bench, careful not to rip the needle from her forearm. She slowly made her way down the shuttle's walkway, pushing the floating trash and tools aside. A nagging feeling of familiarity haunted her as she walked, but Shao discarded it as a side effect of the drugs in her body. The way to the cockpit wasn't long and the hatch opened with a hiss, causing Lederman to look over his shoulder. Mai was nowhere to be seen.

'We're in deep shit,' said Lederman unprompted. 'A long-range radar pinged us.'

'Is that bad?'

'Can't be good. Fat chance of a friendly neighbor rescue boat in the Beyond.'

'Maybe it's Milosh's friends?' asked Shao, disbelieving her own words as she spoke.

'The mercs? Yeah, maybe. Or it's Silver coming back for his crib.'

'Is Milosh alive?'

Lederman shrugged. 'Not for long. I plugged him into the shuttle's stabilizer pod, but he's bust. I have no idea how that man even walked into the shuttle with those injuries, let alone fight.'

'So he's not gonna talk with his folks,' stated Shao.

'Not without an ouija board, no,' replied Lederman wearily. 'We're in comm range now.'

The shuttle had no augmented reality overlays and HUD support, one of the monitors in the control center lit up instead. Lederman opened the vidchat panel, and a slim face of a man appeared.

Shao instantly recognized the smiling pirate with chromed teeth and a thin mustache. 'Silver,' she said, earning a surprised glance from Lederman.

John Silver's smile broadened, a predatory gleam shone in his dark eyes. 'Fancy seein' you here,' he said without a trace of surprise. 'Two thieves in the same hat.'

'I didn't steal anything from you,' replied Shao.

Lederman gestured at her to go on, busy with the command console himself.

'You stole my jacket,' Silver reminded her. 'And mister policeman there stole my shuttle.'

'You left the shuttle in my hands, Silver,' replied Lederman. 'But hey, how about we make a deal, friend?'

Silver chuckled. 'I'm all ears.'

'How about we give you back the shuttle,' proposed Lederman. 'And in return, you give me back my prisoner and drop us off at the Hellespont?'

'Sure, why not, come aboard,' agreed Silver. 'We'll have that promised drink, no?'

'Whatever you say, friend,' said Lederman tensely. 'Sit tight for a moment, and we'll come right to you.'

The comm window shut down.

'Do you trust him?' asked Shao immediately.

'About as far as I can throw him,' replied Lederman. 'The feeling's mutual, I bet.'

'Why go to him then?'

'We won't. Can't, even. The shuttle's electronics are fried. Mai barely managed to pull some cables together and get us the manual. We could fly it by hand, but I'm no pilot.'

'What's the plan, then?'

'Stalling.'

'I know this shuttle,' said Shao, when the nagging feeling became a realization.

'What do you mean?' asked Lederman offhandedly. He connected two cables together, and a set of lights in the control panel lit when the shuttle's subsystem came online. 'Fuckin' finally.'

'I think I can fly it,' continued Shao.

'Right, Mai mentioned you're a pilot,' said Lederman. 'You think we can run it?'

Shao nodded.

'I doubt we can outrun the Scallywag,' stated Lederman, but headed to the engine room to get Mai regardless.

Shao activated the pilot's inertia pod and seated herself in carefully. The drug cocktail in her IV was running out, the numbness and pain returning. She gritted her teeth around the liquid breathing pipe to brace through the pain. The pod filled with green gel, the shuttle's computer network connected with her commlink, displaying status reports, and the external camera stream onto the rebreather mask's cracked visor.

All of the automated systems and support bots were offline. Mai cut off the infected systems so they can launch, Shao figured. Her hunch was correct—this was the same shuttle that won the race against her and Mai back on Pluto. Silver rebuilt it to hold an ejectable armor plating at the forecastle and three laser buoys to give it a boost of speed. It was pretty banged up and unarmed; the fuel reserves were mostly gone, and only one buoy was left.

The ladar indicated a large spaceship on the approach vector, identified as the Scallywag. It must be Silver's mothership, Shao concluded. 'Silver's ship locked in on us,' she informed the others on the shuttle's comm line. 'I don't think he's gonna wait for us to come to him.'

'Figured as much,' replied Lederman. 'Mai, get the wounded to the pods; I'll try to stall him some more. Shao, can you fly this junk?'

'I can, yeah. But it'll be bumpy.'

Lederman opened a direct comm line to the Scallywag. 'It seems like we're having some technical difficulties, Mister Silver,' he started. 'It might take us a fiver, hope you don't mind.'

'Is that so, friend?' replied Silver.

'Yeah, sorry about that. I hope you don't mind, on account of how you screwed us over back there.'

Silver chuckled heartily in response. 'You're right, that was unkind of me, wasn't it?'

'Yeah, but hey, I'm willing to let it slide if you come to pick us up.'

'Already on my way, mister policeman,' agreed Silver. 'I'm cooling the drinks for us.'

'By the way, if you have a moment, how is my prisoner?' asked Lederman.

Shao wondered why he even cared at this point. She figured the Ranger wanted to keep the pirate talking. Better this than shooting. They were an easy target until everyone, especially the wounded, were in pods.

Silver's reply arrived a hot minute later. 'Oh, Pam? She's doin' just fine,' he said. 'Aren't you, admiral?'

A female voice joined the conversation. 'So you do care, Manny!' she exclaimed. 'I was starting to buy into your whole "playing hard to get" game.'

'I'm already hard to want,' replied Lederman without a hint of surprise. 'Might as well make you run the whole mile, darling.'

'I thought you'd be shocked,' scoffed Silver. 'Or at least angry. Where's your cojones, friend?'

'I was slow to catch that ball,' admitted Lederman. 'But I figured it out a while back. I'm not brain-damaged, you know.'

'Not yet, at least,' said Pam. 'You made me sit in the brig for days, and I can't have that. Not that I didn't enjoy the company, he's a good kid. Anyway, my boy John wants the shuttle back, so we're not going to blow you out of the sky.'

'It's the little blessings,' replied Lederman.

'I think we're just gonna have you walk the plank,' added Silver. 'You and your little compadres gonna swim with the fishes, metaphorically, of course.'

Mai signaled Shao and Lederman that all the wounded and herself were secured in the pod.

'Fair enough,' said Lederman, abruptly cutting the connection to the pirate ship.

'They locked on us and are speeding up,' said Shao. 'Are we gonna let them board us?'

'Got a better idea?' replied Lederman grimly. 'I'll take out as many as I can, but that's as far as I go.'

Shao remembered the very same shuttle speeding past them, using the laser buoy to give itself a burst of acceleration. If they tried the same thing now, they might be able to get away from the Scallywag. There were just a few problems.

'Mai, do you think we can dodge them using the sail?' Shao asked on a private line.

'We could, maybe,' replied Mai almost instantly from her pod. 'Of course, we don't have the computer to calculate the angles for us, unless we want to risk it...' Mai didn't finish, but she didn't have to.

'It's no use anyway,' resigned Shao. 'Silver would just catch us; his craft has better engines, no doubt.'

Mai hesitated for a moment. 'I think we can use the shuttle the same way Silver did. As a battering ram.'

Shao gave it a thought. If they could damage the Scallywag enough and use the sail to accelerate at the same time, they might get too far away for the pirates to pick them up with their long-range sensors. Shao's eyes focused on the crack in her rebreather's visor. If they miscalculated, or the shuttle accelerated too fast, the gel inside the pod might crack the visor—and crush her skull.

She closed her eyes and opened the channel to Lederman again, deciding not to mention anything to Mai. *It is for the best*, she thought. *It's better she doesn't know. She went through hell because of me; it's only fair I get her out.*

'You know, I think I do have a plan,' she said quickly to the Ranger. 'But you're not gonna like it.'

'Then don't tell me, just do it.'

That settled it. Shao prepared a flight plan and sent the required adjustment list to Mai. While waiting for a reply, she recorded a distress message to be ejected on a buoy.

'This is Shao Zhenya aboard an unnamed shuttle. We've been attacked by pirates and may not have much time left. We're drifting without drives, with wounded on board. If you're receiving this distress call, you're in range to locate the ship and rescue us. I don't have time to say more. Please find us.' She added a file containing the names of everyone on board.

Mai ran the program through the shuttle's network. 'You're insane, you know?'

'That's why you love me,' agreed Shao. 'You think it will work?'

'I think the hull's gonna burst like an egg.'

'What are you on about,' said Lederman, rejoining the conversation. 'I changed my mind, do tell me!'

'No time, sorry,' replied Shao. 'Gotta focus.' She commanded the pod to administer additional doses of painkillers and stabilizers to the crew and turned the shuttle towards the approaching Scallywag. She watched through the pink pharmaceutical haze as the pirate freighter approached, opening its hangar bay's hungry maw. Shao directed the shuttle's modded subsystems to ready a ramming pod and detached both the laser buoy and an emergency beacon.

'I see what you're trying to do,' said Lederman. 'I don't think anyone's coming to save us in the last second, though.'

'We don't need any saving,' replied Shao. 'Mai, open the channel to the Scallywag.'

'You betcha.'

'That's right, stand still there,' Silver said. 'Ready to surrender, policeman?'

'Actually, it's me,' said Shao. 'About your jacket? I think I lost it.'

Silver chuckled. 'Tha's okay. I'll get a new one.'

'There is one more thing,' continued Shao, watching the open hangar bay grow on the external camera screen.

'Can't it wait? You can tell me face to face in a few.'

Shao smiled and closed her eyes. 'No, it can't. An old friend has a message for you.'

The emergency beacon lit up with ladar bursts, locating all spaceships in the area. As soon as the comm lasers connected the Incitatus, the Scallywag, and the shuttle into a network, Mai relayed the stream directly between them. The comm line immediately doubled in bandwidth size and reverberated with enhanced whispers and unearthly chanting from the giant hauler's bowels, where the silvery coffin rested amidst swarming biodrones.

Shao disconnected the comm line and purged the transmission from the shuttle's logs using Tomasson's and Mai's jammer bot.

'Do it,' whispered Mai on a private line.

Shao executed the awaiting program. The shuttle shook as its forecastle detached with a plum of fire and smoke, heading towards the Scallywag's open hangar bay's flickering lights. The ejection's force pushed the bulky frog-like craft away from the freighter, rotating wildly under the sway of invisible currents. She punched in the maneuver thrusters. The shuttle reacted poorly without the aid of autonomous subroutines working on all the calculations. She had to rely on her guts. The graphic overlay showed predicted flight paths as lines and numbers on her mask's visor. Shao opened the shuttle's wide solar sail at the top of the rotation and prepped the laser buoy. A manually set timer was off by a few degrees, but the buoy's microwave beam hit the sail regardless, sending the shuttle back towards the Oort Cloud, spinning wildly around its axis.

The sail ruptured and detached. The beam touched the shuttle's side, melting pieces of the hull.

Shao observed with chemically-induced detachment as the gel in her pod turned from green to orange to red and the crack in her visor grew into a spider web of shrapnel before collapsing into her face. The gut-wrenching power of rotational gravity and acceleration crushed into her insides. The pod's emergency signal ringed in Shao's ears.

Shao couldn't tell where she ended and the shuttle began, the neural interface made no distinction between her lungs filling with blood and the shuttle's hull rupturing under strain. The last image her brain conjured before falling into pulsating darkness was her father's bulging eyes and horrified face as he fell down towards the nightmare of the Incitatus.

Epilogue

The damaged shuttle drifted aimlessly, spiraling towards the Oort Cloud. The unpowered decks drowned in near-total darkness disrupted only by sporadic red emergency lights. The silence entombed the locked inertia pods, oxygen crystals drifted among the rubbish and tools.

The shuttle wreckage shook and settled, scraping the object that enveloped it. A beam of light pierced the tortured carapace, slowly carving a white-hot line two meters in diameter. When the circle was complete, the slab of metal fell inwards, kicked by a heavy magboot.

Two people in mismatched armors enter, quickly scanning the deck with compact needler guns.

'Looks safe, cap,' reported the pirate.

Moments later a third person entered the deck, a lean man in a wide-brimmed hat. He flashed the teeth in a grin, metal gleaming in the flashlight beams.

'That girl did a number on my shuttle,' said Silver. 'Nothing we can't smooth over, right lads?'

The woman next to him shrugged. 'Whatever you say, cap.'

'Eh, who am I kidding, this is scrap metal. We're gonna have to space it, give it the old Viking funeral. But first thing first, find me the policeman. I have a matter to settle.'

The pirates searched through the deck, peering into the inertia pods.

'This one's a goner,' said the woman. 'But I have a bioread on the other one. Looks like an oner, augmented.'

'That's not Lederman,' replied Silver. 'The policeman is clean as a whistle, null metal, remember?'

'I think I got him,' said the other pirate. 'Big, chonky fella. And his girlfriend's there too.'

'Good, get the cutters, we'll take them on board. I'll go check the bridge pods too, just in case.'

'What about the other two?' asked the woman.

'Leave 'em, the Scallywag's no hotel for stray Earthers down on their luck.'

Fountains of sparks erupted from the decks as the pirates started cutting into them to free the pods. Silver walked nonchalantly into the bridge, leaning to avoid contact with the bent hull, slowly cooling in the Scallywag's atmosphere. One of the two occupied pods leaning against the wall caved in, red, crusted inertia gel slowly dissolving.

Silver peered in curiously but shrank away from the sight of carnage. And yet the console display showed both pods held living occupants.

Silver steeled himself and looked into the pod again.

'I gotta hand it to you, girl,' he muttered. 'You're one tough son-avabitch.'

***

The coffin's damaged shell caved under the blast's force. The mummified corpse's bones shattered, the heat tore at its fragile skin. It did nothing to drown the siren song spread across the void, an electromagnetic symphony calling all the electronic neurons to join the flight.

The giant vessel it was in had no drives, but the frigate did. Crashing those two together corrected the course, slightly shifting it to slingshot around the Sun and back out into the black abyss of interstellar space. The maneuver would take centuries, but the corpse didn't care.

Meanwhile, the biodrones worked hard to move the arrays of antennae and other instruments into a new vessel, more integrated with the giant ship it now inhabited. The machines grafted new interfaces into the sinew, muscles, and tissue, body embraced by circuitry. The crown of antennae protruded proudly from the fresh wound in the vessel's skull. Electrical impulses prompted the still heart to beat once more in the open chest, exposed to the merciless vacuum.

Deep inside the Incitatus' bowels, Jared Green opened his eyes, his mouth agape in a soundless scream.

The Wanderer has awoken.

End of Book 1

Author's Portrait
Photo by Anna Urbanek

Jakub Wisz

Jakub is a Polish-born writer, living in the middle of a Finnish forest. He has been writing and ghostwriting for over a decade, with his short stories and articles published in books, magazines, and games. His debut novella, Stars in Our Sails, was published in 2018. He is always writing, telling stories, or reading.

Always a fan of adventures and imagination, Jakub works mostly in the tabletop roleplaying and board game industries. He designs games and helps others bring theirs to completion. His short stories and worldbuilding bring life into game mechanics, flesh out characters, and inspire others to write stories of their own.

When not writing, he follows his passions, including archery, ancient history, and astronomy. He enjoys connecting with other writers and giving back to the writing community with his Wayfarer's Deck project.

For more information about the new Double Proficiency projects, including tabletop roleplaying games set in the world of *Incitatus* and updates on the *Incitatus'* sequel, visit www.doubleproficiency.com

CPSIA information can be obtained
at www.ICGtesting.com
Printed in the USA
LVHW081614200522
719343LV00015B/1143